About the

Lynne Graham lives in Northern Ireland and has been a keen romance reader since her teens. Happily married, Lynne has five children. Her eldest is her only natural child. Her other children, who are every bit as dear to her heart, are adopted. The family has a variety of pets, and Lynne loves gardening, cooking, collecting all sorts, and is crazy about every aspect of Christmas.

Millie Adams has always loved books. She considers herself a mix of Anne Shirley – loquacious, but charming, and willing to break a slate over a boy's head if need be – and Charlotte Doyle – a lady at heart but with the spirit to become a mutineer should the occasion arise. Millie lives in a small house on the edge of the woods, which she finds allows her to escape in the way she loves best: in the pages of a book. She loves intense alpha heroes and the women who dare to go toe-to-toe with them. Or break a slate over their heads...

Jane Porter loves central California's golden foothills and miles of farmland, rich with the sweet and heady fragrance of orange blossoms. Her parents fed her imagination by taking Jane to Europe for a year where she became passionate about Italy and those gorgeous Italian men! Jane never minds a rainy day – that's when she sits at her desk and writes stories about far-away places, fascinating people, and most important of all, love. Visit her website at janeporter.com

The Crown

April 2023
Duty to the Crown

May 2023
Promised to the Crown

June 2023
Reunited with the Crown

July 2023
Protecting the Crown

August 2023
Trading the Crown

September 2023
Falling for the Crown

Promised to the Crown

LYNNE GRAHAM

MILLIE ADAMS

JANE PORTER

MILLS & BOON

First Published in Great Britain 2023
by Mills & Boon, an imprint of HarperCollins*Publishers* Ltd,
1 London Bridge Street, London, SE1 9GF

www.harpercollins.co.uk

HarperCollins*Publishers*
Macken House, 39/40 Mayor Street Upper,
Dublin 1, D01 C9W8, Ireland

ISBN: 978-0-263-31907-1

MIX
Paper | Supporting
responsible forestry
FSC™ C007454
www.fsc.org

This book is produced from independently certified FSC™ paper to ensure responsible forest management.

For more information visit: www.harpercollins.co.uk/green

Printed and Bound in the UK using 100% Renewable Electricity at CPI Group (UK) Ltd, Croydon, CR0 4YY

JEWEL IN HIS CROWN

LYNNE GRAHAM

CHAPTER ONE

THE BEAUTIFUL BRUNETTE lay in the tangled bed sheets watching her lover get dressed. Prince Raja al-Somari had black hair and exotic dark golden eyes. Exceptionally handsome, he was pure leashed power, muscle and magnetic attraction. He was also a wild force of nature in bed, she reflected with a languorous look of sensual satisfaction on her face.

As his mistress, Chloe, one of the world's top fashion models, certainly had no complaints. But then Chloe was excessively fond of rich men, money and fabulous jewellery. Her prince from the oil-rich country of Najar in the Persian Gulf was staggeringly wealthy and he delivered on every count, so naturally she didn't want to lose him. When a plane crash had killed the bride in the arranged marriage being planned for Raja, Chloe had breathed a secret sigh of relief for such an alliance could well lead to the end of the most profitable relationship she had ever had. And even if another arranged marriage lurked on the horizon, Chloe was determined to hold onto her lover.

Raja watched Chloe finger the glittering new diamond bracelet encircling one slender wrist as if it were a talisman and his mouth quirked at her predictability. Although the demands of his position had made it difficult for him to see her in recent months, Chloe had subjected him to neither tantrums nor tears. Like most Western women he had met since his university days in England, she was as easy to placate as a child with a shiny new toy. In return for the complete discretion he demanded from his lovers, he was extremely generous but he never thought about his bed partners when he was away from them. Sex might be a necessity to a man of his appetites, but it was also simply an amusement and an escape from the weight of responsibility he carried. As acting Regent and ruler of conservative Najar, he could not openly enjoy a sex life without causing offence.

Furthermore, Raja was always aware that he had much more important issues to worry about. The recent appalling plane crash had devastated the people of Najar and its neighbour and former enemy, Ashur. The future of both countries stood on the edge of catastrophe. For seven years war had raged between oil-rich Najar and poverty stricken Ashur and when peace had finally been brokered by the Scandinavian state leading the talks, the two countries had added a more personal cultural twist to the agreement before they were satisfied that the peace would hold firm. That twist had been an arranged marriage between the two royal families and joint rulership that would ultimately unite Najar with Ashur. Having spent most of his adult life as a businessman before serving his country, Raja had accepted that he had to marry Princess Bariah of Ashur. That she was a widow well into her thirties while he was still in his twenties he had accepted as his royal duty to put the needs of his country first.

And his country and his people did desperately *need* a fresh blueprint for a lasting peace.

Unfortunately for all concerned, a tragedy had lurked in the wings of the peace accord. A fortnight earlier, Bariah and her parents had died in a plane crash. Shorn of its entire ruling family in one fell swoop, Ashur was in deep crisis and the court officials were searching frantically through the Shakarian family tree for a suitable heir to the throne who could take Bariah's place as Raja's bride and consort.

His mobile phone buzzed and he lifted it.

'You have to come home,' his younger brother Haroun told him heavily. 'Wajid Sulieman, the Ashuri court advisor, is already on his way here. According to his aide, he is very excited so I expect that means they've found another bride for you.'

It was the news that Raja had been waiting for, the news that honour demanded he hope for, but he still had to fight the crushing sensation of a rock settling on his chest to shorten his breathing. 'We must hope for the best—'

'The best would be if they *couldn't* find anyone else to marry you!' his youthful sibling opined without hesitation. 'Why are you letting yourself be forced into an arranged marriage? Are we still living in the Dark Ages?'

Raja's lean bronzed features were as impassive as he had learned to make them in the presence of others. He rarely spoke without consideration. His wheelchair-bound father had taught him everything he knew about kingship. 'It is necessary that I do this.'

'Trouble?' Chloe asked, blue eyes bright with curiosity as Raja set down the phone and lifted his shirt.

'I have to leave immediately.'

Chloe scrambled out of bed and pressed her lithe pale body to his. 'But we were going out tonight,' she protested, looking up at him with wide, wounded eyes while being careful to look and sound hurt and disappointed rather than accusing, for there was very little Chloe didn't know about keeping a man happy.

'I'll make up for it on my next visit,' Raja promised, setting her to one side to resume dressing.

He was trying not to wonder *who* the Ashuri representatives had found for him to marry. What did the woman's identity matter? Hopefully she would be reasonably attractive. That was the most he could hope for. Anything more would be icing on the cake. He suppressed the thought that he was as imprisoned by his royal birth as an animal in a trap. Such reflections were unnecessarily dramatic and in no way productive.

His private jet whisked him back to Najar within hours and his brother was waiting in the limo that met him at the airport.

'I wouldn't marry a stranger!' Haroun told him heatedly.

'I do it gladly for you.' Raja was grateful that his kid brother had no such future sacrifice to fear. 'Right now, after a long period of instability, tradition is exactly what the people in both countries long to have back—'

'The Ashuris are broke. Their country is in ruins. Why don't you offer them a portion of our oil revenues instead?'

'Haroun!' Raja censured. 'Watch your mouth. Until

we find a feasible framework for this peace agreement we all need to practise great diplomacy.'

'Since when has the truth been a hanging offence?' Haroun argued. 'We won the war yet you're being bartered off to a bunch of boundary thieves, who were still herding sheep when our great-great-grandfather, Rashid, was a king!'

Conscious that many Najaris would agree with his sibling, for the war had sown deep enmity and prejudice between the people of both countries, Raja merely dealt the younger man an impatient appraisal. 'I expect a more balanced outlook from a young man as well educated as you are.'

At the royal palace, the grey-haired and excessively precise Ashuri court advisor awaited Raja's arrival with an assistant and both men were, indeed, wreathed in smiles.

'My apologies if our timing has proved inconvenient, Your Royal Highness. Thank you for seeing us at such short notice.' Bowing very low, Wajid wasted no time in making small talk. A man on a mission, he spread open a file on the polished table between them. 'We have discovered that the only legal and marriageable female heir to the Ashuri throne is the daughter of the late King Anwar and a British citizen—'

'A British citizen?' Haroun repeated, intrigued. 'Anwar was ruler before Princess Bariah's father, King Tamim, wasn't he?'

'He was Tamim's elder brother. I recall that King Anwar made more than one marriage,' Raja remarked. 'Who was the lady's mother?'

The older man's mouth compressed. 'His first wife

was an Englishwoman. The alliance was brief and she returned with the child to England after the divorce.'

'And what age is Anwar's daughter now?' Haroun was full of lively curiosity.

'Twenty-one years old. She has never been married.'

'Half English,' Prince Raja mused. 'And still very young. Of good character?'

Wajid stiffened. 'Of course.'

Raja was not so easily impressed. In his experience women who coveted the attentions of a prince were only looking for a good time and something sparkly to sweeten the deal. 'Why did King Anwar divorce her mother?'

'She was unable to have more children. It was a love match and short-lived,' the older man commented with a scornful compression of his lips. 'The king had two sons with his second wife, both of whom were killed during the war.'

Although Wajid was repeating information he was already well acquainted with, Raja dipped his head in respectful acknowledgement for a generation of young men who had been decimated by the conflict that had raged for so long. As far as he was concerned if his marriage could persuade bitter enemies to live together in peace, it was a small sacrifice in comparison to the endless funerals he had once been forced to attend.

'The name of Anwar's daughter?'

'The princess's name is Ruby. As her mother chose to leave Ashur, the royal family took no further interest in either mother or daughter. Unfortunately Princess Ruby has had no training or preparation for a royal role.'

Raja frowned. 'In which case she would find the lifestyle and the expectations very challenging.'

'The princess is young enough to learn quickly.' The court advisor rubbed his hands together with unfeigned enthusiasm. 'Our advisors believe she can be easily moulded.'

'Have you a photograph to show my brother?' Haroun questioned eagerly.

Wajid leafed through the file and extracted a small photo. 'I'm afraid this is several years old but the most recent photograph we have.'

Raja studied the slender blonde in the miniskirt and T-shirt, captured outside the Ashuri cathedral in their capital city. It was a tourist snap and the girl still had the legginess and slightly chubby and unformed features of adolescence. Her pale colouring was very unusual in his culture and that long blonde hair was exceptionally attractive and he immediately felt guilty for that shallow reflection with his former fiancée, Bariah, so recently laid to rest. But in truth he had only met Bariah briefly on one formal occasion and she had remained a stranger to him.

Less guarded than his elder brother, Haroun studied Princess Ruby and loosed a long low whistle of boyish approval.

'That is enough,' Raja rebuked the younger man in exasperation. 'When can I hope to meet her?'

'As soon as we can arrange it, Your Royal Highness.' Not displeased by the compliment entailed in Haroun's whistle of admiration, Wajid beamed, relieved by Raja's practical response to the offer of another bride. Not for the first time, Wajid felt that Prince Raja would be a king he could do business with. The Najari regent accepted his responsibilities without fuss and if there was one thing he knew inside out, it was *how* to be royal. A young woman blessed with his support and guidance would soon learn the ropes.

'*PLEASE*, RUBY,' STEVE PLEADED, gripping Ruby's small waist with possessive hands.

'No!' Ruby told her boyfriend without hesitation. She pushed his hands from below her sweater. Although it didn't appear to bother him she felt foolish grappling with him in broad daylight in a car parked in the shadiest corner of the pub car park.

Steve dealt her a sulky look of resentment before finally retreating back into the driver's seat. Ruby, with her big brown eyes, blonde hair and fabulous figure, was a trophy and he was the envy of all his friends, but when she dug her heels in, she was as immovable as a granite rock. 'Can I come over tonight?'

'I'm tired,' Ruby lied. 'I should get back to work. I don't want to be late.'

Steve dropped her back at the busy legal practice where she was a receptionist. They lived in the same Yorkshire market town. A salesman in an estate agency, Steve worked across the street from her and he was fighting a last-ditch battle to persuade Ruby that sex was a desirable activity. She had wondered if Steve might be the one to change her mind on that score for she had initially thought him very attractive. He had the blond hair and blue eyes she had always admired in men, but his kisses were wet and his roving hands squeezed her as if she were a piece of ripening fruit for sale on a stall. Steve had taught her that a man could be good-looking without being sexy.

'You're ten minutes late, Ruby,' the office manager, a thin, bespectacled woman in her thirties, remarked sourly. 'You need to watch your timekeeping.'

Ruby apologised and got back to work, letting her mind drift to escape the boredom of the routine tasks that made up her working day. When she had first started working at Collins, Jones & Fowler, she had been eighteen years old, her mother had just died and she had badly needed a job. Her colleagues were all female and older and the middle-aged trio of solicitors they worked for were an equally uninteresting bunch. Conversations were about elderly parents, children and the evening meal, never gossip, fashion or men. Ruby enjoyed the familiar faces of the regular clients and the brief snatches of friendly chatter they exchanged with her but continually wished that life offered more variety and excitement.

In comparison, her late mother, Vanessa, had had more than a taste of excitement while she was still young enough to enjoy it, Ruby recalled affectionately. As a youthful catwalk model in London, Vanessa had caught the eye of an Arab prince, who had married her after a whirlwind romance. Ruby's birthplace was the country of Ashur in the Persian Gulf. Her father, Anwar, however, had chosen to take a second wife while still married to her mother and that had been the ignominious end of what Vanessa had afterwards referred to as her 'royal fling'. Vanessa had got a divorce and had returned to the UK with her child. In Ashur daughters were rarely valued as much as sons and

Ruby's father had promptly chosen to forget her existence.

A year later, Vanessa, armed with a substantial pay-off and very much on the rebound, had married Curtis Sommerton, a Yorkshire businessman. She had immediately begun calling her daughter by her second husband's surname in the belief that it would enable Ruby to forget the family that had rejected them. Meanwhile Curtis had sneakily run through her mother's financial nest egg and had deserted her once the money was spent. Heartbroken, Vanessa had grieved long and hard over that second betrayal of trust and had died of a premature heart attack soon afterwards.

'My mistake was letting myself get carried away with my feelings,' Vanessa had often told her daughter. 'Anwar promised me the moon and I bet he promised the other wife he took the moon, as well. The proof of the pudding is in the eating, my love. Don't go falling for sweet-talking womanisers like I did!'

Fiery and intelligent, Ruby was very practical and quick to spot anyone trying to take too much advantage of her good nature. She had loved her mother very much and preferred to remember Vanessa as a warm and loving woman, who was rather naive about men. Her stepfather, on the other hand, had been a total creep, whom Ruby had hated and feared. Vanessa had had touching faith in love and romance but, to date, life had only taught Ruby that what men seemed to want most was sex. Finer feelings like commitment, loyalty and romance were much harder to find or awaken. Like so many men before him, Steve had made Ruby feel grubby and she was determined not to go out with him again.

After work she walked home, to the tiny terraced house that she rented, for the second time that day. Her lunch breaks were always cut short by her need to go home and take her dog out for a quick walk but she didn't mind. Hermione, the light of Ruby's life, was a Jack Russell terrier, who adored Ruby and disliked men. Hermione had protected Ruby from her stepfather, Curtis, on more than one occasion. Creeping into Ruby's bedroom at night had been a very dangerous exercise with Hermione in residence.

Ruby shared the small house with her friend Stella Carter, who worked as a supermarket cashier. Now she was surprised to see an opulent BMW car complete with a driver parked outside her home and she had not even contrived to get her key into the front door before it shot abruptly open.

'Thank goodness, you're home!' Stella exclaimed, her round face flushed and uneasy. 'You've got visitors in the lounge...' she informed Ruby in a suitable whisper.

Ruby frowned. 'Who are they?'

'They're something to do with your father's family... No, not Curtis the perv, the *real* one!' That distinction was hissed into Ruby's ear.

Completely bewildered, Ruby went into the compact front room, which seemed uncomfortably full of people. A small grey-haired man beamed at her and bowed very low. The middle aged woman with him and the younger man followed suit, so that Ruby found herself staring in wonderment at three downbent heads.

'Your Royal Highness,' the older man breathed in a tone of reverent enthusiasm. 'May I say what a very great pleasure it is to meet you at last?'

'He's been going on about you being a princess ever since he arrived,' Stella told her worriedly out of the corner of her mouth.

'I'm not a princess. I'm not a royal anything,' Ruby declared with a frown of wryly amused discomfiture. 'What's this all about? Who are you?'

Wajid Sulieman introduced himself and his wife, Haniyah, and his assistant. 'I represent the interests of the Ashuri royal family and I am afraid I must first give you bad news.'

Striving to recall her manners and contain her impatience, Ruby asked her visitors to take a seat. Wajid informed her that her uncle, Tamim, his wife and his daughter, Bariah, had died in a plane crash over the desert three weeks earlier. The names rang a very vague bell of familiarity from Ruby's one and only visit to Ashur when she was a schoolgirl of fourteen. 'My uncle was the king...' she said hesitantly, not even quite sure of that fact.

'And until a year ago your eldest brother was his heir,' Wajid completed.

Ruby's big brown eyes opened very wide in surprise. 'I have a brother?'

Wajid had the grace to flush at the level of her ignorance about her relatives. 'Your late father had two sons by his second wife.'

Ruby emitted a rueful laugh. 'So I have two half-brothers I never knew about. Do they know about me?'

Wajid looked grave. 'Once again it is my sad duty

to inform you that your brothers died bravely as soldiers in Ashur's recent war with Najar.'

Stunned, Ruby struggled to speak. 'Oh…yes, I've read about the war in the newspapers. That's very sad about my brothers. They must've been very young, as well,' Ruby remarked uncertainly, feeling hopelessly out of her depth.

The Ashuri side of her family was a complete blank to Ruby. She had never met her father or his relations and knew virtually nothing about them. On her one and only visit to Ashur, her once powerful curiosity had been cured when her mother's attempt to claim a connection to the ruling family was heartily rejected. Vanessa had written in advance of their visit but there had been no reply. Her phone calls once they arrived in Ashur had also failed to win them an invitation to the palace. Indeed, Vanessa and her daughter had finally been humiliatingly turned away from the gates of the royal palace when her father's relatives had not deigned to meet their estranged British relatives. From that moment on Ruby had proudly suppressed her curiosity about the Ashuri portion of her genes.

'Your brothers were brave young men,' Wajid told her. 'They died fighting for their country.'

Ruby nodded with a respectful smile and thought sadly about the two younger brothers she had never got the chance to meet. Had they ever wondered what she was like? She suspected that royal protocol might well have divided them even if, unlike the rest of their family, they had had sufficient interest to want to get to know her.

'I share these tragedies with you so that you can understand that you are now the present heir to the throne of Ashur, Your Royal Highness.'

'I'm the heir?' Ruby laughed out loud in sheer disbelief. 'How is that possible? I'm a girl, for goodness' sake! And why do you keep on calling me Your Royal Highness as if I have a title?'

'Whether you use it or otherwise, you have carried the title of Princess since the day you were born,' Wajid asserted with confidence. 'It is your birthright as the daughter of a king.'

It all sounded very impressive but Ruby was well aware that in reality, Ashur was still picking up the pieces in the aftermath of the conflict. That such a country had fought a war with its wealthy neighbour over the oil fields on their disputed boundary was a testament to their dogged pride and determination in spite of the odds against them. Even so she had been hugely relieved when she heard on the news that the war was finally over.

She struggled to appear composed when she was actually shaken by the assurance that she had a legal right to call herself a princess and then her natural common sense reasserted its sway. Could there be anything more ridiculously inappropriate than a princess who worked as a humble receptionist and had to struggle to pay her rent most months? Even with few extras in her budget Ruby was invariably broke and she often did a weekend shift at Stella's supermarket to help make ends meet.

'There's no room for titles and such things in my life,' she said gently, reluctant to cause offence by being any more blunt. 'I'm a very ordinary girl.'

'But that is exactly what our people would like most

about you. We are a country of ordinary hard-working people,' Wajid declared with ringing pride. 'You are the only heir to the throne of Ashur and you must take your rightful place.'

Ruby's soft pink lips parted in astonishment. 'Let me get this straight—you are asking me to come out to Ashur and live there as a princess?'

'Yes. That is why we are here, to make you aware of your position and to bring you home.' Wajid spread his arms expansively to emphasise his enthusiasm for the venture.

A good deal less expressive, Ruby tensed and shook her fair head in a quiet negative motion. 'Ashur is not my home. Nobody in the royal family has even seen me since I left the country as a baby. There has been no contact and no interest.'

The older man looked grave. 'That is true, but the tragedies that have almost wiped out the Shakarian family have ensured that everything has changed. You are now a very important person in Ashur, a princess, the daughter of a recent king and the niece of another, with a strong legal claim to the throne—'

'But I don't want to claim the throne, and in any case I do know enough about Ashur to know that women don't rule there,' Ruby cut in, her impatience growing, for she felt she was being fed a rather hypocritical official line that was a whitewash of the less palatable truth. 'I'm quite sure there is some man hovering in the wings ready to do the ruling in Ashur.'

The court advisor would have squirmed with dismay had he not possessed the carriage of a man with an iron bar welded to his short spine. Visibly, however, he stiffened even more. 'You are, of course, correct when you say that women do not rule in Ashur. Our country has long practised male preference primogeniture—'

'So I am really not quite as important as you would like to make out?' Ruby marvelled that he could ever have believed she might be so ignorant of the hereditary male role of kingship in Ashur. After all, hadn't her poor mother's marriage ended in tears and divorce thanks to those strict rules? Her father had taken another wife in a desperate attempt to have a son.

Placed in an awkward spot when he had least expected it, Wajid reddened and revised up his assumptions about the level of the princess's intelligence. 'I am sorry to contradict you but you are unquestionably a very important young woman in the eyes of our people. Without you there can be no King,' he admitted baldly.

'Excuse me?' Her fine brows were pleating. 'I'm sorry, I don't understand what you mean.'

Wajid hesitated. 'Ashur and Najar are to be united and jointly ruled by a marriage between the two royal families. That was integral to the peace terms that were agreed to at the end of the war.'

Ruby froze at that grudging explanation and resisted the urge to release an incredulous laugh, for she suddenly grasped what her true value was to this stern little man. They needed a princess to marry off, a princess who could claim to be in line to the throne of Ashur. And here she was young and single. Nothing personal or even complimentary as such in her selection, she reflected with a stab of resentment and regret. It did, however, make more sense to her that she was only finally being acknowledged in Ashur as a member of the royal family because there was nobody else more suitable available.

'I didn't know that arranged marriages still took place in Ashur.'

'Mainly within the royal family,' Wajid conceded grudgingly. 'Sometimes parents know their children better than their children know themselves.'

'Well, I no longer have parents to make that decision for me. In any case, *my* father never took the time to get to know me at all. I'm afraid you're wasting your time here, Mr Sulieman. I don't want to be a princess and I don't want to marry a stranger, either. I'm quite content with my life as it is.' Rising to her feet to indicate that she felt it was time that her visitors took their leave, Ruby felt sorry enough for the older man in his ignorance of contemporary Western values to offer him a look of sympathy. 'These days few young women would be attracted by an arrangement of that nature.'

Long after the limousine had disappeared from view Ruby and Stella sat discussing the visit.

'A princess?' Stella kept on repeating, studying the girl she had known from primary school with growing fascination. 'And you honestly didn't know?'

'I don't think they can have wanted Mum to know,' Ruby offered evenly. 'After the divorce my father and his family were happy for her to leave Ashur and from then on they preferred to pretend that she and I didn't exist.'

'I wonder what the guy they want you to marry is like,' Stella remarked, twirling her dark fringe with dreamy eyes, her imagination clearly caught.

'If he's anything like as callous as my father I'm

not missing anything. My father was willing to break Mum's heart to have a son and no doubt the man they want me to marry would do *anything* to become King of Ashur—'

'The guy has to be from the other country, right?'

'Najar? Must be. Probably some ambitious poor relation of their royal family looking for a leg up the ladder,' Ruby contended with rich cynicism, her scorn unconcealed.

'I'm not sure I would have been so quick to send your visitors packing. I mean, if you leave the husband out of it, being a princess might have been very exciting.'

'There was nothing exciting about Ashur,' Ruby assured her friend with a guilty wince at still being bitter about the country that had rejected her, for she had recognised Wajid Sulieman's sincere love for his country and the news of that awful trail of family deaths had been sobering and had left her feeling sad.

After a normal weekend during which her impressions of that astounding visit from the court advisor faded a little, Ruby went back to work. She had met up with Steve briefly on the Saturday afternoon and had told him that their relationship was over. He had taken it badly and had texted her repeatedly since then, alternately asking for another chance and then truculently criticising her and demanding to know what was wrong with him. She began ignoring the texts, wishing she had never gone out with him in the first place. He was acting a bit obsessive for a man she had only dated for a few weeks.

'Men always go mad over you,' Stella had sighed

enviously when the texts started coming through again at breakfast, which the girls snatched standing up in the tiny kitchen. 'I know Steve's being a nuisance but I wouldn't mind the attention.'

'That kind of attention you'd be welcome to,' Ruby declared without hesitation and she felt the same at work when her phone began buzzing before lunchtime with more messages, for she had nothing left to say to Steve.

A tall guy with luxuriant black hair strode through the door. There was something about him that immediately grabbed attention and Ruby found herself helplessly staring. Maybe it was his clothes, which stood out in a town where decent suits were only seen at weddings and then usually hired. He wore a strikingly elegant dark business suit that would have looked right at home in a designer advertisement in an exclusive magazine. It was perfectly modelled on his tall, well-built frame and long powerful legs. His razor-edged cheekbones were perfectly chiselled too, and as for those eyes, deep set, dark as sloes and brooding. *Wow*, Ruby thought for the very first time in her life as she looked at a man....

CHAPTER TWO

WHEN PRINCE RAJA walked into the solicitor's office, Ruby was the first person he saw and indeed, in spite of the number of other people milling about the busy reception area, pretty much the *only* person he saw. The pretty schoolgirl in the holiday snap had grown into a strikingly beautiful woman with a tumbling mane of blonde hair, sparkling eyes and a soft, full mouth that put him in mind of a succulent peach.

'You are Ruby Shakarian?' the prince asked as a tall, even more powerfully built man came through the door behind him to station himself several feet away.

'I don't use that surname.' Ruby frowned, wondering how many more royal dignitaries she would have to deflect before they got the hint and dropped this ridiculous idea that she was a princess. 'Where did you get it from?'

'Wajid Sulieman gave it to me and asked me to speak to you on his behalf. Shakarian is your family name,' Raja pointed out with an irrefutable logic that set her small white teeth on edge.

'I'm at work right now and not in a position to speak to you.' But Ruby continued to study him covertly, absorbing the lush black lashes semi-screening those mesmerising eyes, the twin slashes of his well-marked ebony brows, the smooth olive-toned skin moulding his strong cheekbones and the faint dark shadow of stubble accentuating his strong jaw and wide, sensual lips. Her prolonged scrutiny only served to confirm her original assessment that he was a stunningly beautiful man. Her heart was hammering so hard inside her chest that she felt seriously short of breath. It was a reaction that thoroughly infuriated her, for Ruby had always prided herself on her armour-plated indifference around men and the role of admirer was new to her.

'Aren't you going for lunch yet?' one of her co-workers enquired, walking past her desk.

'We could have lunch,' Raja pronounced, pouncing on the idea with relief.

Since his private jet had wafted him to Yorkshire and the cool spring temperature that morning, Prince Raja had felt rather like an alien set down on a strange planet. He was not used to small towns and checking into a third-rate local hotel had not improved his mood. He was cold, he was on edge and he did not relish the task foisted on him.

'If you're connected to that Wajid guy, no thanks to lunch,' Ruby pronounced as she got to her feet and reached for her bag regardless because she always went home at lunchtime.

The impression created by her seemingly long legs in that photo had been deceptive, for she was much smaller than Raja had expected and the top of her head barely reached halfway up his chest. Startled by that difference and bemused by that hitch in his concentration, Raja frowned. 'Connected?' he queried, confused by her use of the word.

'If you want to talk about the same thing that Wajid did, I've already heard all I need to hear on that subject,' Ruby extended ruefully. 'I mean…' she leant purposefully closer, not wishing to be overheard, and her intonation was gently mocking '…do I look like a princess to you?'

'You look like a goddess,' the prince heard himself say, speaking his thoughts out loud in a manner that was most unusual for him. His jaw tensed, for he would have preferred not to admit that her dazzling oval face had reminded him of a poster of a film star he recalled from his time serving with the Najari armed forces.

'A goddess?' Equally taken aback, Ruby suddenly grinned, dimples adorning her rounded cheeks. 'Well, that's a new one. Not something any of the men I know would come up with anyway.'

In the face of that glorious smile, Raja's fluent English vocabulary seized up entirely. 'Lunch,' he pronounced again stiltedly.

On the brink of saying no, Ruby recognised Steve waiting outside the door and almost groaned out loud. She knew the one infallible way of shaking a man off was generally to let him see her in the company of another. 'Lunch,' Ruby agreed abruptly, and she planted a determined hand on Raja's sleeve as if to take control of the situation. 'But first I have to go home and take my dog out.'

Raja was taken aback by that sudden physical contact, for people were never so familiar in the presence of royalty, and his breath rasped between his lips. 'That is acceptable.'

'Who is that guy over there watching us?' Ruby

asked in a suspicious whisper, long blonde hair brushing his shoulder and releasing a tide of perfume as fragrant as summer flowers into the air.

'One of my bodyguards.' Raja advanced with the relaxed attitude of a male who took a constant security presence entirely for granted. 'My car is waiting outside.'

The bodyguard went out first, looked to either side, almost bumping into Steve, and then spread the door wide again for their exit.

'Ruby?' Steve questioned, frowning at the tall dark male by her side as she emerged. 'Who is this guy? Where are you going with him?'

'I don't have anything more to say to you, Steve,' Ruby stated firmly.

'I have a right to ask who this guy is!' Steve snapped argumentatively, his face turning an angry red below his fair, floppy fringe.

'You have no rights over me at all,' Ruby told him in exasperation.

As Steve moved forward the prince made an almost infinitesimal signal with one hand and suddenly a big bodyguard was blocking the younger man's attempt to get closer to Ruby. At the same time the other bodyguard had whipped open the passenger door to a long sleek limousine.

'I can't possibly get into a car with a stranger,' Ruby objected, trying not to stare at the sheer size and opulence of the car and its interior.

Raja was unaccustomed to meeting with such suspicious treatment and it off balanced him for it was not what he had expected from her. In truth he had expected her to scramble eagerly into the limo and gush about the built-in bar while helping herself to his champagne like the usual women he dated. But if the angry lovelorn young man shouting Ruby's name was typical of the men she met perhaps she was sensible to be mistrustful of his sex.

'I live close by. I'll walk back home first and meet you there.' Ruby gave him her address and sped across the street at a smart pace, deliberately not turning her head or looking back when Steve called her name.

The prince watched her walk away briskly. The breeze blew back her hair in a glorious fan of golden strands and whipped pink into her pale cheeks. She had big eyes the colour of milk chocolate and the sort of lashes that graced cartoon characters in the films that Raja's youngest relatives loved to watch. A conspicuously feminine woman, she had a small waist and fine curves above and below it. Great legs, delicate at ankle and knee. He wondered if Steve had lain between those legs and the shock of that startlingly intimate thought sliced through Raja as the limo wafted him past and he got a last look at her. A woman with a face and body like that would make an arranged marriage tempting to any hot-blooded male, he told himself impatiently. And just at that moment Raja's blood was running very hot indeed and there was a heavy tightness at his groin that signified a rare loss of control for him.

Ruby took Hermione out on her lead and by the time she unlocked the front door again, with the little black-and-white dog trotting at her heels, the limousine was parked outside waiting for her. This time she noticed that as well as the bodyguard in the front passenger seat there was also a separate car evidently packed with bodyguards parked behind it. Why was so much security necessary? Who was this guy? For the first time it occurred to Ruby that this particular visitor had to be someone more important than Wajid Sulieman and his wife. Certainly he travelled in much greater style. Checking her watch then, she frowned. There really wasn't time for her to have lunch with anyone and she dug out her phone to ring work and ask if she could take an extended lunch hour. The office manager advanced grudging agreement only after she promised to catch up with her work by staying later that evening.

As she stood in the doorway, Hermione having retreated to her furry basket in the living room, the passenger door of the limo was opened by one of the bodyguards. Biting her full lower lip in confusion, Ruby finally pulled the door of her home closed behind her and crossed the pavement.

'I really do need to know who you are,' she spelt out tautly.

For the first time in more years than he cared to recall, Raja had the challenge of introducing himself.

'Raja and you're a prince?' she repeated blankly, his complex surname leaving her head as soon as she heard the unfamiliar syllables. 'But *who* are you?'

His wide, sensual mouth quirked and he surrendered to the inevitable. 'I'm the man Wajid Sulieman wants you to marry.'

And so great was the surprise of that admission that Ruby got into the car and sat back without further comment. This gorgeous guy was the man they wanted her to marry? He bore no resemblance whatsoever to her vague imaginings.

'Obviously you're from the other country, Najar,' she specified, recovering her ready tongue. 'A member of their royal family?'

'I am acting Regent of Najar. My father, King Ahmed, suffered a serious stroke some years ago and is now an invalid. I carry out his role in public because he is no longer able to do so.'

Ruby grasped the fine distinction he was making. Although his father suffered from ill health the older man remained the power behind the throne, doubtless restricting his son's ability to make his own decisions. Was that why Raja was willing to marry a stranger? Was he eager to assume power in Ashur where he could rule without his father's interference? Ruby hated being so ignorant. But what did she know about the politics of power and influence within the two countries?

One thing was for sure, however, Raja was very far from being the poor and accommodating royal hanger-on she had envisaged. Entrapped by her growing curiosity, she stole a long sidewise glance at him, noting the curling density of his lush black lashes, the high sculpted cheekbones that gave his profile such definition, the stubborn set of his masculine jaw line. Young, no more than thirty years of age at most, she estimated. Young, extremely good-looking *and* rich if the car and the security presence were anything to go by, she reasoned, all of which made it even harder for her to understand why he would be willing to even consider an arranged marriage.

'Someone digs up a total stranger, who just happens

to be a long-lost relative of the Shakarian family, and you're immediately willing to marry her?' she jibed.

'I have very good reasons for my compliance and that is why I was willing to fly here to speak to you personally,' Raja fielded with more than a hint of quelling ice in his deep, dark drawl and he waved a hand in a fluid gesture of emphasis that caught her attention. His movements were very graceful and yet amazingly masculine at the same time. He commanded her attention in a way she had never experienced before.

An involuntary flush at that reflection warmed Ruby's cheeks, for in general aggressively male men irritated her. Her stepfather had been just such a man, full of sports repartee, beer and sexist comments while he perved on her behind closed doors. 'Nothing you could say is likely to change my mind,' she warned Raja ruefully.

Unsettled by the effect he had on her and feeling inordinately like an insecure teenager, Ruby lowered her eyes defensively and her gaze fell on the male leg positioned nearest to hers. The fine, expensive material of his tailored trousers outlined the lean, muscular power of his thigh while the snug fit over the bulge at his crotch defined his male attributes. As soon as she realised where her attention had lodged she glanced hurriedly away, her face hot enough to fry eggs on and shock reverberating through her, for it was the very first time she had looked at a man as if he were solely a sex object. When she thought of how she hated men checking her out she could only feel embarrassed.

The prince took her to the town's only decent hotel for lunch. He attracted a good deal of attention there, particularly from women, Ruby registered with growing irritation. It didn't help that he walked across the busy dining room like the royal prince that he was, emanating a positive force field of sleek sophistication and assurance that set him apart from more ordinary mortals. Beside him she felt seriously underdressed in her plain skirt and raincoat. She just knew the other female diners were looking at her and wondering what such a magnificent male specimen was doing with her. The head waiter seated them in a quiet alcove where, mercifully, Ruby felt less on show and more at ease.

While they ate, and the food was excellent, Raja began to tell her about the war between Najar and Ashur and the current state of recovery in her birth country. The whole time he talked her attention was locked on him. It was as if they were the only two people left on the planet. He shifted a shapely hand and she wondered what it would feel like to have that hand touching her body. The surprise of the thought made her face flame. She absorbed the velvet nuances of his accented drawl and recognised that he had a beautiful speaking voice. But worst of all when she met the steady glitter of his dark, reflective, midnight gaze she felt positively light-headed and her mouth ran dry.

'Ashur's entire infrastructure was ruined and unemployment and poverty are rising,' Raja spelt out. 'Ashur needs massive investment to rebuild the roads, hospitals and schools that have been destroyed. Najar will make that investment but only if you and I marry. Peace was agreed solely on the basis of a marriage that would eventually unite our two countries as one.'

Gulping down some water in an attempt to ground

herself to planet earth again, Ruby was surprised by the willpower she had to muster simply to drag her gaze from his darkly handsome features and she said in an almost defiant tone, 'That's completely crazy.'

The prince angled his proud dark head in a position that signified unapologetic disagreement. 'Far from it. It is at present the only effective route to reconciliation which can be undertaken without either country losing face.' As he made that statement his classic cheekbones were taut with tension, accentuating the smooth planes of the olive-tinted skin stretched over his superb bone structure.

'Obviously I can see that nobody with a brain would want the war to kick off again,' Ruby cut in ruefully, more shaken than she was prepared to admit by the serious nature of Ashur's plight. She had not appreciated how grave the problems might be and even though the ruling family of her birth country had refused to acknowledge her existence, she was ashamed of the level of her ignorance.

'Precisely, and that is where *our* role comes in,' Raja imparted smoothly. 'Ashur can only accept my country's economic intervention if it comes wrapped in the reassurance of a traditional royal marriage.'

Ruby nodded in comprehension, her expression carefully blank as she asked what was for her the obvious question. 'So what's going to happen when this marriage fails to take place?'

In the dragging silence that fell in receipt of that leading query, his brilliant dark eyes narrowed and his lean, strong face took on a forbidding aspect. 'As the marriage was an established element of the peace accord, many will argue that if no marriage takes place the agreement has broken down and hostilities could easily break out again. Our families are well respected. Given the right approach, we could act as a unifying force and our people would support us in that endeavour for the sake of a lasting peace.'

'And you're willing to sacrifice your own freedom for the sake of that peace?' Ruby asked, wearing a dubious expression.

'It is not a choice. It is a duty,' Raja pronounced with a fluid shift of his beautifully shaped fingers. He said more with his hands than with his tongue, Ruby decided, for that eloquent gesture encompassed his complete acceptance of a sacrifice he clearly saw as unavoidable.

Ruby surveyed him steadily before saying without hesitation, 'I think that's a load of nonsense. How can you be so accepting of your duty?'

Raja breathed in deep and slow before responding to her challenge. 'As a member of the royal family I have led a privileged life and I was brought up to appreciate that what is best for my country should be my prime motivation.'

Unimpressed by that zealous statement, Ruby rolled her eyes in cynical dismissal. 'Well, I haven't led a privileged life and I'm afraid I don't have that kind of motivation to fall back on. I'm not sure I can believe that you do, either.'

Under rare attack for his conservative views and for the depth of his sincerity, Raja squared his broad shoulders, his lean, dark features setting hard. He was offended but determined to keep his emotions in check.

He suspected that the real problem was that Ruby rarely thought before she spoke and he virtually never met with challenge or criticism. 'Meaning?'

'Did you fight in the war?' Ruby prompted suddenly.

'Yes.'

Ruby's appetite ebbed and she rested back in her chair, milk-chocolate eyes telegraphing her contempt in a look that her quarry was not accustomed to receiving.

His tough jaw line clenched. 'That is the reality of war.'

'And now you think you can buy your way out of that reality by marrying me and becoming a saviour where you were once the aggressor?' Ruby fired back with a curled lip as she pushed away her plate. 'Sorry, I have no intention of being a pawn in a power struggle or of helping you to come to terms with your conscience. I'd like to leave now.'

On a wave of angry frustration Raja studied her truculent little face, his glittering eyes hostile. 'You haven't listened to me—'

Confident of her own opinion, Ruby lifted her chin in direct challenge of that charge. 'On the contrary, I've listened and I've heard as much as I need to hear. I can't be the woman you want me to be. I'm not a princess and I have no desire to sacrifice myself for the people or the country that broke my mother's heart.'

At that melodramatic response, Raja only just resisted the urge to groan out loud. 'You're talking like a child.'

A red-hot flush ran up to the very roots of Ruby's pale hair. 'How dare you?' she ground out, outraged.

'I dare because I need you to think like an adult to deal with this dilemma. You may be prejudiced against the country where you were born but don't drag up old history as an excuse—'

'There's nothing old about the way I grew up without a father,' Ruby argued vehemently, starting to rise from her chair in tune with her rapidly rising temper. 'Or the fact that he married another woman while he was still married to my mum! If that's what you call prejudice then I'm not ashamed to own up to it!'

'Lower your voice and sit down!' the prince ground out in a biting undertone.

Ruby was so stunned by that command that she instinctively fell back into her seat and stared across the table at him with a shaken frown of disbelief that he could think he had the right to order her around. 'Don't speak to me like that—'

'Then calm down and think of those less fortunate than you are.'

'It still won't make me willing to marry a stranger, who would marry a dancing bear if he was asked!' Ruby shot back at him angrily.

'What on earth are you trying to suggest?' Raja demanded, dark eyes blazing like angry golden flames above them.

More than ready to tell him what she thought of him, Ruby tossed down her napkin with a positive flourish. 'Did you think that I would be too stupid to work out what you're really after?' she asked him sharply. 'You want the throne in Ashur and I'm the only way you have of getting it! Without me and a ring on my finger, you get nothing!'

Subjecting her to a stunned look of proud incredulity, Raja watched with even greater astonishment as Ruby plunged upright, abandoned their meal and stalked away, hair flying, narrow back rigid, skirt riding up on those slender shapely thighs. Had she no manners? No concept of restraint in public places? She actually believed that he *wanted* the throne in Ashur? Was that her idea of a joke? She had no grasp of realities whatsoever. He was the future hereditary ruler of one of the most sophisticated and rich countries in the Persian Gulf, he did not need to rule Ashur, as well.

A BRISK WALK of twenty minutes brought Ruby back to work. A little breathless and flustered after the time she had had to consider that fiery exchange over lunch, she was still trying to decide whether or not she had been unfair in her assessment of Prince Raja. Waiting on her desktop for her attention was a pile of work, however, and her head was already aching from the stress of the information he had dumped on her.

At spare moments during the afternoon that followed she mulled over what she had learned about her birth country's predicament. It was not her fault all that had happened between Ashur and Najar, was it? But if Raja was correct and the peace broke down over the reality that their marriage and therefore the planned unification of the two countries did not take place, how would she feel about things then? That was a much less straightforward question and Ruby resolved to do some Internet research that evening to settle the questions she needed answered.

While Stella was cooking a late dinner, Ruby lifted

the laptop the two young women shared, let Herm-ione curl up by her feet and sought information on the recent events in Ashur. Unfortunately a good deal of what she discovered was distressing stuff. Her late fa-ther's country, Ashur, she slowly recognised, desper-ately needed help getting back on its feet and people everywhere were praying that the peace would hold. Reading a charity worker's blog about the rising num-ber of homeless people and orphans, Ruby felt tears sting her eyes and she blinked them back hurriedly and went to eat her dinner without an appetite. She could tell herself that Ashur was nothing to do with her but she was learning that her gut reaction was not guided by intellect. The war might be over but there was a huge job of rebuilding to be done and not enough resources to pay for it. In the meantime the people of Ashur were suffering. Could the future of an entire country and its people be resting on what she chose to do?

Sobered by that thought and the heavy responsi-bility that accompanied it, Ruby started to carefully consider her possible options. Stella ate and hurried out on a date. While Ruby was still deep in thought and tidying up the tiny kitchen, the doorbell buzzed. This time she was not surprised to find Najar's much-decorated fighter-pilot prince on her doorstep again, for even she was now prepared to admit that they still had stuff to talk about. The sheer, dark masculine beauty of his bronzed features still took her by storm though and mesmerised her into stunned stillness. Those lustrous eyes set between sooty lashes in that stunningly mas-culine face exerted a powerful magnetic pull. She felt a tug at the heart of her and a prickling surge of heat.

Once again, dragging her attention from him was like trying to leap single-handed out of a swamp.

'You'd better come in—we have to talk,' she acknowledged in a brittle breathless aside, exasperated by the way he made her stare and turning on her heel with hot cheeks to leave him to follow her.

'It's rude in my culture to turn your back on a guest or on royalty,' Raja informed her almost carelessly.

With a sound of annoyance, Ruby whipped her blonde head around to study him with frowning brown eyes. 'We have bigger problems than my ignorance of etiquette!'

As the tall, powerful man entered the room in Ruby's wake Hermione peered out of her basket, beady, dark eyes full of suspicion. A low warning growl vibrated in the dog's throat.

'No!' Ruby told her pet firmly.

'You were expecting my visit,' Raja acknowledged, taking a seat at her invitation and striving not to notice the way her tight black leggings and shrunken tee hugged her pert, rounded curves at breast and hip. The fluffy pink bunny slippers she wore on her tiny feet, however, made him compress his handsome mouth. He did not want to be reminded of just how young and unprepared she was for the role being offered to her.

Ruby breathed in deep, fighting the arrowing slide of shameless awareness keeping her unnaturally tense as she took a seat opposite him. Even at rest, the intoxicating strength of his tall, long-limbed, muscular body was obvious and she was suddenly conscious that her nipples had tightened into hard bullet points. She sucked in another breath, desperate to regain her usual composure. 'Yes, I was expecting you.'

Raja did not break the silence when her voice faltered. He waited patiently for her to continue with a quality of confident cool and calm that she found fantastically sexy.

'It's best if I lay my cards on the table this time. First of all, I would never, *ever* be prepared to agree to a normal marriage with a stranger, so that option isn't even a possibility,' Ruby declared without apology, knowing that she needed to tell him that upfront. 'But if you genuinely believe that only our marriage could ensure peace for Ashur, I feel I have to consider some way of bringing that about that we can both live with.'

Approbation gleamed in Raja's dark gaze because he believed that she was finally beginning to see sense. He was also in the act of reflecting that he could contrive to live with her without any great problem. He pinned his attention to the stunning contours of her face while remaining painfully aware of the full soft, rounded curves of her unbound breasts outlined in thin cotton. Clear indentations in the fabric marked the pointed evidence of her nipples and the flame of nagging heat at his groin would not quit. Angry at his loss of concentration at so important a meeting, however, he compressed his wide, sensual mouth and willed his undisciplined body back under his control.

'I *do* believe that only our marriage can give our countries the hope of an enduring peace,' he admitted. 'But if you are not prepared to consider a normal marriage, what are you suggesting?'

'A total fake,' Ruby replied without hesitation, a

hint of amusement lightening her unusually serious eyes. 'I marry you and we make occasional public appearances together to satisfy expectations but behind closed doors we're just pretending to be an ordinary married couple.'

The prince concealed his surprise and mastered his expression lest he make the mistake of revealing that inflicting such a massive deception on so many people would be abhorrent to his principles. 'A platonic arrangement?'

Ruby nodded with enthusiasm. 'No offence intended but I'm really not into sex—'

'With me? Or with anyone?' Raja could not resist demanding that she make that distinction.

'Anyone. It's nothing personal,' she hastened to assure a male who was taking it all very personally indeed. 'And it will also give you the perfect future excuse to divorce me.'

Hopelessly engaged in wondering what had happened to her to give her such a distaste for intimacy, Raja frowned in bewilderment. 'How?'

'Well, obviously there won't be a child. I'm not stupid, Raja. Obviously if we get married a son and heir is what everyone will be hoping for,' she pointed out wryly. 'But when there is no pregnancy and no child, you can use that as a very good reason to divorce me and then marry someone much more suitable.'

'It would not be that simple. I fully understand where you got this idea from though,' he imparted wryly. 'But while your father may have divorced your mother in such circumstances, there has never been a divorce within my family and our people and yours would be very much shocked and disturbed by such a development.'

Ruby shrugged a slight shoulder in disinterested dismissal of that possibility. 'There isn't going to be a *perfect* solution to our dilemma,' she told him impatiently. 'And I think that a fake marriage could well be as good as it gets. Take it or leave it, Raja.'

Raja almost laughed out loud at that impudent closing speech. What a child she still was! He could only begin to imagine how deeply offended the Ashuri people would be were he to divorce their princess while seeking to continue to rule their country. What she was suggesting was only a stopgap solution, not a permanent remedy to the dilemma.

'Well, that's one angle but not the only one,' Ruby continued ruefully. 'I have to be very blunt here...'

An unexpected grin slanted across Raja's beautifully moulded mouth, for in his opinion she had already been exceedingly frank. 'By all means, be blunt.'

'I would have to have equal billing in the ruling stakes,' she told him squarely. 'I can't see how you can be trusted to look out for the interests of both countries when you're from Najar. You would have an unfair advantage. I will only agree to marry you if I have as much of a say in all major decisions as you do.'

'That is a revolutionary idea and not without its merits,' Raja commented, striving not to picture Wajid Sulieman's shattered face when he learned that his princess was not, after all, prepared to be a powerless puppet on the throne. 'You should have that right but it will not be easy to convince the councils of old men, who act as the real government in our respective countries. In addition, you will surely concede that you know nothing about our culture—'

'But I can certainly learn,' Ruby broke in with stubborn determination. 'Well, those are my terms.'

'You won't negotiate?' the prince prompted.

'There is no room for negotiation.'

Raja was grimly amused by that uncompromising stance. In many ways it only emphasised her naivety. She assumed that she could break all the rules and remain untouched by the consequences yet she had no idea of what real life was like in her native country. Without that knowledge she could not understand how much was at stake. He knew his own role too well to require advice on how to respond to her demands.

Royal life had taught him early that he did not have the luxury of personal choice. His primary duty was to persuade the princess to take up her official role in Ashur and to marry her, twin objectives that he was expected to achieve by using any and every means within his power. His father had made it clear that the need for peace must overrule every other consideration. Any natural reluctance to agree to a celibate marriage in a society where extramarital sex was regarded as a serious evil did not even weigh in the balance.

I'm really not into sex, she had confided and, like any man, he was intrigued. Since she could not make such an announcement and still be an innocent he could only assume that she had suffered from the attentions of at least one clumsy lover. Far from being an amateur in the same field, Raja surveyed her with a gleam of sensual speculation in his dark eyes. He was convinced that given the right opportunity he could change her mind on that score.

'Well, what do you think?' Ruby pressed edgily as she rose to her feet again.

'I will consider your proposition,' the prince conceded non-committally, springing upright to look down at her with hooded, dark eyes.

His ability to conceal his thoughts from his lean, dark features infuriated Ruby, who had always found the male sex fairly easy to read. For once she had not a clue what a man might be thinking and her ignorance intimidated and frustrated her. Like the truly stunning dark good looks that probably turned heads wherever he went, the prince's reticence was one of his most noticeable attributes. He had the skills of a natural-born diplomat, she conceded, grudgingly recognising how well equipped he was to deal with opposing viewpoints and sensitive political issues.

'I thought time was a real matter of concern,' Ruby could not help remarking, irritated by his silence.

A highly attractive grin slanted his wide sensual mouth. 'If you give me your phone number I will contact you later this evening with my answer.'

Ruby gave him that information and walked out to the front door. As she began to open it he rested a hand on her shoulder, staying her, and she glanced up from below her lashes, eyes questioning. Hermione growled. Raja ignored the animal, sliding his hand lightly down Ruby's arm and up again, his handsome head lowering, his proud gaze glittering as bright as diamonds from below the fringe of his dense black lashes. She stopped breathing, moving, even thinking, trapped in

the humming silence while a buzz of excitement unlike anything she had ever experienced trailed along
her nerve endings like a taunting touch.

His breath warmed her cheek and she focused on
his strong sensual mouth, the surge of heat and warmth
between her thighs going crazy. Desire was shooting
through her veins like adrenaline and she didn't understand it, couldn't control it either, any more than
she could defy the temptation to rest up against him,
palms spread across his chest to absorb the muscular
strength of his powerful frame and remain upright.
Eyes wide, she stared up at him, trembling with anticipation and he did not disappoint her. On the passage to her mouth his lips grazed the pulse quivering
in her neck and an almost violent shimmy of sensation
shot down through her slight length. His hand sliding
down to her waist to steady her, he circled her mouth
with a kiss as hot as a blowtorch. The heat of his passion sent a shock wave of sexual response spiralling
down straight into her pelvis.

Raja only lifted his head again when Hermione's
noisy assault on his ankles became too violent to ignore. 'Call off your dog,' he urged her huskily.

Grateful for the excuse to move, Ruby wasted no
time in capturing her snarling pet and depositing her
back in the living room. Her hands were shaking. Nervous perspiration beaded her upper lip. Ruby was in
serious shock from finally feeling what a man had
never made her feel before. She was still light-headed
from the experience, and her temper surged when she
caught Raja studying her intently. Consumed by a sense
of foolishness, she was afraid that he might have no-

ticed that she was trembling and her condemnation was shrill. 'You had no right to touch me!'

His lustrous dark eyes glinted like rapier blades over her angry face. 'I had no right but I was very curious,' he countered with a studied insolence that pushed a tide of colour into her cheeks. 'And you were worth the risk.'

A moment later he was gone and she closed the door, only just resisting the urge to slam it noisily. She was still as wound up as a clock spring. Men didn't speak to Ruby in that condescending tone and they rarely, if ever, offered her provocation. Invariably they tried to please her and utilised every ploy from flattery to gifts to achieve that end. Raja, on the other hand, had subjected her to a cool measuring scrutiny and had remained resolutely unimpressed and in control while she fell apart and she could only hate him for that: *she* had shown weakness and susceptibility, he had not.

Her phone rang at eleven when she was getting ready for bed.

'It's Raja.' His dark drawl was very businesslike in tone and delivery. 'I hope you're prepared to move quickly on this as time is of the essence.'

Taut with strain and with her teeth gritted, for it was an effort to be polite to him with her pride still stinging from that kiss that she had failed to rebuff, Ruby said stiffly, 'That depends on whether or not you're prepared to stand by my terms.'

'You have my agreement. While I make arrangements for our marriage to take place here—'

'Like soon...*now*? And we're to get married *here*?'

Ruby interrupted, unable to swallow back her astonishment.

'It would be safer and more straightforward if the
deed were already done before you even set foot in
Ashur because our respective representatives will very
likely quarrel about the when and the where and the
how of our wedding for months on end,' the prince informed her wryly. 'In those circumstances, staging a
quiet ceremony here in the UK makes the most sense.'

Infuriatingly at home giving orders and impervious
to her tart comments, Raja advised her to resign from
her job immediately and start packing. Ruby stayed
out of bed purely to tell Stella that she was getting
married. Her friend was stunned and less moved than
Ruby by stories of Ashur's current instability and economic hardship.

'You're not thinking about what you're doing,' Stella
exclaimed, her pretty face troubled. 'You've let this
prince talk you round. He made you feel bad but, let's
face it, your life is here. What's your father's country
got to do with you?'

Only forty-eight hours earlier, Ruby would have
agreed with that sentiment. But matters were not so cut
and dried now. Ashur's problems were no longer distant, impersonal issues and she could not ignore their
claim on her conscience. In her mind the suffering
there now bore the faces of the ordinary people whose
lives had been ruined by the long conflict.

Ruby compressed her generous mouth. 'I just feel
that if I can do something to help, I should do it. It
won't be a proper marriage, for goodness' sake.'

'You might get over there and find out that the prince already has a wife,' Stella said with a curled lip.

'I don't think so. He wouldn't be here if I wasn't needed.'

Unaccustomed to Ruby being so serious, Stella pulled a face. 'Well, look what happened to your mother when she married a man from a different culture.'

'But Mum was in love while I would just be acting out a role. I won't get hurt the way she did. I'm not stuffed full of stupid romantic ideas,' Ruby declared, her chin coming up. 'I'm much tougher and I can look after myself.'

'I suppose you know yourself best,' Stella conceded, taken aback by Ruby's vehemence.

Ruby couldn't sleep that night. The idea of marrying Najar's Prince still felt unreal. She could have done without her friend's honest reminder that her mother's royal marriage had gone badly wrong. Although Ruby knew that she had absolutely no romantic interest in Raja and was therefore safe from being hurt or disappointed by him, she could not forget the heartbreak her mother had suffered when she had attempted to adapt to a very different way of life.

At the same time the haunting images Ruby had seen of the devastation in Ashur kept her awake until the early hours. The plight of her father's people was the only reason she was willing to agree to such a marriage, she reflected ruefully. Even though she was being driven by good intentions the prospect of marrying a prince and making her home in a strange land filled her to overflowing with doubts and insecurity.

In recent years she had often regretted the lack of excitement in her life, but now all of a sudden she was being confronted with the truth of that old adage: *Be careful of what you wish for....*

CHAPTER THREE

THE SALESWOMAN DISPLAYED a ghastly, shapeless plum-coloured suit that could only have pleased a woman who had lost interest in her appearance. Of course it was not the saleswoman's fault, Ruby reasoned in growing frustration; it was Raja's insistence on the outfit being 'very conservative and plain' that had encouraged the misunderstanding of what Ruby might be prepared to wear at her wedding.

'That's not me, that's really not my style!' Ruby declared with a grimace.

'Then choose something and quickly,' the prince urged in an impatient aside for he was not a patient shopper. 'Show some initiative!'

Raja did not understand why what she wore should matter so much. After all, even in her current outfit of faded jeans and a blue sweater she looked beautiful enough in his opinion to stop traffic. Luxuriant honey-blonde hair tumbled round her narrow shoulders. Denim moulded her curvy derrière and slim thighs, wool cupped the swell of her pouting breasts and emphasised her small waist. Even unadorned, she had buckets of utterly natural sex appeal. As he recognised the swelling heaviness of arousal at his groin his lean dark features clenched hard and he fixed his attention on the wall instead.

Show some initiative? Dull coins of aggravated red blossomed over Ruby's cheekbones and her sultry pink mouth compressed. Where did someone who had so far dismissed all her helpful suggestions get the nerve to taunt her with her lack of initiative? It was only an hour and a half since she had met her future husband at his hotel to sign the various forms that would enable them to get married in a civil ceremony and he was already getting on her nerves so much that she wanted to kill him! Or at the very least kick him! A high-ranking London diplomat had also attended that meeting to explain that a special licence was being advanced to facilitate their speedy marriage. Raja, she had learned, enjoyed diplomatic immunity. He was equally immune, she was discovering, to any sense of fashion or any appreciation of female superiority.

Stalking up to the rail of the town's most expensive boutique, Ruby began to leaf through it, eventually pulling a red suit out. 'I'll try this one on.'

The prince's beautifully shaped mouth curled. 'It is very bright.'

'You did say that a formal publicity photo would be taken and I don't want to vanish into the woodwork,' Ruby told him sweetly, big brown eyes wide with innocence but swiftly narrowing to stare intently at his glorious face. He was gorgeous. That fabulous bone structure and those dark deep-set eyes set below that slightly curly but ruthlessly cropped black hair took her breath away every time.

The saleswoman took the suit to hang it in a dressing room. With fluid grace Raja lifted his hand and let his thumb graze along the fullness of Ruby's luscious lower lip. His dark eyes glittered hot as coals as he felt that softness and remembered the sweet heady taste of that succulent mouth beneath his own. Tensing, Ruby dealt him a startled look, her lips tingling at his touch while alarm tugged at her nerves. As his hand dropped she moved closer and muttered in taut warning, 'This is business, just business between us.'

'Business,' the prince repeated, his accent scissoring round the label like a razor-sharp blade. Business was straightforward and Ruby Shakarian was anything but. He watched her sashay into the dressing room, little shoulders squared, hair bouncing, all cheeky attitude and surplus energy. He wanted to laugh but he had far too much tact. He didn't agree with her description. Business? No, he wanted to have sex with her. He wanted to have sex with her very, very much. He knew that and accepted it as a natural consequence of his male libido. Desire was a predictable response in a young and healthy man when he was with a beautiful woman. It was also a positive advantage in a royal marriage. Sex was sex, after all, little more than an entertaining means to an end when children were required. Finer feelings were neither required nor advisable. Been there, done that, Raja acknowledged in a bleak burst of recollection from the past. He had had his heart broken once and had sworn he would never put it up for a woman's target practice again.

Even so, once Ruby was his wife Raja had every intention of ensuring that the marriage followed a much more conventional path than she presently intended.

Obviously he didn't want a divorce. A divorce would mean he had failed in his duty, failed his family and *failed* his very country. He breathed in deep and slow at that aggrieved acknowledgement, mentally tasting the bite of such a far-reaching failure and striving not to flinch from it. After all there was only so much that he *could* do. It was unfair that so much should rest on his ability to make a success of an arranged marriage but Raja al-Somari had long understood that life was rarely fair. The bottom line was that he and everyone who depended on them needed their prince and princess to build a relationship with a future. And a fake marriage could never achieve that objective.

Over the three days that followed Ruby was much too busy to get cold feet about the upheaval in her life. She resigned from her job without much regret and began packing, systematically working through all her possessions and discarding the clutter while Stella lamented her approaching departure and placed an ad in the local paper for a new housemate. The day before the wedding, Hermione, accompanied by her favourite squeaky toy and copious instructions regarding her care and diet, was collected to be transported out to Ashur in advance. The memory of her pet's frightened little eyes above her greying muzzle as she looked out through the barred door of her pet carrier kept her mistress awake that night.

The wedding was staged with the maximum possible discretion in a private room at the hotel with two diplomats acting as official witnesses. Accompanied only by Stella, Ruby arrived and took her place by Raja's side. His black hair displaying a glossy blue-black sheen below the lights, dark eyes brilliant shards of light between the thick fringe of his lashes, Raja looked impossibly handsome in a formal, dark pinstripe suit. When he met her appraisal he didn't smile and his lean bronzed features remained grave. She wondered what he was thinking. Not knowing annoyed her. Her heart was beating uncomfortably fast by the time that the middle-aged registrar began the short service. Raja slid a gold ring onto her finger and because it was too big she had to crook her finger to keep the ring from falling off. The poorly fitting ring struck her as an appropriate addition to a ceremony that, shorn of all bridal and emotional frills, left her feeling distinctly unmarried.

It was done, goal achieved, Raja reflected with considerable satisfaction. His bride had not succumbed to a last-minute change of heart as he had feared. He studied Ruby's delicately drawn profile with appreciation. She might look fragile as a wild flower but she had a core of steel, for she had given her word and although he had sensed her mounting tension and uncertainty she had defied his expectations and stuck to it.

One of the diplomats shook Ruby's hand and addressed her as 'Your Royal Highness', which felt seriously weird to her.

'I'm never ever going to be able to see you as a princess,' Stella confided with a giggle.

'Give Ruby time,' Raja remarked silkily.

Colour tinged Ruby's cheeks. 'I'm not going to change, Stella.'

'Of course you will,' the prince contradicted with unassailable confidence, escorting his bride over to a floral display on a table where the photographer awaited them. 'You're about to enter a different life and I believe you'll pick up the rules quickly. Smile.'

'Raja,' Ruby whispered sweetly, and as he inclined his arrogant, dark head down to hers she snapped, '*Don't* tell me what to do!'

'Petty,' he told her smoothly, his shrewd gaze encompassing the photographer within earshot.

And foolish as it was over so minor an exchange, Ruby's blood boiled in her veins. She hated that sensation of being ignorant and in the position that she was likely to do something wrong. Even more did she hate being bossed around and told what to do and Raja al-Somari rapped out commands to the manner born. No doubt she would make the occasional mistake but she was determined to learn even quicker than he expected for both their sakes.

Chin at a defiant angle, Ruby gave Stella a quick hug, promised to phone and climbed into the limousine to travel to the airport. She would have liked the chance to change into something more comfortable in which to travel but Raja had stopped her from doing so, advising her that while she was in her official capacity as a princess of Ashur and his wife she was on duty and had to embrace the conservative wardrobe. His wife, Ruby thought in a daze of disbelief, thinking back to the previous week when she had been kissing Steve in his car. How could her life have changed so much in so short a time?

But she comforted herself with the knowledge that she wasn't *really* his wife, she was only pretending. Boarding the unbelievably opulent private jet awaiting them and seeing the unconcealed curiosity in the eyes of the cabin staff, Ruby finally appreciated that pretending to be a princess married to Raja was likely to demand a fair degree of acting from her. Instead of kicking off her shoes and curling up in one of the cream leather seats in the cabin, she found herself sitting down sedately and striving for a dignified pose for the first time in her life.

Soon after take-off, Raja rose from his seat and settled a file down in front of her. 'I asked my staff to prepare this for you.' He flipped it open. 'It contains photos and names for the main members of the two royal households and various VIPs in both countries as well as other useful information—'

'Homework,' Ruby commented dulcetly. 'To think I thought I'd left that behind when I left school.'

'Careful preparation should make the transition a little easier for you.'

Ruby could not credit how many names and faces he expected her to memorise, and the lengthy sections encompassing history, geography and culture in both countries made distinctly heavy reading. After a light lunch was served, Ruby took a break and watched Raja working on his laptop, lean fingers deft and fast. Her husband? It still didn't feel credible. His black lashes shaded his eyes like silk fans and when he glanced at her with those dark deep-set eyes that gleamed like polished bronze, something tripped in her throat and strangled her breathing. He was drop-dead gorgeous and naturally she was staring. Any woman would, she told herself irritably. She didn't fancy him; she did *not*.

Raja left the main cabin to change and reappeared

in a white, full-length, desert-style robe worn with a headdress bound with a black and gold cord.

'You look just like you're starring in an old black-and-white movie set in the desert,' she confided helplessly, totally taken aback by the transformation.

'That is not a comment I would repeat in Najar, where such a mode of dress is the norm,' Raja advised her drily. 'I do not flaunt a Western lifestyle at home.'

Embarrassment stirring red heat in her cheeks, Ruby dealt him a look of annoyance. 'Or a sense of humour.'

But in truth there was nothing funny about his appearance. He actually looked amazingly dignified and royal and shockingly handsome. Even so his statement that he did not follow a Western lifestyle sent an arrow of apprehension winging through her. What other surprises might lie in wait for her?

A few minutes later he warned her that the jet would be landing in Najar in thirty minutes. When she returned after freshening up he announced with the utmost casualness that they would be parting once the jet landed. She would be flying straight on to Ashur where he would join her later in the week.

Ruby was shattered by that unexpected news and her head swivelled, eyes filled with disbelief. 'You're leaving me to travel on alone to Ashur?'

'Only for thirty-six hours at most. I'm afraid that I can't be in two places at once.'

'Even on what's supposed to be our wedding night?' Ruby launched at him.

The prince shut his laptop and shot her a veiled look as silky as melted honey and somehow that appraisal made her tummy perform acrobatics. 'Are you offering me one?'

The silence simmered like a kettle on the boil. Her cheeks washed with heat, Ruby scrambled to her feet. 'Of course, I'm not!'

'I thought not. So, what's the problem? The exact date of our marriage will not be publicly announced. Very few people will be aware that this is our wedding night.'

Ruby almost screamed. He was not that stupid. He was seriously not that stupid and his casual reaction to her criticism enraged her. She breathed in so deep and long she was vaguely surprised that her head didn't lift off her shoulders and float. 'You're asking me what the problem is? Is that a joke?'

Raja uncoiled from his seat with the fluid grace of a martial arts expert. Standing very straight and tall, broad shoulders hard as a blade, Raja rested cool eyes on her, for he was not accustomed to being shouted at and he was in no mood to become accustomed to the experience. 'Naturally I am not joking.'

'And you can't see anything wrong with dumping me with a bunch of strangers in a foreign country? I don't know anyone, don't speak the language, don't even know *how* to behave,' Ruby yelled back at him full volume, causing the steward entering the cabin with a trolley to hastily backtrack and close the door again. 'How can you abandon me like that?'

The prince gazed down at her with frowning dark eyes, exasperated by her ignorance. Clearly she had no concept of the extensive planning and detailed security arrangements that accompanied his every movement and that would soon apply equally to hers. Familiar as Raja was with the military precision of planning a royal schedule set in stone often months in advance, he saw no room for manoeuvre or a change of heart. 'Abandon you? How am I abandoning you?'

Made to feel as if she was being melodramatic, Ruby reddened and pursed her sultry mouth. 'You're supposed to be my husband.'

Taken aback by the reminder, Raja quirked an expressive ebony brow. 'But according to you we're only faking it.'

'Well, you're not faking it worth a damn!' Ruby condemned with furious bite, strands of hair shimmying round her flushed cheekbones, eyes accusing. 'A husband should be loyal and supportive. I don't know how to be a princess yet and if I make mistakes I'm likely to offend people. Hasn't that occurred to you? You can't leave me alone in a strange place. I don't know how to give these people what they expect and deserve and I was depending on you to tell me!'

Unprepared for his gutsy bride to reveal panic, Raja frowned, setting his features into a stern mask. 'Unfortunately arrangements are already in place for us to go our separate ways this afternoon. It is virtually impossible to make last-minute changes to that schedule. We're about to land in Najar, I'm expected home and you're flying on to Ashur by yourself.'

Suddenly mortified by the nerves that had got the better of her composure, Ruby screened her apprehensive gaze and said stiffly as she took her seat with determination again, 'Fine. Don't worry about it—I'm sure I'll manage. I'm used to being on my own.'

Ruby didn't speak another word. She was furious with herself for revealing her insecurity. What on earth had she expected from him? Support? When had she ever known a man to be supportive? Raja had his own priorities and they were not the same as hers. As he had reminded her, their marriage, their very relationship, was a fake. As, to be fair, she had requested. Her soft, full mouth curved down. Clearly if she wasn't sleeping with him she was on her own and that was nothing new....

CHAPTER FOUR

THE INSTANT RUBY stepped out of the plane the heat of the sun engulfed her in a powerful wave, dewing her upper lip with perspiration and giving the skin below her clothes a sticky feeling. In the distance an architectural triumph of an airport building glinted in the sun. A man bowed low in front of her and indicated a small plane about fifty yards away. Breathing in deep and slow to steady her nerves, Ruby followed him.

At the top of the steps and mere seconds in her wake, the prince came to a dead halt, rare indecision gripping him.

'You're supposed to be my husband...loyal and supportive.'

'How can you abandon me?'

His stubborn jaw line clenched. He gritted his teeth. He could not fault her expectations. Would he not expect similar consideration from her? He was also a very masculine guy and it went against the grain to ignore her plea for help. At a time when her role was still so new to her, even a temporary separation was a bad idea. Of course she was feeling overwhelmed and he was well aware that people would be only too willing to find fault when she made innocent mistakes. He strode down the steps, addressed the court official waiting to greet him and politely ignored the surprise, dismay and the sudden burst of speech that followed his declaration of a change of plan. All the signs were that the little plane parked on the asphalt was almost ready to take off and, determined not to miss his chance to join his bride, Raja headed straight for it. His security chief ran after him only to be waved away for so small a craft had only limited room for passengers.

Ruby buckled her belt in the small, stiflingly hot compartment. She had never flown in so small a plane before and she felt utterly unnerved by her solitary state. When a young man approached her with a bent head and a tray to proffer a glass she was quick to mutter grateful thanks and grasp it, drinking down the fragrantly scented chilled drink, only to wince at the bitter aftertaste it left in her mouth. She set the empty glass back on the tray with a strained smile and the steward retreated again.

A split second later, she heard someone else board and Raja dropped down into the seat by her side. Astonished by his reappearance, Ruby twisted round to study him. 'You've changed your mind? You're coming with me?'

Raja basked in the glowing smile of instant relief and appreciation she awarded him.

Ruby recalled him asking her if she was offering him a wedding night. Although she had said no, his change of heart made her worry that they had got their wires crossed. But wasn't that a stupid suspicion to cherish? A guy with his looks would scarcely be so desperate that he would nurture such a desire for an unwilling woman.

The same young man reappeared with a second glass but when he focused on Raja, he suddenly froze and then he fell to his knees in the aisle and bowed his head very low, almost dropping the tray in the process.

Raja reached for the drink. The steward drew the tray back in apparent dismay and Raja had to lean out of his seat to grasp the glass.

'What's wrong with him?' Ruby whispered as the steward backed nervously out of the plane again. As the door slammed shut the engines began revving.

'He didn't realise who I was until he saw me up close. He must have assumed I was one of your guards when I boarded.'

The plane was turning. 'I have guards now?'

'I assume they're seated with the pilot. Of course you have guards,' Raja advanced, gulping back the drink and frowning at the acidic flavour. 'Wajid will have organised protection for you.'

As a wave of dizziness ran over Ruby she blinked and took a deep breath to clear her head. 'I'm feeling dizzy…it's probably nerves. I don't like small planes.'

'You'll be fine,' Raja reassured her.

Ruby's head was starting to feel too heavy for her neck and she propped her chin on the upturned palm of her hand.

'Are you feeling all right?' Raja asked as her head lowered.

'Just very, very tired,' she framed, her hands gripping the arms of her seat while the plane raced down the runway and rose into the air, the craft juddering while the engines roared.

'Not up to a wedding night?' Raja could not resist teasing her in an effort to take her mind off her nerves.

At that crack Ruby's head lifted and she turned to look at him. The plane was mercifully airborne.

The pupils of her eyes had shrunk to tiny pinpoints and Raja stared. 'Have you taken medication?' he asked her abruptly.

'No.' Ruby heard her voice slur. All of a sudden her tongue felt too big and clumsy for her mouth. 'Why?'

Raja could feel his own head reeling. 'There must have been something in that drink!' he exclaimed in disbelief, thrusting his hands down to rise out of the seat in one powerful movement.

'What…you…mean?' Ruby mumbled, her cheek sliding down onto her shoulder, her lashes drooping.

Raja staggered in the aisle and stretched out a hand to the door that led into the cockpit. But it was locked. Blinking rapidly, he shook his fuzzy head and hammered on the door, his arm dropping heavily down by his side again. Everything felt as if it were happening to him in slow motion. His legs crumpled beneath him and he fell on his knees, a bout of frustrated incredulous rage roaring up inside him and threatening to consume him. Ruby was slumped unconscious in her seat, her face hidden by her hair and he was in no state to protect her.

RUBY OPENED HER eyes to darkness and strange sounds. Something was flapping and creaking and she could smell leather along with the faint aromatic hint of coffee. She was totally disorientated. Add in a pounding headache and the reality that her teeth were chattering with cold and she was absolutely miserable. She began slowly to shift her stiff, aching limbs and sit up. She was fully dressed but for her shoes and the ground was hard as a rock beneath her.

'What…where am I?' she mumbled thickly, the inside of her mouth as dry as a bone.

'Ruby?' It was Raja's deep accented drawl and she stiffened nervously at the awareness of movement and rustling in the darkness.

A match was struck and an oil lamp hanging on a tent pole cast illumination on the shadowy interior and the man towering over her. She blinked rapidly, relief engulfing her when she recognised Raja's powerful physique. Adjusting to the flickering light, her eyes clung to his hard bronzed features. In shocking defiance of the cold biting into her bones *he* was bare chested, well-defined hair-roughened pectorals flexing above the corrugated musculature of his abdomen. He was wearing only boxer shorts.

'My goodness, what happened to us?' Ruby demanded starkly, shivering violently as the chill of the air settled deeper into her clammy flesh. 'What are we doing in a tent?'

Raja crouched down on a level with her, long, strong thighs splayed. His stunning bone structure, composed of razor-sharp cheekbones, slashing angles and forbidding hollows, momentarily paralysed her and she simply stared, mesmerised by a glorious masculine perfection only enhanced by a dark haze of stubble.

'We were kidnapped and dumped out in the Ashuri desert. We have no phones, no way of communicating our whereabouts—'

'K-kidnapped?' Ruby stammered through rattling teeth. 'Why on earth would anyone want to kidnap us?'

'Someone who intended to prevent our marriage.'

'But we're *already*—'

'Married,' he slotted in flatly for her, handsome mouth hardening into a look of grim restraint as if being married was the worst thing that had ever happened to him but he was too polite to mention it. 'Obviously the kidnappers weren't aware of that when they planned this outrage. Apparently they assumed that our wedding would take place at the cathedral in Simis the day after tomorrow. In fact I believe a reconciliation and blessing service is actually planned for that afternoon.'

'Oh, my word,' she framed shakily, struggling to think clearly again. 'The kidnappers were trying to *stop* us from getting married? But if we're in the desert why is it so cold?'

'It *is* very cold here at night.' He swept up the quilt lying in a heap at her feet and wrapped it round her narrow shoulders.

'You're not cold,' she breathed almost resentfully, huddling into the folds of the quilt.

'No,' he acknowledged.

'Kidnapped,' she repeated shakily. 'That's not what I came out here for.'

'It may not be a comfort but I'm convinced that no harm was intended to come to you. I was not supposed to be with you. I invited that risk by changing my travel plans at the eleventh hour and boarding the same flight,' the prince explained with sardonic cool. 'The kidnappers only wanted to prevent you from turning up for our wedding, a development which would have offended my people enough to bring protesters out into the streets.'

'So not everybody wants us to get married,' Ruby registered with a frown, shooting him an accusing glance. 'You didn't tell me that some people were so hostile to the idea of us marrying.'

'Common sense should have told you that but the objectors are in a minority in both countries.'

'How do you know all this?'

'Our captors were keen to explain their motives. The drugged drink didn't knock me out for as long as you. I began recovering consciousness as a pair of masked men were dragging us into this tent. Unfortunately I was so dizzy I could barely focus or stand and they pulled a gun on me. I don't think they had any intention of using it unless I managed to interfere with their escape,' he explained heavily and she could tell from his discomfited expression just how challenging he had found it to choose caution over courage. 'It would have been foolish to risk injury out here while you were incapacitated and without protection. I believe the men were mercenaries hired by a group of our subjects to ensure that you didn't turn up for the wedding—'

'*Our*...subjects?' she queried.

'We are in Ashur and the masked men were of Western origin... I think. Members of both royal households were aware of our travel plans so it will be hard to establish where the security leak occurred and who chose to take advantage of it and risk our lives. But it must be done—'

'At least we're not hurt.'

'That doesn't diminish the gravity of the crime.'
Raja dealt her a stern appraisal. 'One of us could have
had an allergic reaction to the drug we were given. Vi-
olence could have been used against us. Although our
captors tried to talk as though this was intended to be
a harmless prank, you might easily have suffered illness or injury alone out here. In addition, our disap-
pearance will have cast both our countries into a very
dangerous state of turmoil and panic.'

'Oh, hell,' Ruby groaned as he finished that sobering speech and she pushed her tousled hair off her
brow and muttered in a small voice, 'My head hurts.'

He touched her hand, realised her fingers were cold
as ice and concern indented his brow. 'I'll light a fire—
there is enough wood.'

'What on earth are we going to do?'

With relaxed but economical movements, Raja
began to light a small fire. 'A search for us will already
have begun. The Najari air force will mount an efficient
rescue mission but they have a very large area to cover.
We have food and shelter. This is an oasis and *bedu*
tribesmen must come here sometimes to water their
flocks. Many of them have phones and could quickly
summon help. I could trek out to find the nearest settlement but I am reluctant to leave you alone—'

'I would manage,' Ruby declared.

'I don't think so,' the prince told her without apology as a spark flared and he fed it with what appeared
to be dried foliage. 'I will make tea.'

'I could come with you—'

'You couldn't stand the heat by day or keep up with
me, which would put both of us at greater risk.'

Stymied by his conviction of her lack of stamina, Ruby dug her toes into the quilt in an effort to defrost them. 'How come you're so calm?'

'When all else fails, celebrate the positive and...we *are* safe and healthy.'

The warm drink did satisfy her thirst and drive off her inner chill though even the effort of sitting up to drink made her very aware of how tired and dizzy she still was.

'Try to get some sleep,' the prince advised.

The thin mat that was all that lay between her and the ground provided little padding. She curled up. Raja tucked the quilt round her as if she were a small child. The cold of the earth below pierced the mat, making her shiver again and, expelling his breath in an impatient hiss, Raja got below the quilt with her and melded his heated body to the back of hers.

'What are you doing?' Ruby squeaked, her slight figure stiff as a metal strut in the loose circle of his strong arms.

'There's no need for you to be cold while I am here.'

'You're not a hot-water bottle!' Ruby spat, unimpressed, her innate distrust of men rising like a shot of hot steam inside her.

'And you're not as irresistible as you seem to think,' Raja imparted silkily.

The heat of her angry suspicion blazed into mortification and if possible she became even more rigid. Ignoring the fact, Raja curled her back firmly into his amazingly warm body.

'I don't like this,' she admitted starchily.

'Neither do I,' Raja confided without skipping a beat. 'I'm more into sex than cuddling.'

Outrage glittered in her eyes in the flickering light from the dying fire. She wanted to thump him but the horrible cold was steadily receding from her body and she was afraid that she would look comically prudish if she fought physically free of his embrace.

'And just think,' Raja remarked lazily above her head. 'All those miserable old diehards who think we shouldn't be getting married will be so pleased to find out we *are* married now.'

'Why?'

'If you were still single your reputation would be ruined by spending the night out here alone with me. As it is you're a married woman and safe from the embarrassment of a scandal, if not much of a catch in the wife stakes.'

Ruby twisted her head around, brown eyes blazing. 'And what's that supposed to mean?'

'A sex ban would exude zero appeal for the average male in either one of our countries.'

'You signed up for it,' Ruby reminded him stubbornly, furious that he could be so basic that he deemed sex with a virtual stranger a necessary extra to a successful civilised relationship with a woman.

Raja was not thinking with intellect alone. In fact his brain had little to do with his reactions for he had a raging hard-on. Strands of fragrant silky blonde hair were brushing his shoulder, her pert derrière braced against his thighs while he had one hand resting just below the swell of a plump breast. He raised a knee to keep her out of contact with the seat of his arousal and tried to think of something, *anything* capable of cooling down the sexual fire in his blood.

CHAPTER FIVE

WHEN RUBY WAKENED she was immediately conscious of the heat and the crumpled state of her clothing. What she wanted more than anything at that moment was access to a long, refreshing shower and opening her eyes on the interior of the roughly made and claustrophobic tent was not a heartening experience. She checked her watch and was taken aback to realise how long she had slept for it was already almost one in the afternoon.

Raja was nowhere to be seen and she sat up in a rush, pushing off the quilt and registering the presence of her suitcase in one corner. Mentally she leafed through what she recalled packing for what she had assumed would be short-term requirements while the majority of her wardrobe was shipped out in advance of her arrival. Just as Hermione had been shipped out, she recalled, her eyes suddenly stinging, for she missed her dog and knew her quirky little pet would be sadly missing her. She scrambled up and looked in vain for her shoes before peering out of the tent in search of Raja. It was not that she needed him, it was just she wanted to know where he was, she told herself staunchly.

That angle forgotten, however, Ruby remained standing stock still to stare out of the tent with a dropped jaw at the view of an alien world that shook her to the core. As far as the eye could see there was nothing but sand and the occasional small bush on a wide flat plain overarched by a bright blue sky and baked by a sun so bright and hot she couldn't look directly at it.

'Coffee? You slept soundly,' Raja commented from the side of the small fire he had lit below the ample tent canopy.

'Like the proverbial log.' One glance in his direction and Ruby's teeth grated together in exasperation. As if it weren't hot as hell already he had to build a fire to sit beside! And there he sat, infuriatingly immaculate in the same long off-white robe he had donned the day before and seemingly as comfortable living in the desert as he might have been in a five-star hotel. Only the reality that he was unshaven marked his departure from his usual standards of perfect grooming.

'Where did you get more water to make coffee?' Ruby was struggling not to care that her hair was probably standing on end and mascara had to be smeared all round her eyes.

'This is an oasis. I established that last night. An underground stream feeds a pool below the cliff and our water supply is secure.' He gestured to the other side of the tent. 'Do you want a drink?'

Ruby flipped round to belatedly note the towering cliff of rock on the far side of the tent. A large grove of flourishing date palms and other vegetation made it clear that a water source had to exist somewhere near by. 'I'd sooner not take the risk. After what happened on the plane, I'm only drinking water that comes out of a bottle,' she told him thinly.

The prince compressed his sensual mouth on the laugh he almost let escape. She looked very small, young and unsure of herself, standing there with tousled hair and bare feet, clearly unsettled by her surroundings but struggling not to reveal the fact. She hated to betray weakness and it was a trait he implicitly understood. Dishevelled though she was, however, her hair still glinted like polished silk and her flawless skin had the subdued glow of a pearl. Her beauty was not dependent on cosmetics or the flattering cut and gloss of designer clothing, he recognised, very much impressed by how good she looked without those trimmings. 'There is no bottled water to be had here.'

'Yes, I know that… I'm not stupid!' Ruby snapped back at him in furious self-defence. 'I just don't do the camping thing… OK? Never did do it, never saw the appeal of it and don't want to be roughing it out here now!'

'That is very understandable,' the prince responded with the utmost cool.

Far from impervious to the likely impression she had to be making on a guy who had probably majored in advanced desert survival skills during the war, Ruby dealt him a dirty look. 'I don't care if you laugh at me!'

Retreating crossly back into the tent because she cared very much indeed, Ruby hauled her case to the ground and opened it. She was grateful she hadn't bothered to lock it because, like her shoes, her handbag in which she would have stowed a key was missing. Only when she saw the state of the tumbled contents did she realise how naive she was being: their kidnappers had clearly rummaged through the contents before unloading it from the plane, doubtless keen to ensure that she hadn't packed a phone. She dug out her wash bag and a towel as well as a change of clothing and a pair of sneakers, suddenly very grateful indeed to be in possession of such necessities. A quick inspection of the tent interior warned her that Raja had not been so fortunate.

Donning fresh underwear and tee, she wrapped a sarong round her waist and tried to move more slowly because the heat was making her perspire. She came to a reluctant halt on the edge of the sparse shade offered by the canopy. 'I have a new toothbrush and a razor you can have and you can share my towel.'

In the mood his wife was in, Raja considered that a surprisingly generous offer. A wolfish grin of appreciation slashed his bold, bronzed features and he looked so ravishingly handsome at that instant that Ruby stared fixedly at him, her tummy flipping like an acrobat on a high wire, the warmth of awareness sending hot colour surging into her oval face.

She climbed up the slope and saw the pool that had formed in a gully densely shaded by the massive bulk of the rock formation behind it. Raja strode up from the tent to join her and fell into step beside her, his hand first at her elbow and then at her spine to help her ascend the rougher ground and to steady her when she wavered. He had incredibly good manners and, unused as she was to that consideration from a man, she could only be pleased that he was willing to make the effort. She was uneasily aware that so far she had not been the most heartening companion. Even worse in so challenging and harsh an environment she could only be at a loss.

They hovered by the side of the palm-fringed, crystal-clear pool formed by the water seeping out from a crack low in the rock face. Ruby moved first, taking off her sneakers to dip her toes in the water. The temperature was deliciously cool on her skin in the intense heat. Lifting her chin and refusing to be self-conscious, she wasted no time in pulling her T-shirt off and untying the sarong. In bra and knickers she reckoned that she was as well covered as she would have been in a bikini. Raja followed suit, stripping off his long tunic and draping it over a rock beside her clothing. Wide-eyed, Ruby watched the sleek muscles working in his strong back and shoulders and then hurriedly averted her gaze, reminding herself how much she had always hated her stepfather leering at her body. It was a clumsy comparison though, she reflected, for she suspected that Raja might well enjoy her admiration.

Standing thigh deep in the pool, Raja watched Ruby wash, his masculine body quickening with hungrily appreciative male interest. Wet through, her underwear was very revealing. He could see the prominent pink nipples poking through the sheer cups of her bra and he wondered how sensitive she would be if he put his mouth to those delicate peaks. As she waded out of the pool again, the clinging fabric of her panties clearly outlined the cleft between her thighs and the forbidden aspect of what he was seeing was a much more stimulating sight than complete nudity. Hard as steel in response, he studied the rippling surface of the water instead. On a very basic level his thoughts were reminding him that she was his wife, that at the very least he was entitled to look while at the same time his brain was recalling their agreement. No sex, no touching. Why the hell had he ever agreed to that? He reckoned that if he touched her the way he was feeling the force of his desire would frighten her.

Ruby walked out of the water and reached for the towel to dab herself dry, moving out of the shade in the expectation that the sun would dry her off more quickly.

'This is the hottest hour of the day. Cover up or you'll burn,' Raja warned her, knowing that he was burning already in an altogether more primitive way.

Reckoning that he was bone-deep bossy in the same unalterable way that holly leaves were prickly, Ruby ignored the stricture and left off her tee. She knotted the sarong just above her bra and began to comb out her damp hair, her attention quite naturally straying to his sleek powerful physique as he stood in the water that had covered her to the waist. His torso was a streamlined wall of muscle, his bulging upper arms, narrow hips and long thighs whipcord taut with lean tensile strength. As he splashed water up over his magnificent body, droplets glistening like diamonds in the bright light, she noticed the revealing fit of his boxer shorts which clearly defined his manhood. Feeling like a voyeur invading his privacy, she quickly looked away but she was shocked.

Was the presence of her only minimally clad body responsible for putting him in that condition? Her face stung with mortified red at the suspicion. What else was she supposed to think? She might not be irresistible as he had quipped the night before but she evidently did have what it took to awaken the most basic chemistry of all. It also occurred to her that she really had not realised until now that an aroused male would be quite so...*large* in that department.

A heavy ache stirred low within her own body and she was taken aback by the recognition that seeing Raja aroused, and knowing that her body was responsible for that development, excited her. And it was the first time ever that a man had had that astounding effect on Ruby. Indeed as a rule she felt uneasy and apprehensive when boyfriends became too enthusiastic in her arms. But then Ruby had never been comfortable with either her body or her own sexuality. How could she have been? During the years that had seen her steadily transform from child to young woman she had been forced to live with her stepfather's obscene comments and the lecherous looks he had constantly aimed at her developing body. While being careful to ensure that her mother neither heard nor saw anything amiss, Curtis Sommerton had taught his stepdaughter to be ashamed of her femininity. His barely concealed lust had made Ruby feel soiled. Although he had never managed to unleash that lust on her, he had taught her an aversion to the male body and the kind of crude sexist comments that some men found amusing.

The prince draped the damp towel carefully round Ruby's bare shoulders. 'Your skin is very fair. Sit in the shadows while I finish here.'

And because Ruby was getting too hot under the sun and her confusing thoughts preoccupied her she did as she was told in most un-Ruby-like silence. She watched him peer into the tiny compact mirror she had produced for his use and shave and then clean those perfect, even white teeth. Her curiosity about him on a personal level was leapfrogging up the scale at an embarrassing rate. Had she had access to the Internet she would have been searching out information about his social life. He *had* to have one. As much of a pin-up as a movie star, rich as sin and obviously possessed of a healthy male libido, Raja al-Somari had to have women in his life. Did he enjoy discreet affairs? He would have to be discreet because Najar was a conservative country just like Ashur. Did he seek out lovers only when he was abroad? Or did he have a lover stashed away somewhere more convenient? The intimate aspect of her thoughts mortified her. What was it to her, for goodness' sake? Even if he had a constant procession of women eager to provide him with an outlet for his sexual needs, it was none of her business!

Having replaced the long tunic, his black hair curling back damply from his brow, Raja approached her. 'We should eat now.'

He showed her the ancient refrigerator operating off a car battery in the back of the tent.

'You understand this way of life,' Ruby remarked.

'When I was a child my father often sent me to stay with my uncle in the desert. He is the ruling sheikh of a nomadic tribe,' he explained. 'But in Najar there are few true nomads left now. The *bedu* have settled so that their children can attend school and they have easier access to jobs and medical facilities. But the nomadic way of life is still quite popular in Ashur.'

There was only fruit, some vegetables, meat and

bread in the refrigerator and several tins of indistin-
guishable supplies. 'I assume we're not expected to
be here for very long,' Raja commented, handing her
a cup of coffee.

Ruby frowned up at what looked like a red flag rippling on top of the cliff. 'What's that up there?'

'A blanket I tied to a stick. It will be easily visible
from the air and unusual enough to attract attention—'

'You *climbed* up there?' Ruby exclaimed, aghast,
for the cliff rose to a pinnacle of almost vertical rock.

'It was not so difficult.' Raja shrugged a broad
shoulder that dismissed the risk involved in so dangerous a climb. 'I went up to take advantage of the view
and see if there was any sign of human habitation but
there is nothing within sight.'

'Obviously this particular place was chosen because
it was isolated,' Ruby said wryly. 'At least I don't have
any family to worry about me—what about you?'

'A father, a younger brother and two sisters and a
whole host of other relatives. But I'm most worried
about my father. He is not strong. The stress my dis-
appearance will cause will endanger his health,' he
proffered, his wide sensual mouth compressing, his
handsome features taut with concern. 'But there is
nothing I can do about it.'

Her generous heart was troubled by his apprehension. 'I have no relatives in Ashur, have I?'

'None close that I'm aware of. Distant cousins, certainly.'

His ability to efficiently feed them both set Ruby's
teeth on edge. He could cook on an open fire with very
limited ingredients and produce an edible meal while

she would have been challenged to do so even in a modern kitchen. Her mother had been a poor cook and Ruby's own repertoire was limited to the making or heating of simple snacks. While she lived with Stella, a very competent cook, her lack in that field had not seemed important but somehow in Raja's presence it annoyed the hell out of her.

Feeling helpless stung Ruby's strong pride. She hated feeling reliant on Raja and was painfully conscious that to date she had proved more of a burden than a help. That sense of inadequacy drove her into ceaseless activity that afternoon. She tidied up her clothes, ashamed of the fact she had left the garments lying in a tumbled heap beside her suitcase. She folded the quilts, shook the sand off the mats and took care of the few dishes and then she wandered round the grove of date palms busily gathering twigs and dried foliage to keep the fire going. The heat sapped her energy fast and she was filled with dismay at the prospect of what the much higher summer temperatures had to be like to live with. Her hair sticking to the back of her neck, she headed up to the pool to cool off again. The cold water felt glorious. Wrapped in the sarong, she sat down wearily on a rock in the deep shade to knot her hair and hold it off her perspiring face, wishing she had something to tie it back with. She looked across the pool to see her desert prince approaching, all six feet plus of his leanly muscled commanding figure pure poetry in motion, and she pursed her lips.

There he was drop-dead gorgeous and rich and he could cook, as well. She marvelled that he had stayed single so long. Of course that authoritarian streak might be a problem for some. He knew best...*always*. Her shoulders were pink and slightly burned as he had warned before lunch and she wasn't one bit grateful that his forecast had come true but she knew that she ought to be grateful that he was so well able to cope when she was not. He was also equally keen to protect her from her own mistakes.

'Watch out for—'

Ruby lifted her hands in a sudden silencing motion, brown eyes lightening with temper. 'Just let it go, Raja. I'll take my chances against whatever it is! You're just about perfect and you know everything and you could probably live out here all year but I'm afraid I'm not cut from the same cloth.'

'The desert is home to my people and yours,' the prince contradicted in a tone of reproof. 'We design and maintain beautiful gardens and parks in Najar but when our people want to get back to basics they come out into the desert.'

Ruby snatched in a sustaining breath and she kicked a rock with a sneaker-clad foot to expel her extreme irritation.

'Ruby!'

As the rock rolled over and something moved and darted from beneath it Raja almost leapt forward in his haste to haul her out of harm's way. From several feet away, plastered back against the solid support of his hard muscular frame, Ruby stared in horror at the greenish yellow insects rushing out.

'Scorpions. They shelter in dark places during the day. Their sting is very painful,' Raja informed her as she went limp against him, sick with repulsion at how close she had come to injury. He removed her to a safe distance.

'I don't like insects either,' Ruby confided in a shaken rush. 'Especially ones that size and anything that stings—'

'There are also poisonous snakes—'

'Shut up...*shut up*!' she launched at him fiercely. 'I'm not on an educational trip. I don't want to know!'

Raja turned her round and stared down at her, eyes shimmering with reluctant amusement.

'I don't care what you say either,' Ruby added truculently. 'Give it a rest—stop trying to train me into being a stuffy royal who never puts a foot wrong!'

This time Raja al-Somari laughed out loud, his ready sense of humour finally breaking free of his innate reserve, for Ruby was very much an original and not at all like the women he was accustomed to meeting. She didn't flirt—at least if she did, she didn't bother to do it with him. Indeed she used no feminine wiles that he could identify. She staged no enticing poses to draw attention to her body. She made no attempt to appeal to his ego with compliments or to pay him any especially gratifying attention and she had not told him a single story calculated to present her in a flattering light. He had never in his entire life met a woman as uncomplicated as she was and the more he was exposed to her frank, fearless style, the more he liked it.

'So, you do have a sense of humour after all. My goodness, is that a relief!' Ruby exclaimed, shaking her head in emphasis, a wealth of damp strands escaping her loose knot and spilling across her shoulders.

Raja stared down at her stunning face and the teasing smile on her ripe rosy lips. He lowered his handsome, dark head almost jerkily as if he were being yanked down to her level by some mysterious but very powerful outside force. He found her soft, sultry mouth with his and although that kiss started out gentle and searching it heated up at supersonic speed. Desire rose to gush through Ruby in a floodtide. Nothing had ever felt so necessary as the hard pressure of that sensual mouth on hers and the taste of him drowned her senses like a shot of alcohol on a weak head.

Without a word, Raja released her with startling abruptness and pressed a hand to her spine to urge her back down the slope towards the tent.

Ruby had never experienced such a charge of hunger before and, suddenly deprived of that connection with him, she was in a daze. The tip of her tongue snaked out to explore the reddened and swollen contours of her lips and all she could think about was how much she wanted his hot, hungry mouth back on hers again. The strength of that craving shook her. Her nipples were tight and tingling and her legs felt shaky. Putting one foot in front of another was a challenge. And at the same time, gallingly she was desperate to know what he was thinking.

Outside the tent Ruby shot Raja a sidewise glance brimming with curiosity. His hard profile was taut and he skimmed a look back at her, eyes brilliant with a wealth of stormy emotion. That shook her and in response her heart started beating very, very fast. 'Don't play games with me, Ruby,' he spelled out in a roughened undertone.

Games? Ruby was offended by the suggestion and she lifted her chin in denial. 'I don't know what you're talking about—*you* kissed *me*—'

'But you made no objection. When you have said that you don't want me to touch you what else is that but a game?'

'I don't calculate things to that extent. You are so suspicious,' Ruby condemned, flushed and flustered by the reminder and by the embarrassment of her own un-characteristic behaviour. 'It's being in this situation... I simply forgot and got carried away for a moment.'

'Every action has consequences,' Raja pronounced, rigid with the pent-up force of arousal he was restrain-ing, his lean hands clenching into fists, for his body was not one half as disciplined as his quick and clever brain.

Ruby sank down on a mat inside the tent. It was hot but nothing was as hot and disturbing as the hum of unnatural warmth at the centre of her body, which was shockingly new and demanding. She could not relax. She lifted a hand, watched it tremble and tried and failed to laugh at the state she was in. One kiss and it had been earth-shattering, even more so than the last. Now she felt cheated. She wanted more, she wanted to know what it felt like to make love with a man who attracted her to that extent. The hurricane-force po-tency of that attraction was certainly a first. She had not experienced anything comparable with other men when intimacy had often felt like more of a threat and a nuisance than a potential source of pleasure. More than once her unenthusiastic response had led to her being asked if she was frigid or gay. She had often had to fight her way out of over-keen encounters. She had had to shout, she had had to defend and justify her boundaries because the easy availability of sex was often taken for granted in relationships. But not once, not once in the five years since she began dating had she actually *wanted* to make love.

And now what was she doing about it? Here she was taking refuge in the tent and avoiding Raja as if she were ashamed of herself or afraid when she was neither, she conceded uncertainly. It was not as though she could fall pregnant either, she reminded herself squarely. Some months earlier her doctor had advised her to agree to a course of contraceptive pills in the hope of correcting an irregular menstrual cycle. Although she had no supply with her in the desert she assumed she would still be protected for some time against conception. She lifted her head high. She had not been playing some sexual game with Raja, she was not a tease and didn't want him thinking that she was. In an impatient movement she scrambled upright again.

Raja was staring into the dying embers of the fire, black lashes lowered and as spectacular even in profile as glossy black fringes, his high cheekbones prominent, sculptured mouth clenched.

'I wasn't playing games,' Ruby declared defiantly.

He flung his proud dark head back and looked straight at her. 'I want you so much I ache...'

And his admission sizzled through Ruby like a hot knife gliding through butter. His confidence shocked her, for she had believed that she was being bold but his words made hers meaningless and little more than a sulky expression of innocence. Indeed almost a lie, she adjusted uncomfortably, jolted by her sudden unexpected collision with the scorching challenge of his gaze. Just at that moment she knew that she had sought him out again quite deliberately and that he was experienced enough to know it.

'A woman hasn't made me ache since I was younger than you are now,' Raja told her huskily, vaulting upright with an easy grace of movement that tensed every muscle in her slim body. 'You're very beautiful...'

So was he, but she was too wary and proud to tell him that that lean dark-angel beauty of his had taken up residence in her brain and dug talon claws of need and desire into her very soul. When he kissed her she felt as dizzy and uncoordinated as though she had drunk too much alcohol. He made her feel out of control and she didn't like that but, regardless of that fact, every time she looked at him it was a tougher challenge to look away again. She moved closer and somehow he met her in the middle, a possessive hand closing on her slight shoulder to hold her in place, his mouth or was it her mouth eagerly melding with the temptation of his again. And that crushing kiss was good, *so* good, her bare toes curled and her nerve endings sang. Her arms went round him, her fingers spearing into his hair, and with her eager encouragement his mouth got rougher and harder, his lean, powerful length sealing more forcefully to her softer curves.

It was too much: she couldn't breathe, broke her mouth free to pant for breath and yet immediately sought him out again with renewed hunger and blindly impatient hands. In the midst of it he eased back from her to haul off his robe but just as quickly he pulled her back into his arms. The sarong fell at her feet but she didn't notice because Raja was already lowering her down on the quilts while pressing taut open-mouthed kisses along the slender expanse of her neck. She squirmed helplessly as the tip of his tongue scored the pulse there and then he nipped at her responsive flesh with his strong white teeth. Need was driving her now, all the while the heat in her pelvis was building and building into a furnace.

Her bra fell away. His palm closed over a small, pert breast and she gasped, back arching as he plunged his mouth down to the swollen pink tip and let his teeth graze the straining nipple. She dragged him up to kiss him again and ran an appreciative palm down over the hair-roughened expanse of his superb torso. He caught her hand in his and brought her fingers down to the rampant length of the shaft straining against his hard flat stomach. A shudder ran through his big frame as she took that invitation and stroked him, moulding the smooth hard heat and promise of him with reverent fingers.

He moved her beneath him and again put his carnal mouth to her tender nipples. He was gentle at first but still she writhed and when he got a little more ardent she cried out, struggling to find herself again in the thunderous, greedy surge of the hunger he had awakened.

'Very beautiful,' Raja groaned in reply. 'And wonderfully passionate…'

The hollow ache between her thighs had her hips shifting back and forth. He traced the tender pink flesh there and she shivered, violently and with longing, driven by feverish want and need. He slid a finger into her and she was hot and wet and tight and he groaned with masculine appreciation, capturing her lips with his again, letting his tongue dart into the sensitive interior of her mouth with a skilful flick that made the blood drum insanely fast through her veins.

He teased the tiny bundle of nerve endings that controlled her entire body and she writhed in the storm of intoxicating sensation. 'Don't stop...whatever you do, don't stop!' she warned him through gritted teeth, reacting to an overload of pleasure that wiped out every thought and consideration and left frantic desire in charge.

Black hair tousled, golden eyes hot as flames, the prince rose over her. 'After this, there is no going back.'

In the merciless grip of unsated need, Ruby could barely focus on his darkly handsome features. 'No going back?' she repeated blankly.

Raja, as eager for completion as she was, was already pressing back her thighs and impatiently splaying his hands below her hips to raise her to him. As he positioned himself and pushed into her a sharp pain arrowed through her and she cried out. He stopped moving to gaze down at her with a bemused frown. 'What's wrong?'

'Nothing...don't stop,' Ruby told him, taut with discomfiture for it had not occurred to her that losing her virginity might hurt. Her more experienced friend, Stella, might have told her a lot of things but that possibility had not been mentioned.

Dark eyes confused, he stared down at her. 'But I hurt you.'

Ruby could feel her face getting hotter and hotter.
'It's my first time…that's all. No big deal.'

It was Raja's turn to be surprised and it was a very
big deal on his terms. His bride was a virgin? The
level of his ignorance about her annoyed him. He had
made the wrong assumptions but not without her encouragement to do so. A slight shudder racked him as
he endeavoured to remain still while every fibre of his
being craved the completion of sinking into her as far
and as fast as he could go.

'It's all right…it really is,' Ruby whispered, deeply
embarrassed by the enforced pause in their lovemaking.

The prince lowered his head and pressed a kiss to
the rosy invitation of her mouth. For the very first time
he allowed himself to think of her as his wife. It was
a powerful source of attachment for a man given to
ruthlessly guarding his emotions. Lithe as a cat, he
shifted inside her and her eyes widened with wondering appreciation as the first swirl of sensation circled
her pelvis and melted her inside to hot, liquid honey.

'Oh…' she framed, taken aback by that feeling of
exquisite fullness, lips parting, eyes drifting shut on a
heady vocal sound of appreciation.

'I want it to be good for you…'

Ruby looked up at him, her entire body buzzing with
electrified arousal. 'It's better than good…'

Raja shifted again, initially slow and sure, patiently
teaching her his rhythm while he revelled in the vel-
vety grip of her slick passage. In the still heat of the
tent, perspiration gleaming on his sleek bronzed length,
he pleasured her with long driving strokes. Excite-

ment gripped her as the pace quickened and the only thing that mattered then was the pounding surge of his body into hers. Delirious with the pulsing pleasure, she arched her back and wild tremors tore through her. With a feverish cry she splintered into the electrifying heat of an earth-shattering climax.

Afterwards, Raja held her close, soothing fingers caressing the smooth skin of her abdomen while little quivers, aftershocks of that intense physical crescendo, still coursed through her. 'I'm sorry I hurt you. If I had known that you were not experienced I would have been more gentle.'

Hugging a glorious unfamiliar sense of well-being along with the feeling that she was still floating on a fluffy cloud, Ruby fixed dazed eyes on his face. 'I'm not sure gentle would have been quite so exciting.'

Raja laughed with easy appreciation and vaulted upright. He pulled on his boxers and strode out of the tent. She wondered what he was doing but was too lazy to ask or follow as she lay there with limbs that felt weighted down. At the corner of her mind a kernel of unease was nagging at her, keen to remind her that she had trashed the platonic agreement she had forged with Raja and made their relationship much more personal, much more intimate than she had ever envisaged.

Just at that moment such serious reflections seemed ridiculously irrelevant. They were marooned in the desert in circumstances neither of them could ever have foreseen and, as far as she was concerned, the normal rules no longer applied. It was just sex, she told herself urgently, not worth getting worked up about. Creating a fuss about it would only make her look deeply uncool.

Raja strode back in and knelt down by her side. One glimpse of that strong, dark face and sleek physique and her tummy flipped and her brain seemed to turn to mush. He smiled down at her, and it was, without a doubt, the most spectacular smile. Evidently her approval rating had gone from zero to through the roof. He reached down to uncurl her legs for she was lying coiled in a ball.

'What are you doing?' she muttered in bewilderment.

He didn't answer, he simply showed her. He had soaked the towel in the pool and wrung it out. Beneath her stunned gaze he began to run that very welcome cold, wet cloth over her hot, damp body, cooling her feverish temperature, leaving her fresh and revitalised and unexpectedly touched by his thoughtfulness.

They ate in a surprisingly comfortable silence below the tent canopy. 'I don't think we'll be here for much longer,' Raja admitted quietly. 'Once the fact that we were married in the UK is publicly announced there can be no reason for leaving us here.'

'But that means that someone would have to own up to knowing where we are.'

'There are many ways of passing information without the source being identified,' the man by her side remarked shrewdly.

When she finished her drink and began to get up he rose with her and pulled her up against his powerful frame. Hot eyes raked her flushed and uncertain face and for an instant she was stiff, suddenly disturbingly lost in the brave new world of intimacy she had created with him. The balance of power had changed irrevocably. A low-pitched growl vibrating in his throat, Raja closed a hand into her tumbled hair and kissed her, hard and hungrily, unleashing a passion that was uninhibited. He thrust aside the sarong and cupped her bare breasts, teasing the tips between thumb and finger. An arrowing tingle of damp heat speared between her thighs and she ached. She quivered and clung, wanting and needing again even more than she had the first time.

CHAPTER SIX

RUBY SUFFERED A rude awakening the next morning. Raja was shaking her shoulder, the tent walls were flapping loudly and her ears were ringing with noise.

'Get dressed,' he framed urgently as she blinked in bewilderment. 'We've been found and we're leaving!'

As he strode from the tent she peered out after him and saw a pair of what looked like heavy-duty military helicopters coming in to land. Galvanised into action as she registered that their desert sojourn appeared to be at an end, she yanked open her case in search of something decent to wear. She dressed in haste, choosing cropped trousers and a vest top teamed with a light shirt. As she hastily brushed her hair every movement she made ensured that she remained mortifyingly conscious of the intimate ache between her legs.

The events of the past twelve hours raced through her memory and her slender hands fisted in defensive rejection of her reckless behaviour. As a rule, Ruby didn't *do* reckless. Ruby was usually thoughtful and cautious, never impulsive, yet she had, with very little thought, utterly destroyed the platonic marital agreement she had insisted on. All for what? Great sex, she acknowledged shamefacedly, but in the aftermath even greater regrets.

They had agreed to a fake marriage and now how was their relationship to be defined? The agreement had been broken, the boundaries blurred and their respective roles were no longer clear-cut. Raja's unqualified passion had enthralled her. She had to be honest with herself about that. She found the Najari prince regent incredibly attractive. He fascinated her and he had tempted her from that first kiss back in England. No other man had ever had that effect on her. She had been eager to know what sex was all about, had wanted to feel what other women felt and had sensed from the outset that he might well be the guy who could show her. And he had, unquestionably, shown her. Over and over and over again, she recalled, her face burning. In bed her desert prince ditched all reserve and cool in favour of a scorching-hot sexual intensity that had lit a fire inside her that she could neither resist nor quench.

As Ruby emerged from the tent she saw Raja standing in conversation with several men, all of whom wore military uniform. Every male eye turned towards her and then heads inclined and lowered and a respectful murmur of greeting acknowledged her presence. Raja drew her forward with an assured hand to introduce her to the various air-force personnel before assisting her into the nearest helicopter.

'We will breakfast in Najar—'

'I think I should stay in Ashur for the moment,' Ruby told him quietly. 'I ought to continue on to where I was heading when we were kidnapped.'

The tall black-haired male by her side frowned down at her.

'Naturally you want to let your father see that

you're OK as soon as possible. I'll be fine,' she asserted lightly.

Raja captured her hand in his. 'Where's your wedding ring?'

Ruby glanced down at her bare fingers. 'Oh, dear, I didn't notice. It was very loose and it must've fallen off. I don't think it was still on my finger when we arrived here.'

His wide sensual mouth compressed. 'I will find a replacement.'

A slight hint of amusement on her gaze, Ruby sent him an airy glance as though the matter was too trivial to discuss. 'No hurry...'

His face hardened, inky lashes dropping low over his intent scrutiny. 'We must agree to disagree,' he traded huskily. 'I will see you tonight—'

'Tonight?' Ruby was surprised, having assumed that their separation would last somewhat longer. She was also rather keen to have a decent breathing space in which to regroup.

'Tonight,' Raja confirmed, striding off to speak to the pilot before climbing aboard the second helicopter.

During the flight, when Ruby felt nervous tension beginning to rise at the prospect of what expectations might await her in Simis, the capital of Ashur, she breathed in deep. She reminded herself that she was reasonably intelligent, even-tempered and willing to learn, not to mention being filled with good intentions. She didn't need Raja by her side telling her what to do every minute of the day.

The airport building outside Simis was a large temporary shed. Surrounded by soldiers and police who made her nervous, Ruby was greeted by Wajid Sulieman's familiar and surprisingly welcome face and tucked straight into a waiting car. His concerned questions about her health and how she had managed in the desert brought a smile to her expressive mouth.

'I was lucky to have the prince with me,' she admitted, willing to award honour where it was due. 'How did you find us?'

'Someone contacted the media with your location,' Wajid told her. 'From the moment that we announced that you were missing, people began gathering outside the palace gates to wait for news. There was great anger and concern on your behalf. Some were quick to suspect the Najaris of duplicity and there were protests. It was a very tense situation.'

'I'm sure feelings ran equally high in Najar,' Ruby remarked as the car cut around a horse and cart.

'Even higher. Your husband is a war hero and tremendously popular,' Wajid said. 'It is unfortunate that he was unable to accompany you here but I understand that he will be arriving later.'

'Yes.' Crowds lined the old-fashioned city streets and necks were craned to get a better view of her car. 'Are those people actually waiting to see me?' Ruby whispered incredulously.

'There is great excitement and curiosity about your arrival. It is a positive event after so many years of bad news,' the older man volunteered wryly. 'For the next few days you will be out and about a good deal to allow people to become familiar with you. The photograph taken after your wedding was very well received. I cannot praise Prince Raja highly enough for having had the foresight to organise it.'

'Raja thinks of everything,' Ruby agreed, thinking sunburn, scorpions…sex. A little tremor of heated recollection rippled low in her body and she stiffened, annoyed that even memory could make her so sensually susceptible.

On her short visit to Ashur as a teenager she had seen the imposing grey building that comprised the palace only from the vantage point of the tall wrought-iron gates. A step in the imperious wake of Wajid, she entered the palace from a side entrance where a group of staff bowed low and several introductions were offered. From the hall she was escorted up a staircase.

'Your uncle, the late King Tamim, and his family used the east wing. I thought you might be more comfortable in this more modern corner of the palace.'

Ruby reckoned that only in Wajid's parlance could a decor at least sixty years out of date be deemed modern. 'What was my uncle like?'

'He was rather set in his ways, as was his daughter, Princess Bariah—'

'My cousin.'

'A fine young woman, who was of course destined to marry Prince Raja before the accident that took her life and that of her parents,' the older man remarked in his pedantic manner, quite unaware of Ruby coming to a sudden halt and shooting him a look of dismay.

Her cousin had originally been contracted to marry Raja? Of course that made sense but it was still the first time that that fact had been mentioned to Ruby. And like a bolt from the blue that little fact cut Ruby to the bone. Just at that moment it was a deeply unwelcome reminder that there was nothing personal, private or indeed special about her relationship with the future king of Najar and Ashur, for Raja had been equally willing, it seemed, to marry her cousin. Fate had simply served Ruby up in her cousin's stead. But how had Raja really felt about that sudden exchange of brides? Had he been attached to her royal cousin, Princess Bariah? A sliver like a shard of ice sliced through Ruby, who was affronted and hurt by the idea that she might well have been a second-best choice on her husband's terms. No doubt he would have been equally willing to share a bed with her cousin. How could she have been foolish enough to allow such intimacy without good reason? And how could desire alone ever be sufficient justification?

As she stepped through a door a little dog barked wildly and hurled itself at her legs. Smiling happily, Ruby got down on her knees to pet Hermione, who gave her a frantic squirming welcome before finally snuggling into her owner's arms and tucking her little head blissfully below Ruby's chin. Wajid mentioned the reconciliation service to be held at the cathedral that afternoon, which Ruby had to attend, as well as an evening reception at which she was to meet many important people. She stifled a groan at the thought of her inadequate wardrobe and wondered if the red suit could be freshened up for the occasion.

A knock sounded on the door and a young woman joined them. 'This is Zuhrah, Your Royal Highness, who with the assistance of your personal staff will take care of all your needs,' Wajid explained. 'She speaks excellent English.'

Zuhrah explained that she would look after Ruby's diary and take care of all the invitations she received. Wajid departed while the pretty brunette showed Ruby through the spacious suite of rooms that had been set aside for her use. Over the light lunch that was served in the dining area Ruby mentioned the red suit and Zuhrah wasted no time in going off to track it down. As soon as she had eaten Ruby took advantage of the bathroom—she would never take one for granted again—and enjoyed a long, invigorating shower. Having dried her hair, she returned to the drawing room, clad in a wrap, and asked Zuhrah, who was tapping out notes on a netbook, if her missing handbag had turned up. Apparently it had not and Ruby knew she would have to see a doctor if she wanted another contraceptive pill. But did she need to take that precaution now? Was she planning to continue sleeping with Raja?

She thought not. Her brain said no, a very firm no. A mistake was a mistake and better acknowledged as such. There was another consequence to be feared as well, she reminded herself ruefully. She had missed taking her contraceptive pills while she was in the desert and there had to be a risk that she might already have conceived a child by Raja. What was she going to do if that happened? A chill ran down Ruby's spine at the prospect of such a dilemma. She loved babies but a baby that would be deemed royal would severely complicate her practical marriage and ultimately wreck any hope of them establishing a civilised relationship. She was convinced that if she had a child there was no way that Raja would agree to her taking that child back home to the UK with her again.

The service at the cathedral late that afternoon required nothing more from Ruby than her presence. Police stood outside the historic building with linked arms to hold back the crowds struggling to catch a glimpse of the new princess. The evening reception was a great deal more taxing, however, for while she was perfectly able to make small talk she was embarrassed several times by more probing questions concerning her background than she wished to answer. People were extremely curious about her and as yet she did not have the skill to deflect unwelcome queries. Later she would register that she had known the exact moment when Raja entered the big reception room for a flutter of excitement seemed to run through the gathered cliques. With a muttered apology, Wajid left her side and heads turned away from her, eyes swerving towards the door while a low buzz of comment sounded.

'*Real* royalty,' someone whispered appreciatively within Ruby's hearing. 'And you can definitely tell the difference.'

Mortified heat burnished Ruby's fair complexion. *Real* royalty? Had she performed her role so badly? But then she knew that she could only be a pretend princess by virtue of her birth. How could she be anything else when she had spent all her life to date living as an ordinary person? But she was *trying*, she was trying very hard to be polite, reserved and dignified as Wajid had advised her she must be at all times while carefully avoiding controversial subjects. It was tough advice for a bubbly and naturally outspoken young woman to follow. To Ruby it also felt like trying to be something she was not while putting on airs and graces that went against the grain.

His tall powerful physique sheathed in a dove-grey suit, her husband looked devastatingly handsome. Her *husband*? Why was she thinking of Raja in such terms? He wasn't her husband, not really, she told herself angrily, irritated by the mental mistake. A woman chose her husband with her heart but she had not. Guilty colour mantling her face, Ruby studied that lean, strong, wondrously handsome face and she steeled herself to feel nothing, absolutely nothing. She watched Raja work the room like a professional, smooth and practised and yet charming as well with a word here, a greeting there, for some a smile, for others a more serious aspect. He was a class act socially, everything she was not. Hovering at his elbow, Wajid Sulieman looked as though all his Christmases had come at once.

When refreshments were served, Raja was finally free to join Ruby. Lustrous dark eyes gleaming like polished amber flared down into hers while he rested a light hand at her spine. She went rigid, rejecting the temptation of even that much familiarity while recalling Bariah, who would never have been ill-at-ease in such a social gathering.

'My family were very disappointed not to meet you today,' the prince told her quietly.

'Whereas here everyone is disappointed that I'm not you—you carry the accolade of being *real* royalty, unlike me,' Ruby retorted, only to bite her lip a few seconds after that hot rejoinder had escaped her for she would have preferred to keep that particular thought to herself.

'You are imagining that. A beautiful woman in fashionable apparel is almost always more welcome than a man,' Raja fielded without skipping a beat.

Wajid introduced them to an older couple, who represented a charity that ran an orphanage just outside Simis, which Ruby, apparently, would be visiting the next day. In the wake of that casual announcement, which was news to Ruby, she appreciated how little freedom she now had when it came to how she might choose to spend her time. Her time evidently now belonged to an ever-growing list of duties, engagements and activities, not least of which was her need to learn the language so that a translator did not have to dog her every footstep.

'You're very quiet. What's wrong?' Raja enquired as Ruby mounted the stairs that led back to her suite.

'It's not important.' Ruby pushed open the door and sped through to the bedroom to change into something more comfortable. A maid was engaged in hanging clothes in a closet there, *male* clothes. Her soft full mouth compressing as she recognised that fact, Ruby walked back into the main reception room where Raja was poised by the window.

'You're staying in this suite with me?'

'Married couples usually share the same accommodation,' Raja pointed out evenly.

Temper roused by that tranquil response skittered up through Ruby in an uneasy rush. He made it sound so simple but their relationship was anything but simple. 'I didn't realise that but for that plane crash you would have married my cousin Bariah,' she admitted. 'I hadn't worked that out yet.'

'A marriage would hardly have been included in the peace accord if the royal families did not have a bride and a groom in mind.'

As usual what Raja said made perfect sense and her teeth gritted in frustration. 'I'm sure you would have preferred a proper Ashuri princess!'

Face deadpan, Raja gazed steadily back at her, patently refusing to be drawn on that touchy topic.

Tension roared through Ruby's rigid stance like a hurricane seeking an outlet. 'I *said*—'

'I am not deaf,' Raja cut in very drily. 'But I do wonder what you expect me to say in reply to such an assumption.'

Flushed and furious, Ruby surveyed him. 'Is an honest answer too much for me to ask for?'

'Not at all, but I will not insult either you or your late cousin with the suggestion that I might compare two completely different women and voice a preference for either,' Raja advanced, eyes cool while his strong jawline set hard as iron. 'That is not a reasonable request.'

'Well, as far as I'm concerned, it's perfectly reasonable!' Ruby slung back heatedly.

'But to answer you would be disrespectful.'

'Unlike you I'm only human. Naturally I want to know although I don't know why I'm bothering to ask. Bariah was a real princess and would've had much more in common with you than I have.'

'No comment,' the prince pronounced stonily and with much bowing and scraping the little maid emerged from the bedroom and left the suite.

'Bariah spoke the language, *knew* this country.' Ruby's statement was pained for after spending only hours in the Ashuri palace she was all too conscious of her deficiencies.

'Given time and patience you will learn,' Raja murmured quietly, his lack of tension merely increasing the adrenaline surge ready to charge through Ruby's veins.

Ruby was in no mood to be comforted. 'My cousin would have known automatically how to behave in every situation—'

'Wajid already thinks you're doing a marvellous job,' Raja imparted gently.

As she stiffened defensively her eyes flared bright as topaz gemstones. 'Don't patronise me!'

'I'm going for a shower,' Raja breathed, casting his jacket down on a chair and striding into the bedroom.

Ruby stilled in her restive stalk round the spacious room and shot a startled glance in his direction as she followed him into the bedroom. 'You're actually planning to sleep in here with me?'

In the act of unbuttoning his shirt, Raja dealt her an impatient glance and said nothing.

For a timeless moment Ruby watched a wedge of masculine torso appear between the parted edges of the shirt. 'There are two big sofas in the room next door,' she pointed out, in case he had not yet noticed the possibility of that option.

Raja treated that reminder to the contempt he evidently felt it deserved. His eyes burned hot gold below his black, spiky lashes, his jaw squared, giving his face a dangerous edge.

'All right… I'll take a sofa,' Ruby pronounced, determined to stick to her guns. It was her belief that if she reinforced their separation they would both soon forget those boundaries they had unwisely crossed and return to their original agreement.

Raja elevated a deeply unimpressed and sardonic black brow and stripped off his boxers to walk fluidly into the bathroom. As nude exits went it scored an impressive ten in the cooler-than-cool stakes. While the shower was running, Ruby made up a bed on a sofa for herself, donned her pyjamas, doused the lights and climbed in. Hermione snuggled in next to her feet.

A little while later, a wild burst of barking drove her from the brink of slumber.

'Call off the dog or I will put her out to the kennels,' Raja growled, his face grim in the light spilling from the bedroom.

Ruby leapt off the sofa, snatched the snarling Hermione up into her arms and attempted to soothe her overexcited pet. 'What are you doing in here?'

'Retrieving my wife,' Raja traded in a wrathful tone of warning.

'I'm not your wife, not your proper wife!' Ruby launched furiously back at him, inflamed by that insistence and the label.

'So you're not a real princess or a proper wife. Then what are you?' Raja challenged impatiently, bending down from his considerable height to haul her up into his arms while she clutched Hermione frantically to her chest. 'My sex buddy? A friend with benefits?'

He then went on to employ a third term of description, which was crude enough to make Ruby's soft, full lips fall open in shock and her big, brown eyes flame. 'How *dare* you?'

Raja settled her down on the bed with a good deal more care than she had grounds to expect from an angry man. Hermione tried to bite him. Composed in the face of that attempted attack, he scooped up the animal and put Ruby's pet out of the room. From the other side of the door Hermione whined and scraped the wood.

'Are you planning to do the same to me if I stand up to you?' Ruby enquired furiously. 'I am not sleeping with you again—'

'I'm not very interested in sleeping right now either.' At least six feet three inches tall and magnificently male, Raja threw back the sheet and slid into bed beside her.

'I am not your sex buddy or that other thing you mentioned!' Ruby proclaimed in a rage.

'No, you're my wife,' Raja repeated again, immovably stubborn on that point.

Ruby was taken aback when he got out of bed again and crossed the room to reach for his jacket and retrieve something from a pocket. He returned to bed and reached for her hand.

'What are you doing?' she demanded apprehensively.

'I'm replacing your wedding ring.' And this time the ring on her finger was a perfect fit as well as being very different from its predecessor. The first ring had been a plain gold band but the second struck her as a good deal more personalised for it was a slender platinum ring chased with ornate decoration.

'Don't call me your wife again,' Ruby muttered helplessly, twirling the ring round her finger with a restless hand. 'It makes me feel trapped.'

This time Raja did not hide his anger. His nostrils flared and his dark golden eyes scorched hers like burning arrows, leaving her feeling alarmingly short of breath. 'You should be proud to be my wife,' he told her without hesitation.

Her breath rattled in her tight throat. She had not meant to insult or offend. Without warning things had become terrifyingly personal. 'I'm sure I would be proud if I loved you,' she whispered in a response intended to soothe.

'Love!' Raja loosed a derisive laugh of disagreement. 'What need have we of that with the fire that burns between us?'

Well, so much for the emotional angle, she was thinking irately, for clearly she had not married a romantic guy, when sure fingers trailed across her cheekbone and captured her chin. His other hand curving to her waist, Raja lowered his proud, dark head and claimed her full, pink mouth hungrily with his. There was a split second when she might have pushed him away and her slim body braced and her hands rose in protest against his broad shoulders to do exactly that. But the moist slide of his tongue between her lips and the hand rising below her pyjama top to curve to the plump swell of her breast sent a flood of damp heat to the tender flesh between her thighs and a surge of such hunger that she shivered in shock. The dark force of desire took her by storm, every fibre of her being sitting up, begging and clawing for more.

CHAPTER SEVEN

'WE SHOULDN'T DO THIS!' Ruby gasped in a last-ditch attempt to reclaim control of the situation while she mustered sufficient self-discipline to drag her tingling mouth from the unadulterated magnetic allure of his.

Having already whisked her free of her pyjama bottoms, Raja threw back his tousled dark head and angled his lean hips to let her feel the hard evidence of his erection against her stomach. She quivered, fighting her desire for him with all her might, for at that instant desire had as much of a hold on her as a powerful addiction in her bloodstream.

'You mustn't get me pregnant!' Ruby exclaimed in a sudden panic, anxiety gripping her at the thought of suffering such a far-reaching and serious consequence. Just for a moment she could barely credit that she had ever been stupid enough to run that level of risk.

A hand spread below her hips to raise her to him. 'We took no precautions in the desert,' Raja reminded her with a frown.

'But we don't need to run that risk now. I take contraceptive pills but I missed some when we were there so for the rest of the month I need to take extra precautions.'

Raja found it deeply ironic that the potential pregnancy from which she was so keen to protect herself would have been a source of much rejoicing in both their countries. He suppressed that knowledge, for once uninterested in the bigger picture and concentrating on his own reactions for a change. As he studied her stunning oval face with burnished golden eyes of anticipation, he was startled to discover that he was willing to want whatever would make her happy. 'It's OK. Don't worry about it. I will protect you—'

'We can't be sex buddies…it's indecent—'

'I like indecent,' Raja confided huskily, trailing provocative fingertips very gently along the tender skin of her thigh so that she became even more painfully aware of the awesome strength of her own craving. 'In fact I could live beautifully with indecent.'

To silence the argument he sensed brimming on her lips he tasted her sultry pink mouth with the lingering eroticism that came so naturally to him, sensually teasing the soft fullness of her lower lip before penetrating her mouth in a smooth, explicit thrust. And while he kissed her he was skimming the ball of his thumb against the most sensitive spot on her entire body with a shocking expertise that made her stifle a scream while she writhed and gasped her response.

Before she could catch her breath from that onslaught, Raja leant back from her to rip open a foil packet and make use of a condom. Her heart thudded violently up tempo. She would not let herself think about what she was doing. She was rebelling against everything she knew because she had never wanted anything so much as she wanted him in that moment. And without a doubt she was ashamed of it, ashamed of the wild seething longing that controlled her, befuddling her brain and enslaving her body.

Raja sank into her in a long, slow surge, stroking her tender flesh with his. It felt so indescribably good that she cried out and her inner muscles clenched and convulsed around him. In the throes of extreme pleasure, he shuddered violently, as entrapped in that hunger as she was. 'It's never been like this for me before...' he confided.

Or for her, her brain echoed but speech was beyond her. Her whole body was attuned to every movement of his. With every subtle shift of that lean, powerful physique of his the dark pleasure rose in a sweet suffocating tide. He withdrew and then delved deep, moving faster and faster and her spine arched and she moaned in frantic excitement, defenceless against the feverish beat of exquisite sensation. Her climax finally rippled through her in an unstoppable force and she flamed into countless burning pieces before she dropped back to planet earth again. Another cry was dragged from her as the violent tremors of his final pleasure rocked her slight body with renewed sensitivity and sensation.

Raja eased back from her to study her with appreciation. He bent his head to press a kiss to her cheekbone. 'You're amazing,' he told her breathlessly.

'What have we done?' Ruby lamented out loud, already gritting her teeth, aware that in yielding to her hunger for him she had given way to weakness for the first time in her life. And that acknowledgement hurt her pride, really hurt.

Laughing, Raja described what they had done in the

most graphic terms and she curled a hand into a fist and struck his shoulder in reproach. 'This is not a joke.'

'You're my wife. We had sex. Our desire was mutual and natural and the slaking of it rather wonderful. Why the fuss?' Raja enquired with a slumberous smile of satisfaction while he marvelled at the unfathomable way in which she drew out the lighter side of his nature.

Ruby was jolted by the reality that he was in a totally different frame of mind and mood. He was celebrating while she was filled with regrets. 'It's not that simple—you know it's not. We made an agreement—'

'A foolish agreement destined to be broken from the outset,' Raja countered without an ounce of uneasiness. 'How could we marry and live in such proximity and not surrender to the attraction between us?'

In rejection of that stance, Ruby twisted free of his arms and rolled away to the far side of the bed. 'That's not what you said to me at the time.'

At that precise reminder, an impatient look skimmed across Raja's face. 'Choice didn't come into it—I had to win your agreement to marry me—'

'*Had* to?' Ruby prompted stiffly, her whole attention lodged to him with unwavering force.

Far from impervious to the threat of the drama waiting in the wings, Raja raked his fingers through the black hair falling into curls at his brow and sent her a look of reproach. 'You are not that naive, Ruby. With this marriage we brought the end to a war and created a framework for a peaceful future for both our countries. There is nothing more important than that and I never pretended otherwise. We sacrificed personal freedom for the greater good.'

That grim little speech, voiced without sentiment, froze Ruby to the marrow and felt like an ice spear thrust through her heart. He had torn any possibility of fluffy illusion from their relationship to insist on showing it to her as it truly was. But had she ever been in doubt of what their relationship entailed? A marriage that was part of a peace treaty between warring countries? A royal husband, who had married her because it was his duty to do so? Exactly when had she begun to imagine that finer feelings might be incorporated in that logical and unemotional package?

Scrambling out of bed because she was hugely uncomfortable with any physical reminder of what had just taken place there, Ruby pulled on her wrap and folded her arms. She would be reasonable, totally reasonable and practical just as he was, she told herself urgently. 'You said that we made a foolish agreement. On what grounds do you base that charge?'

'When we made that agreement, we were already strongly attracted to each other.'

'But you didn't argue that at the time,' Ruby protested.

'Sometimes you can be very naive.' Raja sighed, expelling his breath in a measured hiss and stretching back against the tumbled pillows, a gloriously uninhibited vision of male magnificence. 'Why do you think I went to the UK to meet you? My job was to persuade you to marry me as quickly as possible and assume your rightful place as a royal here in Ashur.'

Ruby lost colour as he made that explanation. 'Your...*job*?'

'There is nothing warm and fuzzy about that peace

treaty, Ruby, or the stability that rests on the terms being upheld to the letter of the law. Obviously I was prepared to do pretty much whatever it took to win your agreement,' Raja admitted tautly.

'Obviously,' Ruby repeated, feeling horribly hollow inside as if she had been gutted with a fish knife. 'So, are you saying that you deliberately set out to get me into bed in the desert?'

'I desired you greatly.' Brilliant dark eyes struck challenging sparks off her critical and suspicious scrutiny.

'That's not what I asked you,' Ruby declared. 'I asked you if I was seduced to order, another box to be ticked on your list of duties.'

His clever brow furrowed, his darkly handsome features still and uninformative. 'To order?' he queried huskily.

'Your English is as good as mine, possibly even better!' Ruby snapped, her temper hanging by a fingernail to a cliff edge as she forced herself to seek a clarification that stung her shrinking self like acid. 'Stop faking incomprehension to play for time when I ask an awkward question!'

Unmoved by that indictment, Raja stretched, hard muscle rippling across his broad shoulders and abdomen as he shifted position with the fluidity and grace of a tiger about to spring. 'Is that what I'm doing?' he traded with an indolence she suspected to be entirely deceptive.

Being stonewalled merely aggravated Ruby more and her chin came up, eyes bright with antagonism and resentment now. 'Let me bring this down to the simplest level. Did you or did you not take off your boxers and lie down with me that night for the sake of your precious country?'

Raja very nearly laughed out loud at that demand but restrained the urge, aware it would go down like a lead balloon. 'I am willing to confess that I never had any true intention of allowing our marriage to be a fake. I hoped to make our marriage real from the day of our wedding.'

The barefaced cool with which he made that shattering admission shook Ruby, whose nature was the direct opposite of calculating, to her very depths. 'So, you deceived me.'

'You put me in a position where I could do little else. A divorce between us would be a political and economic disaster. Any goodwill gained by our marriage would be destroyed and offence and enmity would take its place. And how could I continue to rule this country without an Ashuri princess by my side?' he demanded bluntly. 'Your people would not accept me in such a role.'

Unfortunately for him, Ruby was in no mood to recognise the difficulties of his position or to make allowances. Deep hurt allied with a stark sense of humiliation were washing through her slight body in poisonous waves. 'You deceived me,' she said again, her voice brittle with angry bitter condemnation. 'I gave you my trust and you deceived me.'

'I always intended to do whatever it takes to make you happy in our marriage,' Raja breathed in a driven undertone, his dark eyes alight with annoyance and discomfiture, for he was well aware that he had been less than honest with her and that went against the grain with him, as well. 'That is the only justification I can offer you for my behaviour.'

'But if it takes a divorce to make me happy you're going to make it difficult,' Ruby guessed, her face pale and tight with the self-control she was exerting as she turned on her heel. 'I'm sleeping on the sofa tonight.'

As the door eased shut on her quiet exit Raja swore, jolted by a powerful wave of dissatisfaction more biting than any he had ever known. He had wounded her and he had never wanted to do that. Although it would have been very much out of character he badly wanted to unleash his temper and punch walls and shout. But the discipline of a lifetime held, forcing him to stop, think and reason. Pursuing her to continue the altercation in the state of mind she was in would only exacerbate the situation. He had chosen honesty and maybe he should have lied but he believed that the woman he had married deserved the truth from him.

Ironically, Raja believed that he knew what his wife wanted from him. After all, almost every decent woman he had ever spent time with had wanted the same thing from him: eternal devotion and commitment and all the empty words and promises that went along with them. At a young age Raja had learned to avoid getting involved with that kind of woman. His mistress Chloe's unconcealed greed was a great deal easier to satisfy and the main reason why Raja much preferred relationships based on practicality and mutual convenience.

Ruby, however, was very emotional and she would demand more than he had to offer. Ruby would want things that would make him grossly uncomfortable. He looked back down the years to when he had been a student deeply in love for the one and only time in his life. She would want romance and poetry, hand-holding and constant attention and if he even looked at another woman she might threaten to kill herself, he recalled with a barely repressed shudder. He was no woman's lapdog and, although his father was a noted poet in Najar, Raja secretly hated poetry. He groaned in increasing frustration. Why were some women so difficult? So highly strung and demanding? Her meta-phoric cup was half empty but in comparison his was almost full to overflowing. Ruby was a very beautiful and very entertaining woman and he had just enjoyed the most fantastic sex with her. That was enough for him and an excellent foundation for a royal marriage between strangers. He was more than content with what they already had together. Why couldn't she be con-tent? And how was he to persuade her of the value of his more rational and reserved approach?

On the sofa, which had all the lumps if not the worn appearance of a piece of furniture that had served be-yond its time, Ruby tossed and turned. She was stunned that Raja could admit to telling her a barefaced lie. He had agreed to her terms. He had said the words but he hadn't *meant* them. Clearly he had been diametrically opposed to a platonic marriage and the first chance he got to change that status quo he had snatched at it.

Just as Ruby had snatched at Raja out in the desert, craving the hot, hard passion of that lean, strong body against hers! Lust, that was all it could have been, and she had given way to that lust and without much of a struggle. It didn't matter how much she blamed the up-setting circumstances of their kidnapping for what had transpired. In her heart she knew that nothing would ever have happened between them had she not found Raja al-Somari downright irresistible in the flesh.

But it seemed that Raja had made love to her for much more prosaic reasons than mere desire. He had slept with her to consummate their marriage, to make it a *real* marriage and ensure that she was less able to walk away easily. How much did he really find her at-tractive? Was it even possible that he was the sort of guy who had set out to bring her down simply because she defied his wishes and expectations? How many women had actually said no to Prince Raja with his fabulous looks and even more fabulous wealth? Had she only made herself an irresistible challenge?

Her eyes prickled with stinging tears of humiliation that rolled slowly down her face in the moonlight that filtered through the windows, which had no curtains. She had never had the power to guess what went on in Raja's arrogant, dark head. Their confrontation tonight had been an education. He had been a total mystery to her and a dangerously fascinating one at that, she ac-knowledged painfully.

Possibly she had been overdue for the experience of meeting a man who affected her more than she affected him. Had she got too full of herself? Too convinced she could not be fooled or hurt by a man? She had as-sumed she could call the shots with Raja and he had just proved that she could not. The guy she had stupidly married was much colder, more astute and ruthless than she could ever be. Raja had manipulated her into doing what he wanted her to do when she slept with him and in doing so he had crushed Ruby's pride to dust.

Hermione was standing guard over Ruby's sleep when Raja entered the room soon after dawn. With a snarl, the little dog launched herself at him and he caught the animal. He suffered a bite on his arm before he got the frenzied little dog under control and deposited her outside the suite with a word of command to the guards standing outside to take care of her. Raja then strolled quietly back across the room to study his soundly sleeping wife. She didn't take up much space on the sofa and she looked achingly young. Below the tousled mane of blonde hair, only her profile was visible. He could see the silvery tear tracks marking her cheek and he cursed under his breath, his conscience pierced afresh. He had screwed up, he had screwed up royally. He should have kept his mouth shut. Lying didn't come easily to him but the truth had done way too much damage.

Somehow he had to redress that damage and make their marriage work. With no previous experience in the marital department and only a long unhelpful history of unscrupulous mistresses to fall back on, Raja felt unusually weak on the necessary strategy required to make a wife happy. Particularly a wife as unusual as Ruby. An apology would probably be in order. It was not that he had done anything he shouldn't have done, he reasoned in frustration, more a question of accepting that in her eyes he was guilty and that for the sake of better marital relations he had to respond accordingly. He would buy her something as a gift, as well. Flowers? His nostrils flared and he grimaced. Flowers had the same nauseous effect on him as poetry. Diamonds? He had never met a woman who didn't melt when he gave her diamonds...

CHAPTER EIGHT

FROM HER SMALL collection of clothing, Ruby selected a black dress she had bought to wear at her mother's funeral and a beige cotton casual jacket. She would be too warm in the garments but they would have to do because she couldn't wear the red suit again. Some minimal make-up applied to conceal the puffiness of her eyes and her pallor, her hair caught up in a high ponytail for coolness, Ruby forced herself to walk out to the dining area and join Raja for breakfast.

'Good morning...' Raja murmured lazily as if they had not parted at odds the night before.

'Good morning.' One glance at that handsome face and her mouth ran dry and her heart thumped loudly behind her breastbone, while a tiny heated knot of reaction pulled taut in her pelvis and made her clench her thighs together as she took a seat opposite him. Face burning with discomfiture, she suddenly didn't blame herself any more for succumbing to Raja's lethal sex appeal. He was a heartbreakingly beautiful man. Her biggest weakness was her failure to appreciate how clever and calculating he might be, but now that she did know she would be a great deal more cautious.

'I've made arrangements for a new wardrobe to be assembled for you in Najar,' Raja informed her.

'I do need more clothes. I don't own dressy outfits but I wouldn't want anything too expensive or flashy,' Ruby responded thoughtfully as he poured tea for her and she buttered a roll. 'The state this country is in, it wouldn't be appropriate for me to be dressed up like some sort of celebrity.'

'Wajid would disagree with you. He thinks life is too dull here and that you will bring some much-needed colour and the promise that brighter times lie ahead. Here you *are* a celebrity, whether you like it or not, and celebrities dress up.'

Zuhrah joined them along with her male administrative counterpart, Asim, who organised Raja's diary. Ruby's engagements at the orphanage and at a school were discussed and useful sheets of facts tucked into a file for her. She could not help noticing that the heavy-duty visits, like one to a homeless camp and another to a makeshift hospital, fell on Raja's shoulders, Wajid evidently having decided such venues were no place for a lady. A lighter note was struck when a maid appeared with a crystal vase filled with the most exquisite white roses, which she placed on the table.

'Oh, how lovely!' Ruby got to her feet to lean down and draw in the rich opulent perfume of the perfect blooms and only then noticed the gift envelope inscribed with her name. She recognised Raja's distinctive handwriting immediately. Eyes veiling, her facial muscles freezing, she took the card and sat down again to open it with pronounced reluctance.

I am sorry for upsetting you. Raja

Her teeth gritted. She reckoned there was never a truer word written than that apt phrase but she was unimpressed by the apology, for a wife barely able to look at him never mind speak to him was naturally a problem he had to fix. No doubt any effort made towards that objective would be all for the greater good and the peace treaty, as well.

'Thank you,' she said with the wooden intonation of a robot and gave him an even more wooden smile purely for the benefit of their audience of staff. Wajid would have been proud of her, she reflected bleakly. Instead of throwing the vase at her royal husband she had smiled at him, showing a restraint in her opinion that raised her near to sainthood. After all, had he been sincerely sorry would he not just have apologised across the table?

Ruby didn't do a good fake smile, Raja acknowledged wryly while he wondered if it had been accidental or deliberate that at one point she had actually pushed the vase of roses out of her way to lay down her file. And then he could not credit that he had actually spared the brain power to wonder about something so trivial! He left the room to phone his jeweller and explain what he wanted: a diamond of the very highest calibre. Raja did not embarrass easily but her silence over breakfast had embarrassed him. He did not want their differences paraded in front of their staff for inevitably it would lead to gossip and the news that their marriage was in trouble would enter the public domain very soon afterwards.

Wajid accompanied Ruby to the orphanage and revealed that Raja had requested that he do so as soon as he had realised that Wajid had scheduled them to make visits separately.

'His Royal Highness is very protective of you,' Wajid told her with approval. 'When he is unable to be with you he wants you to have every possible means of support.'

It occurred to Ruby that that was paradoxical when Raja seemed to have the power to wound her more than anyone else. His protectiveness meant nothing, she reasoned unhappily. The prince was simply one of those very masculine men who deemed a woman to be more helpless and instinctively expected to have to take care of her. That in the desert she had proven him right on that score still blasted a giant hole in her self-esteem. But why did she feel so unhappy? Why had he hurt her as no other man had ever succeeded in doing since her stepfather had gone out of her life?

It hadn't just been sex for her, Ruby conceded reluctantly, striving to be honest about that. Raja was strong and clever and resourceful and she admired those traits. Add in his looks, boundless sex appeal and equally extensive charm and her defensive barriers had begun crumbling so fast she had barely registered the fact. Of course she had never met the equal of Raja al-Somari before. He came from a different world and culture but he had also been shaped by every educational advantage and great wealth and status. Twenty-odd years earlier, Ruby's mother, Vanessa, had made the mistake of falling in love with just such a man. Was Ruby about to make the same mistake? Not if she could help it.

The limousine in which she was travelling drew up outside the orphanage, a cluster of relatively modern buildings that had mercifully not been targeted by the Najari soldiers. As the older couple she had met at the reception the night before appeared on the steps to welcome them, Ruby had no more time for introspection. She had always loved children. As her visit progressed she was alternately appalled by the scale of loss many of the children had suffered in losing their entire families and then touched by the resilience of their spirits. The orphanage was in dire need of more trained staff, bedding and toys but most of the children were still able to laugh and smile and play.

One little girl attached herself to Ruby almost as soon as she appeared by sliding her tiny hand into hers. About three years old, Leyla had big dark eyes, a tangle of black curls and a thumb firmly lodged in her rosebud mouth.

The orphanage director was surprised by the little girl's behaviour and explained that she was rather withdrawn with the staff. Leyla's parents had died during the war. Unfortunately there was no tradition of adoption in Ashuri society and many people were struggling just to feed their own families. Leyla clinging to her skirt, Ruby spent the most time with the younger children and listened while a story was being told. When the time came for Ruby to leave, Leyla clung to Ruby as if her life depended on it and, lifted from her, wept inconsolably. Ruby was surprised at how difficult she found it to part with Leyla. Just the feel and scent of that warm little body curled trustingly in her arms had made her eyes sting with tears. All of a sudden her own problems seemed to shrink in comparison.

Ignoring Wajid's disapproving expression, Ruby promised to come back and visit in the evening. Their next visit to a temporary school housed in tents was a good deal more brisk but also less formal as Ruby mingled with teenagers and answered their questions as best she could, trying not to wince or stiffen when the court advisor admonished those he considered were being too familiar with his royal companion.

'I don't like formality. I'm more of a hands-on person and that's the only style I'm comfortable with,' Ruby informed the older man as they drove off.

'Royalty should be more reserved,' Wajid preached.

A determined look in her level eyes that Raja would have recognised, Ruby said quietly, 'I'll carry out my engagements as the ordinary person that I am, Wajid. I can only do this kind of thing because I like mingling with people and chatting to them.'

'Princess Bariah would not have dreamt of lifting a crying child,' the older man was reduced to telling her.

'I am not Bariah. I grew up in a different society.'

'One day soon you will be a queen and such familiarity from your subjects would seem disrespectful.'

Aware that a man old enough to be her grandfather was almost certain to cherish a less liberal viewpoint on suitable behaviour, Ruby dropped the subject. But she had not noticed Raja standing on ceremony with their guests at the reception the evening before. He had appeared equally friendly and courteous with everybody.

When she got back to the palace she was so tired she lay down. For quite some time she thought sadly about Leyla. The little girl had touched her heart and she was wishing that there were something she could do to help her before she finally fell asleep for several hours. She wakened when a maid knocked to deliver a garment bag. Unzipping it, she extracted an opulent sapphire-blue evening dress and high-heeled shoes. Her expression thoughtful, she checked the size of both.

Only minutes later, Raja joined her in the bedroom.

'Did you organise this?' she asked, extending the dress.

'Yes. This evening you'll be meeting friends and relatives of your late uncle and his family. You would feel ill at ease if you were underdressed in such a gathering,' Raja forecast smoothly.

'You even got my sizes right,' Ruby remarked, thinking how very, very handsome he was, even when in need of a good shave, for dark stubble clearly accentuated the sensual curve of his sculpted mouth. 'You're obviously used to buying clothes for women.'

A slight frown at that remark drawing his ebony brows together, Raja swung fluidly away to remove his jacket and made no response.

But Ruby was not so easily deflected. 'Are you in the habit of buying for your sisters?'

'They do their own shopping,' Raja admitted.

'So, you are accustomed to buying clothes for the other women in your life,' Ruby gathered, not a bit averse to making him uncomfortable if she could.

'No comment. I'm glad you like the dress.'

Her brown eyes flamed amber. 'Your hide is as tough as steel, isn't it?'

'I never said I was a virgin,' Raja shot back at her with sardonic cool, his strong features taut.

'Oh, I had already worked that out for myself,' Ruby retorted, thinking of how smoothly he had seduced and bedded her.

In retrospect the level of his experience with her sex was obvious to her and to her annoyance that awareness loosed a whole flock of curious questions inside her head. How had she compared to his other lovers? Did he go for blondes, brunettes or redheads or any of the above? Would he even have found her attractive had she not been a long-lost and almost forgotten Ashuri princess? Every question of that ilk that crossed Ruby's mind infuriated her. Why was she letting him make her feel insecure and vulnerable? Now that she knew the truth behind their consummated marriage, she would be better able to protect herself.

'There will not be another woman in my bed while you remain my wife,' Raja volunteered abruptly, his brilliant, dark eyes welded to her expressive face.

'My goodness, do you think I care?' Ruby forced a laugh and then plastered an amused and scornful smile to her lips. 'I couldn't care less what you do. I have to take account of the reality that we're stuck with each other for the foreseeable future so there's no sense in fighting every step of the way.'

'You make a good point,' Raja responded although outrage had shot flames of gold into his gaze when she declared that she didn't care what he did.

'And I'm not asking you to sleep on the sofa tonight and I'm not sleeping on it either. We're adults. I'm asking you to respect that agreement you think is so foolish and forget that we ever had sex.'

Wonderment consumed Raja as she spoke. Forget about the sex? She stood there looking like every fantasy he had ever had in her little black dress with her beautiful eyes, sultry pink mouth and glorious legs

tempting him and she thought he could easily return
to treating her like a sexless stranger? He *had* deceived
her by cloaking his true intentions, he reminded himself fiercely. This was the punishment, the payoff. He
had to give her time to adjust to her new role.

'I will do my best,' Raja replied flatly.

He emanated angry vibrations and she wondered
why that was. The need to get inside Raja's head and
understand what made him tick was, Ruby was discovering, a constant craving. Did he only want to make
love to her because he thought that should be his right
as a husband? Or would he have wanted her anyway
just for herself? And why, when she had never planned
to become intimate with him, should that distinction
matter to her?

Later he did up the zip on the blue dress and it fit her
like a tailor-made glove, the rich colour flattering her
fair colouring. As she sat at the dressing table straight-
ening her hair Raja came to her side and handed her a
jewellery box. 'It is a small gift.'

Ruby lifted the lid and stared down dumbstruck at
the flawless glittering teardrop diamond on a pendant.
Small wasn't the right word. It was a *big* diamond and,
although she knew next to nothing about the value of
jewellery because she had never owned any beyond a
wristwatch, she guessed that a diamond that large had
to be worth a small fortune.

'Thanks,' she mumbled in shock.

'Allow me.' While she lifted her hair out of the way,
Raja clasped the pendant at the nape of her neck. She
shivered as his fingertips brushed her sensitive skin
and that little knot of sexual hunger in the pit of her

stomach tightened up a notch. 'I would've given you earrings but your ears aren't pierced.'

'No, I'm a total unbelievable coward. I once went with a friend and she fainted when they did her ears. She bled all over the place too—it put me right off!' Ruby confided, suddenly desperate to fill the awkward silence.

His shrewd, dark eyes screened in his reflection in the mirror, Raja rested a hand on her taut shoulder. 'Ruby…'

'My mother said my father chose my name, you know,' she volunteered abruptly. 'He said that a virtuous wife was worth more than rubies. It's kind of insulting that the only future he could see for me was as someone's wife.'

'But I am grateful to have you as my wife.'

'Only because I was part of the peace treaty,' Ruby fielded, flatly unimpressed by that declaration. 'Spoils of war and all that.'

TWO WEEKS LATER, the night before Ruby's first visit to Najar, Raja was enjoying a pleasant daydream. A century or so earlier had he acquired Ruby as the spoils of war, she would have belonged to him…*utterly*. It was a heady masculine fantasy to toy with while he was being driven to the orphanage that his wife had contrived to visit alone almost every evening since her initial official visit there. He had Wajid to thank for that information, for Ruby had kept very quiet about where she took off to during their rare moments of leisure.

Ruby took care not to share that time with him. It was yet another vote of no confidence from his wife, who was not his wife in any way that mattered, Raja conceded grimly. They might still share the same bed but she had placed a bolster pillow down the middle of it. That had made him laugh the first night, but within a week the comedy aspect had worn very thin.

His cell phone pinged with a message and he checked, frowning as the snap Chloe had put in of herself shone up at him, all blonde hair and a wide, perfect smile. Ruby did not possess that perfection of feature. Her nose turned up at the tip and she had the cutest little gap between her front teeth. Yet whenever he saw Ruby there was no one else in the room capable of commanding his attention. His handsome mouth curled as he read the suggestive text from his mistress. He had no desire to exchange sexy texts. That didn't excite him. Chloe was becoming a liability. On the other hand if Ruby had felt the urge to send him a suggestive text he would have responded with imagination and enthusiasm, he acknowledged with self-derision. Unfortunately there was as much chance of a sext coming from Ruby as of Ashur sending a rocket to the moon.

Raja, however, remained conscious that he had no real grounds for complaint. His bride was already performing her duties as a future queen with considerable grace and good humour. Her naturally warm personality had great appeal. The Ashuri people liked her easy manner and chatty approach, not to mention her frankness in referring to the days when she had led the life of a young working woman.

Forewarned by a call of his impending unofficial visit, the orphanage director greeted him in the hall and took him straight to Ruby. Ruby was in the nursery with a little girl on her lap, painstakingly reading out a few brief words from a picture book in the basic Ashuri language, which she was working so hard to learn. A cluster of children sat on the floor round her feet.

'The princess is a natural with children. It's unfortunate that the child she is holding—Leyla—is becoming a little too attached to your wife,' the older woman told him in a guarded undertone.

Raja got the message intended. He watched the little girl raise a hand to pat Ruby's cheek and then beam adoringly up at her, her other hand clutching possessively at Ruby's top. He watched Ruby look down at the child and realised that he had a problem that cut both ways, for his wife's lovely face softened into a deeply affectionate smile. Raja would have been elated to receive such a smile but he never had. When Ruby saw him in the doorway, she leapt almost guiltily upright, arms locking protectively round the child in her arms. A staff member approached to take the little girl and Ruby handed her over, visibly troubled when the child began to sob in protest.

'Raja...' Ruby framed in a jerky, almost soundless whisper, for she was so astonished to see him standing there that her voice just deserted her.

Clad in the long off-white tunic called a *thaub* that he wore most days, Raja looked fantastically handsome, the smooth golden planes of his classic masculine features demarcated by the exotic set of his lustrous dark eyes and high cheekbones. Her tummy flipped like a teenager's and she froze, feeling foolish and very much aware that she was hopelessly infatuated with her husband, which was one reason why she avoided his company as much as was humanly possible. He was like an ever-growing fever she was trying to starve into subjection in her bloodstream.

'I had some news I wished to share with you,' Raja imparted lightly. 'Until Wajid mentioned it, I had no idea that this was where you were coming most evenings.'

'I enjoy being with the children. There's no formality here—it's relaxing,' she told him.

'Mrs Baldwin said you're fond of one particular child—'

'Leyla...there's just something about her that grabs my heart every time I see her,' Ruby admitted, opting for honesty. 'I really love spending time with her. She's so sweet and smart.'

Installed in the limo he had arrived in, Ruby said, 'What news wouldn't wait until I got back to the palace?'

'There have been arrests here and in Najar. The members of the royal households who shared our itinerary with the kidnappers have been identified and arrested, as have their supporters.'

Taken by surprise by that information, Ruby frowned and asked, 'Who were they?'

'An aide on my father's staff and a private secretary from Wajid's team here in the palace. Wajid is very ashamed of that link. Be tactful with him if he raises the subject. He is very much aware that the kidnapping could have ended tragically.'

'But we were unhurt,' Ruby hastened to remind him.

Her husband looked grave, his sensual mouth compressing. 'Ruby...tempers run high with memories of the war still so fresh. Fighting could have broken out again. Our lives and those of others were put at risk. The mercenaries whom the perpetrators hired to act for them have fled the country and are unlikely to be apprehended but a prison sentence is inevitable for the citizens involved.'

'I understand.' The justice system was rigid and retribution fell swift and hard on those who broke the laws in their countries. Ruby was already learning to temper her opinions in the light of the society in which she now lived, but it still occasionally annoyed her to depend so much on Raja's interpretation of events and personalities.

Just weeks earlier she had claimed that she intended to be as much involved as Raja in ruling Ashur and could only marvel at her innocence, for the longer she lived in the palace, the more she appreciated how much she still had to learn about the constantly squabbling local factions and the council of elderly men who stalled and argued more than they made decisions. Raja spent a good deal of his time soothing difficult people and in meetings with the Najari investors financing the rebuilding of Ashur. His duties seemed endless and he was working very long hours because he was also dealing with his duties as Regent of Najar from a distance. Unable to offer much in the way of support, Ruby felt guilty.

Indeed the longer she stayed in Ashur, the more confused and unsure of her own wishes Ruby was becoming. She was fully conscious that Raja had married her with the best of intentions and acted as he saw fit in an effort to turn their platonic marriage into a lasting relationship. He had played the hand he had been given without intending to hurt or humiliate her. He wanted her to stay married to him but to date he had put no pressure on her to do so and she respected him for that. Yet while he was bearing the blame for the dissension between them she knew that she had played a sizeable part in her own downfall by being so violently attracted to him. Her decision to surrender to that attraction had badly muddied the water and her thinking processes and encouraged her to want more from him than he was ever likely to give her. When she had specified and demanded a marriage of convenience, how could she blame him for *her* change of heart?

At the same time avoiding Raja and keeping to the other side of the bolster in the bed was beginning to feel a little childish. She was also living on her nerves because her period was currently overdue. She had told herself that her menstrual cycle could just be acting up. But in her heart of hearts she was terrified that her misfiring cycle combined with the new tenderness of her breasts meant that she had fallen pregnant. She had abandoned all restraint in the desert with Raja and it looked as though she might well be about to pay a price for that recklessness.

'The little girl you were with,' Raja commented quietly.

Instantly, Ruby tensed. 'Leyla? What about her?'

'Have you gone to the orphanage every evening?'

'Have you a problem with that?' Ruby countered defensively.

'The child seems very attached to you. Is that wise?'

he prompted gently. 'She will be hurt when you disappear from her life again.'

Annoyance hurtled up through Ruby and she closed her hands together very tightly to control her feelings. 'I have no plans to disappear.'

Sensing her distress at what he had suggested, Raja stretched out a hand to rest it on top of her tensely knotted fingers. 'We're leaving Ashur tomorrow for a couple of weeks. You have many claims on your time now.'

'I… I was thinking of adopting Leyla!' Ruby flung at him, finally putting into words the idea that had been growing at the back of her mind for two weeks and working on her until it began to seem a possibility rather than a wild idea. 'I know you'll probably think I'm crazy but I've become very fond of Leyla. Whatever it takes, I'd very much like to give her a home.'

Astonished by that outspoken admission, Raja studied her. 'But you're planning to divorce me…'

Ruby frowned. 'Well, eventually, yes, *but*—'

'Then I suspect that you have not thought this idea through,' Raja intoned. 'The Ashuri Court of Family Law would not countenance foreign adoption and would wish the child to be raised here where she was born with her own language and people. I doubt that you are willing to offer her that option.'

'I would love her,' Ruby breathed in stark disagreement as the limo drew up outside the side entrance to the palace. 'Leyla needs *love* more than she needs anything else!'

'Love is not always enough,' Raja drawled softly.

In receipt of that hoary old chestnut, Ruby shot him a furious look of disagreement and took the stairs to their suite two at a time. Her heart was hammering like mad behind her breastbone because she was genuinely upset. Having finally got up the courage to voice her hopes with regard to Leyla, she had been shot down in flames. The hard facts Raja had voiced rankled and hurt. Evidently there was no question of her trying to adopt Leyla if she was planning to ultimately divorce Raja. But *was* she planning to divorce him?

Exactly when would she be able to walk away from Raja without that decision impacting on the stability of Ashur? She could not imagine a date even on the horizon when she might leave her marriage without there being a risk of it leading to political upheaval in her late father's country. Her decision to marry Raja had been rash in the extreme, she conceded ruefully. She had not looked into the future. She had failed to recognise that a short-term fix might be almost worse for her country of birth than her refusing outright to marry Raja. A divorce would unleash more political and economic turmoil. Raja was right about that, for she had listened to people talking and seen for herself how much weight rested on their marriage as a symbol of unity and reconciliation. An image of Leyla's tear-stained little face swam before her now and her heart turned over inside her chest.

'What do you know about love?' Ruby demanded, challenging Raja as she poured the mint tea waiting for them on a tray. 'Have you ever been in love?'

'Once was enough,' he admitted sardonically.

Ironically Ruby felt affronted by that admission. He didn't love her but he had fallen for someone else? 'Who was she?'

His lean strong face took on a wry expression. 'Her name was Isabel. We met as students at Oxford. I was besotted with her.' He grimaced, openly inviting her amusement. 'We read poetry and went everywhere together holding hands.'

'People apparently do stuff like that when they're in love,' Ruby remarked stiltedly, well aware that he had never shown any desire to read her a poem or to hold her hand and, as a result, feeling distinctly short-changed rather than amused.

'The romance turned into a nightmare,' Raja confided tight-mouthed, his beautiful dark eyes bleak with recollection. 'She was very jealous and possessive. Everything was a drama with her. If I even spoke to another woman she threw a scene. I was nineteen years old and totally inexperienced with your sex.'

Sipping the mint tea, which she had learned to find refreshing, Ruby was touched by his honesty, for baring his soul did not come naturally to a man accustomed to keeping his own counsel and concealing his feelings. 'At that age you must have found a volatile woman hard to cope with.'

'She threatened to kill herself when I tried to break it off. I stood up to her but she carried through her threat—she *did* take an overdose,' he admitted gravely, acknowledging her wince of sympathy with compressed lips. 'When I said it was a nightmare I wasn't exaggerating. Eventually Isabel's parents put her into a clinic to be treated for depression. It took me a long time to extract myself from my entanglement with her.'

'And of course it put you off what she saw as love,' Ruby conceded thoughtfully, understanding that perfectly, her brown eyes soft as she tried to picture him as a naive teenager spouting poetry and holding hands. 'But Isabel sounds as if she had a very twisted idea of love. It was just your bad luck to meet a woman like that and get burned.'

Raja shrugged a broad shoulder in a fatalistic gesture.

'My mum, though—she got burned twice over,' Ruby volunteered, startling him. 'She lacked good judgement. She just fell in love and believed the man would be perfect. My father married his second wife behind her back and then told Mum he had no choice because he needed a son and she had had to have a hysterectomy after giving birth to me.'

'And the second burning?' Raja queried curiously, for he was already familiar with the first, although he had been given a rather different version.

Ruby grimaced. 'The reason Hermione distrusts men around me—my stepfather, Curtis. He was always trying it on with me—'

'Your stepfather tried to abuse you?' Raja ground out in an appalled tone, black brows drawing together.

Ruby nodded in uneasy confirmation. 'He started bothering me when I was about twelve. By then Mum was going out several nights a week to a part-time job and I was left alone in the house with him.'

Raja was outraged that she had been targeted at such a tender age by a man within her own home where she should have been safe. For the first time he understood what had given Ruby her essentially feisty and independent nature as well as her distrust of his sex. Angry concern in his gaze, Raja was frowning. 'You didn't tell your mother what he was doing, did you?' he guessed. 'Why not?'

'Because it would've broken her heart,' Ruby proffered heavily. 'She adored Curtis and she'd had a bad enough time with my father.'

'Your stepfather never actually managed to touch you?'

'No, but I lived in terror that he would. It was such a relief for me when he walked out on us. He made me very suspicious of men. He also left Mum absolutely broke.' Ruby set down her cup and began to move towards the bedroom.

'Ruby?'

Ruby glanced back at him warily.

'How much do you want to give Leyla a home?'

Ruby paled and contrived to look both very young and very determined. 'I've never wanted anything more...' *Apart from you*, but that was a truth she refused to voice, watching him as he stood there poised, darkly beautiful and dangerous to her every sense and emotion.

'I will make enquiries on our behalf—'

'*Our?*'

'Only a couple could be considered to adopt her. It would have to be a joint application from us both.'

Astonished by that speech, Ruby trembled with emotion. 'Is that an offer?'

Raja surveyed her steadily. 'No, it is my assurance of support in whatever you decide to do.'

And Ruby knew very well what was going unsaid in that statement. A married couple naturally meant a couple planning to stay married. Lashes lowering, she was too enervated to respond and she turned away and went for a shower. Towelling herself dry in the bathroom, she took stock of her situation. She was in love with him. Why not just come clean about that? She was madly, hopelessly in love with Raja al-Somari! Aside from that sense of duty of his, which had hit her pride squarely where it hurt, she liked everything about Raja. His strength, his intelligence, his generosity. His protectiveness, his understanding, his tolerance. He was no longer just a very good-looking, sexy guy, he was the one she had learned to love to distraction even though she had done her utmost to resist his considerable appeal.

The bedroom was empty. But she left the bolster pillow in the foot of the wardrobe where it stayed by day. Tonight she saw no need for a barrier. In fact she was not quite sure which of them had required the restraint imposed by the presence of the bolster the most.

Thirty minutes later, Raja came to bed and the very first thing he noticed was the missing bolster. He slid into the bed in semi-darkness and lay there. There might as well have been a ten-foot wall down the middle of the bed, he reflected wryly. He refused to give her the excuse of believing that there had been any sort of a price attached to his support in the adoption application she was hoping that they would make. He was very much impressed by her commitment to the child, her willingness to become a mother at a young age when so many women would have chosen only to make the most of his unlimited wealth.

Barely a foot away Ruby lay wide awake, as well. She knew that she wanted him quite unbearably. She also knew that suddenly bringing the sex factor back in before other things were sorted out between them would be extremely imprudent but she was still madly hoping that he would take her unspoken invitation.

But the invitation was ignored and it took her a long time to get to sleep. Hours crept past while she thought about Leyla, wondering if they would be allowed to offer the little girl a home and if Raja would learn to love her, as well. She should have discussed the subject more with him. She had to learn how to be half of a couple and wondered why that skill seemed to come so much more naturally to him. It felt as though she had barely slept when she woke up and recalled that this was the day when she would finally meet Raja's family and see Najar for the first time.

CHAPTER NINE

'WAJID SAID THAT adopting an Ashuri child would be a fantastic PR exercise,' Raja revealed with a look of distaste mid-morning the following day as they travelled to the airport for their flight. 'The orphanage director is pleased about our decision because she hopes that our example will encourage people to consider the other children available for adoption.'

'My goodness, you've been busy,' Ruby commented a tad guiltily at his obvious industry with regard to her hopes concerning the little girl. Having woken soon after dawn when Raja always got up, she had felt distinctly nauseous and had returned to bed only to sleep in late and have a rushed breakfast. A stomach upset, she was wondering now that she felt perfectly fine again, or a symptom of a more challenging condition? Could she be pregnant? How soon would she be able to find out? And how could she check discreetly without anyone finding out?

She was startled when the limousine turned in the orphanage gates.

'I think it's time that I met Leyla properly,' Raja announced, recognising her surprise at that change to their itinerary. 'And I believe that you would be glad of the opportunity to see her again before we leave.'

The Baldwins met them on the doorstep to express voluble thanks for the sizeable donation that Raja had made to the orphanage. He had not shared that fact with Ruby and was clearly uncomfortable with the couple's gratitude. They were ushered into an office and Leyla was brought to them there. Her little face lit up when she saw Ruby and she ran in her eagerness to greet her, only to fall to a halt when she saw Raja. He crouched down to a less intimidating height and produced a ball from his pocket. Leyla clutched the ball in a tiny fist while surveying Raja with great suspicion. But Raja was perfectly at home with her, talking to her, smiling and teasing until the child began to giggle and hide her face.

Witnessing that surprising show, Ruby was learning something she hadn't known. 'You're used to kids.'

'I ought to be. My sisters have five children between them and my cousins must have about thirty,' he volunteered, finally standing up with Leyla content to be held in his arms, her thumb stuck in her mouth, her eyes bright.

The effort he was making, the kindness he displayed, Ruby reflected on a tide of quiet appreciation, just made her love him all the more. Suddenly the fact he had taken advantage of her susceptibility to him in the desert no longer mattered and her resentment melted away. Hadn't she encouraged him and taken the final decision? As she had good reason to know he was a very practical and dutiful guy, loyal to his country, his family, faithful to his promises and keen to meet every expectation no matter how unreasonable it might be. And at its most basic, all Raja had ever wanted from her was the willingness to make their marriage work. But the man whom she had resented for that no-nonsense aspiration was also the same one holding the little girl she had come to care for and he was willing for both their sakes to consider making her a part of his illustrious family. And no man Ruby had ever met had been willing to expend even a tenth of Raja's effort and thoughtfulness into making her happy.

ARRIVING IN THE country of Najar was not remotely like flying into Ashur. For a start there was a proper airport that was very large and sophisticated. In fact as Ruby looked out open-mouthed at the busy streets through which they were being driven with a police escort and motorcycle outriders, Najar seemed to have nothing at all in common with Ashur. Towering office blocks, apartment buildings, fancy shopping malls and exotically domed mosques all blended together in a well-designed city with wide, clean streets. She saw at once why Raja had looked at her in disbelief when she had accused him of wanting the throne of Ashur. Her birth country was very much the poor relation, decades behind its rich neighbour in technology and development.

In contrast, the royal palace was still housed in an ancient citadel separated from the aggressively modern city by the huge green public park that stretched outside its extensive walls.

And the palace might be ancient on the outside but, from the inside, Ruby soon appreciated that Raja's family home bore a closer resemblance to a glossy spread from an exclusive design magazine. The interior was so grand and opulent that she was stunned by the eye-watering expanse of marble flooring and the glimpses of fabulously gilded and furnished rooms. Her steps had slowed and she was fingering the plain dark dress she had chosen to wear with her nervous tension rising to gigantic heights when a door opened and a group of women appeared. And, oh, my goodness, Ruby's sense of being intimidated went into overdrive as shrieks of excitement sounded and high heels clattered across the incredible floor. Ruby and Raja were engulfed by an enthusiastic welcome.

Raja drew her forward in her little black chainstore dress. 'This is Ruby...' and she wanted to kick him for not warning her that the women in his family wore haute couture even in the afternoon. Indeed one look at Raja's female relatives and she felt like the ugly duckling before the swan transformation. All of them were dressed as if they were attending a cocktail party. They sported elaborate hairdos, full make-up, jewel-coloured silks and satins and fantastic jewellery.

They entered the room the women had just vacated on a tide of welcoming chatter and questions. Fortunately everybody seemed to speak at least some English. Children joined their mothers in the crowd surrounding Ruby. There was an incredible amount of noise. Most of the men standing around in the big room attempted to act as though they were not as curious about Raja's bride as their womenfolk were. One tall young man made no such attempt at concealment and he strode across the room to seize her hand and shake it with a formality at odds with his wide grin and assessing eyes. 'Raja said you were even more gorgeous than you looked in your photo and he was right. I'm his brother, Haroun,' he told her cheerfully.

Ruby thought that it was heartening to know that Raja paid her compliments behind her back that he would never have dreamt of making to her face. Was he afraid she might get big-headed? Or did compliments fall under the dubious heading of romance? Or did a woman in a platonic relationship just not qualify for such ego-boosting frills? Haroun looked like a smaller, slighter, younger version of his big brother and he was rather more light-hearted, for he was cracking politically incorrect jokes about Ashur within seconds. Drinks and snacks were served by uniformed staff and Raja's sisters, Amineh and Hadeel, were quick to come and speak to her.

'You are very beautiful,' Hadeel, a tall, shapely woman in her mid-twenties, told her with an admiring smile. 'And a much more suitable match for my brother than your unfortunate cousin.'

'Am I?' Ruby studied her sister-in-law hopefully. 'I never met my cousin so I know nothing about her.'

'Bariah was thirty-seven years old and a widow,' Amineh told her wryly.

'But she was also a very good and well-respected woman,' Hadeel hastened to add, clearly afraid that her sister might have caused offence.

Ruby, however, was just revelling in the promise of such indiscreet gossip. She had missed that aspect of female companionship and felt that when Raja's sisters were willing to be so frank with her it boded well for her future relationship with them. Learning that Bariah had been eight years older than Raja and had also been married before was something Ruby could have found out for herself from Wajid, but she had been too proud to reveal her curiosity and ask more questions. She met Amineh's and Hadeel's husbands and a whole gaggle of children followed by a long parade of more distant relatives. Everyone was very friendly and welcoming and she was thoroughly relaxed by the time that Raja came to find her. He explained that his father found large family gatherings very tiring and that he was waiting in the next room to meet her in private.

King Ahmed was in a wheelchair and frail in appearance. He had Raja's eyes and white hair and, although he spoke only a few words of English, his quiet smile and the warm clasp of his hand were sufficient to express his acceptance of Ruby as the latest member of his extensive family. Ruby was surprised to learn that Raja had already told his father about Leyla and their plans. The older man was warmly supportive of their intentions and talked at some length about his sadness over the suffering and disruption inflicted on families during the war.

'I didn't realise that you were so close to your father that you would already have told him about Leyla,' Ruby commented on the way back into the party at the end of their audience with the king.

Raja laughed. 'No matter where I am in the world we talk on the phone every day. I think he would have been very shocked to hear the news about Leyla from anyone else!'

'I wish I'd known my father,' Ruby confided, feeling a slight nauseous lurch in her stomach and tensing slightly, for she had assumed her tummy upset at the start of the day had gone away and she didn't want it revisiting her while she was in company.

Raja paused to look down at her with his dramatic, dark, deep-set eyes. 'The loss was his, Ruby. I fear that you suffered because he and your mother parted on bad terms.'

'Well, after what he did to Mum, naturally they did.'

'The story of your background that I heard suggested that your mother was aware that your father might well take another wife after they were married. It was a lifestyle practised by several of your ancestors over the past hundred years,' Raja told her quietly. 'Perhaps your mother didn't understand what she was getting into when she agreed to marry him.'

'That's very possible...' Ruby focused wide brown eyes on him that were suddenly full of dismay. 'I can't believe I didn't ask you *but*—'

Raja laughed and rested a silencing forefinger against her parted lips. 'No, do not ask me that question, *habibi*. I would be mortally offended. One wife has always been sufficient for the men in my family and the thought of more than one of you is actually quite unnerving.'

'Unnerving? *How?*' Ruby demanded and just at that moment her fractious insides clenched and went to war with her dignity again. Forced to hurry off to the nearest cloakroom, Ruby was so embarrassed by her digestive weakness that her eyes flooded with tears. Her mood was not improved when Raja's sisters insisted on waiting outside the door for her to ensure that she was all right, for she would rather have suffered the sickness without a concerned audience close by.

When the emergency was over, she was ushered
into the building that acted as Raja's secluded home
within the rambling fortress. He had his own staff, one
of whom showed her up a flight of stairs to a superbly
decorated bedroom suite. It was a relief to slip off her
shoes there and lie down on top of the bed. A drink
reputed to soothe a troubled stomach was brought to
her and a little while after that as her tension eased and
she relaxed she began feeling fine and eventually and
surprisingly rather hungry.

A pair of Saluki hounds trotting at his heels, Raja
walked in to study her from the foot of the bed. Hermione had accompanied them and the little dog jumped
up at the side of the bed to nuzzle her cold nose against
Ruby's hand, the Salukis following to make her ac-
quaintance. 'Oh, they're beautiful, Raja!' Ruby exclaimed, leaning out of bed to pat their silky heads.
'Do they belong to you?'

'Yes. Hermione seems to like them well enough.
How are you feeling?' Raja asked

'Great now, believe it or not,' she told him with a
hesitant smile. 'I'm going to have a shower and then
I'd like something to eat. I'm sorry about all the fuss.'

'Are you sure that you're feeling well enough to
get up?'

Ruby slid easily off the bed and scolded Hermione
for trying to jump up on it. She could not help noticing
that Raja's dogs, who had retreated to sit by the door,
seemed to be very well trained. 'Very sure.'

'I'll order a meal.'

'Haven't you eaten either?'

'I wanted to see how you were first.'

Ruby checked out the dressing room in search of her wrap and found the closets and drawers were already packed with unfamiliar clothes in her sizes. 'That's some new wardrobe you've bought me!' she called to Raja.

'It won't matter what you wear. You will still outshine every outfit,' Raja responded huskily.

Ruby was surprised by that tribute. A flowing blue negligee set draped over one arm, she emerged from the dressing room to study him, the colour of awareness lighting up her face. Having discarded his traditional robe, he was in the act of changing into designer jeans and a shirt. The fluid grace and strength of that muscular physique of his still had enough impact to take her breath away. It didn't matter how much exposure she had to Raja al-Somari, he still had the power to trip her heartbeat inside her and make her mouth run dry with excitement.

'Shower,' she reminded herself a little awkwardly.

The bathroom was as palatial as the bedroom and the invigorating beat of the water from multi-jets restored her energy levels. She wondered how Raja had tolerated the weak water flow of the old-fashioned shower in their suite of rooms in Ashur. Since her arrival in Najar she had come to realise that he was accustomed to a lifestyle in which every possible modern convenience and luxury was available to ensure the last word in comfort. She admired him for not having uttered a single complaint while he was forced to stay in the palace in Ashur.

When she returned to the bedroom Raja was talking on the phone in Arabic. He glanced up and then stilled to stare, lustrous dark eyes flaming gold at the sight of her. A wealth of blonde hair falling round her lovely face, her slim shapely figure framed by the flowing blue nightwear, she was a picture. With an abstracted final word he concluded his call and pushed the phone into his pocket.

As she met that intense appraisal Ruby's face flushed, her nipples tightening into prominence while a melting sensation of warmth pulsed between her thighs. As he crossed the room, his eyes holding her gaze with a stormy sensuality that filled her with yearning, she was welded to the spot.

Without a word, Raja pushed the tumble of silky blonde hair back from her cheekbone and lowered his head to trace the seam of her closed mouth with his tongue and then pry her lips apart. Fingers stroking her slender neck, he plundered her mouth with a hungry ferocity that blew Ruby away. Staggered by the passion he made no attempt to contain, she angled her head back, snatching in a ragged breath as she looked up at him through her lashes and collided with the smouldering urgency in his stunning eyes. Her tummy flipped. One kiss and she felt as if he had switched a light on inside her, bathing her in warmth and dazzling brilliance.

'I am already so hot and ready for you,' Raja breathed thickly.

Ruby trembled, insanely aware of the surging dampness and the ache at the heart of her body. She was so wound up she couldn't make her throat produce a recognisable sound. But it was also one of those moments when she knew not a shred of doubt about what she wanted to happen next. Her hands lifted of their own volition to unbutton his shirt.

A wolfish smile tilted Raja's handsome mouth. He bent his head to kiss her again with lingering eroticism. 'I will make it so good for you, *aziz*,' he husked in a tone of anticipation that slivered through her like a depth charge of promise.

And the breath rattled in Ruby's tight throat and her knees went weak because she had every faith in his ability to deliver on that score. He would drive her out of her mind with pleasure and she was way past the stage where she could deny either of them what they both needed. She wasn't quite sure when wanting had become a much more demanding *need* and self-denial an impossible challenge. Mesmerised by Raja's raw sensuality, she stretched up to touch his face with delicate fingertips, tracing those slashing angular cheekbones, and those beautiful sculpted lips. She gasped beneath that carnal mouth as it captured hers with delicious masculine savagery. Suddenly, as if her caress had unlocked his self-control to free his elemental passion, he trailed off the peignoir with impatient hands and pushed her back on the bed. Throwing off his shirt, he came down beside her bare-chested.

Breathing shallowly, the level of his hunger for her unhidden, Raja stared down at her. 'I don't know how I've kept my hands off you for so long. It was pure torment.'

As she pushed up on her elbows, feeling marvellously irresistible, Ruby's eyes brightened and she stretched closer to unzip his jeans. The bulge of his arousal made that exercise a challenge and she laughed when he had to help her and then stopped laughing altogether when he drew her hand down to the long, hard length of his erection in an expression of need that was a huge turn-on for her.

She bent her head and took him in her mouth, silky blonde hair brushing his hair-roughened thighs. Watching her, Raja groaned with intense pleasure, knotting his hands in her hair and then finally pulling away at the peak and surprising her.

'Raja...?'

'I want to come inside you,' he told her raggedly. 'And once isn't going to be enough...'

Shivering in reaction to the coiled-tight ache of need in her, Ruby let him move her. Her body was eager and ready, charged by a hunger so strong it made her tremble. He filled her with a single thrust, sinking into her with a power and energy that almost made her pass out with pleasure. She cried out as he lifted her legs onto his shoulders and rose over her to plunge down into her honeyed sheath again and again. Uncontrollable excitement gripped her as he drove her slowly, surely to a delirious climax. At the apex of delight she came apart under him, writhing and sobbing with mindless satisfaction as the wild spasms of pleasure ripped through her in wave after wave. Afterwards he cradled her close, murmuring in his own language, stroking her cheek with caressing fingers while his lustrous eyes studied her with unashamed appreciation.

It was the middle of the night before they ate.

Ruby wakened feeling sick again at dawn and Raja was very insistent on the point that in his opinion it was time for her to see a doctor. He was worried that she had contracted food poisoning. While Ruby lay as still as she could and fought the debilitating waves of nausea Raja made arrangements for a doctor's visit and got dressed.

An hour and a half later, Ruby received the answer to the big question she had been asking herself for more than a week.

'Congratulations,' Dr Sema Mansour pronounced with a wide smile. 'I am honoured to be the doctor to give you such important news.'

Ruby smiled back so hard her facial muscles ached under the strain. 'Please don't tell anyone else,' she urged, although even as she said that she appreciated that it was not a secret that she could hope to keep for long.

'Of course not. It is a confidential matter.' Lifting her doctor's bag, the young female medic, recommended by Princess Hadeel, took her leave.

A light breakfast was served to Ruby in bed and the maid plumped up her pillows first to ensure her comfort. Indeed all the staff involved in her care in the magnificent bedroom displayed a heart-warming level of concern for her welfare. Munching on a piece of roll without much appetite, Ruby stared into space and wondered how Raja would feel once she made her announcement. Last night they had made love and she had felt buoyant at the knowledge that her husband desired her so much.

But starting a family wasn't something they had ever discussed or planned, although he had proved keen to encourage her desire to adopt Leyla.

Ruby had always assumed that some day she would

want children. But until she had met Leyla and Mother
Nature had turned her broody, she had believed that the
family she might ultimately have lay somewhere far
into her future. Leyla, however, had stolen into Ruby's
heart and she had experienced such a strong longing
to be Leyla's new mum that she had been amazed at
herself. And now she was carrying Raja's baby. That
hadn't taken long, although it was true that they had
been very active in that line in the desert. Ruby flushed
hotly at the recollection of a night when she had barely
slept, indeed had behaved like a sex addict wonderfully
well matched with another sex addict. Wretchedly vir-
ile fertile man, she thought ruefully and in shock, for
there was no denying that a royal baby in the offing
would change everything.

In the short term Ruby had been willing to ditch the
concept of divorce and future freedom if it meant she
could qualify to adopt little Leyla and raise her as her
daughter. In spite of that though, she had still believed
somewhere in the back of her mind that there remained
a slight possibility that ten years or more down the line
she and Raja might be able to separate from each other
and lead their own lives without causing too much of
a furore within their respective countries. Now with
the needs of a second child entering the equation she
felt that she had to be a good deal more practical. She
had to ask herself if she was willing to subject possibly Leyla and her future child to the rigours of a broken home solely because she wanted a husband who
loved her the way she already loved him. Children
got attached to their parents living together as a couple. She had seen the heartbreak among school friends

when their parents broke up and one parent moved out. Although in many cases there was no alternative to a separation, Ruby felt that she was in a position where she was still lucky enough to have choices to make.

Raja appeared in the doorway, brilliant dark eyes alive with concern, the taut line of his handsome mouth easing with relief when he saw that she was eating. 'It was a stomach upset, probably the result of you being given so much unfamiliar food,' he reasoned. 'Perhaps we should ask one of the chefs to cook English meals for you.'

'No, what we needed was better birth control,' Ruby contradicted, taking tiny sips of tea to moisten her dry mouth while she stared mournfully back at her husband. 'And I'm afraid that ship has sailed.'

Raja was staring fixedly at her, shapely ebony brows quirked, bewilderment stamped in the angles of his strong face. 'Better birth control?'

'We didn't use any in the desert—didn't *have* any to use,' she conceded heavily for so far being pregnant, between the nausea and the sore breasts, was not proving to be a lot of fun. '*And*…you've knocked me up.'

Raja had never bothered to try and imagine how he might hear that he was to become a father for the first time, but had he done so he was certain that not once would the colloquial British phrase 'knocked up' have featured on his dream wife's lips. 'You're…' Shaken by the concept, he had to clear his throat to continue. 'You're *pregnant*?'

'Yes, congratulations, you're a real stud.' Ruby sighed in a tone that would not have encouraged him to celebrate. 'But it's such a shock.'

Raja shifted his proud dark head in agreement. In receipt of her announcement, which had rocked him on his feet, he felt a little light-headed. 'I feel rather foolish,' he admitted wryly. 'This possibility didn't once cross my mind.'

'Me neither—until afterwards. I worried after we were rescued,' Ruby told him ruefully.

'You should have told me that you were concerned. I can't believe it but in the excitement of the situation I overlooked the risk of such a development,' Raja declared gravely.

'That's not like you,' Ruby remarked helplessly, for she always got the feeling that Raja worked everything out to the nth degree and rarely got taken by surprise. 'At the beginning I even suspected that conceiving a child might have been part of the seduction plan. After all, once you got me pregnant it would be harder for me to walk away from our marriage.'

'But not impossible and I wouldn't wish an unwilling mother on any child of mine.' Raja scored impatient fingers through his cropped black hair, his clear, dark golden gaze melding to hers in reproach. 'I am not a Machiavelli. My desire for you was very strong and I acted on it for the most natural of reasons.'

It disturbed Ruby that she could not work out how he felt about her revelation that she was pregnant. She had originally assumed that he would be pleased, which was why she had announced it in that quirky fashion, striving to be cool. But now she was no longer so certain of his reaction because his innate reserve concealed his true reaction from her. 'I bet you that Wajid turns wheelies when he finds out—it's another piece of good PR, isn't it? Three weeks of marriage and I'm pregnant?'

'And you feel even more trapped than you did already,' Raja assumed, his stubborn jaw line clenching, a muscle pulling taut at the edge of his handsome mouth. 'I know you had already decided that you wanted to offer a home to Leyla, but you are very young to take on the responsibility of parenthood—'

'Raja…girls of fourteen were falling pregnant when I was at secondary school. At twenty-one I'm mature enough or I wouldn't have been talking about trying to adopt Leyla,' Ruby argued, feeling insulted and wondering if he considered her immature.

Raja strolled over to the window and looked out at the lush tranquil garden in the courtyard. His lean classic profile was taut. 'I *do* understand how you must feel. Such massive changes in your life are a challenge to cope with. Be honest with yourself and with me—'

Tension made Ruby sit up a little straighter in the bed. 'Honest about what? And how do you feel?'

'I felt incredibly trapped when I knew I had to get married as part of the peace accord,' he admitted without warning, the words escaping him in a low-pitched driven surge. 'I didn't want a wife I didn't choose for myself. My father reminded me that he didn't even meet my mother before he married her but, as I pointed out to him, he was raised in a different world with exactly that expectation. I never dreamt that I would be asked to make an arranged marriage. I had to man up.'

With that confession, which Ruby was quite unprepared to receive at that moment, she felt as though he had driven a knife into her. It shook her that she had been happy to feel like a victim while ignoring the reality that he might have felt equally powerless on his own behalf. *I didn't want a wife I didn't choose for myself.* That one sentence really said all she needed to know. At heart they had always had much more in common than she was prepared to accept. No doubt he had not shared his feelings on the score of their marriage when they first met for fear of influencing her into a negative response. She could understand that. Yet even so, regardless of how she had felt at the beginning, she had adapted, a little voice pointed out in her head—adapted, without even appreciating the fact, to her new position and responsibilities to live a life that was a great deal more demanding but also more interesting than the life she had left behind her in England.

Paradoxically it had wounded Ruby to hear her husband admit that he too had felt trapped when he had learned that he had to marry her. It was a case of very bad timing to learn that truth at the same time as she told him she had already conceived his child. But perhaps once again she was being unfair to him, Ruby reasoned uncertainly, reluctant to come over all dramatic like his first love. After all, how much enthusiasm could she reasonably expect from him? A baby with a woman he didn't love could only feel like another chain to bind him even though he had already agreed to take on Leyla.

Raja sank down on the side of the bed and reached for her hand. 'We will have two children. We will be a family before we have learned how to be a couple.'

'Not how you would have planned it?' Ruby prompted.

'When it comes to us nothing seems to go as planned and who is to say that what we have now is not all the better for that?' Expression reflective, he sounded more as if he was trying to convince her of that possibility than himself. 'I'm accustomed to change and I will handle this, but you have already had so many challenges to overcome in so short a space of time. This is a tough time for you to fall pregnant.'

Ruby was bewildered. 'I—'

'Naturally I feel guilty. I should have been more careful with you,' Raja breathed curtly. 'You have enough to deal with right now without this added responsibility.'

'You still haven't told me how you feel about the baby. Don't you want it?' Ruby queried anxiously.

Raja dealt her an astonished appraisal. 'Of course I want my own child, but not at the cost of your health and emotional well-being.'

'I'll be fine.' Ruby was disappointed that he had said nothing more personal. 'But most of those fancy clothes you bought me aren't likely to fit in a few months.'

'Not a problem. I like buying you things,' Raja volunteered, his thumb rubbing gently over the pulse in her narrow wrist. 'I want you to spend the next couple of days just acclimatising and catching up on your rest.'

Ruby gave him an impish grin. 'No more all-night sex sessions, then?'

Dark colour highlighted his superb bone structure and his eloquent mouth quirked in reluctant appreciation of that sally. 'Oh, Ruby...' he breathed, his hands gathering her slight body up so that he could kiss her with all the devastating expertise that sent her defensive barriers crashing flat like a domino run.

Feeling daring, Ruby pushed the sheet back. 'You could rest with me,' she muttered in an intuitive invitation.

'I have only fifteen minutes to make a meeting on the far side of the city,' Raja groaned, pausing to extract a second driving kiss, his breathing fracturing as he stared down at her with unalloyed hunger before finally springing up again, adjusting the fit of his trousers to accommodate his response to her. 'You're a constant temptation. I'll see you mid-afternoon and we'll go over the adoption papers we need to lodge to apply for Leyla.'

He found her very attractive, Ruby told herself consolingly. It wasn't love, it was lust, but marriages had survived on less. He was taking the advent of an unplanned baby very much in his stride, but then Raja was the sort of guy who typically rose to every challenge. The very worst thing she could do was brood about what they didn't have as opposed to what they did. In time he might almost come to love her out of habit. What was wrong with that? Did she need the poetry and the hand-holding? It would have been much worse had she fallen in love with a man she couldn't have. A man, for example, who belonged to another woman. Here she was safely married to a very handsome, sexy and exciting man and she was still feeling sorry for herself. Why was that? Was she one of those perennially dissatisfied personalities who always wanted more than she could have?

Ruby was dozing when she heard a mobile phone

going off somewhere very close to her ear. With a sound of exasperation she lifted her head and focused in surprise on the slim cell phone flashing lights and lying semi-concealed in a fold of the bedding. It was Raja's phone. It must have fallen out of his pocket while he was kissing her. She closed a hand round it and immediately noticed the photo of the gorgeous blonde.

And that was that. Ruby suffered not one moral pang rifling through Raja's phone and discovering that someone called Chloe had sent him a series of suggestive texts in English. Obviously a woman who was a lover, a woman who had shared a bed with him, enjoying all the intimacies and no doubt many more than Ruby had ever had with him. In shock Ruby read the texts again. The skank, she thought furiously, appalled by the sexy little comments calculated to titillate the average male. Raja's healthy libido did not require stimulation yet he had been receiving those texts ever since they got married. She went through his phone. If he had sent any texts back to Chloe he had clearly had the wit to delete them.

So, who was Chloe and what was Ruby going to do about her? Was she his most recent girlfriend? Why hadn't he told Chloe to leave him alone? Why hadn't he told her that his relationship with her was over? He had promised Ruby that he would be faithful and that there would be no other woman in his life while he was with her. Suddenly the cocoon of shock that had kept Ruby unnaturally calm was cracking right down the middle...

CHAPTER TEN

DISTRESS FLOODED RUBY and for a horrible timeless period she was too upset even to think straight. Men had cheated on Ruby before but invariably because she refused to sleep with them and it had never hurt so much that she wanted to scream and sob and rage all at the same time.

Yet she had instinctively trusted Raja—why was that? She peered down at the photo. Chloe was a very beautiful woman. Few men would feel obligated to ditch a woman with Chloe's looks and penchant for provocative texts just because they had made an arranged marriage. Why would Raja award Ruby that amount of loyalty when he didn't love her?

I felt incredibly trapped. I didn't want a wife I didn't choose for myself. Today the revelation about the baby had proved such a shock that Raja had at last chosen to be honest with her, sharing what was on his mind and in his heart. All the time that she had subjected him to her bad temper and resentment over the head of their need to marry he had suffered in silence rather than admit that he felt *exactly* the same way. That truth had cut deep. Was Raja planning to keep Chloe in the background of his life while he pretended to be a devoted husband? Was Chloe to be his secret comfort and escape from the exigencies of his royal life and arranged marriage?

The advent of two children was unlikely to lock Raja closer to home and hearth. In all probability children would make him feel more trapped than ever. The demands of a family and all the accompanying domesticity would never be able to compete with the freewheeling appeal of a Chloe, willing to send him sexy texts about what she longed to do to him between the sheets.

Ruby was devastated. She had understood what Raja meant when he had said that they should have had the time to get to know each other as a couple before they considered becoming parents. She also knew that she had literally shot herself in the foot. Tears trickling down her cheeks, Ruby thought about Leyla and yet she knew she could have done nothing different where that little girl was concerned. Her need to give Leyla the love she craved had been overwhelming. But hadn't she railroaded Raja into that commitment with her? She missed the little girl a great deal and could hardly wait for the magical day when she would have the right to take Leyla out of the orphanage and bring her home as her daughter. She had already pictured sharing that special day with Raja but Chloe's texts and the intimate pledges within them might well be much more of an attraction for him.

Having dressed in a denim skirt and tee and slid her bare feet into sandals, Ruby ate a chicken salad in the shaded arbour in the courtyard. Her stomach was mercifully at peace again. It was a beautiful spot with trees, lush greenery and flowers softening the impact of the massive medieval walls that provided a boundary. In the centre water from a tranquil fountain streamed down into a mosaic tiled basin, cooling the temperature. Had she been in a happier mood she would have thought she was in paradise.

She wondered exactly what she was going to say to Raja about those texts. She would have to be blunt and he would have to be honest. How important was Chloe to him? He had to answer that question.

A burst of barking from Hermione warned Ruby that Raja had arrived. Steps sounded on the tiles and Raja appeared, tall and sleek and darkly attractive in a lightweight designer suit.

'I left my phone here?' Lean brown fingers immediately descended on the cell phone lying on the table top and swept it up. 'I've been looking for it. I use my phone for everything...'

Ruby's pensive face tensed. 'I *know*,' she said feelingly. 'I'm going to be totally frank with you—I've read Chloe's texts. Her photo flashed up and I'm afraid I just had to go digging and I'm glad that I did.'

For a split second, Raja was paralysed to the spot, black brows drawing together, lush lashes flying up on disconcerted dark eyes, his dismay unhidden. 'Chloe,' he repeated flatly. 'That's over, done with.'

'If it's over, why was she still texting you as recently as last week?'

Raja was frowning at her. 'Did you read my texts?'

Ruby lifted her chin but her colour was rising. 'We're married. I felt I had the right.'

Faint colour defined his stunning cheekbones. His

proud gaze challenged that assumption. 'Even married I am entitled to a certain amount of privacy.'

'Not if you're going to be married to me, you're not. All right—I snooped. But I stand by what I did,' Ruby told him resolutely and without an instant of hesitation. 'It cuts both ways. Everything in my life is open to you.'

His face was impassive. A smouldering silence stretched between them in the hot, still air and during it a servant delivered mint tea and a plate of the tiny decorative cakes that Raja loved to the table. Drymouthed, Ruby poured the tea into the cups, her heart beating very fast.

Raja studied her from semi-screened eyes. Without warning a surprising smile curved his beautiful mouth. 'The idea of you reading those texts embarrasses me,' he admitted.

'Receiving that kind of thing *should* embarrass you,' Ruby told him forthrightly, but the ease of his confession and that charismatic smile reduced the worst of her tension, for she could not credit that he could smile like that if there was anything serious going on between him and Chloe.

'My affair with Chloe is over—it was over the moment you and I consummated our marriage,' he added.

'I'm willing to believe that but, if it's over as you say, why was she still sending you texts like that?' Ruby pressed uncomfortably.

'Think about it,' Raja urged wryly. 'From my point of view, Chloe was a sexual outlet. From hers, my greatest advantage was that I spent a great deal of money on her and she is naturally reluctant to lose that benefit. As I didn't wish to see her again I arranged to pay her a settlement through my lawyer last week. I can only assume that the texts are supposed to tempt me back to her bed. I didn't reply. I thought to reply would only encourage her.'

'She was your mistress,' Ruby remarked uneasily, relieved that no deeper feelings had been involved, but troubled by the obvious truth that he could so efficiently separate sex from emotion. 'That arrangement sounds so...so *cold.*'

'It suited both of us. I didn't want complications or hassle.' Raja shrugged a broad shoulder, his face reflective. 'But now I have you and as long as I have you I have no need of any other woman.'

There was something wonderfully soothing about that statement, voiced as it was with such rock-solid assurance in her ability to replace his sexually sophisticated mistress. The worst of the stress holding Ruby taut drained away.

'I was really upset when I saw those texts,' Ruby admitted reluctantly.

'I regret that you saw them and had reason to doubt my integrity. In that field, you can trust me, Ruby,' he murmured levelly, his sincerity patent. 'I believe in trust and honesty. I would not deceive you with another woman.'

Her eyes stung like mad and she widened them in an effort to keep the tears from overflowing, but some of them escaped, trickling down her cheeks. 'I believe you,' she said in a wobbly voice. 'And I don't know why I'm crying.'

'Hadeel said you might be very emotional over the

next few months because of your hormones,' Raja told her, startling her with that forecast and belatedly adding, 'I told her that you were pregnant.'

Ruby was disconcerted by that admission. 'You've told your family already?'

'Only Hadeel, the sister I am closest to, and she will keep our news a secret until we are ready to share it with the rest of the family. It's such exciting news—I could not keep quiet. I *had* to tell someone!' Raja exclaimed, a mixture of apology, appeal and distinct pride in his delivery that touched her heart.

It was the first sign that she had seen that he was genuinely pleased about the baby and a stifled sob escaped her convulsed throat because inexplicably, even though he had set her worst fears to rest, she felt more like having a good cry than ever. 'I don't know what's the m-matter with me.'

Murmuring soothing things, Raja scooped her up in his arms and carried her back indoors, shouldering open the bedroom door to settle her down onto the comfortable bed.

'Do you want me to start sending you texts like that?' Ruby asked him abruptly. 'I mean, I haven't done anything like that before but I'm sure I could learn the knack.'

Raja dealt her a startled look and then he laughed with rich appreciation of that proposal. 'No, thanks for the offer but I can get by without that sort of thing. To be truthful it's not really my style.'

'Honestly?' Ruby pressed anxiously.

'Honestly. I would much rather do it than talk about it, *aziz*,' he husked with considerable amusement gleaming in his lustrous eyes. 'And of course I have to have you to do it with. That goes without saying.'

'Am I really going to be enough for you?'

'Oh, yes,' Raja asserted. 'More than enough.'

'How can you be so sure?'

'You're special and you were from the start. My first introduction to you was a photo of you when you were fourteen. It was taken outside the cathedral in Simis. Wajid had it in his possession—'

'My goodness, you saw that snap? Mum sent it after we came home from that holiday in Ashur when we were turned away from the palace gates,' Ruby explained. 'I think it was her way of saying that we were perfectly happy whether the royal family ignored us or otherwise.'

'I was very impressed with the photo, and when I saw you for real I was stunned by your impact on me and by how much you challenged me,' Raja confided. 'I only had to look at you to want you. I couldn't take my eyes off you.'

'I couldn't take my eyes off you either,' Ruby said. 'But you admitted earlier that you were very resentful of the need for us to marry...'

'The instant I saw my beautiful bride my fate became instantly more bearable,' Raja told her, laughing at the face she pulled. 'Yes, I'm a very predictable guy—I desired you at first glance and I'm afraid that went a long way towards settling my objections to our arranged marriage.'

Ruby frowned, studying him in disbelief. 'That is just so *basic*.'

Raja spread his hands as if to ask her to hold that

opinion. 'But then when I was least expecting it I fell in love with you…'

'And then you…*what*?' Ruby gasped, utterly bemused by that declaration.

'At first it was just sexual desire that motivated me and then it was your smile, your strength and your sense of fun that had even more appeal. I fell in love without even realising what was happening to me,' Raja declared, gazing at her with hot golden eyes in which possessiveness was laced with pride. 'All of a sudden you became the most important element in my world.'

'I don't believe you. You said you slept with me in the desert because you wanted to make our marriage a real marriage.'

'I slept with you purely because I wanted you. Any other aspirations which I cherished were secondary to that simple fact,' Raja intoned levelly. 'I'm not too proud to admit that I wanted you any way I could get you. I was very hurt when you said later that you didn't care what I did.'

Ruby was beginning to believe but she wasn't prepared to let him off the hook too easily. 'But there was a seduction plan?'

Raja curled her fingers into his palm. 'I couldn't resist you.'

'I was pretty horrible to you in the desert. I mean, it wasn't your fault that we were there but I behaved as though it was.'

'You were scared and trying not to show it. I understood that.' Raja bent his dark, arrogant head and brushed his sensual mouth very slowly and silkily across her soft pink lips. 'And then you gave me your body and there was nothing I wouldn't have done for you, nothing I wouldn't have forgiven.'

'I thought that night was amazing but it can't have been so special to you.'

'It was, *aziz*.' Raja extracted a deep drugging kiss that made her tremble and look up at him with dazed eyes. 'But I think I fell in love with you when you said over that hotel lunch you walked out on that I would have been equally willing to marry a dancing bear. No other woman would ever have said such a thing to me. Or maybe our defining moment came when you said very ungraciously that you would only drink *bottled* water from now on—'

'Stop teasing me.' Her fingers speared into his thick black hair and she kissed him back with all her heart and soul, the longing he could awaken slivering through her in a piercing arrow of need.

'That second night we spent together was extraordinary. It was our wedding night,' Raja pointed out, his brilliant eyes resting appreciatively on her beautiful face. 'And wonderful.'

'Yes, it was, wasn't it?' Ruby agreed, arching up to taste his mouth again for herself and hauling him back down to her again with greedy hands.

'I thought I would never love a woman again and then I met you and it was a done deal right from the start. I was so resentful of the need to marry you until I actually met you. You got right under my skin. I tried to stay in control but it didn't work. And then after we were rescued you made it clear that you wanted nothing more to do with me. The flowers and the diamonds didn't make much of an impression and that's about all

I had in my repertoire. You vanished every evening and only spoke to me when you had to. I'm not used to being ignored.'

'It probably did you the world of good. I felt stupid.' Ruby wrinkled her nose. 'I'd demanded a platonic marriage and then got intimate with you the first chance I got. I didn't know how to behave after that.'

'I lay in that bed every night burning for you.' Raja groaned, his body shuddering against hers in recollection. 'I have never felt so frustrated and yet so aware that I would be putting unfair pressure on you if I made another move.'

'I did need breathing space.' Ruby rubbed her cheek comfortingly against his hand in a belated apology, hating the idea that he had been unhappy, as well. 'I wanted you as well but I had so many other things— like my new royal life—to worry about. I was exhausted and living on my nerves and afraid that it would be a mistake to trust you too much.'

'The greatest mistakes were mine. I was too impatient, too hungry for you.' Raja sighed, discomfiture darkening his beautiful eyes and stamping his features with regret. 'I should never have touched you in that tent. I rushed you into something you weren't ready for and almost lost you in the process.'

'You can't plan stuff like that. I fell in love with you too,' Ruby murmured, looking at him with loving eyes, revelling in the tenderness of his embrace and loving his strength and assurance. 'But I was so scared I was going to get hurt, that I was falling for a guy who would never feel the same way about me.'

'I won't hurt you, *aziz*. You are my beloved and I can only be happy if you are happy with me—'

'Obviously you got over that trapped feeling—'

'I trapped you with me,' Raja pointed out, dropping the mask of his reserve completely. 'I felt so guilty about letting you fall pregnant. That shouldn't have happened. I was selfish, thoughtless. I should have abstained from sex when I couldn't protect you.'

'That night was worth the risk. I would make the same choice again,' Ruby told him, running a caressing hand across the muscular wall of his warm hard torso and smiling with satisfaction when he pushed against her and sought out her mouth again with barely restrained passion.

'Some day I would like to take you back into the desert and show you its wonders.'

'You were enough of a wonder for me,' Ruby countered, in no hurry to recapture the magic of sand and scorpions, before he kissed her breathless and all sensible conversation was forgotten.

'I really do love you,' he told her some time later when they had sated their desire and they lay close and satisfied simply to be together.

'I love you too but words are cheap—you didn't give me the poetry or the hand-holding,' she complained with dancing eyes.

'Not the poetry, please,' he groaned, wincing at the prospect. 'I don't have a literary bone in my body.'

Unconcerned, Ruby squeezed the fingers laced with hers and kissed his stubborn jaw line, loving the scent of his skin. She was very happy and she would settle quite happily for the hand-holding.

EPILOGUE

A LITTLE LESS than two years later, Ruby smiled as Leyla told her brother, Hamid, to put away his toys and began showing him how to go about the task.

A lively little girl of five years, Leyla was very protective of her little brother but bossy, as well. For the sake of peace, Hamid toddled across to the toy box on his sturdy little legs and dumped a toy car in it, ignoring the rest of the cars scattered across the rug. Of course, even as a toddler Hamid was accustomed to the reality that servants would cheerfully tidy up after him and go out of their way to fulfil his every need and wish.

Hamid, the heir to the united throne of Najar and Ashur, was treated like the eighth wonder of the world in both palaces. Hamid might easily have become spoilt by overindulgence but Raja was very aware of the potential problem and he was a strict but loving father. With his black curly hair and big dark eyes, Ruby's son was the very image of his father and an energetic child with a quick temper and a wilful streak. Ruby tried not to laugh as Leyla tried to pressure her brother into lifting more cars and he sat down and refused to move another step in silent protest.

Ruby still felt surprised to be the mother of two

young children, nor did it seem possible to her that she and Raja had already reached their second wedding anniversary. The two years had flown by, packed with events and precious moments. Leyla's adoption had been a joy. Ruby still remembered the memorable day when she and Raja had collected the little girl from the orphanage and explained that they would now be acting as her mother and father and that she would be living with them from then on. A decree from the throne had made Leyla an honorary princess so that she would not be the odd one out among any siblings born to her adoptive parents. Happily many of the other inmates of the orphanage had also found adoptive homes since then.

Hamid's birth a couple of months later had provided an excuse for huge public celebrations in Najar and Ashur. Their son was the next generation of their ruling family and a very welcome reminder of all that had changed between the two countries. Ashur was no longer a devastated country on the edge of economic meltdown. Slowly but surely the infrastructure had been rebuilt and the unemployment figures had steadily fallen while more liberal laws had encouraged the development of trade and tourism. As the standard of living improved accordingly the Ashuri people had become more content and travel between the two countries had become much more common.

Raja and Ruby enjoyed great popularity. Ruby had never got the chance to have much input into the ruling aspect of their royal roles because soon after Raja's father, King Ahmed's death the previous year elections had been held to pick a government and the monarchy now held more of a constitutional role. Raja had been devastated by the older man's demise and he and Ruby had grown even closer when he shared his grief with her.

Ruby had never even dared to dream that she might be so happy in her marriage. But Raja made her feel incredibly happy and secure. He was wonderfully patient and loving with the children and endlessly supportive of her. Living with Raja, she felt irresistible and very much loved.

Tall, breathtakingly handsome and still very much the focus of his wife's daydreams, Raja appeared in the doorway of the nursery and smiled at Ruby, making her heart lurch in response. 'It's time for us to leave.'

Ruby emerged from her reverie as Hamid and Leyla pelted over to their father and jumped into his arms. Raja hugged the children and then set them down with the suggestion of firmness, nodding to the staff waiting to take over and extending a hand to Ruby to hurry her away.

'Why won't you tell me where we're going?' she pressed as he walked her out of the palace and led her over to the helicopter parked on the landing pad he had had built.

'It's an anniversary surprise,' he told her again.

When she realised that the helicopter was flying over the desert her heart sank a little. A surprise including a tent would not be welcome. As the craft began to land a glimpse of a familiar rock formation made her soft mouth curve down.

Raja sprang out and swung round to assist her out.

'I've organised electric and a bathroom but I'm afraid there's no supermarket,' he teased her.

Ruby blinked in astonishment at the vast tented structure within view. 'What on earth?'

'The sort of desert lifestyle you can enjoy, *habibi*,' Raja pronounced with satisfaction. 'Every convenience and comfort possible has been organised so that we can celebrate our wedding anniversary and remember how we first came together here...'

'That is so romantic.' In the shade of the tent canopy, Ruby turned in the circle of his arms, her eyes tender. She knew that for his sake she was going to pretend to enjoy every moment of the desert sojourn he had arranged for them.

'I would have done this last year but Hamid was so young I knew you wouldn't want to leave him even for a night,' he explained earnestly.

As she entered the main body of the tent Ruby's jaw dropped at the opulence. There was carpet and proper seats and even overhead fans to cool the interior. There was a proper bedroom and when she found the bathroom at the back of the structure she beamed at him in wondering approval. 'You really do know the way to a girl's heart,' she told her husband. 'How the heck did you arrange all this without me finding out about it?'

'With a great deal of ingenuity and secrecy. I've been planning it for weeks,' he confessed, closing his hands over hers to draw her close and kiss her with hungry fervour. 'Happy anniversary, Your Majesty. May we enjoy many many more together...'

Gazing up into his brilliant dark golden eyes, Ruby felt dizzy with love and longing and thought with a little inner quiver of bathing naked in the cliffside pool with him later. She knew her demand for a bathroom had persuaded him that she wouldn't wish to revisit that particular experience but she was already planning to surprise him with her contrariness.

'I love you so much,' Raja breathed huskily.

'You were going to get all your favourite food for dinner tonight—now you're going to miss out—'

'No, we won't. We have a chef coming in a few hours to take care of our evening meal,' Raja whispered.

'You think of absolutely everything.' Ruby was entranced and she leant up against his lean, muscular chest, listening to the solid reassuring thump of his heartbeat. 'That's one of the reasons I love you. You cross every t and dot every i—'

Tipping up her chin, Raja sealed his mouth to hers and the world spun dizzily on its axis for Ruby. He swept her up in his arms and carried her through to the comfortable bed awaiting them. Happiness bubbling through her, she made the most of his passion, which was only another one of the many reasons why she loved him to distraction.

* * * * *

STEALING THE
PROMISED PRINCESS

MILLIE ADAMS

For all the Mills & Boon Modern Romance
that came before this one.

It is the other books, and the other authors, that
brought me my love of romance.

And it is why I'm writing them now.

CHAPTER ONE

"I HAVE A debt to collect, Violet King."

Violet stared out the windows of her office, glass all around, providing a wonderful view of the Pacific Ocean directly across her desk, with a view of her staff behind her. There were no private walls in her office space. She preferred for the team to work collaboratively. Creatively.

Her forward-thinking approach to business, makeup and fashion was part of why she had become one of the youngest self-made billionaires in the world.

Though, self-made might be a bit of a stretch considering that her father, Robert King, had given her the initial injection of cash that she needed to get her business off the ground. Everyone worked with investors, she supposed. That hers was genetically related to her was not unheard-of nor, she supposed, did it fully exclude her from that self-made title. But she was conscious of it. Still, she had made that money back and then some.

And she did *not* have debt.

Which meant this man had nothing to say to her.

"You must have the wrong number," she said.

"No. I don't."

The voice on the other end of the phone was rich and dark, faintly accented, though she couldn't quite nail down what accent it was. Different to her family friend, now her sister's husband, Dante, who was from Italy and had spent many years in the States since then. Spanish, perhaps, but with a hint of Brit that seemed to elongate his vowels.

"Very confident," she said. "But I am in debt to no man."

"Oh, perhaps I misspoke then. You are not in debt. You are the payment."

Ice settled in her stomach. "How did you get this number?"

In this social media age where she was seemingly accessible at all hours, she guarded her private line with all the ferocity of a small mammal guarding its burrow. She—or her assistants—might be available twenty-four hours a day on the internet, but she could only be reached at this line by business associates, family or personal friends. This man was none of those, and yet somehow he was calling her. And saying the most outlandish things.

"How I got this number is not important to the conversation."

She huffed. "To the contrary, it is extremely important."

Suddenly, she felt the hairs on the back of her neck stand on end and she turned around. The office building was empty, just as she thought it was. It was late in the day and everyone had gone home. Her employees often worked from home, or at the beach, wherever creativity struck them.

Her team wanted to be there, and she didn't need to enforce long office hours for them to do their work. The glass walls of the building made it possible for her to see who was in residence at all times, again, not so she could check up on them, but so there was a sense of collaboration.

It also made it easy to see now that she was alone here.

Of course she was. A person couldn't simply walk into this building. Security was tight, and anyone wanting entrance would have to be buzzed in.

But then suddenly she saw a ripple of movement through the outermost layer of glass, motion as a door opened. A dark shape moved through each clear barrier, from room to room, like a shark gliding beneath the surface of clear water. As each door opened, the shape moved closer, revealing itself to be the figure of a man.

Her chest began to get tight. Fear gripped her, her heart beating faster, her palms damp.

"Are you here?" she whispered.

But the line went dead, and she was left standing frozen in her office, her eyes glued to the man steadily making his way deeper and deeper into the office building. The glass, however transparent, was bulletproof, so there was that.

There were so many weirdos in the world that an abundance of caution never went amiss. She had learned about that at a fairly early age. Her father being one of the wealthiest businessmen in California had put her in the public eye very young. The media had always been fascinated with their family; with her brother, who was incredibly successful in his own right; her mother, who was a great beauty. And then, with her for the same reason.

It had always felt so…unearned to her. This great and intense attention for doing nothing at all. It had never sat well with her.

Her father had told her to simply enjoy it. That she was under no obligation to do anything, considering he'd done all the work already.

He'd always been bemused by her desire to get into business, but he'd helped her get started. He'd been humoring her, that much had been clear. But she'd been determined to prove to him that she was smart. That she could make it on her own.

Even now she had the feeling he regarded her billion-dollar empire as a hobby.

The only one of them who had seemingly escaped without massive amounts of attention was her younger sister, Minerva, who Violet had always thought might have been the smartest of them all. Minerva had made herself into the shape of something unremarkable so that she could live life on her own terms.

Violet had taken a different approach, and there were times when the lack of privacy grated and she regretted living the life that she had.

Sometimes she felt an ache for what might have been. She wondered why she had this life. Why she was blessed with money and a certain amount of success instead of being anonymous or impoverished.

Some of that was eased by the charity she ran with her sister, which made it feel like all of it did mean something. That she had been granted this for a reason. And it made the invasions of privacy bearable.

Though not so much now. She felt vulnerable, and far too visible, trapped in a glass bowl of her own making, only able to watch as a predator approached her, and she was unable to do anything but wait.

She tried to call the police, her fingers fumbling on the old-fashioned landline buttons. It wasn't working. She had that landline for security. For privacy. And it was failing her on every level.

Of course she had her cell phone, but it was…

Sitting on the table just outside the office door.

And then suddenly he was *there*. Standing right on the other side of her office door. Tall, broad, clad all in black, wearing a suit that molded to his exquisitely hard-looking body, following every cut line from the breadth of his shoulders to his tapered waist, on down his long muscular legs. He turned around, and how he saw she was thinking of him in those terms she didn't know. Only that he was a force. Like looking at a sheer rock face with no footholds.

Hard and imposing, looming before her.

His face was...

Like a fallen Angel. Beautiful, and a sharp, strange contrast to the rest of him.

There was one imperfection on that face. A slashed scar that ran from the top of his high cheekbone down to the corner of his mouth. A warning.

This man was dangerous.

Lethal.

"Shall we have a chat?"

The barrier of the glass between them made that deep, rich voice echo across the surface of it, and she could feel it reverberating inside of her.

She hated it.

"How did you get in here?"

"My darling, I have a key."

She shrank back. "I'm not your darling."

"True," he said. "You are not. But you are my quarry. And I have found you."

"I'm not very hard to find," she said. She lifted her chin, trying to appear confident. "I'm one of the most famous women in the world."

"So you are. And that has me questioning my brother's sanity. But I am not here to do anything but follow orders."

"If you're here to follow orders, then perhaps you should follow one of mine. Leave."

"I answer to only one man. To only one person. And it is not you."

"A true regret," she said tightly.

"Not for me."

"What do you want?"

"I told you. I am here to collect payment. And that payment is you."

She was beautiful. But he had been prepared for that. When his brother had told him that it was finally time for him to make good on a promise given to him by Robert King ten years ago, Prince Javier de la Cruz had held back a litany of questions for his lord and master. He wondered why his brother wished to collect the debt now. And why he wished to collect it at all, at least in the form of this woman.

She was conspicuous. And she was everything his brother was not. Modern. Painfully so in contrast with the near medieval landscape of Monte Blanco. Yes, the kingdom had come a long way under his brother's rule during the last two years, but there was still a long way to go to bring it out of the Dark Ages their father had preferred. If a woman such as Violet King would be something so foreign to their people, then imagining her his queen was impossible.

But then, on some level, Javier imagined that was his brother's aim. Still, it was not Javier's position to question. Javier was as he had ever been. The greatest weapon Monte Blanco possessed. For years, he had undermined his father, kept the nation from going to war, kept his people safe. Had freed prisoners when they were wrongfully withheld. Had done all that he could to ensure that his father's impact on their people was as minimal as possible. And he had done so all under the oversight of his older brother, who—when he had taken control—had immediately begun to revive the country, using the money that he had earned with his business acumen. The Tycoon King, he was called.

And this—this deal with Robert King—had been one of those bargains he'd struck in secret. Apparently this deal had been made long ago, over drinks in a casino in Monte Carlo. A bet the other man had lost.

Javier was surprised his brother would hold a man to a drunken bargain.

And yet, here he was.

But Matteo was not a thoroughly modern man, whatever moves he was making to reform the country, and this sort of medieval bargain was just the type he knew his brother might favor.

Still…

Looking at her now, Javier could not imagine it.

She was wearing a white suit. A crisp jacket and loose-fitting pants. Her makeup was like a mask in his estimation. Eyelashes that seemed impossibly long, full lips played up by the gloss that she wore on her mouth. A severe sort of contour created in her cheeks by whatever color she had brushed onto them.

Her dark hair was in a low ponytail, sleek and held back away from her face.

She was stunningly beautiful. And very young. The direct opposite of their poor mother, who had been so pale and defeated by the end of her life. And perhaps that was the point.

Still, forcing a woman into marriage was possibly not the best way to go about proving your modernity.

But again. He was not in a position to argue.

What mattered most was his brother's vision for the country, and he would see it done.

He was a blunt instrument. Not a strategist.

Something he was comfortable with. There was an honesty to it. His brother had to feign diplomacy. Had to hide his agenda to make the world comfortable.

Javier had to do no such thing.

"I don't know who you are. And I don't know what you're talking about," she said.

He made his way over to the door, entered in the code and it unlocked.

Her father had given him all that information. Because he knew that there was no other choice.

She backed against her desk, her eyes wide with fear.

"What are you doing?"

"This is growing tiresome. I'm Prince Javier de la Cruz, of Monte Blanco. And you, Violet King, are my brother's chosen bride."

"What?" She did something he did not expect at all. She guffawed. It was the most unladylike sound he had ever heard. "I am *nobody's* chosen bride."

"You are. Your father owes my brother a debt. Apparently, he ran out of capital at a gambling table and was quite…in his cups, so to speak. He offered you. And I have come to collect you."

"My father would not do such a thing. He would not… gamble me away. My brother, on the other hand, might play a prank on me that was this ridiculous. Are there cameras somewhere? Am I on camera?"

"You are not on camera," he said.

She laughed again. "I must be. If this is your attempt to get a viral video or something, you better try again. My father is one of the most modern men that I have ever known. He would never, ever sell one of his daughters into marriage. You know my sister came home from studying abroad with a baby, and he didn't even ask where the baby came from. He just kind of let her bring it into his house. He does not treat his daughters like commodities, and he does not act like he can sell us to the highest bidder."

"Well, then perhaps you need to speak to him."

"I don't need to speak to him, because this is ridiculous."

"If you say so."

And so he closed the distance between them, lifted her up off the ground and threw her over his shoulder. He was running low on time and patience, and he didn't have time to stand around being laughed at by some silly girl. That earned him a yelp and a sharp kick to his chest. Followed by another one, and then another.

Pain was only pain. It did not bother him.

He ignored her.

He ignored her until he had successfully transported her out of the building, which was conveniently empty, and down to the parking lot where his limo was waiting. Only then, when he had her inside with the doors closed and locked, did she actually stare at him with fear. Did she actually look like she might believe him?

"Violet King, I am taking you back to my country. Where you are to be Queen."

CHAPTER TWO

SHE DIDN'T HAVE her phone. She might as well have had her right hand amputated. She had no way to reach anybody. She was an undisputed queen of social media. And here she was, sentenced to silence, told she was going to be Queen of a nation, which was something else entirely.

But this guy was clearly sick in the head, so whatever was happening…

She looked around the limousine. He might be sick in the head, but he also had someone bankrolling his crazy fantasy.

"Is this your limousine?"

He looked around and rolled his shoulders back, settling into the soft leather. "No."

"Who are you working for?"

"I told you. My brother. The King of Monte Blanco."

"I don't even know where that is."

She searched her brain, trying to think if she had ever heard of the place. Geography wasn't her strong suit, but she was fairly well traveled, considering her job required it. Also, she loved it. Loved seeing new places and meeting new people. But Monte Blanco was not on her radar.

"It's not exactly a hot tourist destination," he said.

"Well."

"It's not my brother's limousine either, if you are curious. Neither of us would own something so…" His lip curled. "Ostentatious."

Old money. She was familiar enough with old money and the disdain that came with it. She was new money. And often, the disdain spilled over onto her. She was flashy. And she was obvious. But her fortune was made by selling beauty. By selling flash. Asking women to draw attention to themselves, telling them that it was all right. To dress for themselves. To put makeup on to please themselves, not necessarily to please men.

So yes, of course Violet herself was flashy. And if he had an issue with it, he could go… Well, jump out of the limo and onto the busy San Diego Freeway. She would not mourn him.

"Right. So you're a snob. A snob who's somehow involved in a kidnapping plot?" She supposed, again, he could be an actor. Not someone wealthy at all. Somebody hired to play a prank on her.

Somebody hired to hurt her.

That thought sent a sliver of dread through her body. She wouldn't show it. After all, what good were layers of makeup if you couldn't use them to hide your true face?

"I'm not a snob. I'm a prince."

"Right. Of a country I've never heard of."

"Your American centric viewpoint is hardly my problem, is it, Ms. King? It seems to me that your lack of education does not speak to my authenticity."

"Yes. Well. That is something you would say." The car was still moving, farther and farther away from where they had originated. And she supposed that she had to face the fact that this might not be a joke. That this man really thought she was going to go back to his country with him. If that country existed. Really, she had nothing but his word for it, and considering that he seemed to think that she was going to marry his brother, he might be delusional on multiple levels.

"I want to call my dad."

"You're welcome to," he said, handing her the phone.

She snatched it from him and dialed her father's personal number as quickly as possible. Robert King picked up on the second ring.

"Dad," she said, launching into her proclamation without preamble. "A madman has bundled me up and put me in his limousine, and he's claiming that you made a deal with him some decade ago, and I'm supposed to marry his brother?"

"I didn't make a deal with your dad," Javier said. "My brother did."

"It doesn't matter," she hissed. And then she sat there, waiting for her father to respond. With shock, she assumed. Yes, she assumed that he would respond with shock. Because of course this was insane. And of course it was the first time her father was hearing such a thing. Because there was no way he had anything to do with this. "So anyway, if you could just tell him that he's crazy…"

She realized how stupid it was the minute she said that. Because of course her father telling Javier he was crazy wouldn't likely reinforce it if the act of flinging her into his limousine hadn't done it.

"Violet…" Her father's voice was suddenly rough, completely uncharacteristic of the smooth, confident man that she had always looked up to.

Her father was imperfect. She wasn't blind to that. The fact that he was completely uninvested in her success was obvious to her. When it came to her brother, he was always happy to talk business. But because her business centered around female things, and she herself was a woman, she could never escape the feeling that her father thought it was some kind of hobby. Something insubstantial and less somehow.

But surely he wouldn't... Surely that didn't mean he saw her as currency.

"He's crazy, right?"

"I never thought that he would follow up on this," her father said. "And when you reached your twenties and he didn't... I assumed that there would be no recourse."

"You promised me to a king?"

"It could've been worse. I could have promised you to the used car salesman."

"You can't just promise *someone else* to *someone else*. I'm a person, not a... A cow."

"I'm sorry," he said. "Violet, I honestly didn't think that..."

"I won't stand for it. I will not do it. What's to stop me from jumping out of the car right now—" she looked out the window and saw the scenery flying by at an alarming clip, and she knew that that would keep her from jumping out of the car, but her father didn't need to know that "—and running for freedom?"

"The businesses. They will go to him."

"The businesses?"

"Yours and mine. Remember we sheltered yours under mine for taxes and..."

"Maximus's too?"

Because if he had sheltered her business, surely he had sheltered her brothers as well...

"No," her father said slowly.

"What's the real reason you kept mine underneath your corporation? Was it for this?"

"No. Just that I worried about you. And I thought that perhaps..."

"Because you don't think anything of me. You don't

think that I'm equal to Maximus. If you did, then you wouldn't have done this to me. I can't believe... I can't believe you."

She could keep on arguing with her father, or she could accept the fact that he had sold her as chattel to a stranger. And with that realization, she knew that she needed to simply get off the phone. There was no redeeming this. Nothing at all that would fix it.

She had come face-to-face with how little she meant to her father, how little he thought of her.

She had taken his reaction to Minerva coming home with the baby to mean that he was enlightened, but that wasn't it at all. Minerva was being traditional, even if she hadn't had a husband initially when she had brought the baby home.

Still, he would rather have seen Minerva, in all her quirky glory, with a baby, than see Violet as a serious businesswoman.

There was no talking to him. She stared across the limo at the man who had taken her captive, and she realized...

That he was a saner option than arguing with her father.

She hung up the phone.

"So you are telling the truth."

"I have no investment in lying to you," Javier said. "I also have no investment in this deal as a whole. My brother has asked that I retrieve you, and so I have done it."

"So, you're a Saint Bernard, then?"

A flash of icy amusement shot through his dark eyes, the corner of his mouth curving up in a humorless smile. "You will find that I am not so easily brought to heel, I think."

"And yet here you are," she said. "Doing the bidding of someone else."

"Of my king. For my country. My brother and I have

been the stronghold standing between Monte Blanco and total destruction for over a decade. My father was always a dictator, but his behavior spiraled out of control toward the end of his life. We were the only thing that kept his iron fist from crushing our people. And now we seek to rebuild. Who my brother wants as his choice of bride is his business. And if you'll excuse me… I don't care one bit for your American sensibilities. For your money. For your achievements. I care only that he has asked for you, and so I will bring you to him."

"Good boy," she said.

His movements were like liquid fury. One minute he was sitting across from her in the limousine, and the other he was beside her. He gripped her chin and held her fast, forcing her to look into his eyes. But there was no anger there. It was black, and it was cold. And it was the absence of all feeling that truly terrified her.

She did not think he would hurt her.

There was too much control in his hold. He was not causing her any pain. She could feel the leashed strength at the point where his thumb and forefinger met her chin.

"I am loyal," he said. "But I am not good. The cost of keeping my country going, the cost of my subterfuge has been great. Do not ever make the mistake of thinking that I'm good."

And then he withdrew from her. It was like she had imagined it. Except she shivered with the cold from those eyes, so she knew she hadn't.

"How are you going to make me get on the plane?"

"I will carry you," he said. "Or you could get on with your own two feet. Your father won't harbor you. I assume that he told you as much. So there's no use you running back home, is there?"

She was faced then with a very difficult decision.

Because he was right—she could try to run away. But he would overpower her. And she had a feeling that no one would pay much attention to what would look like a screaming match between two rich people, culminating with her being carried onto a private plane. They were far too adjacent to Hollywood for anybody to consider that out of the ordinary.

And even if she did escape… Her father had verified what he'd said. Her father saw nothing wrong with using her to get out of a bad situation. He had sacrificed not only her, but her livelihood.

"You're not going to hurt me," she said. And she searched those eyes for something. All right, he'd said that he wasn't good. But she had a feeling that he was honest. Otherwise, there would have been no reason for him to tell her he wasn't good, except to hit back at her, and she had a feeling that wasn't it. That wasn't why.

There was more to it than that.

Somehow she knew that if she asked this question, he would answer. Even if the answer was yes, he was going to hurt her. He had no reason to lie to her, that was the thing. She was at his mercy and he knew it.

"No," he said. "I swear to you that no harm will come to you. My brother intends to make you his bride, not his slave. And as far as I go… I'm your protector, Violet, not your enemy. I have been charged with transporting you back to Monte Blanco and if I were to allow any harm to come to you, you can rest assured that my brother would see me rotting in my father's favorite dungeon."

"Your father had a favorite dungeon?"

"More than one, actually."

"Wow."

She didn't know why she felt mollified by his assurance that he wouldn't hurt her. Especially not considering he had just said his father had a favorite dungeon. But he made it clear that he and his brother weren't like their father. So if she could believe that…

It was insane that she believed him. But the thing was, he hadn't lied to her. Not once. Her father had tricked her. Had made her believe that the life she was living was different than the one she actually had. That their relationship was different.

But this man had never lied.

Her world felt turned upside down, and suddenly, her kidnapper seemed about the most trustworthy person.

A sad state of affairs.

The car halted on the tarmac, and there was a plane. It didn't look like a private charter, because it was the size of a commercial jet.

But the royal crest on the side seemed to indicate that it was in fact his jet.

Or his brother's. However that worked.

"This way," he said, getting out of the limousine and holding the door for her.

The driver had gotten out and stood there feebly. "I think he was going to hold the door," she said, looking up at Javier.

Her heart scampered up into her throat as her eyes connected with his again. Looking at him was like getting hit with a force. She had never experienced anything quite like it.

It wasn't simply that he was beautiful—though he was—it was the hardness to him. The overwhelming feeling of rampant masculinity coming at her like a testosterone-fueled train.

Admittedly, she was not exposed to men like him all that often. Not in her line of work.

She actually hadn't been certain that men like him existed.

Well, there was her brother-in-law, Dante, who was a hard man indeed, but still, he looked approachable in comparison to Javier.

This man was like a throwback from a medieval era. The circumstances of her meeting him—the ones where she was being sold into marriage pit debt—certainly contributing to this feeling.

"Too bad for him," Javier shot back. "I don't wait."

And that, she concluded, was her signal to get out of the limo. She decided to take her time. Because he might not wait, but she did not take orders.

And if she was going to retain any kind of power in the situation, she had better do it now. Hoard little pieces of it as best she could, because he wasn't going to give her any. No. So she would not surrender what she might be able to claim.

"Good to know." She made small micromovements, sliding across the seat and then flexing her ankles before her feet made contact with the ground. Then she scooted forward a bit more, put her hands on her knees.

And he stood there, not saying anything.

She stood, and as she did so, he bent down, and her face came within scant inches of his. She forgot to breathe. But she did not forget to move. She pitched herself forward and nearly came into contact with the asphalt. He wrapped his arm around her waist and pulled her back against him. Her shoulder blades came into stark contact with his hard chest. It all lasted only a moment, because he released her and allowed her to stand on her own feet as soon as she was steady. But she could still feel him. The impression of him. Burning her.

"If I walk on my own two feet to the airplane, it is not a kidnapping, is it?"

"I'm certainly not married to the narrative of it being a kidnapping. Call it whatever you need to."

She straightened her shoulders and began to walk toward the plane.

Toward her doom.

Violet didn't know which it was.

But she did know that she was going to have to find her control in this, one way or another.

Even if it were only in the simple act of carrying *herself* aboard the plane.

CHAPTER THREE

JAVIER STUDIED THE woman sitting across from him. Her rage had shrunk slightly and was now emanating off her in small waves rather than whole tsunamis.

She had not accepted a drink, and he had made a show of drinking in front of her, to prove that no one was attempting to poison her, or whatever she seemed to imagine.

He was going to have to have words with Matteo once he arrived in Monte Blanco. "You might want to lower your shields," he said.

"Sure," she said. "Allow me to relax. In front of the man who is holding me against my will."

"Remember, you walked on your own two feet to the airplane, which you felt was the difference between a kidnapping and an impromptu vacation."

"It's a kidnapping," she said. "And I'll have some champagne."

"Now that you've watched me drink a glass and a half and are satisfied that I'm not going to fall down dead?"

"Something like that."

"Why are you in a temper now when you were fine before?"

"This is absurd. I haven't been able to check my social media for hours."

"Is that a problem for you?"

"It's my entire business," she said. "It's built off that. Off connectivity. And viral posts. If I can't make posts, I can't go viral."

"That sounds like something you would want to avoid."

"You're being obtuse. Surely you know what *going viral* means."

"I've heard it," he said. "I can't say that I cared to look too deeply into it. The internet is the least of our concerns in Monte Blanco."

"Well, it's one of my primary concerns, considering it's how I make my living. All fine for you to be able to ignore it, but I can't."

"Also not going to allow you to post from the plane. Anyway. We don't have Wi-Fi up here."

"How do you not have Wi-Fi? Every airplane has that."

"My father didn't have it installed. And my brother has not seen the use for it."

"I find that hard to believe. He's running a country."

"Again. That is not a primary concern in my country. You may find that we have different priorities than you."

"Do you have electricity?" she asked, in what he assumed was mock horror.

"We have electricity."

"Do you live in a moldering castle?"

"It's quite a bit less moldering than when my brother took the throne. But it is a bit medieval, I'm not going to lie."

"Well. All of this is a bit medieval, isn't it?"

"I felt it was quite modern, given you weren't traded for a pair of sheep."

"No. Just my father's gambling debt, extracted from him when he was drunk. What kind of man is your brother that he would do that?"

"I would say honorable. But his primary concern is the

country, and while I don't know what his ultimate plans are for you, or why he wants you specifically, I do know there is a reason. One thing I know about him is that he has his reasons."

"Woof," she said.

In spite of himself, amusement tightened his stomach. And that was the last thing he expected to feel at her insolence. She had no idea who he was. He was a weapon. A human blade.

And she… She taunted him.

He was used to women reacting to him with awe. Sometimes they trembled with fear, but in a way that they seemed to enjoy. He was not blind to the effect he had on women. No indeed. He was a powerful man. A man with a title. A man with wealth.

He commanded a military.

Violet King did not tremble with fear when she looked at him.

He took a champagne glass from the table next to him and poured her a measure of liquid, reaching across the space and handing it to her. She didn't move.

"You'll have to come and get it. Contrary to what you may have heard, I don't fetch or deliver."

She scowled and leaned forward, grabbing hold of the glass and clutching it to her chest as she settled back in her chair.

She looked around the expansive airplane. "Do you think this thing is a little bit big?"

"I've never had any complaints."

Color mounted in her cheeks. "Well. Indeed." She downed half the glass of champagne without taking a breath. "I really do wish there was an internet connection."

"But there isn't. Anyway, we left your phone back in your office."

She looked truly panicked at that. "What if somebody else gets a hold of it? I can't have anybody posting on my social media who wasn't approved."

"Such strange concerns you have. Websites. You know, I've been fighting for the life and health of my people for the last several years. I can't imagine being concerned that somebody might post something on a website in my name."

"Optics," she snapped.

"Optics are no concern of mine. I'm concerned with reality. That which you can touch and see. Smell. Feel. That is my concern. Reality."

"It's no less real. It changes people's lives. It affects them profoundly. I built an entire business off of influence."

"You make a product. I did a cursory amount of research on you, Violet. You don't simply post air."

"No. But for want of that air my products wouldn't sell. It's what exposes me to all those people. It's what makes me relevant."

"I should hope that more than a piece of code floating out in cyberspace would make you relevant."

Her lips twitched and she took another sip of champagne. "I'm not going to argue about this with a man who thinks it's perfectly reasonable to bundle me up and take me back to his country."

"I didn't say it was reasonable," he said. "Only that it was going to be done."

After that, they didn't speak.

Upon arrival in Monte Blanco, Javier parted with Violet and made a straight path for his brother's office.

"I've returned," he said.

"Good," Matteo said, barely looking up from his desk. "I assume you have brought the woman with you?"

"Yes. As promised."

"I knew I could count on you. Did she come quietly?"

He thought of the constant barbs that he had been subjected to on the trip.

"No. She is *never* quiet."

Matteo grimaced. "That could be a problem."

"Your Highness."

Javier turned around at the sound of the breathy voice. Matteo's assistant, Livia, had come into the room. She was a small, drab creature, and he had no idea why his brother kept her on. But Matteo was ridiculously attached to her.

"Yes," Matteo said, his voice gentling slightly.

"It's only that the United Council chief called, and he is requesting the presence of Monte Blanco at a meeting. It's about your inclusion."

This was something his brother had been waiting for. His father had stayed out of international affairs, but it was important to both Matteo and Javier that Monte Blanco have a voice in worldwide matters.

"Then I shall call him."

"I don't know that that will be necessary. He only wishes to know if you will accept his invitation to come to the summit this week."

"Well, I'm a bit busy," Matteo said, gesturing toward Javier.

"Oh?" she asked.

"Yes," he responded. "Javier has brought my bride to me."

Livia's eyes widened, but only for a moment. "Of course." That slight widening was the only emotional reaction given by the assistant. But Javier knew how to read people, and he could see that she was disturbed.

He could also see that his brother did not notice. "It is of no consequence," he said. "We must attend. Javier, you will make sure that Violet acclimates while I'm gone."

"Of course," he said. What he did not say was that he was not a trained babysitter for spoiled socialites, but a soldier. Still, he thought it.

"See that my things are collected immediately," Matteo said, addressing Livia. "All the details handled."

He spoke in such incomplete sentences to the woman, and yet she scurried to do his bidding, asking for no clarification at all.

"Don't you think this is a bit outlandish, even for you?"

"My mouse will have no trouble taking care of things," he said, using his nickname for Livia.

"Yes. I forgot. She is your mouse, living only to do as you ask. Though your appalling treatment of your assistant was not actually what I was referring to. That you had me drag this woman across the world, and you will not be in residence."

"It's perfect," he said. "A more traditional sort of relationship, yes? Hearkening back to the days of old. We won't meet until the wedding."

"You forget, she's an American. A thoroughly modern one."

"*You* forget: she has no choice."

"Why exactly do you want Violet King? That's something that I don't understand."

"Because we need to modernize. Because we need to change the way that the world perceives Monte Blanco."

"I was told by your fiancée that the world does not perceive it at all."

"A blessing," Matteo said. "Because if the world did have a perception of us before now, it would not be a good one."

"And you want to change that." He thought of everything Violet had said to him regarding the internet. "Why don't you have Wi-Fi on your plane?"

Matteo blinked. "What does that have to do with anything?"

"Violet seemed to find it odd that you didn't. I told her you weren't concerned with such things. But it appears that you are."

"Well, I've never needed it in the air."

"Your future bride would want it. Otherwise I think she will find traveling with you onerous."

"I didn't realize you would be so concerned for her comfort."

"Well, you put her comfort in my charge."

"And I leave it to you now." Matteo stood from behind the desk. "I understand that it's not ideal, but I know that you'll also trust me when I tell you this is necessary."

"I know," Javier said. "You never do anything that isn't."

"I'm not our father," Matteo said, and not for the first time Javier wondered if he was telling him or telling himself.

He was well familiar with that internal refrain. He knew his brother walked a hard road, but a different one than Javier did.

Javier had been part of his father's army.

Under Javier's oversight, missions had been carried out that had caused harm. He had believed, fully and completely, that he was in the right.

Until one day he'd seen the truth. Seen what love and loyalty had blinded him to.

And he had learned.

That a man could be a villain and not even know.

That with the right lie, a man could commit endless atrocities and call it justice.

"I know," Javier repeated. "You have spent all these past years defying him. I hardly thought that a little bit of power was going to corrupt you entirely."

"But I must be on guard against it. I understand that you may think it medieval for me to force the girl into marriage…"

Javier shrugged. "I have no thoughts on it one way or the other." And it was true. He knew that Violet was unhappy with the situation, but her happiness was not his concern.

Swaths of unhappiness had been cut through his country for decades, and he and his brother were working as hard as they could to undo it. If Matteo thought that making Violet his queen would help with the situation, then it was collateral damage Javier was willing to accept.

"You say that," Matteo said. "But I have a feeling that you always have thoughts."

"Are they relevant, My King?"

"I told you, I am not our father. But for the fact that I'm a few years older than you, you would be King. Or, if I were dead."

"Stay alive," Javier said. "I have no desire to bear the burden of the crown."

"And yet, the burden is heavy enough that I daresay you can feel the weight of it. It is not like you are immune to the responsibilities we face."

"What is the point of sharing blood with our father if we don't do everything, to the point of spilling it, to correct his wrongs?"

"No point at all," Matteo said, nodding. "I must go check on my mouse's progress."

"You call her that to her face?"

"Yes. She finds it endearing."

He thought back to the stricken look on Livia's face when Matteo had mentioned his fiancée. But Javier also thought of the slight note of warmth in his brother's voice when he said it. *Mouse.* He didn't say it as if she were small or gray, though in Javier's opinion she was both. No, he said it as if she were fragile. His to care for.

"She may."

"No. It is because of how I found her. Shivering and gray, and far too small. Like a mouse."

Javier was not certain that Livia liked to be reminded of her origins. However much Matteo might find his name for her affectionate. He meant what he had said to Violet. Javier was not a good man. Matteo might be, but for the two of them it was more honor than it was anything quite so human as goodness.

In fact, the only real evidence Javier had ever seen of softness in his brother was the presence of Livia in the palace. He didn't know the full story of how he had come into... Possession of her, only that he had found her in quite an unfortunate situation and for some reason had decided it was his responsibility to fix that situation.

"You will keep things running while I'm gone," Matteo said, a command and not a question.

"Of course I will."

"And I will endeavor to make sure these meetings go well. You remember what I told you."

"Of course. If ever you were to exhibit characteristics of our father, it would be better that you were dead."

"I meant that."

"And I would kill you myself."

His brother smiled and walked forward clasping his forearm, and Javier clasped his in return. "And that is why I trust you. Because I believe you would."

They were blood brothers. Bonded by blood they hated. The blood of their father. But their bond was unshakable and had always been. Because they had known early on that if they were ever going to overcome the evil of their line, they would have to transcend it.

And they could only do that together.

Their relationship was the most important thing in Javier's life. Because it was the moral ballast for them both. Because Javier knew how easy it was to upset morality. How emotion could cloud it.

How it could cause pain.

Whether he understood Matteo's being so intent to marry Violet or not, he would support it. All that mattered was Monte Blanco. Violet's feelings were a nonissue.

All that mattered was the kingdom.

CHAPTER FOUR

VIOLET HAD BEEN essentially born into money. So she was used to grandeur. She was used to the glittering opulence of sparkling shows of wealth. But the palace and Monte Blanco were something else entirely.

It wasn't that the walls were gilded—they were entirely made of gold. The floor, obsidian inlaid with precious metals, rubies and emeralds. The doorframes were gold, shot through with panels of diamond.

Given what Javier had said about the limo, she was somewhat surprised to see such a glaring display of wealth, but then she imagined the palace had been standing for centuries. She could feel it. As if it were built down into the mountain.

And it was indeed on a mountain. Made of white granite, likely the namesake of the country.

It reminded her of Javier himself. Imposing, commanding, and entirely made of rock. The view down below was... Spectacular.

A carpet of deep, dense pines swooping down before climbing back upward to yet more mountains. She could barely make out what she thought might be a city buried somewhere in there, but if it was, it was very small. The mountains loomed large, fading to blue and purple the farther away they were. Until they nearly turned to mist against the sky. A completely different color than she had ever seen before. As if it were more ice than sky.

She had not thought it would be cold, given that she didn't think of cold when she thought of this region, but nestled as it was between France and Spain at such a high elevation, it was shockingly frigid and much more rugged than she had thought.

Queen of the wilderness. He had brought her out here to be Queen of the wilderness.

The thought made her shiver.

Then she turned away from the view and back toward the bedroom she had been installed in by a helpful member of staff, and she couldn't think of wilderness at all. It was ornate to the point of ridiculousness.

The bed was made of gold. The canopy was comprised of layers of fabric, a glittering and a gauzy layer, with heavy brocade beneath. The covers were velvet, rich purple and gold.

It made the clean, modern lines of her all-white apartment stark in her memory.

She wasn't going to waste time pondering the room, though. What she needed to do was figure out how to talk the King out of this ridiculous idea that they needed to get married. First, she needed to figure out what his motives were. Obviously if he were crazed by lust where she was concerned, there wasn't much she could offer him. At least, nothing much that she was willing to offer.

Violet knew that no one would believe it if she told them, but she had no physical experience with men. She had never been carried away on a tide of passion, and she fully intended to be carried away on a tide of passion when she allowed a man to… Do any of that.

The problem was, she had met so many kinds of men in her life. Hazard of being well connected and well traveled. She had met rich men. Talented men. Actors, chefs, rock stars. CEOs.

Javier is the first prince you ever met...

Well. That didn't matter. The point was, she'd been exposed to a variety of powerful men early on, and inevitably she found them to be... Disappointments.

They either revealed themselves to be arrogant jerks with overinflated opinions of themselves, secret perverts who had only been pretending to listen to her while they contemplated making a move on her, or aggressive nightmares with more hands than a centipede and less sense.

And she had just always thought there could be more than that. More than shrugging and giving in to a wet kiss that she hadn't wanted anyway.

The richer she had become, the more men had seemed to find her a challenge. Whether she was actually issuing one or not.

And that had made her even more disenchanted with them.

And she hadn't held out for passion for all this time to just...

To just be taken by some king that she didn't even know.

She could Google him if she had any devices. But there was no damned internet in this place.

The first active business would be to find out what he wanted. Because she had a lot. She was a billionaire, after all. And, she was well connected. He could break off a chunk of this castle, and it would probably equal her net worth, so there was that. But there had to be something. There had to be. Otherwise, it wouldn't matter if it was her.

Which brought her back to sexually obsessed. Which really creeped her out.

There was a knock on the chamber door, and she jumped. "Come in."

She expected it to be the same woman who had led her to her room, but it wasn't. It was Javier. And when he came in he brought with him all of the tension that she'd felt in her chest the entire time they were together on the plane ride over.

"I wasn't expecting you," she said.

"What were you expecting exactly?"

She realized there was no point in being difficult. Because Javier might be the key to this. "Where is your brother?"

"Eager to see him?"

"No," she said, and she found that was honest. Better the devil she knew, after all. Even if said devil was as unyielding as a rock face. "Did he tell you why he wants to marry me?"

She needed to know. Because she needed to formulate a plan. She needed to get some power back. Or, rather than getting it back, needed to get some of it in the first place.

"Yes," Javier said.

He just stood there. Broad, tall and imposing.

"Would you care to share with the class?"

"I don't think it matters."

"You don't get that it matters to me why this stranger wants to marry me? I would like to know if it has to do with him harboring some sort of obsession for my body."

That made him laugh. And it offended her. "No. My brother has no designs on your body. He thinks that you will be useful in improving the world's view of Monte Blanco. It is in fact his sole focus. Which is what I came to tell you. He is not here."

"He's not here?"

"No. He has gone to the United Council summit. It is very important to him that Monte Blanco be granted inclusion into the Council. For too long, we have been without the benefit of allies. For too long, we have not had a say in how the world works. And it is something my brother feels is key to bringing us into the twenty-first century."

"So he wants my... Influencer reach?"

That was ridiculous. But she could work with that. "He wants me to make the country look better."

"Yes," Javier said.

"Well. That's easy. I can do that without marrying him."

"I'm not sure that's on his agenda."

"Well, then I'll just have to convince him that it's a better agenda. I'm very convincing. I entered a very crowded market, and I managed to essentially dominate it. You know that I'm the youngest self-made billionaire in the world?"

"Yes," Javier said. "We did in fact look at the basic headlines about you."

"Then he should know that I'll be of much more use to him as a business consultant."

"You sell makeup," he said.

She bristled. "Yes. And I sell it well. Enough that he seems to have taken notice of the impact that I've made on the world. So don't belittle it." She huffed a breath. "Anyway. All I need is a chance to get to know the country."

"Excellent. I'm glad that you think so. Because I believe that my brother's mouse is making an agenda for while they are away."

"His what?"

"His assistant. We have assignments for while he is away. And I am to oversee."

"Are you *babysitting* me?"

"In a sense."

"You know," she said, keeping her voice carefully deadpan. "I seem to recall a Saint Bernard that acted as Nana in a classic cartoon..."

"Don't push it. I can always tell him you met with an unfortunate accident."

"You said you wouldn't hurt me," she said, meeting his gaze, keeping her eyes as stern as possible.

He inclined his head. "So I did."

"Are you a man of your word, Javier?"

"I am."

The simple confidence in those words made her stomach tighten. "Somehow I knew that."

His eyes narrowed. "How?"

She shrugged. "I don't know. I'm a good judge of character, I think. I was born into wealth, and I will tell you that it's an easier life than most. But I had access to... Anything. Any excess that I wanted. Any sort of mischief that I might want to get into. Drugs and older men and parties. People were always after me to do favors for them. And I had to learn very quickly who my real friends might be. Because let me tell you... What people say and what they do are two very different things. Words don't mean anything if they're not backed up by actions."

"Well, I've kidnapped you. What does that action tell you?"

"I didn't think we were going with *kidnap*?"

"That was your call, not mine."

"Well, you're loyal to your brother. I also think you're loyal to... Your own sense of honor. You might say that you aren't good. But you have a moral code. And even if it does extend to allowing you to kidnap me if your brother says it's the right thing to do, I do not think it would ever extend to hurting someone who couldn't defend themselves against you."

He inclined his head. "Fair enough. My father enjoyed inflicting pain upon the weak. He enjoyed exploiting his power. I have no desire to ever involve myself in such a thing. It is an act of cowardice."

"And you're not a coward," she said confidently. "And I think that you might even want to help me prove to your brother that I don't need to marry him so that I can get back to my real life."

"That's where you're wrong. I genuinely don't care about your plan. Not one way or the other. Happiness, in that fleeting immediate sense, is quite immaterial to me. What matters is the greater good. If my brother feels the greater good is served by marrying you, then that is the goal I will help him accomplish. Not what will make you... Happier. As you said, you had a happier life than most. Drugs, parties and rich men, from the sounds of things."

"But I had none of those things," she said, not sure where she had lost the conversation. "It's just that I had access to them. I haven't experienced them. I have too much to live for. Too much experience to explore."

"It seems to me that you had ample opportunity to do so prior to your engagement to my brother."

"I am not engaged. I am *kidnapped*, as you just stated."

"Walked onto the plane with your own two feet, I think you mean."

"You were the one that introduced *kidnap* again."

"You're the one who seems hung up on the terminology."

"I'll prove it. I'll prove that we don't need marriage."

"Fantastic. Feel free. In the meantime, I will set about to fulfill the items on my brother's list. Because that is all I care about."

He turned and began to walk away from her. "Do you have any feelings about anything?"

When he turned back to face her, his eyes were blank. "No."

"You must be a great time in bed," she shot back, not

sure where that came from. Except she knew it made men angry when you called their prowess into question, and if she couldn't elicit sympathy from him, then she would be happy to elicit some rage.

"Thankfully for you," he said, his tone hard, "my bedroom skills will never be a concern of yours. You are not meant for me."

And then he was gone. Leaving her in the oppressive silence created by those thick, wealth-laden walls.

And she had a feeling that for the first time in her life she might have bitten off more than she could chew.

Except, it wasn't even her bite. It was her father's. And she was the one left dealing with it.

CHAPTER FIVE

HER WORDS ECHOED in his head all through the next day, and when he finally received the memo from his brother's assistant, his irritation was at an all-time high. Because what Violet King thought about him in bed was none of his concern. She had an acerbic tongue, and she was irritating. Beautiful, certainly, but annoying.

Had he been the sort of man given to marriage, she would not be the woman that he would choose. But then, marriage would never have to be for him. He didn't have to produce heirs.

He charged down the hall, making his way to her room, where he knocked sharply.

"Don't come in!"

"Why not?"

"I'm not decent."

"Are you undressed?" The image of Violet in some state of undress caused his stomach to tighten, and he cursed himself for acting like an untried boy. She was just a woman.

"No," she said.

He opened the door without waiting for further explanation. And there she sat, at the center of the massive bed looking...

Scrubbed clean.

She looked younger than when he had first seen her yesterday, than she did in any picture he had ever seen.

Her lashes were not so noticeable now, shorter, he thought. Her face looked rounder, her skin softer. Her lips were no longer shiny, but plump and soft looking. Her dark hair fell around her shoulders in riotous waves.

"I don't have my makeup," she said.

He couldn't help it. He laughed. He couldn't remember the last time he had felt actual humor. Until now. The woman was concerned because she did not have her makeup.

"And that concerns me why?"

"It's my… It's my trade. I don't go out without it. It would be a bad advertisement."

"Surely you don't think you need all of that layered onto your face to make you presentable?"

"That's not the point. It's not about being presentable, or whatever. It's just… It's not who I am."

"Your makeup is who you are?"

"I built my empire on it. On my look."

"Well. No one is here to see your look. And we have assignments."

"Assignments?"

"Yes. First, time to give you a tour of the palace. Then we are to discuss your… Appearance."

She waved a hand in front of her face. "I have been discussing my appearance this entire time."

"Well. I don't mean that, precisely. Your role as Queen will require a different sort of… A different sort of approach."

"I'm sorry. I've made it very clear that I'm not on board with this whole Queen thing, and you're talking about how you're going to change my appearance?"

"I'm only telling you what's on the list. We also need to go over customs, expectations. Ballroom etiquette."

"Don't tell me that I'm going to have to take dancing lessons."

"Precisely that."

"This is... *Medieval*."

"Tell me what it is you need from home, and I will accommodate you." Looking at the stubborn set of her face, he realized that he could drag her kicking and screaming into completing these tasks, or he could try to meet her in the middle. Compromise was not exactly second nature to him, but sometimes different tactics were required for dealing with different enemies.

He and his brother had been covert by necessity when dealing with their father. He could certainly manage a bit of finesse with one small makeup mogul.

"I... Well, I need all my beauty supplies. I might be able to come up with a queen-level look using my makeup, but nobody's doing it but me."

"We'll see."

"I can't wear someone else's products." She was verging on melodrama and he would not indulge it in the least if it weren't for his brother.

That was all.

"My concern is not centered on your business. And anyway, yours shouldn't be at this point either."

"Untrue. My primary concern is my business, because I think it's what I have to offer here."

"Why don't we discuss this over breakfast."

"I told you. I can't go out looking like this."

He pushed a button on the intercom by the door. Moments later the door opened, and in came breakfast for two.

"Oh," Violet said.

"You keep introducing issues that are not issues for me."

She looked deflated. "Fine. I don't actually care about my makeup."

"Then why exactly are you protesting?"

"Because. I want to win. And I figured if you thought I was this ridiculous and unable to function without a full face of makeup, you might send me back."

"Again. Whether or not you become the next Queen of Monte Blanco is not my decision. So you can go ahead and try to make me believe that you are the silliest creature on planet Earth, but it still won't change what's happening."

He moved the cart closer to her bed. She peered down at the contents. "Is that avocado toast?"

"It is," he said. "Of course, I'm told that it's quite trendy the world over. It has always been eaten here."

"Fascinating," she said. "I didn't realize that you were trendsetters."

He picked up his own plate of breakfast and sat in the chair next to her bed. Then he poured two cups of coffee. Her interest became yet more keen.

"I'm not going to poison you," he said. "You keep staring at me as if I might."

She scrabbled to the edge of the bed and reached down, grabbing hold of the plate of avocado toast, bringing it onto the comforter.

Her eyes met his and held. A shift started, somewhere deep in his gut. She didn't move. Or maybe it only felt like she didn't. Like the moment hung suspended.

Then her fingers brushed his as she took the cup, color mounting in her face as she settled back in the bed, away from him.

The distance, he found, helped with the tightening in his stomach.

She took a sip and smiled. "Perfect," she said. "Strong."

"Did you sleep well?"

"I slept about as well as a prisoner in a foreign land can expect to sleep."

"Good to know."

"The pea under the mattress was a bit uncomfortable."
A smile tugged the edge of her lips.

She was a strange sort of being, this woman. She had
spirit, because God knew in this situation, many other people would have fallen apart completely. But she hadn't. She
was attempting to needle him. To manipulate him. From
calling him a Saint Bernard to pretending she was devastated by her bare face.

And now she was drinking coffee like a perfectly con-
tented cat.

"Why don't you go ahead and say what's on your mind.
I can tell you're dying to."

"I will complete your list," she said. "Down to the dancing lessons. But I want you to show me around the country. Not just the palace."

"To what end?"

"I've been thinking. Your brother wants to bring this
country into the modern era. Well. I am the poster child
for success in the modern era. And I believe that I can
bring some of that to you. I can do it without marrying
your brother."

"As far as I'm concerned it's not up for negotiation."

"Fine. We'll table that. But I want you to give me the
tools to make it a negotiation with him."

"Perhaps," he said, taking a long drag of his own coffee.

"Look. Even if I do marry your brother, you're going
to want me to do this."

"He didn't leave orders to do it. I have no personal feelings on the matter."

"If you get your way, I'm going to live here for the rest
of my life," she said, her voice finally overtaken by emotion. "You don't even want me to see the place? Don't

you think that I should be able to… Envision what my life will be?"

This was not a business negotiation. Finally. She wasn't playing at being sharp and witty, or shallow and vapid. Not holding a board meeting curled up in her canopy bed. This, finally, was something real.

And he was not immune to it, he found.

"I'll see what I can accomplish."

She picked up her toast and took a bite of it with ferocity. "Well. At least I approve of your food." She set the toast back down on the plate and brushed some crumbs away from her lips.

She managed to look imperious and ridiculous all at once.

He could not imagine his brother wrangling this creature. She was as mercurial as she was mystifying, and Javier had never been in a position where he had to deal with a woman on this level.

When it came to his personal relationships with women, they weren't all that personal. They were physical. Suddenly, he was in an entanglement with a beautiful woman that was all… All too much to do with her feelings.

"Finish your toast," he said briskly. "I will send a member of staff to escort you downstairs in roughly an hour. And then, it is time we begin your training."

Violet muttered to herself as she made her way down the vast corridor and toward the ballroom. "Begin your training… Wax on. Wax off."

This was ludicrous. And she was beginning to get severely anxious. She had been in Monte Blanco for more than twelve hours. She had not seen the mysterious King— who had vanished off on some errand, if Javier was to be believed—and she didn't seem to be making any headway when it came to talking herself out of her engagement.

But she was the one who had decided she was better off trying to take the bull by the horns, rather than running and hiding in California. She supposed she had to own the consequences of that rash decision, made in anger.

The castle was vast, and even though she had received rather explicit instructions on how to get to the ballroom, she was a bit concerned that she might just end up lost forever in these winding, glittering halls. Like being at the center of a troll's mountain horde. All gems and glitter and danger.

And as she walked into the vast ballroom and saw Javier standing there at the center, she felt certain she was staring at the Mountain King. She knew he wasn't the King. Javier was acting on his brother's behest; he had said so many times. Except it was impossible for her to imagine that this man took orders from anyone.

It took her a moment to realize there was someone else in the room. A small round woman with an asymmetrical blond haircut and a dress comprised of layers of chiffon draped over her body like petals.

"The future Queen is here," she said excitedly. "We can begin. My name is Sophie. I will be instructing you in basic Monte Blancan ballroom dance techniques."

"They could be anyone's ballroom dance techniques," Violet said. "They would still be completely new to me."

"You say that like it should frighten me," Sophie said. "It doesn't. Especially not with the Prince acting as your partner."

Violet froze. "He dances?" She pointed at him.

"I have been part of the royal family all of my life," he said. "That necessitated learning various customs. Including, of course, ballroom dancing. There is nothing that you will be subjected to over the course of this training that I was not. And a great many things you will be spared."

There was a darkness to that statement that made a tremor resonate inside of her. But before she could respond to it, he had reached his hand out and taken hold of hers, drawing her up against the hardness of his chest.

He was hot.

And her heart stuttered.

And she felt...

She felt the beginnings of something she had read about. Heard about... But never, ever experienced before.

When he looked down at her, for a moment at least, it wasn't nice what she saw there in his dark eyes. No. It was something else entirely.

She looked down at the floor.

"I will start the music. Javier is a very good dancer, and he will make it easy by providing a solid lead."

He was solid all right. And hot. Like a human furnace.

His hand down low on her back was firm, and the one that grasped hers was surprisingly rough. She would have thought that a prince wouldn't have calluses. But he did.

She wondered what sort of physical work he did. Or if it was from grueling workouts. He certainly had the body of somebody who liked to exact punishment on himself in the gym.

Music began to play in the room, an exacting instrumental piece with clear timing. And then she was moving.

Sophie gave instructions, but Violet felt as if her feet were flying, as if she had no control over the movements herself at all. It felt like magic. And she would have said she had no desire to dance like this, in an empty ballroom in a palace that she was being held in, by the man who was essentially her captor, but it was exhilarating.

She hadn't lied to him when she said she had been given

the opportunity to indulge in a great many things in life. She had turned away from most of them. They just hadn't appealed.

But this…

Was this the evidence of being so spoiled that it took some sort of bizarre, singular experience to make her feel? No. She didn't think that was it.

She looked up slightly and could see his mouth. There was something so enticing about the curve of it. Something fascinating about it. She spent a lot of time looking at people's features. Using the natural planes and angles, dips and curves on people's faces to think about ways that makeup might enhance them.

But she had never been entranced by a mouth in quite the way she was now.

She licked her own lips in response to the feeling created inside her when she looked up at him. And she felt him tense. The lines in his body going taut. And when she found the courage inside of herself to look all the way up to his eyes, the ice was completely burned away. And only fire remained.

But she didn't feel threatened. And it wasn't fear that tightened her insides. Wasn't fear that made her feel like she might be burned, scorched from the inside out.

She took a breath and hoped that somehow the quick, decisive movement might cover up the intensity of her re-action to him. But the breath got hung up on a catch in her throat, and her chest locked, as she leaned forward. Her breasts brushed against the hardness of his chest and she felt like she was melting.

She swayed, and he seemed to think she was unsteady, because he locked his arm around her waist and braced her against his body. She felt weightless.

And she had the strangest sense of security. Of protection. She shouldn't. This man was her enemy. After the way he had dismissed her suggestions for finding ways of not being forced into marriage, he was her sworn enemy.

But in his arms she was certain that he would never hurt her. And when she looked up into those eyes, she could easily see an image of him in her mind, holding a sword aloft and pressing her against his body, threatening anyone who might try to claim her. Anyone who might try to take her from him.

She was insane.

She had lost her mind.

She never reacted to men like this. Much less men who were just holding her in captivity until they could marry her off to their brothers.

But looking up into his eyes now, looking at that sculpted, handsome face, made it impossible for her to think of that. It made it impossible for her to think of anything. How isolated she was here. How her friends weren't here, her family wasn't here. She didn't even have her phone. She hadn't thought about her phone from the moment she had woken up this morning.

She had gotten up, scrubbed the makeup off her face, discarded her fake eyelashes and seized on the idea to play a ridiculous damsel in distress. Over eyeliner. And see where that got her. She hadn't been able to stomach it. Because it was too ridiculous.

He might have believed it, but she found that her pride had to come into play somewhere.

So that had been her first waking thought. And then he had appeared.

There had been toast.

He had been handsome.

Now he was touching her.

And somewhere in there logic was turned upside down, twisted, then torn in half.

Because somehow she felt more connected, more present with this man, here in isolation, than she could remember feeling at home for a very long time.

But he's not why you're here.

The thought sent such a cold sliver of dread through her, and it acted like a bucket of icy water dropped over her head.

She was being ridiculous however you sliced it. But feeling… Physical responses to him were ludicrous. Not just because he had brought her here against her will, but because he wasn't even the reason she had been brought here.

It was his brother. His brother who she hadn't even met. She hadn't even googled anything about him, because she didn't have the means to do it.

She extricated herself from Javier's hold, her heart thundering rapidly. "I think I got the hang of it," she said.

"You are doing okay," Sophie said. "I wouldn't call it masterful."

"Well, I'm jet-lagged," Violet said. "Or did you not hear that I was forced onto a plane yesterday afternoon and flown from San Diego."

Sophie looked from Violet to Javier. "I admit I didn't know the whole story."

"Forced," Violet said. "I am being forced to marry King Whatever-his-name-is."

"King Matteo," Javier said.

"Are you?" Sophie's face turned sharp.

"She's fine," Javier said. "Cold feet."

"Oh yes, prewedding jitters are a real issue for kidnapped brides."

"You're clearly terrified for your life," Javier said dryly.

"You definitely treat me like I might kill you via lack of Wi-Fi at any moment."

"I'm in withdrawal."

"Leave us," Javier said to Sophie.

"Should I?" Sophie asked Violet.

"I'm not afraid of him," Violet said, tilting her chin upward.

Sophie inclined her head and left the room, doing what Javier told her. "You have my employees questioning me."

"Good. Maybe we'll start a revolution."

"I would advise against that."

"If you hear the people sing, you might want to make a run for it. And make sure you don't have any guillotines lying around."

"If revolution were that simple, I would have engaged in one a long time ago."

"The history books make it look simple enough."

"And full of casualties. My brother and I did our best to work behind the scenes to keep this country from falling apart. We prevented civil war."

"Good for you," Violet said, but she felt somewhat shamefaced now for making light of something that was apparently a very real issue here. And she shouldn't feel guilty, because she was being held here against her will. There was no place for her to be feeling guilty. He should feel guilty. But of course he wouldn't.

"I have work to do," he said.

"I thought you were going to take me into the city," she called after him.

"I have no desire to spend any more time with a spoiled brat."

"Oh, how awful of me. Do I have a bad attitude about being your prisoner?"

"This is bigger than you. Can't you understand that?"

He really thought that she should be able to take that on board. That she should just be willing to throw her life away because he was convinced that his brother thought she would be the best Queen for the country.

The longer she stood there staring at him, the longer she felt the burn of his conviction going through her skin, the more she realized they might as well be from different planets.

It wasn't a language barrier. It was... An *everything* barrier.

He had sacrificed all his life for the greater good. He could not understand why it didn't make sense to her. Why it wasn't the easiest thing in the world to abandon her expectations about her life and simply throw herself on the pyre of the good of many.

"Javier," she said.

His expression became haughty. "You know people don't simply address me by my first name."

"What do they call you?"

"His Royal Highness, Prince Javier of Monte Blanco."

"That's a mouthful. I'm going to stick with Javier."

"Did I give you permission?"

Tension rolled between them, but it was an irritation. She had a terrible feeling she knew what it was. That maybe he had felt the same thing she had when they had been close earlier.

She chose to ignore it.

She chose to poke at him.

"No. But then, did you ask me if I cared to get it?"

"What is it you want, Violet?"

Her throat went dry, and she almost lost her nerve to ask him what she had intended to.

"Do you do anything for yourself?" She decided that since she was already acting against what would be most people's better judgment, she might as well go ahead and keep doing it.

"No," he said. Then a smile curved the edges of his lips. "One thing. But I keep it separate. In general, no. Because that kind of selfishness leads to the sort of disaster my brother and I just saved our nation from."

"But you know that's not the way the rest of the world works."

"The rest of the world is not responsible for the fates of millions of people. I am. My brother is."

"We just don't expect that, growing up in Southern California."

"That isn't true. Because you're here."

"Because of my business," she said.

"And your father," he said. "Because whatever you think, you feel an obligation toward something other than yourself. Toward your father. Your family. You know what it is to live for those that you love more than you love your own self. Magnify that. That is having a country to protect."

Then he turned and left her standing there, and she found that she had been holding her breath. She hadn't even been aware of that.

She looked around the room. She was now left to her own devices. And that meant… That she would be able to find a computer. She was sure of that. And once she had the internet at her disposal, she would be able to figure out some things that she needed to know.

It occurred to her that she could contact home. If her brother had any idea what had happened to her…

She could also contact the media.

But something had her pushing that thought out of her mind. If she needed to. If she needed to, she could make an international incident. But for some reason she believed everything that Javier told her. And since she did, she truly believed that things in their country had been dire, and that he and his brother were working to make them better.

She didn't want to undo that.

So she supposed he was right. She did have some sense of broader responsibility.

But that was why she needed a better idea of what she was dealing with. Of who she was dealing with. And that meant she was going exploring.

CHAPTER SIX

JAVIER IMMEDIATELY WENT to the gym. He needed to punish his body. Needed to destroy the fire that had ignited in his veins when he had touched Violet King. It was an aberration. He knew he had to turn his desires on and off like a switch.

In his life, it had been a necessity. Sometimes he had to go months without the touch of a woman, when he and Matteo were deep in trying to redirect one of his father's plans from behind the scenes, or when they were actively harboring refugees, helping wrongly convicted citizens escape from prison… Well, sometimes there was no time for sex. When he wanted a woman, he went and found one.

Weekends in Monaco. Paris. Women who had appetites that matched his own. Voracious. Experience to match the darkness that lived inside of him.

And never, ever a woman who was meant for his brother.

He had far too much self-control for this.

Perhaps the issue was he had been too long without a woman.

It had been several months while he and Matteo worked to right the balance of Monte Blanco. And though he did not think they had been entirely celibate—either of them—since his brother had taken the throne, it had left little time for them to pursue personal pleasure.

Javier was feeling it now.

He growled and did another pull-up before dropping down to the floor, his breath coming hard and fast.

And he could still feel the impression of her softness in his arms. He had been in the gym for hours now, and it had not dissipated.

He would find a woman. He would have one flown in.

At this point, he felt deeply uncomfortable finding his pleasure with women in his own country. The power imbalance was too great.

And he was wary of being like his father.

So you're more comfortable lusting after the woman you're holding captive?

No, he was not comfortable with it. It was why he was here.

Because she was in his care, if one could say that of a captive. And he could so easily… Crush her.

He had harmed people before in the service of his father. A blot on his soul he would never scrub out.

"Oh."

He whirled around and he saw the object of his torment standing there, her mouth dropped open, her eyes wide.

"What the hell are you doing in here?"

"I asked around. They said that you might be in the gym. And I had found a computer, so I found an internal schematic for the palace and… Anyway. I found my way down here."

"A computer?"

"Yes," she said. "You see, conveniently, your staff doesn't know that I'm a prisoner. They all think that I'm here of my own accord. So of course there is nothing wrong setting me up with a computer that has internet. Really. You need to watch me more closely."

He crossed his arms over his bare chest. "I hear no helicopters. So I assume you did not call in the cavalry?"

"No. I figured I would wait for that."

Her eyes skittered down from his face, landed on his chest and held. Color mounted in her face.

He gritted his teeth. It was a dangerous game she was playing. Whether she knew it or not.

"If you have something to say," he said, his temper coming to an end point, "say it. I'm busy."

"I can see that," she said. "Do you suppose you could find a… You don't have a shirt on hand, do you?"

He didn't particularly care if she was uncomfortable. Not given the state of his own physical comfort over the last several hours. "No. And I'm in the middle of a workout. So I won't be needing a shirt after you leave. It would be wasted effort. Continue."

It was only then that he noticed she was clutching a portfolio in her hand.

She was still wearing the simple outfit that had been provided for her by the staff earlier in the day. Her hair was still loose, her face still free of makeup.

It was unconscionable, how attractive he found that.

He was a busy man. And consequently, his needs were simple. When he pursued a woman for a physical relationship, he liked her to be clearly sophisticated.

A very specific, sleek sort of look with glossy makeup, tight dresses and high-heeled shoes.

Obvious.

Because when you were short on time, *obvious* was the easiest thing.

Violet was anything but, particularly now, and yet she still made his blood boil.

Perhaps this was it. The taint of his father's blood coming to the fore. Bubbling up the moment there was a woman in proximity who was forbidden. Who was forbidden to him? No one and nothing. And so what had he done?

What had he done? He had made the forbidden the most attractive thing.

And that was it. It had to be his body creating this situation. Because there was nothing truly special about her.

Except that tongue of hers.

Razor-sharp and quick.

Her bravery in the face of an uncertain future.

He gritted his teeth again. None of those things mattered to him. A woman's personality meant nothing. She would serve his brother well when it came to a choice of bride, provided Matteo could handle the sharper edges of her, that was. But those things, Javier presumed, would make her a good queen.

When it came to a bedmate… No. It wasn't desirable at all. A construct. A fabrication.

Brought to him by the less desirable parts of him.

He and his brother had always known those things lurked inside of them.

How could they be of their father and consider themselves immune to such things? They didn't. They couldn't.

And so, Javier had to be realistic about it now.

"I have put together a portfolio. Everything I learned about your country. And the ways in which I think I could help by bringing my business here."

"What do you mean?"

"You used to have manufacturing here. You don't anymore. I do most of my manufacturing in the United States, but with products coming to Europe… I don't see why I couldn't have some of it manufactured here. In fact, I think it would be a good thing. It would allow me to keep costs down. And it would bring a substantial amount of employment to your country."

"We are not impoverished."

"No. But particularly the women here are underemployed. Child marriages are still happening in the more rural villages. I know your father looked the other way..."

"Yes," he said, his teeth gritted. "We fought to stop that. We did not look the other way."

"I know. And I know you're still fighting for it. Again. I did a lot of reading today. I feel like I understand... More of what you're trying to do here. Well. I believe in it. And you're right. It doesn't do us any good to live a life to serve only ourselves. And that has never been my goal. Don't you know I have a charity with my sister, for women who are abused?"

He shook his head. "I regret that I do not."

"My sister... She ended up raising her best friend's baby after her friend's ex-lover murdered her. My sister has always been so regretful that she couldn't do more. And so the two of us established a foundation in her honor. I've been looking for more ways to help vulnerable women. Minerva inspired me." She blinked. "I did work only for myself for a while. To try and make my father..." She shook her head. "It doesn't matter. Working on this charity has made me feel better about myself than anything else ever has. Making Monte Blanco my European base will bring an entirely new light to the country."

"You think very highly of yourself."

She shook her head. "No. But I do know a lot about public perception. And I'm very good with it. Gauging it, manipulating it, I suppose. If you want to call it that. I can help."

"Well. I don't think Matteo would be opposed to that."

"I know he wouldn't. And what does he think, anyway? That he could just put me on ice here until he gets back?"

Javier laughed. "I guarantee you he thinks exactly that."

"I'm to believe that he is the softest, most compassionate ruler this country has ever known?"

Javier nodded. "He is. You may find that hard to believe, but it's true."

"I have a question for you."

"Why bother to let me know? You don't seem to have any issue saying exactly what you think or asking for exactly what you want to know."

"All right. So tell me this. How did you know that what your father was doing was wrong? And what inspired you to try to fix it? How did you see outside of the way you were raised? Because a few hours ago when you were facing me down, I realized something. We were not speaking the same language. We expect different things. Because of our realities. For you… Caring about this entire nation of people is part of you the same as breathing. But it wasn't for your father. You weren't taught this… How did you know it?"

It was something he would have wondered, had the memory not been so emblazoned in his mind.

"The answer is the same as it always is. The moment you see the world outside of the little bubble you're raised in, is the moment you stop believing that your perspective is infallible. It is the moment that you begin to question whether or not your reality is in fact the true reality of the world. It was a child marriage. I was newly in the military. Sixteen years old. I happened upon a village. A six-year-old girl was being married off, and she was terrified."

Even now the memory made his teeth set on edge. Made him burn for blood.

"I put a stop to it. Rallied the military, ordered them to hold her father and the groom captive. I remember picking the child up. She was terrified. When I went to my father and told him I was appalled to see that these things were still happening in our country… He scolded me. He said it was not up to me to impose my beliefs on our citizens. My father was no great believer in liberty, Violet. His motivations were related to money. Peace, border protection. Not freedom." He stared hard against the back wall of the gym. "The minute I knew that was the minute that I stopped believing what I saw. It didn't take me long to realize my brother was in a similar crisis of faith. And that was when the two of us began to work to affect change."

"It's amazing," she said. And somehow, he truly believed her. He had never felt particularly amazing. Only like a grim soldier carrying out marching orders that he had never received. But the ones that should have existed. If their leader had had any integrity.

"Most people look away, you know," she said.

"Not me," he said.

"No. Will you please take me out into town?"

"Yes," he agreed.

Because he saw her purpose now. Saw her intent. And because she was correct. It wasn't reasonable for Matteo to keep her here on ice, so to speak.

Anyway, he did not have to check with his brother on every last thing. They had to trust each other. With the way things had been for the past decade and a half, they had no choice. And so, Matteo would have to trust him in this as well.

"Perfect. But I need… I need a phone."

"Your phone, along with your makeup, is making its way here. You will have it tomorrow. And then I promise you, we will go on your field trip."

"Thank you," she said.

It occurred to him then, the ludicrousness of it all. Of her thanking him when she hated him. Of him standing there, desire coursing through his veins when she was off-limits.

But it didn't matter. Nothing mattered more than Monte Blanco. Nothing mattered more than the good of the nation.

Certainly not his own errant lust.

But tomorrow everything would be as it should be.

He was a man of control. A man of honor.

And he would not forget.

CHAPTER SEVEN

IT HAD TAKEN her several hours to regain her breath after seeing him without his shirt. There it was. She was that basic.

She had known that he was spectacular. Had known that he was muscular and well-built. Because she wasn't blind, and it didn't take a physique detective to know that he was in very good shape underneath those clothes.

But then she had seen it.

His body. All that golden, perfect skin, the dark hair that covered his chest—she would have said that she didn't like chest hair, but apparently she did—and created an enticing line that ran through the center of his abdominal muscles.

He was hot.

Her captor was hot.

She did not have time to ponder that. She had a mission.

She steeled herself and took one last look in the mirror before leaving her room. She had told him they could meet in the antechamber. She was pretty sure she knew which room the antechamber was. She had made it her business to figure out the layout of the palace. It was difficult. But she had done it.

And she had her phone back.

She had been feeling gleeful about that since the moment it had been deposited into her hand this morning.

And yet… And yet.

She hadn't been able to think of a single thing to update her account with.

If she still didn't want to call home.

Because she was mad.

Because she didn't even know what to say.

She tucked her phone in her purse and made her way to the appointed meeting place. He was already there. She tried to force her eyes to skim over him, not to cling to the hard lines and angles of his body. To the terrifying symmetry of his face.

Terrifying and beautiful.

Saved only by that scar along his cheekbone.

She wanted to know how he got it.

She shouldn't want to know how he got it. She shouldn't want to know anything about him.

"Good morning. As you can see," she said, waving her hand over her face, "I'm restored to my former glory."

His eyes moved over her dispassionately. And she felt thoroughly dismissed. Insulted.

She shouldn't care.

"All right. Where are we going to first?"

"The capital city. I thought that would be the perfect place to start. It's about thirty minutes away. Down the mountain."

"Excellent."

Her stomach tightened, her hand shaking. And she didn't know if it was because of the idea of being in close proximity with him in a car for that long or if it was stepping outside of this palace for the first time in several days.

The lack of reality in the situation was underlined here. By her containment. In this glittering palace of jewels it was easy to believe it was all a dream. Some kind of childhood fantasy hallucination with the very adult inclusion of a massive, muscular male.

But once they left the palace, the world would expand. And the fantasy that it was a dream would dissolve. Completely.

There was no limousine waiting for them. Instead, there was a sleek black car that was somehow both intensely expensive looking and understated. She didn't know how it accomplished both of those things. But it did.

And it seemed right, somehow, because the car's owner was not understated and could not be if he tried.

Looking at him now in his exquisitely cut dark suit, she had a feeling that he was trying.

That this was the most inconspicuous he could possibly be. But he was six and a half feet tall, arrestingly beautiful and looked like he could kill a hundred people using only his thumb. So. Blending wasn't exactly an option for him.

He opened the door for her, and she got inside.

When he went to the driver's seat, her tension wound up a notch.

It was even smaller than she had imagined. She had thought they might have a driver. Someone to help defuse this thing between them.

Between them. He probably felt nothing.

Why would he?

He was carved out of rock.

Well. One thing.

She thought of his response to her question yesterday. The way that his lips had curved up into a smile.

One thing.

The idea of this rock as a sexual being just about made her combust. She did not need those thoughts. No, she did not.

He was not the kind of man for her. Even in fantasy.

She needed a sexual fantasy with training wheels. An accountant, maybe. Soft. One who wore pleated-front khakis and emanated concern. A nice man named Stephen.

The kind of man that would bring her cinnamon rolls in bed.

After... Making tender love to her.

Nothing about that appealed.

She had no idea why her sexuality was being so specific. She had never intended to make it to twenty-six a virgin.

And she had certainly never intended for this man to awaken her desire.

No. It was just exacerbated by the fact that this felt like a dream. That was all. She wasn't connected to reality. And she was... Stockholm syndrome. That was it. She was suffering from sexual Stockholm syndrome.

When the car started moving, she unrolled the window and stuck her head out of it. Breathed in the crystal mountain air and hoped that it would inject her with some sense.

It didn't.

It did nothing to alleviate the bigness of his presence in the tiny vehicle.

"Are you going to roll the window up? Because you know I don't make a habit of driving to public spaces with women hanging out my car."

She shot him a look and rolled the window up. It really did her no good to oppose him now. She was on a mission. Trying to prove something. "I was enjoying the air."

"Now which one of us is a Saint Bernard?"

"Did you just make a joke?" She looked at his stern profile and saw the corner of his lip tip upward. "You did. You made a joke. That's incredible."

"Don't get used to it."

It felt like a deeper warning of something else. But she

went ahead and ignored it. Along with the shiver of sensation that went through her body.

They were silent after that. And she watched as the trees thinned, gave way to civilization. The dirt becoming loose rocks, and then cobblestone.

The town itself was not modern. And she would have been disappointed if it was. The streets were made of interlocking stones, the sidewalks the same, only in a different pattern. Tight spirals and sunbursts, some of them bleeding up the sides of the buildings that seemed somehow rooted to the earth.

The streets were narrow, the businesses packed tightly together. There were little cafés and a surprising number of appealing-looking designer shops that Violet suddenly felt eager to explore.

"This is beautiful," she said. "If people knew… Well, if people knew, this would be a huge tourist spot."

"It was not encouraged under the rule of my father. And in these past years businesses have rebounded. But still…"

"There is ground to gain. Understood. Pull over."

"What?"

"Pull over."

She saw a bright yellow bicycle leaned against a wall. And right next to it was a window planter with bright red geraniums bursting over the top of it.

All backed by that charming gray stone.

"We need to take a photo."

He obeyed her, but was clearly skeptical about her intent.

She got out of the car quickly and raced over to the bike. Then she looked over into the courtyard of the neighboring café. People were sitting outside drinking coffee. "Excuse me? Is this your bike?" She asked the young woman sitting there working on her computer.

The woman looked at her warily and then saw Javier, standing behind her. Her eyes widened.

"It's fine," Violet said. "He's harmless. I just want to take a picture with your bike."

"Of course," the woman said.

She still looked completely frazzled, but Violet scampered to where it was, positioning herself right next to it and putting her hand over the handlebars. "A picture," she said. She reached into her purse and pulled her phone out, handing it to him.

"That's what all this is about? Also. I am not harmless."

"Yes. Very ferocious. Take my picture."

She looked straight ahead, offering him her profile, and tousled her hair lightly before positioning her hand delicately at her hip.

"There," he said. "Satisfied?"

"Let me verify." She snatched the phone from his hand and looked at the photo.

It had done exactly what she wanted to do, and with some tweaking, the colors would look beautiful against the simple gray stone.

"Yes," she confirmed. "I am."

She pulled up her account, touched the picture up quickly and typed:

Exploring new places is one of my favorite things. Stay tuned for more information on your next favorite vacation spot.

"There," she said. "That's bound to create speculation. Excitement."

He looked down at the picture with great skepticism. "That?"

"Yes."

"I do not understand people."

"Maybe they don't understand you," she said.

He looked completely unamused by that.

"Sorry. Joke. I thought you were getting to where you understood those sometimes."

The look he gave her was inscrutable.

"Show me the rest of this place," she said. "I'm curious."

He looked at her as if she had grown a second head. "You realize that I'm slightly conspicuous?"

"Usually I am too," she said. "I guess... I just figure you ignore it."

"You're not conspicuous here."

"No," she said. "But that won't last long, will it? I mean, if I'm going to be the Queen..."

"You're not going to be inconspicuous as long as you're walking around with me. That's a pretty decent indicator that you might be important."

"Wow. No points for humility."

"Do you have false humility about the degree to which you're recognized? Or what your status means? You've been throwing all sorts of statistics at me about your wealth and importance ever since we first met."

"All right," she said. "Fair enough."

They walked on in silence for a moment. She paid attention to the way her feet connected to the cobblestones. It was therapeutic in a way. There was something so quaint about this. It was more village than city, but it contained a lot more places of interest than she would normally think you would find in a village.

"What is the chief export here?"

"There isn't any. We are quite self-contained. What we make tends to stay here, tends to fuel the citizens."

"That's very unusual."

"Yes. It also feels precarious."

"So… If we were to manufacture my products here, I would be your chief export."

"In point of fact, yes."

"Though, if your other products became desirable because of tourism…"

"Yes. I understand it would mean a great deal of cash injection for the country. Though, thanks to my brother's personal fortune, the coffers of the country have been boosted as it is."

"Yes, I did some research on him. He's quite a successful businessman."

"You would like him. Other than the fact that he's a bit of a tyrant."

"More than you?"

"Different than me." He relented. "Perhaps not more."

"A family of softies."

The sound he made was somewhere between a huff of indignation and a growl. "I have never been called soft."

She looked at him. The wall of muscle that was his chest. The granite set of his jaw. She meant her response to be light. Funny. But looking at him took her breath. "No. I don't suppose you have."

There was a small ice-cream parlor up the way, and she was more than grateful for the distraction. "I want ice cream," she said.

"*Ice cream?* Are you a child?"

"Ice cream is not just for children," she said gravely. "Surely you know that, Javier."

"I don't eat ice cream."

"Nonsense. Everyone needs ice cream. Well, unless they're lactose intolerant. In which case, they just need to find a good nondairy replacement. And let me tell you, in Southern California they're plentiful."

"I'm not intolerant of anything."

She tried, and failed, to hold back a laugh. "Well, that just isn't true. I've only spent a few days in your company, but I can tell you that you're clearly intolerant of a whole host of things. But, it's good to know that dairy isn't among them."

"You are incredibly irritating."

"*Not* the first time I've heard that."

"And who told you that?"

"My older brother, for a start. Also, my surrogate older brother, Dante. He's now my brother-in-law, incidentally."

"That seems convoluted."

"It's not really. Not at all. Just the way things ended up. My father quite literally found him on a business trip and brought him home. Took care of him. I think my sister was in love with him for most of her life."

"But you weren't."

She laughed. "I remember very clearly telling Minerva that I didn't like men who were quite as hard as Dante."

A tense silence settled between the two of them. She hadn't meant to say that. Because of course that implied that perhaps it had changed. And perhaps there was a hard man that she might find appealing after all.

She gritted her teeth.

"And I still don't," she said. "So. Just so we're both clear."

"Very clear," he said.

"Now. Ice cream." She increased her pace and breezed straight into the shop. And she did not miss the look of absolute shock on the faces of the proprietors inside. It wasn't to do with her. It was to do with Javier.

"I saw that there was ice cream," she said cheerily. She approached the counter and looked at all the flavors.

"We make them all here," the woman behind the counter said, her voice somewhat timid. "The milk comes from our own cows."

"Well, that's wonderful," Violet said. "And makes me even more excited to try it." There was one called Spanish chocolate, and she elected to get a cone with two scoops of that. She kept her eyes on Javier the entire time.

"You don't want anything?"

"No," he said, his voice uncompromising.

"You're missing out," she said.

She went to pay for the treat, and he stepped in, taking his wallet from his pocket.

"Of course we cannot ask Your Royal Highness to pay," the woman said.

"On the contrary," Javier said, his voice decisive. "You should be asking me to pay double. Consider it repayment."

The woman did not charge Javier double, but she did allow him to pay.

"I didn't need you to buy my ice cream," she said when they were out on the street.

"It's not about need. It is about... What feels right."

"You're that kind of man, huh? The kind that holds open doors and pays for dinner?"

He laughed, a dark, short sound. "You make me sound quite a bit more conventional than I am."

"A regular gentleman."

"I would not say that."

"Well, what would you say, then? You're single-handedly setting out to save the country, and you saved a little girl from child marriage. You worked for years to undo the rule of your father." She took a short lick of her ice cream. It was amazing. "I would say that runs toward gentlemanly behavior, don't you?"

"I think that's overstating human decency. I would like to think that any man with a spine would do what I did in my position. Inaction in my position would be complicity. And I refused to be complicit in my father's actions."

"Well. Many people would be, for their comfort."

She looked down the alleyway and saw a lovely hand-painted mural. She darted there, and he followed. It was secluded, ivy growing over the walls, creeping between the brick.

"I just need a picture of this."

She held out her hand, extending her ice-cream cone to him. "Can you hold this?"

He took it gingerly from her grasp, looking at it like it might bite him. She lifted her brows, then turned away from him, snapping a quick picture and then another for good measure.

He was still holding the ice-cream cone and looking aggrieved, so when she returned, she leaned in, licking the ice-cream cone while he held it still.

His posture went stiff.

He was reacting to her, she realized. The same way that she reacted to him. And she didn't like how it made her feel. Giddy and jittery and excited in a way she couldn't remember feeling before.

And she should pull away. She should.

But instead, she wrapped her hand around his, and sent electric sensation shooting through her body.

"You should taste it," she said.

"I told you, I didn't want any."

"But I think you do," she insisted. "You should have some."

She pushed his hand, moving the cone in his direction, and she could see the moment that he realized it was better to take the path of least resistance. He licked the ice cream slowly, his dark eyes connecting with hers.

She realized she had miscalculated.

Because he had his mouth where hers had been.

Because she was touching him and he was looking at her.

Because something in his dark eyes told her that he would be just as happy licking her as he was this ice cream.

And all of it was wrong.

Why couldn't she hate him? She should.

Why couldn't she get it into her head that this was real? That it was insane. That she should want to kick him in the shins and run as far and fast as she could. Call for help at the nearest business, rather than lingering here in an alley with him.

"It's good," she said, her throat dry.

"Yes," he agreed, his voice rough.

Then he thrust it back into her hand. "I think I've had enough."

"Right."

Her heart clenched, sank. And she didn't know what was happening inside of her. Didn't know why her body was reacting this way, now, to him. Didn't know why she felt like crying, and not for any of the reasons that she should.

"I'm not done exploring the city, though. And I wouldn't want to take my ice cream back in your car. I might make a mess."

But the rest of the outing was completely muted. Not at all what it had been before.

And that it disappointed her confused her even more than anything else.

When she was back at the palace, back in her room, she lay down and covered her head. And only then did she allow herself to think the truth.

She was attracted to the man who was holding her captive.

She was attracted to the brother of the man she was being forced to marry.

But more important, he was attracted to her. She had seen it.

She had very nearly tasted it.

Thankfully, they had come to their senses.

She spent the rest of the night trying fitfully to be thankful when all she felt was frustrated.

And she knew that she had come up with a plan, no matter how it made her stomach churn to think of putting it into action.

She had no choice.

CHAPTER EIGHT

HIS BROTHER STILL hadn't returned.

Javier was tired of being tested. He had been avoiding Violet since they had come back from the city the other day. The temptation that she had presented to him was unacceptable.

That he had the capacity to be tempted was not something that he had first seen. But Violet King had tested him at every turn, and the true issue was that he feared he might fail a test if she continued.

He curled his fingers into fists. No. He was not a weak man.

Even before he had turned on his father, he had not had an easy life. He had faithfully served in his father's army. And that had required work guarding the borders in the forests, camping out for long periods of time. His father's paranoia meant that he was certain that enemies were lurking behind every tree.

And Javier had found that to be so. His father had had many enemies. And Javier had done his job in arresting them.

He wasn't sure what he wished to avoid thinking about more. That period of time in his life, or his current attraction to Violet.

"Of course, the architecture is nothing compared to the

natural beauty. You got a little peek outside the window, but more to come later on this beautiful vacation spot."

He heard Violet's voice drifting down the corridor, coming from the expansive dining room where his brother often held dinner parties.

It was a massive room with a view that stretched on for miles, a large balcony connecting it and the ballroom and making the most of those views.

Violet was standing right next to the window, her cell phone in her hand. She waved—not at him, but at her screen—then put the phone down at her side. "I was filming a live video. Doing more to tease my location."

"Of course you were," he said.

She gave him a bland look. "Just because you don't understand it doesn't mean it's not valid."

"Oh, I would never think that."

"Liar. If you don't understand it, you think it's beneath you."

"I didn't say I didn't understand it."

"But you do think it's beneath you."

"That was implied in my statement, I think."

"You're impossible."

She walked nearer to him, and he tried to keep his focus on the view outside. But he found himself looking at her. She had most definitely regained her precious makeup. She looked much as she did that first day he had seen her, which he assumed was a signature look for her.

"So you must go to all this trouble," he said, indicating her makeup, "to talk to people who aren't even in the room with you."

She winked. "That's how you know I like you. If I talk to you in the same room, and I don't bother to put my eyelashes on."

"Your eyelashes are fake?"

"A lot of people have fake eyelashes," she said sagely. "I used to have them individually glued on every week or so, but I prefer the flexibility of the strips so I can just take them off myself at the end of the day."

"I have to say I vastly don't care about your eyelashes."

He looked down at her, at the dramatic sweep of those coal black lashes they were discussing. And he found that he did care, more than he would like. Not about the application, but that he wished he could see them naturally as they had been the other morning. Dark close to her eyes, lighter at the tips. He appreciated now the intimacy of that sight.

And he should not want more.

"You know what I do care about?" she asked. "Outside. I would like to go outside."

"Well, the garden is fenced in, feel free to wander around. Just don't dig underneath it."

"Very cute. Another joke. We could write that in your baby book. However, I would like a tour."

"A tour of the grounds?"

"Yes."

"Of the garden, or of the entire grounds? Because I warn you, they are quite wild."

"I find I'm in the mood for wild."

She smiled slightly and enigmatically. He could not tell whether she intended for the statement to be a double entendre.

But the moment passed, and he found himself agreeing to take her out of the palace.

One path led to the carefully manicured gardens that had been tamed and kept for generations. A testament to the might of the royal family, he had always thought. And as a result, he had never liked them.

"This way," he said. "This is where Matteo and I used to play when we were boys."

The rocky path led down to a grove of trees. Heavily shaded, and next to a deep, fathomless swimming hole.

A waterfall poured down black, craggy rocks into the depths.

The water was a crystalline blue, utterly and completely clear. The bottom of the river was visible, making it seem like it might not be as deep as it was. But he knew that you could sink and sink and not find the end of it.

He and Matteo had always loved it here. It had seemed like another world. Somewhere separate from the strictures of the palace. Though, at that point he had not yet come to hate it.

Still. He had appreciated the time spent outdoors with his brother. His brother had been most serious at that age.

Perhaps because he had always known that the burden of the crown would be his.

"This is beautiful," she said. He expected her to reach for her phone immediately, but she didn't. Instead, she simply turned in a circle, looking at the unspoiled splendor around them.

"Yes. You know something? I know that my father never set foot down here." He stared at the pool. "And now he's dead."

"That's a tragedy," Violet said. "To live right next to something so beautiful and to never see it."

"There were a great many things my father didn't see. Or care about. He cared about his own power. He cared about his own comfort. This is just one of the many things he never truly looked at. Including the pain that he caused his own people."

"But you did. You do," she said.

"For better or worse."

"You used to swim down here?"

"Yes."

"Did you laugh and have fun?"

"Of course I did."

"I can't imagine you having fun."

"I can assure you I did."

"It's safe?" she asked.

"Yes."

She took her phone out of her pocket and set it on the shore. Then she looked back at him and kicked her shoes off, putting her toe in the water. "It's freezing," she said.

"I said it was safe. I didn't say it wasn't frigid water coming down from an ice melt."

She stared at him, a strange sort of challenge lighting her eyes.

"What?"

"Let's swim."

"No," he said.

He realized right then that the outright denial was a mistake. Because her chin tilted upward in total, stubborn defiance. And the next thing he knew she had gone and done it. Gone in, clothes and all, her dark head disappearing beneath the clear surface. And she swam.

Her hair streaming around her like silken ribbon, her limbs elegant, her dress billowing around her. And he was sure that he could see white cotton panties there beneath the surface. He felt punched in the gut by that. Hard.

"Swim with me," she said.

"No."

She swam up to the edge, giving him an impish grin. "Please."

He remembered her words from the other day. *Don't you do anything for yourself?*

He didn't. He didn't, because there was no point.

But swimming wasn't a betrayal.

He could feel his body's response to that in his teeth.

A twist in his gut. Because he knew what he was doing. Knew that he was pushing at that which was acceptable.

But the water would be cold.

And he would not touch her. Tension rolled from his shoulders, and he unbuttoned his shirt, leaving it on the banks of the river. His shoes, his pants. And leaving himself in only the dark shorts that he wore beneath his clothes.

Then he dived, clearing her completely, sliding beneath the surface of the water at the center of the pool, letting the icy water numb his skin like pinpricks over the surface of it. Maybe it would knock the desire that he felt for her out of his body.

Maybe.

He swam toward her, and he saw something flash in the depths of her eyes. Surprise. Maybe even fear.

He stopped just short of her.

"Is this what you had in mind?"

"I didn't expect the strip show."

The characterization of what had occurred made his stomach tighten. Or the cold water had no effect on his desire.

He couldn't understand why. Why this woman, at this moment, tested him so.

Any retort she might have made, any continuation of the conversation seemed to die on her lips.

And he knew. He knew that he had just gone straight into temptation. Had literally dived right in. Whatever he had told himself in that moment on the shore was a lie. All he had wanted to do was to be closer to her.

He had never experienced anything like this. Had never experienced this kind of draw to a woman before. To anyone.

She had nothing in common with him. A spoiled, sheltered girl from the United States. But when she looked at him, he felt something. And he had not felt anything for a long time.

She began to draw closer to him.

"Don't," he said.

"I just…" A droplet of water slid down her face, and her tongue darted out. She licked it off. She reached out and dragged her thumb over the scar on his cheek. "How did you get this?"

Her touch sent a lightning bolt of desire straight down to his groin. "It's not a good story."

"I don't care."

"You think you don't care, but you haven't heard it."

Her hand was still on him.

"Tell me," she insisted.

"You know you should be afraid of me," he said. "And here you are, pushing me."

"You said you wouldn't hurt me."

"And I wouldn't. Intentionally. But you are here touching me as if I cannot be tempted into anything that we would both regret."

"Who says I would regret it?"

He gritted his teeth. "You would."

"Javier…"

"I was helping a man escape from prison. Wrongfully arrested by my father. One of his guards attempted to put a stop to it. It was war, Violet, and I did what had to be done."

She said nothing. She only looked at him, her eyes wide.

"Yes. It is what you think."

"You did what you had to," she said softly.

"But that's what I am. A man who does what he has to. A man who is barely a man anymore."

She slid her thumb across his skin, and he shuddered beneath her touch. "You feel like a man to me," she whispered.

"You are not for me."

He pushed away from her and swam back to the shore. She watched him dress, the attention that she paid him disconcerting. Then she got out of the water, the thin fabric of her dress molded to her curves. He could see her nipples, clearly visible, and his arousal roared.

"You are not for me."

Then he turned, leaving her there. She would find her way back. Follow the path.

But he had to do them both a favor and remove himself from her. Because if he did not, he would do something that they would both come to bitterly regret.

He was familiar with the sting of failure. The process of deprogramming himself from his father's rule had been a difficult one when he had been sixteen years old and he had wanted to believe with intensity that his father was a benevolent ruler. And he had seen otherwise. The way that it had hurt his soul, torn him in two, to begin to look differently at the world, at his life and at himself, had been the last time he had truly felt pain. Because after that it was over. After that, the numbness had sunk in, had pervaded all that he was.

It was Matteo who had seen him through it. Matteo, who had been struggling with the exact same thing, who made Javier feel like he wasn't losing his mind.

His brother had been his anchor in the most difficult moment of his life.

And now there was another wrenching happening in his soul. It was all because of the luminous, dark eyes of Violet King.

In that alleyway, when she had put her hand over his, when she had tempted him with a bite of ice cream like she was Eve in the garden offering him an apple, he had not been able to think of anything but casting the frozen treat aside and claiming her mouth with his own.

In the water he had longed to drag her to the shore, cover her body with his own. Claim her.

And that was a violation of all that he had become.

He was a man of honor because he had chosen it.

None of it was bred into him. None of it was part of his blood.

He and Matteo knew that, so they were always on guard.

And this woman… This woman enticed him to betray that.

To betray his brother.

The one man to whom he owed his absolute loyalty.

The man he had promised to destroy should that man ever abuse his power. Such was their bond.

Such was his dedication.

But now… Lusting after his brother's fiancée made him compromised.

It compromised that promise. Compromised what he was. What he claimed to be.

His phone rang.

It was Matteo. As if his brother could feel his betrayal from across the continent.

"Yes?"

"We have been successful," Matteo said. "Monte Blanco will now be included in the United Council. My mouse has proven herself indispensable yet again."

"Is she in the room with you?"

"Of course she is."

Javier didn't even have the right to scold his brother for that. Not at this point. He had lost his right to a moral high ground of any kind.

"When do you return?" he said, his voice heavy.

"Two days. We have to make a stop in Paris for a diplomatic meeting."

"I suppose, then, that it is good you spent all those years studying business."

"Yes. Not the way our father did it, but there are similarities to diplomacy in business and when it comes to running a country. Of course, the bottom line is not filling your own pockets in the situation."

"No indeed."

The bottom line was not about satisfying themselves at all.

It stung particularly now. As he thought of Violet. As he thought of the deep, gut-wrenching longing to touch her.

And the anger that crept in beneath his skin. Anger that was not at himself, though it should have been. Anger at the cruelty of fate. That he should want this woman above all others when she was perhaps the only woman in the world who was truly off-limits to him.

He was a prince. He could snap his fingers and demand that which he wished.

Except her.

The insidious doubt inside of him asked the question. Was that why he wanted her? Was that why she presented a particular appeal? Because she was forbidden.

Because she was forbidden to him and no matter how hard he tried to pretend otherwise, he was born a man with a massive ego who didn't feel that a single thing on the earth should be barred from him should he take to it.

No. He would not allow it.

He would not allow that to be true.

"I look forward to your return."

"How is my fiancée?"

"Not exactly amenable to the idea of being your fiancée," he said.

It was the truth. Everything else could be ignored. For now.

"I must say, the connection between myself and her is one of the things that made our meetings the most interesting. She is well liked, world-renowned for her business mind. Such a fantastic asset to me she will be."

"You don't know her."

"And I suppose you do now. I will look forward to hearing how you think I might best manage her."

His brother hung up then. And left Javier standing there with his hand curled so tightly around the phone he thought he might break. Either his bones or the device, he didn't know. Neither did he care.

He gritted his teeth and walked out of his office. Something compelled him down to the ballroom where he had the dance lesson with Violet. Where he held her in his arms and first began to question all that he was. It was unconscionable. That this woman he had known for a scant number of days could undo twenty years' worth of restraint.

And when he flung open the doors to the ballroom... There she was.

Curled up in one of the tufted chairs that sat in the corner of the room, next to the floor-to-ceiling windows, sunlight bathing her beauty in gold.

Her legs were tucked up underneath her, and he could see the edges of her bare toes peeking out from beneath her shapely rear. She was wearing simple, soft-looking clothes, nothing fancy. Neither did she have on any of her makeup. She was reading.

Not on her phone.

And it made him want to dig deeper. To question all that she presented of herself to the world, all that she tried to tell him about who she was and who she actually might be.

She looked up when she heard his footsteps. "Oh," she said. "I didn't expect you to be lurking around the ball-room."

"I didn't expect you to be lurking around at all. Much less away from the computer."

"I found this book in the library," she said. "And the library's beautiful, but it doesn't have the natural lighting of this room."

"Protecting the books," he said.

"Makes sense."

"What is it you're reading?"

"It's a book of fairy tales. Monte Blancan fairy tales. It's very interesting. We all have our versions of these same stories. I guess because they speak to something human inside of us. I think my favorite one that I've read so far is about the Princess who was taken captive by a beast."

"Is that what you think me? A beast?"

She closed the book slowly and set it down on the table beside the chair. "Possibly. Are you under some kind of enchantment?"

"No."

"That's something I found interesting in your version of the story. The Prince was not a beast because of his own sins. He was transformed into one as punishment for something his father had done. And then, much like the story I'm familiar with, the woman is taken captive because of the sins of her father. It feels shockingly close to home, doesn't it?"

"Except I believe in the story my brother would be that enchanted Prince."

Her gaze was too frank. Too direct. "If you say so."

"You were shocked by your father's deal?"

She nodded slowly. "I was. Because I thought that we…

I knew he wasn't perfect. I did. But it's not like he was a raving villain like your father."

"You know, I didn't realize my father was a raving villain until I started to see, really see the things that he had done to our country. And I don't know that your father is a villain so much as he was made a desperate man in a desperate moment. And my brother took advantage of that. My brother does his best to act with honor. But like me, he is not afraid to be ruthless when he must be. I do not envy the man who had to go up against his will."

"He should have protected me. He should never have used me as currency. I can't get over that. I won't."

"Is that why you came? To teach him a lesson?"

Her lips twitched. "Maybe. And I won't lie, I did think that perhaps my notoriety would keep me safe. You know, because people will miss me if I'm not around. But I sort of like not being around. It's been an interesting vacation."

"Except you're going to marry my brother."

"Yes. I know you think so."

"You can take it up with him when he returns. He tells me he'll be back in two days."

Shock flared in the depths of her eyes. "Two days?"

"Yes. Don't look so dismayed."

"I can't help it. I am dismayed."

"Why exactly?"

"I just thought there was more time."

There was something wild in the depths of her eyes then, and he wanted to move closer to it. But he knew that would be a mistake. Still, when she stood, it was to draw closer to him.

"I know that you feel it," she said. "It's crazy, isn't it? I shouldn't feel anything for you. But you… I mean, look, I know it's chemistry, or whatever, I know it's not feelings. But…" She bit her full lower lip and looked up at him from beneath her lashes, the expression both innocent and co-quettish. "Don't you think that maybe we should have a chance to taste it before I'm sold into marriage?"

"I thought you were intent on resisting that," he said, his voice rough.

"With everything I have in me."

"I cannot. I owe my brother my undying loyalty. And I will not compromise that over something as basic as sex. You mistake me, *querida*, if you think that I can be so easily shaken."

"I know that you're a man of honor. A man of loyalty. But I feel no such loyalty to your brother. And it is nothing to me to violate it."

She planted her hand on his chest. And he knew that she could feel it then. Feel his heart raging against the muscle and blood and bone there. Feel it raging against everything that was good and right and real, that which he had placed his faith in all these years.

She let out a shaking breath, and he could feel the heat of it brush his mouth, so close was she. So close was his destruction.

He was iron. He was rock. He had been forced to become so. A man of no emotion. A man of nothing more than allegiance to an ideal. Knowing with absolute certainty that if he should ever turn away from that, he might become lost. That corruption might take hold of him in the way that it had done his father. Because he considered himself immune to nothing.

And so, he had made himself immune to everything.

Except for this. Except for her.

So small and fragile, delicate.

Powerful.

Not because of her success or her money. But because

of the light contained in her beauty. A storm wrapped in soft, exquisite skin that he ached to put his hands on.

And when she stretched up on her toes and pressed her mouth to his, no finesse or skill present in the motion at all, he broke.

He wrapped his arms around her, cupping her head in one of his hands, shifting things, taking control. And he consumed her.

What she had intended to be a tasting, a test, he turned into a feast. If he was going to be destroyed, then he would bring the palace down with him. Then he would crack the very foundations of where they stood. Of all that he had built his life upon. Of all that he was. If he would be a ruined man, then the world would be ruined as a result. As would she.

He nipped her lower lip, slid his tongue against hers, kissed her deep and hard and long until she whimpered with it. Until she had arched against him, going soft and pliant. Until there was no question now who was in charge. Until there was no question now who was driving them to the brink of calamity. It was him.

He had made his choice. He had not fallen into temptation; he had wrapped his arms around it. He had not slid into sin; he had gathered it against his body and made it his air. His oxygen.

And she surrendered to it. Surrendered to him.

The white flag of her desire was present in the way her body molded against his, in the way that she opened for him, the small, sweet sounds of pleasure that she made as he allowed his hands to move, skimming over her curves, then going still, holding her against him so that she could feel the insistence of his desire pressing against her stomach.

He was a man of extremes.

And if she wanted a storm, he would give her a hurricane.

If he could not be a man of honor, then he would be a man of the basest betrayal.

It was the sight of that book sitting on the side table that brought him back to himself. Just a flash of normality. A familiarity. A reminder of who he was supposed to be, that caused him to release his hold on her and set her back on her feet.

She looked dazed. Her lips were swollen. Utterly wrecked.

Just like he was.

"Never," he said. "It will never happen between us."

"But... It already did."

He chuckled, dark and without humor just like the very center of his soul. "If you think that was an example of what could be between us, then you are much more inexperienced than I would have given you credit for."

"I..."

"The things I could do to you. The things I could do to us both. I could ruin you not just for other men, but for sleep. Wearing clothes. Walking down the street. Everything would remind you of me. The slide of fabric against your skin. The warmth of the sun on your body. All of it would make you think of my hands on you. My mouth. And you would try... You would try to use your own hand to bring yourself the kind of satisfaction that I could show you, but you would fail."

"And what about your brother? Would he fail?"

"It is why I won't do it. Because yes. After me. After this... Even he would fail to satisfy you."

And he turned and walked out of the room, leaving her behind. Leaving his broken honor behind, held in her delicate hands. And he knew it. He only hoped that she did not.

The sooner Matteo returned, the sooner Javier could leave this place. Could leave her. Matteo needed to do what he thought was best for the country.

But Javier would not stand by and see it done.

CHAPTER NINE

SHE HAD FAILED. It kept her awake that night. The sting of that failure. She was supposed to seduce him. It had been her one job. Granted, it had all gotten taken out of her hands, and she had a feeling that her own inexperience had been played against her.

Her heart hadn't stopped thundering like it might gallop out of her chest since.

She hadn't expected him to find her in the ballroom. That was the real reason she had been in there. Who hung out in an empty ballroom? But then he had appeared. And she had realized it was her chance.

She hadn't actually been sitting there scheming. She had been avoiding her scheme.

After her failure at the waterfall, and after...

The problem was, he had shared something of his past with her there, and she felt like she knew him better. Felt guilty for her seduction plan even though it felt like the perfect solution to her problem.

Because she knew on some level that if Javier were to sleep with her, Matteo would not want her anymore.

And she had been... She had been excited about it, perversely, because for the first time in her life she was attracted to a man, so why not take advantage of it? She didn't want to marry him. He was... He was an unyielding rock face, and she had no desire to be stuck with a man like that for any length of time.

But then she had been sitting there reading that fairy tale. And not only had she—through those stories—come into a greater understanding of his culture, there was something about the particular story of the beast she'd been reading that had made her understand him.

Transformed into something due to the sins of his father and so convinced that the transformation was a necessity.

That he had to sit in the sins, in the consequence, to avoid becoming a monster on the inside as well as a monster on the outside.

She had been so caught up in that line of thinking that when he had appeared, she had clumsily made an effort at seduction, and she had been carried away in it.

That was the problem with all of this.

She was a reasonable girl. A practical one. A businesswoman. Thoroughly modern and independent in so many ways, but she had been swept up in a fairy tale, and nothing that she knew, nothing that she had ever achieved, had prepared her for the effect that it was having on her.

For the effect that he was having on her.

She had been kissed before.

Every single time it had been easy to turn away. Every single time she had been relieved that it was over. When she could extricate herself from the man's hold and go on with her day, untouched below the neck and very happy about it thank you.

But she wanted Javier to touch her. And she feared very much that the vow he had made to her before he had stormed out of the ballroom was true.

That if it were to become more, she would never, ever be able to forget. That she would be ruined. That she would be altered for all time.

"That's ridiculous," she scolded herself. *It's the kind of ridiculous thing that men think about themselves, but it's never true. You know that. It can't be.*

The idea that she might fail in her objective to avoid marrying Matteo terrified her. But somehow, even more, the idea that she might leave here without… Without knowing what it was like to be with Javier was even more terrifying. And she despised herself for that. For that weakness. Because it was a weakness. It had to be.

Without thinking, she slipped out of bed. She knew where his room was. She had studied the plans to the palace, and she was familiar with it now. Had it committed to memory. She had a great memory; it was one of the things that made her good at business. And, it was going to help her out now.

With shaking hands, she opened up the door to her bedroom and slipped down the corridor. It wasn't close, his chamber.

But suddenly she realized. That wasn't where he would be. She didn't know how she knew it, she just knew.

Where would he be?

His gym. That made sense. She had found him there that day, and the way that he was committed to the physical activity he was doing was like a punishment, and she had a feeling he would be punishing himself after today.

No. She stopped.

He wouldn't be there.

The library.

He would be in the library. Somehow she knew it. He would be looking at the same book that she had been earlier. She could feel it.

It defied reason that she could. And if she was wrong… If she was wrong, she would go straight back to her room. She would abandon this as folly. All of it.

She would leave it behind, and she would find another solution to her predicament. She would use her brain. Her business acumen.

Right. And you're still pretending that this is all about avoiding the marriage?

She pushed that to the side. And she went to the library.

She pushed the door open, and the first thing she saw was the fire in the hearth.

But she didn't see him.

Disappointment rose up to strangle her, warring with relief that filled her lungs.

But then she saw him, standing in the corner next to the bookshelf, a book held open in his palm. The orange glow of the flames illuminated him. The hollows of his face, his sharp cheekbones.

But his eyes remained black. Unreadable.

"What are you doing here?"

"I was looking for you," she said. "And somehow I knew I would find you here."

"How?"

"Because you wanted to read the story. You wanted to see how it ended."

"Happy endings are not real."

"They must be. People have them every day."

"Happy endings are not for beasts who spirit young maidens away to their castle. How about that?"

"I don't know. We all have that story. Every culture. Some version of it. We must want to believe it. That no matter how much of a beast you feel you might be, you can always find a happy ending."

"Simplistic."

"What's wrong with being simplistic? What is the benefit of cynicism? And anyway, what makes cynicism more complex?"

"It's not cynicism. It is a life lived seeing very difficult things. Seeing tragedy unfold all around you. Knowing there is no happy ending possible for some people. Understanding for the first time that when you have power, you must find ways to keep it from corrupting you or you will destroy the world around you. Great power gives life or takes it, it's not neutral."

"All right. But in here… In the library, it's just us, isn't it? What does anyone have to know outside this room? It doesn't have to touch anything. It never has to go beyond here."

That wasn't the point of what she was doing. She should want Matteo to know. She should want there to be consequences.

But she wasn't lying to Javier.

Because suddenly, she just wanted to take that heaviness from his shoulders. For just one moment. She wanted to soften those hard lines on his face. Wanted to ease the suffering she knew he carried around in his soul.

Because he truly thought that he was a monster.

And he believed that he had to be above reproach in order to keep that monster from gaining hold.

She had intended to taunt him. To ask why he was so loyal to a brother who left him behind to be a babysitter.

But she didn't want to. Not now.

She didn't want this moment to have anything to do with the world beyond the two of them.

Beyond these walls.

Beyond this ring of warmth provided by the fire.

The heat created by the desire between them.

She had never wanted a man before.

And whatever the circumstances behind her coming to be in this country, in this castle, she wanted this man.

She had waited for desire, and she had found it here.

But it was somehow more, something deeper than she had imagined attraction might be. But maybe that was just her ignorance. Maybe this was always what desire was supposed to be. Something that went beyond the mere physical need to be touched.

A bone-deep desire to be seen. To be touched deeper than hands ever could.

There was something inside of her that responded to that bleakness in him, and she didn't even know what it was.

Her life had been a whirlwind. Her loud, wonderful family, who she loved, including her father, even though he had wounded her as he had done. Parties. Vacations. Things.

The triumph in her business. The constant roar of social media.

But now all of it had faded away, and for the first time in her life...

For the first time in her life Violet King was truly self-made.

Was truly standing on her own feet.

Was making decisions for herself, and for no other reason at all.

This moment wasn't about proving herself to anyone.

It wasn't a reaction to anyone or anything but the need inside of her.

And she suddenly felt more powerful than she had ever felt before.

As a prisoner in a palace in a faraway land. Standing across from a man who should terrify her, but who filled her with desire instead.

And whatever this resulted in, it would be her choice. This, at least, was her choice.

She didn't have to close the distance between them. Not

this time. He was the one who did it. He wrapped his arm around her waist and brought her against him.

She shivered with anticipation. Because the pleasure that she had found in his kiss surpassed anything else she had ever experienced, and just thinking about it opened up a wide cavern of longing inside of her.

When his mouth connected with hers, she whimpered. With relief. To be touched by him again, consumed by him again...

Only days ago she had never met him. She had been living a life she had worked for. A life that she loved. And she had been missing this one elemental thing without realizing it. Had been completely blind to what desire could feel like. To what it could mean.

And she would have said that obviously if she could wake up tomorrow and just be back at home, back in her bed, if she could never have found out that her father did such a thing to her, then she would have gone back.

Until now. Until this. Until him. And she didn't think it was simplistic. Because as she'd said to him, why was happiness simplistic? Why was desire treated like it was simplistic or base? Desire like this was not cheap, and she knew it. It was not something that came to just everyone, that could occur between any two people. It was a unique kind of magic and she reveled in it.

In him.

His mouth was firm and taut, his tongue certain as it slid between her lips, sliding against her own.

That sweet friction drove her crazy. Made her breasts feel heavy. Made her ache between her thighs. Desperate to be touched.

She felt slick and ready, for what she didn't quite know. Oh, she knew. In a physical sense. But what she was learning was that there was a spiritual component to this sort of attraction that could not be defined. Could not be easily explained in a textbook.

Something that went beyond human biology and went into the realm of human spirituality.

It wasn't basic. It wasn't base.

But it was elemental. Like something ancient and deep that had been dug up from the center of the earth. An old kind of magic, presented as a gift, one she had never even known she needed. But she did know now. Oh, she knew now.

His hands were sure and certain as they roamed over her curves. As if he knew exactly where she needed him most. He slipped his hands upward, cupping her breasts, teasing her nipples with his thumbs. And she gasped. He took advantage of the gasp, tasting her deeper, making it more intense. Impossibly so.

In fact, it was so intense now, she wasn't sure she would survive it. He was not a rock. He was a man. And suddenly, the differences between the two of them felt stark and clear.

And, like everything else that had passed between them, just a little bit magical. That he was strength and hardness and heat and muscle. And he made her feel like her softness might just be strength in and of itself. A match for his.

Her world was suddenly reduced to senses. The texture of his whiskers against her face, the firmness of his mouth. Those rough, calloused hands tugging at her shirt, at her pants. She pushed her hands beneath his shirt, gasped when her palms made contact with his hot, hard muscles.

She lived in Southern California. She saw a lot of beach bodies. She had already seen him shirtless in the gym, and she already knew that visually, he was the most stunning man she had ever beheld. But touching him... Well, maybe it had to do with that chemistry between them. That spiritual element. But there was something that transcended mere aesthetic beauty. It was as if he had been created for her. Carved from stone and had breath infused into him, as if he had been created for this moment, for her to admire.

For her to revel in.

She moved her fingertips over the hard ridges of his abs, and when he sucked in a breath, all those gorgeous muscles bunched and shifted beneath her touch, and the very act of being able to affect him like she did was an intoxicant that transcended anything made by men.

She moved her hands up over his shoulders, across his back. Admired the sheer breadth of him. The strength inherent there.

The whole world rested on his shoulders. So much.

And she kissed him. Not just with all the desire inside of her, but with the formless, indefinable feeling that was expanding in her chest. The deep resonant understanding that was echoing inside of her. Because of him.

Because she saw herself clearly for the first time because of this moment. And whatever happened afterward, that could never be taken from her. This could never be taken from her.

He crushed her body against his, her now bare breasts feeling tender against his chest. Her nipples scraping against his chest hair. And she loved it. The intensity of it. That was another thing. She hadn't realized it would be like this. In her mind, making love was something gauzy and sweet. But this felt raw. A feast for her every sense. The smell of his skin, the touch of his hands. The rough and the soft. Pain and pleasure. Desire that took root so deep it was uncomfortable.

A desperation for satisfaction and a need for the torment to be drawn out, so she could exist like this forever.

Balancing on a wire, precarious and brave, suspended over a glittering and breathless night sky.

If she fell, she was sure she would fall forever.

But if she didn't fall...

Well, then she would never know.

Both were terrifying.

Both were exhilarating.

And when he laid her down on the plush carpet by the fire and pushed his hand beneath the waistband of her panties, she felt her control, along with that wire, begin to fray.

His fingers were deft, finding the center of her need, stoking the fire inside of her and raising the flame of her need to unbearable levels.

Dimly, she thought she should maybe be embarrassed about all of this. It was the first time a man had ever touched her like this. The first time a man had ever seen her naked. But she felt no shame. None at all. Because it was him. And that made no sense, because he was a virtual stranger.

But not in the ways that counted. Not in those places that no one else could see, or reach.

He was a beast, transformed by the sins of his father. And she was a captive because of the sins of hers.

They both had big houses. Wealth. Certain amounts of power.

They were both alone in many ways. But not here. Not now.

So there was nothing to be embarrassed about. Nothing to be ashamed of. When his mouth abandoned hers and began to move downward, her breath hitched, her body growing tense. He moved to her breast first, sucking one tightened bud between his lips, extracting a gasp from her, making her writhe with pleasure. He pressed his hand firmly between her breasts, his touch quieting her before he moved those knowing fingers back down between her legs. Teased her slick folds, pressed a finger inside of her.

She squirmed, trying to wiggle away from the invasion. Until he began to stroke the center of her need with his thumb, the strangeness of the penetration easing as desire began to build.

He kissed a path down her stomach, down farther still, and replaced his thumb with his wicked lips and tongue, stroking her inside in time with those movements.

She shivered, her desire building to unbearable levels.

"My name," he growled against her tender flesh. "Say my name. So that I know."

How could he doubt it? Of course it was only his name. She didn't care at all. Not for anyone else.

"Javier."

He searched upward, claiming her mouth with his, and she could taste her own desire on his lips. She wanted more. Wanted to taste him. Wanted to torment him the way that he had tormented her.

But he was easing himself between her thighs, the blunt head of him right there, causing a tremor of fear to rush through her. But that was stolen when he captured her lips again, kissed her to the point of mindlessness before easing deeper inside of her. Before thrusting all the way home.

The stretching, burning sensation took her breath away, but she didn't want it to stop. Because this was what she had been waiting for. This felt significant. It felt altering. This was the new, this was the different that she had known lay on the other side of this. The transformation.

And when he was fully seated inside of her, she lowered her head against his shoulder, shuddering against the pain, but embracing it all the same.

He froze for a moment, but then he began to move.

She was blinded by the intensity of it. That sense of

him, so large and hard filling her like this. It made it so she couldn't breathe. Couldn't think. Couldn't speak. Couldn't do anything but surrender to this thing that was overtaking them like a storm.

She clung to his shoulders, clung to him to keep herself rooted to the earth. Rooted to the floor. To keep it so that it was still the two of them in this library. So that no other thoughts could invade. No other people. No other expectations.

It was just them.

She didn't have to be the best. She didn't have to be better than her brother. She didn't have to make herself important.

She simply had to be.

All feeling. No calculation. No striving. Just bright, brilliant pleasure, crackling through her like fireworks.

And she was back again, poised on that wire, with the endless sea of nothing and brilliance shining beneath her. She was afraid. Because she didn't know what might happen next. But he was holding her, moving inside of her, over her, in her. And all she could do was cling to him. All she could do was trust in him, in a way that she had never trusted in another person.

But that's what this was. That's what it really was.

The giving of trust, sharing it. Because as vulnerable as she was in this moment, he was too. Because as much as she had to trust him to hold her in his arms, she was holding him as well.

And even as she felt so feminine, vulnerable and small, she had also never felt quite so equal. Quite so happy in those differences.

But then, she couldn't hold on, not any longer. He thrust inside of her one last time, and she was cast into the deep. And what she found there was an endless world of pleasure that she hadn't known existed. So deep and real and intense.

He followed her there. His roar of pleasure reverberating inside of her.

And all the stars around her were made of brilliance and fire. And when she opened her eyes, she realized that the flames were right there. In the fireplace. And she was still in the library.

And Javier was still with her.

She could feel his heart beating just like hers. A little bit too fast. A little bit too hard.

She wanted to cling to him. But he was already moving away.

"This cannot be endured," he growled.

He pushed his fingers through his dark hair, curving his muscular shoulders forward. And even as she realized that the bliss, the connection they had just shared was over, she couldn't help but admire his golden physique, illuminated in the firelight.

"I didn't mind it," she said quietly.

"Why didn't you tell me?"

"Tell you what?"

"You were a virgin."

"Oh. That. Well, if it helps, I didn't really plan to be."

"You realize that makes this worse."

"How?"

"Because I have... I have spoiled you."

"I thought you said that was a promise," she said quietly. "A vow, if I didn't mistake you. That you would ruin me for other men."

"That is not what I mean now," he said, his tone feral. He stood up, and she went dry mouthed at the sight of his naked body.

"No. What do you mean? Perhaps I need clarification?"

"If you were a virgin, then it was meant for him."

"It was meant for who I gave it to."

"Did you give it to me? Or did you fling it away knowing what you were doing."

"No." She winced internally, not because she'd been thinking of her virginity, but she had considered the fact that this would make the marriage to Matteo difficult. But in the end, it wasn't why she had done it. "We don't all live in the Dark Ages, Javier, and you know that. I don't come from this world. Who I decide to sleep with is my choice and my business, and it is not a medieval bargaining tool, however my father treated me and my body. I do not owe you an explanation."

"But I owed my brother my loyalty."

"Then the failure is yours," she spat, feeling defensive and angry, all the beautiful feelings that she had felt only moments before melting away. "It was my first time, and you're ruining it. It was really quite nice before you started talking."

"But it is a reality we must deal with," he said. "You are to marry my brother."

"You can't possibly think that I will go through with it after this."

He stared at her, his eyes dark, bleak.

"You do. You honestly think that whatever this greater good is that your brother plans… You honestly think that it's more important than what I want. Than what passed between us here. You know that I don't want to marry him. Putting aside the fact that we just made love… You know that I want to go home."

Fury filled her. Impotent and fiery. She just wanted to rage. Wanted to turn things over. Because she felt utterly and completely altered, and he remained stone.

"How can nothing have changed for you?"

"Because the world around me did not change. My obligations did not change."

"This was a mistake," she said. "It was a huge mistake."

She began to collect her clothes, and she dressed as quickly as possible. Then she ran out of the library without looking back. Pain lashed at her chest. Her heart felt raw and bloodied.

How could he have devastated her like this? It had been her plan. Her seduction plan to try to gain a bid for freedom, and it had ended…

She felt heartbroken.

Because this thing between them had felt singular and new, and so had she. Because it had felt like maybe it was something worth fighting for.

But not for him.

When she closed the bedroom door behind her, for the first time she truly did feel like a prisoner.

But not a prisoner of this palace, a prisoner of the demons that lurked inside of Javier.

And she didn't know if there would be any escaping them.

When Matteo returned two days later, Javier had only one goal in mind.

He knew that what he was doing was an utter violation of his position. But he had already done that.

But things had become clearer and clearer to him over the past couple of days. And while he knew that his actions had been unforgivable, there was only one course of action to take.

"You need to set her free," he said when he walked into his brother's office.

"Would you excuse us, Livia?"

Like the mouse he often called her, Livia scurried from the room.

"You must be very happy with her performance on the business trip to address her by her first name."

"I am. Now, who exactly do I have to set free?"

"Violet King. You cannot hold her. You cannot possibly be enforcing her father's medieval bargaining."

"I instigated the medieval bargain. So obviously I'm interested in preserving it."

"She will be willing to offer her business services. But she does not wish to marry you."

"Why exactly do you care?" Matteo asked, his brother always too insightful.

"I slept with her," Javier said. "Obviously you can see why it would be problematic for her to remain here."

Matteo appraised him with eyes that were impossible to read. "You know I don't actually care if you've slept with her. As long as you don't sleep with her after I marry her."

"You aren't angry about it?" The idea of Matteo touching Violet filled him with fury. That his brother could feel nothing…

Well, he didn't know her. He didn't deserve her.

Matteo waved a hand. "I have no stronger feelings about her than I do for my assistant. She's a useful potential tool. Nothing more. What she does with her body is her business."

"I betrayed you," Javier said.

"How? She has made no vows to me. And I don't love her."

For the first time, Javier found his brother's complete lack of emotion infuriating. Because he had wasted time having far too many emotions about the entire thing, and apparently it didn't matter after all.

"Let her go."

"Now see, that does bother me, Javier. Because my word is law."

"And you wanted to know when you were overstepping. And it is now. She doesn't wish to marry you. She wishes to leave."

"And her wishes override mine?"

"You would force a woman down the aisle?"

"I told you what I wanted."

"And I'm here to tell you it isn't going to happen. She is mine."

"Then you marry her."

He jerked backward. "What?"

"You marry her."

"Why the hell does anyone have to marry her?"

"Because I made a bargain with her father. And I don't like to go back on a bargain. It was what he promised me in exchange for his freedom. I didn't ask, if you were wondering."

"He simply… Offered her?"

"Yes. I think he liked the idea of a connection with royalty."

"She doesn't want it."

"But you see, I made a business deal with Robert King. He gave me some very tactical business advice that was needed at the time. In exchange I promised that I would make his daughter royalty. Make him a real king, so to speak."

"In exchange for?"

"Manufacturing rights."

"Violet is prepared to offer those for her makeup line."

"Great. I'm glad to hear it. I would like both. Either I marry her or you do it, younger brother, but someone has to."

Javier stared at his brother, more a brick wall than even

Javier was. And for the first time he truly resented that his brother was the leader of the nation and he owed him loyalty. Because he would like to tell him exactly where he could shove his edict. Because they were two alpha males with an equal amount of physical strength and a definite lack of a desire to be ruled by anyone.

But his brother was the oldest. So he was the only one that actually got to give that free rein.

But Javier thought of Violet. Violet.

And he could send her away, or he could keep her.

The beast in the castle.

He could have her. Always. Could keep her for his own and not have to apologize for it.

"Why did you make it sound like her father didn't have any power? Like he'd lost a bet?"

"That's what he told me. He didn't want her to know that he had traded her for a business deal. He instructed me that when the time was right… I should embellish a little bit."

"That bastard."

"Honestly. He's decent enough compared to our father."

"Our father should not be a metric for good parenting in comparison to anyone."

"Perhaps not. So, what's it to be?"

"Even if I marry her, you will still have to marry."

"I'm aware," Matteo said. "I'm sure my mouse can help with that."

"I'm sure she shall be delighted to."

"She is ever delighted to serve my every whim. After all, I am her Savior, am I not?"

"I cannot imagine a worse possible man to serve as Savior. To owe you a debt must be a truly miserable thing. I will marry Violet."

"Interesting," Matteo said. "I did not expect you to accept."

"If you touch her," Javier said, "I will make good on my promise and find an excuse to kill you."

"So you have feelings for her?"

He had, for many years, looked into his soul and seen only darkness. But she had somehow traversed into that darkness and left the tiniest shard of hope in him. A small sliver of light. But it wasn't his. It was hers. He feared that the laughter she'd placed in him, the smile she'd put on his lips…he feared in the end his darkness would consume it.

But like any starving creature, hungry for warmth, he could not turn away either.

Though he knew he should.

Though it went against all he knew he should do, all he knew he should be. "She's mine. I'm not sure why it took this long for me to accept it. I'm the one who went and claimed her. You've kept your hands clean of it the entire time. If I'm going to go to all the trouble of kidnapping a woman, she ought to belong in my bed, don't you think?"

"As you wish."

"I do."

"Congratulations, then. On your upcoming marriage."

CHAPTER TEN

VIOLET'S ANXIETY WAS steadily mounting. Everything had come crashing down on her that moment in the library. The reality of it all. And then in the crushing silence Javier had delivered in the days since, it had all become more and more frightening.

She knew that Matteo was back.

But she still hadn't seen him. Everything was beginning to feel…

Well, it was all beginning to feel far too real.

When she had gone back to her room after they'd made love, her body had ached. Been sore and tender in places she had never been overly conscious of.

And her heart had burned. The sting of his rejection, of pain that she hadn't anticipated.

And she couldn't decide exactly what manner of pain it was.

That he had still been willing to give her to his brother, that he didn't seem to care what she wanted.

That he didn't seem to want her in the way that she wanted him, because if he did then the idea of her being with another man would…

Well, it was unthinkable to her, and on some level she wished it were unthinkable to him.

That he didn't care that she wanted her freedom, because didn't the beast always let the beauty go?

But maybe this was the real lesson.

Because how many times had her female friends been distraught over one-night stands that had ended with silence? How often had they been certain that there was some sort of connection only to discover it was all inside of them? Violet had been certain that what was passing between herself and Javier had been magical. That it had been real, and that it had been real for both of them.

But that had been a virgin's folly. She was certain of that now.

And she was trapped here. Trapped.

For the first time, she knew that she needed to call home.

But not her father. Not her mother.

Instead, she took her phone out and dialed her sister, Minerva.

"Violet," Minerva said as soon as she answered. "Where are you?"

"Monte Blanco," she said, looking out her bedroom window at the mountains below.

Even the view had lost some of its magic. But then it was difficult to enjoy the view when you were finally coming to accept that you were in fact in prison.

"Why?"

It wasn't any surprise to her that her bookish younger sister had heard of the country.

"Well. It's a long story. But it involves Dad making a marriage bargain for me. With a king that I still haven't met."

"I'm sorry, what?"

"I'm serious. I got kidnapped by a prince."

"I… What is your life like?" she asked incredulously.

"Currently or in general?"

"I just don't know very many people who can say they've been kidnapped by a prince. At least not with such flat affect."

"Well, I have been. And it isn't a joke. Anyway. You lied and told the world that you had our brother's billionaire best friend's baby."

"Sure," Minerva said. "But Dante never kidnapped me."

"He did take you off to his private island."

"To protect me. That's different."

"Sure," Violet said. "Look. I don't know if I'm going to be able to get out of this. I'm trying... But I'm here now. I'm in the palace. Then... The worst part is... I... He's not the one that I want."

The door to her bedroom opened, and she turned around, the phone still clutched in her hand, and there Javier was, standing there looking like a forbidding Angel.

"I'm going to have to call you back."

"No. You can't say something cryptic like that and then go away."

"I have to. Sorry."

"Should I call the police?"

"I'm the captive of a king, Minerva. As in an actual king, not our last name. The police can't help me."

She hung the phone up then and stared at Javier. "Have you come to deliver me to my bridegroom?"

They hadn't been face-to-face since that night. The last time she'd seen him he had been naked. And so had she. Her skin burned with the memory.

"Who are you talking to?"

"My sister. Oddly, I have a lot on my mind."

"I spoke to Matteo."

She took a deep breath and braced herself. "And?"

"You are not marrying him."

A roar of relief filled her ears, and suddenly she felt like she might faint.

"You mean I'm free to go?"

"No," he said gravely.

"But you just said that I don't have to marry him."

"No. But you do have to marry me."

"I'm sorry, what?"

"It turns out that neither my brother nor your father were honest about the particulars of the situation. You may want to call him and speak to him. But my brother made a commandment. He said one of us had to marry you. But that sending you home was not an option."

"Except, what's to stop you from letting me go?"

"I refuse," Javier said. "He has turned your charge over to me completely. And that means you're staying here. With me."

"But I have a life, and you know that. We... We know each other."

"And you wanted me to be something other than what I am. You want to believe that I am a man made into a beast. But you never gave space to the idea that I might simply be a beast. Given free rein to keep you, I think that I will. We are very compatible, are we not?"

"You..."

And she realized that the strange, leaping, twisting in her heart was because she was as terrified about this new development as she was exhilarated.

This man, this beautiful man, was demanding she become his wife.

And he was the man that she wanted.

If his words had been filled with happiness. If there had been any indication that he felt emotion for her, then she would have been... She would have only been happy. But there wasn't. Not at all. He was hard and stoic as ever, presenting this as nothing more than another edict as impersonal as the one that came before it, as if they had not been skin to skin. As if he had not rearranged unseen places inside of her. As if he had not been the scene of her greatest act of liberation, and her greatest downfall.

"Just like that. You expect me to marry you."

"Yes," he said.

"I don't understand."

"There is nothing to understand. You will simply do as you're commanded. As you are in Monte Blanco now. And the law here is the law you are beholden to."

"But you don't care at all what I want."

"To be free. To go back to your life. To pretend as if none of this had ever happened. But it has. And you're mine now."

"Why? Why are you marrying me instead of him? I don't seem to matter to you. Not one bit."

That was when he closed the distance between them. He wrapped his arm around her waist and pulled her up against his body. "Because you are mine. No other man will ever touch you. I am the first. I will be the last."

She was angry then that she hadn't had the presence of mind to lie to him when they'd made love. Because it would have been much more satisfying in the end. To take that from him, when it clearly mattered.

"I will be the only one. Didn't I promise you? That no other man would ever satisfy you as I did?"

"Yes," she said, her throat dry.

"I know no man will ever have the chance to try."

"That's all you want. To own me?"

"It's all I can do."

There was a bleakness to that statement that touched something inside of her. This, for him, was as close to emotion as he could come. It was also bound up in his control.

In that deep belief that he was a monster of some kind. He had told her he was not good, but that he had honor.

And she could see now that he was willing to leave her behind, embrace greed.

And on some level she had no one to blame but herself. Because hadn't she appealed to that part of him when she had seduced him in the library? Hadn't it been on the tip of her tongue to ask him why he was so content to let his brother have what he so clearly wanted?

But he didn't need her goading him to embrace those things now. He emanated with them. With raw, masculine intent. With a deep, dark claim that she could see he was intent to stamp upon her body.

Unknowing he had already put one on her soul.

It wasn't that he didn't feel it, she realized. It was that he didn't understand it.

Perhaps she had not felt the depth of those emotions alone. It was only that he did not know how to name them. Only that he did not understand them.

"And what will it mean for me? To be your wife?"

He stared at her, his dark eyes unreadable. "You did not ask me that. About my brother."

"Because I wasn't going to marry him."

She let the implied truth in those words sit there between them. Expand. Let him bring his own meaning to them.

"There will be less responsibility as my wife. I do not have the public face that he does."

"And if I should wish to?"

"Whatever you wish," he said. "It can be accommodated."

"What about charities?"

"You know that we would actively seek to establish

them. We must improve the view of our country with the rest of the world."

"My charity in particular," she said.

"Supported. However much you would like."

"The control of my money?"

He shrugged. "Remains with you."

"And if I refuse…"

"Everything you have will belong to my brother. And you will be bound to us either way."

"Then I suppose there is no choice."

There was. They both knew it. It was just a choice with a consequence she wasn't willing to take on.

And there was a still, small voice inside of her that asked if she still thought she was lost in the fairy tale.

If she was still convinced that she was the maiden sent to tame a beast.

Whatever the reason, she found herself nodding in agreement. Whatever the reason, she knew what her course would be.

"All right. I'll marry you. I will be a princess."

The announcement happened the very next day. Media splashed it all over the world. And she was compelled to put up a post with a photograph of the view outside of her bedchamber and an assortment of vague gushing comments.

"Will I be expected to give up all forms of social media?"

"No," Javier said. "Your visibility is appreciated. An asset."

"Indeed," she mused, looking at the glorious meal spread out before her.

"I will need a ring," she said. "It will have to be spectacular. Don't mistake me. It's not because I have any great need of a massive diamond. Simply that you want me to make some kind of a spectacle. Getting engaged to a prince will require that I have a very strong jewelry game."

"I will bring the Crown Jewels out of the vault for your examination, My Princess."

"Are you teasing me or not?"

"I am not."

The problem was, she couldn't really tell. And the other problem was, in the days since the engagement announcement, there had been no further intimacy between them.

The sense that she had known him had dissipated with their thwarted afterglow, and now she simply felt… Numb.

"Well. I guess… I guess that would be acceptable."

It was more than acceptable to him, apparently, because as soon as they were finished with the meal, he ushered her into the library, which felt pointed, and told her that the jewels would appear.

And appear they did. Members of his staff came in with box after box and laid them all out on the various pieces of furniture throughout the room. On the settee, the different end tables, a coffee table.

She blushed furiously when her eyes fell on the place by the fire, where she had given herself to Javier and cemented her fate.

"This is maybe a little bit much…"

"You said you wanted spectacular. And so I have determined that I won't disappoint you." His dark eyes seemed to glow with black fire. She wondered how she had ever thought them cold. Now she felt the heat in them like a living flame inside her chest.

He moved to one of the end tables and opened the first box. Inside was a ring, ornate, laden with jewels that glittered in the firelight. And she would never be able to see firelight without thinking of his skin. Without thinking of his strong body searching inside of her. It was impossible.

She blushed, focusing on the jewel. Then, those large, capable hands moved to the next box. He opened it, revealing a ring filled with emeralds. The next, champagne diamonds. Citrine, rubies, every gem in every cut and color was revealed.

"There are the rings," he said.

"I…"

"Would you like me to choose for you?"

At first, she bucked against the idea. But what did it matter? Their marriage wasn't going to be a real one anyway. So what did it matter what she wore.

The idea made her eyes feel dry, made her throat feel raw. Because something about this felt real to her. More real than the diamonds that were laid before her. More real than the stones around them. This entire palace was made of gems; why she should be surprised and awed at the splendor laid before her she didn't know. But they were not real. Not in the way that the conviction and need that burned in her heart was.

This man was.

A man. Not a mountain. Not a beast. No matter how much he might want to believe that he was either of the latter.

The ring didn't matter, on that level. But it would matter what he chose for her. In the same way that it mattered the first night they had been together that she had known that he would be in the library. Known that he would be holding that book. Known that whatever he said, he was seeking a connection between the two of them. To deepen it. Because it was real. It was there.

She had spent her life seeking connections. Using connections. She had spent her life trying to show her father that she was worthy. That she was just as good as her brother, Maximus. Just as charming and delightful as her sister, Minerva.

But with Javier it was just there.

Whether they wanted it to be or not. And she had to cling to the fact that something in that was real.

"You can choose," she said.

"Very well."

It was the ruby that he picked up between his thumb and forefinger. He didn't even have to pause to think. With his dark eyes glowing with a black flame, he took her hand in his and he slipped that ring onto her finger.

"Mine," he said.

"Mine," she returned, curling her fingers around his. "If I am yours, then you must be mine."

There was something stark and shocked on his face as she said those words. "I'm a modern woman," she returned. "I believe in equality. If you expect that you will own my body, then I will own yours."

He inclined his head slowly. "As you wish."

"I like it," she said, looking down at the gem.

"Good. Because there is more."

He went to the coffee table, where wider, flatter jewelry boxes were set. He opened first one, then another. Necklaces. Spectacular and glittering with an intensity that mocked the fire.

There was one made of rubies, one that matched the ring. He pulled it out, held it aloft. All of her words were stolen from her. Lost completely in the moment.

And for her, it wasn't about the value of the gems, but about the care of the selection. About the fact that he knew what he wanted to see her wear. That he had chosen them for her. The necklace settled heavily across her breastbone, and he clasped it gently behind her neck.

The metal was cold against her skin and felt erotic somehow. She shivered. Of course, agreeing to be his wife meant more of this. This touching. This need.

This need satisfied and sated when they needed it.

He looked up at her, slid his thumb along her lower lip. And she shivered.

"Last time I had you here you belonged to him."

She shook her head. "No. I never did."

The corner of his mouth curved upward, and she recognized it for what it was: triumph.

"The tradition of what royal marriage means has been lost in my family," he said, his voice rough. "Have you read any of the other books on these shelves?"

She nodded. "A few."

"Did you happen to read about marriage customs?"

"No."

"Then I will explain. Because service is to be given, first to the country. Those who are royal do not belong to themselves. They belong to Monte Blanco. The woman who marries into the family surrenders in the same way."

"What about a man who marries into the family?" she asked.

"Women cannot sit on the throne here."

"That seems...unfair."

"I have seen how heavy the weight of the position is for my brother. I would call it a blessing."

"But it's gender bias either way."

"You may lobby for a change when we are wed."

He didn't even sound all that irritated with her.

It made her want to smile.

"A marriage into the royal family is a surrender of self," he said. "Except...except between the husband and wife there is a bond considered sacred. Nearly supernatural."

He moved his hand behind her back, and on an indrawing of her breath he undid the zipper on her dress with one fluid motion. It fell down her body, pooling onto the floor. Leaving her in her shoes, her underwear, the necklace and that ring.

Her nipples went tight in the cold air, her lack of a bra not a consideration before this moment, but now, with his hungry eyes on her...

She shivered.

"They have surrendered themselves to the greater good. To the nation. But in the walls of their bedchamber they surrender to each other. They belong only to each other. And it is ownership, *querida*. Not a partnership the way you think of it in your modern world."

"But they own each other," she pressed.

He nodded slowly, then he moved to the couch, and picked up another box. He opened it up and revealed two thick, heavy-looking bracelets. Gold and ruby, matching the rest of the jewels.

He moved close to her body and she responded. Being bare as she was with him so near made it impossible for her to breathe. To think.

He took the first bracelet out and clasped it tightly on her wrist. Then he took the second and put it around the other.

She felt the weight of them, heavy in a way that went beyond the materials they were forged from.

He moved again. "Surely there isn't more," she said breathlessly.

"Surely there is," he murmured.

The next box contained cuffs that looked much like the ones on her wrists.

"Do you know what these are?"

"No," she said, the word a whisper.

"These are very ancient. They have been in my family for hundreds of years."

"Oh."

"Out of use for generations. They are deeply symbolic. And they are never worn in public."

"Where are they worn?"

He looked at her with meaning.

"Oh."

"They speak of this ownership that I feel. The ownership I told you about, in these royal marriages."

"Oh," she said again, her throat dry, her heart fluttering in her chest like a trapped bird.

"Permit me."

And she didn't even consider refusing.

He knelt before her. With great care, he removed her shoes and set them aside. Then he lifted his hands, hooked his fingers in the waistband of her underwear and drew them slowly down her legs. A pulse beat hard at the apex of her thighs, and she closed her eyes tight for a moment, trying to find her balance.

She was embarrassed, to be naked with him kneeling down before her like this. And she didn't want to look. But also... She couldn't bear to not watch what he might do next.

So she opened her eyes, looked at him, his dark head bent, his position one of seeming submission.

But she knew better.

He clasped the first cuff to her ankle. Then the second.

Then, nestled in those jewelry boxes she spotted something she hadn't seen before. Gold chains. Without taking his eyes from her, he clasped one end of the first chain to her ring on the left ankle cuff, then attached it to the one on the right.

After that, he rose up, taking the other gold chain in his hand, sliding it between his fingers and looking at her with intent. Then he repeated the same motion he had completed on her ankles with her wrists.

She blinked several times, trying to gather herself. She took a fortifying breath. "I don't understand," she whispered. "Surely these wouldn't actually keep anyone captive. They're far too fine."

"They're not intended to keep anyone captive. Not really. This captivity is a choice," he said, curling his forefinger around the chain that connected her hands. He tugged gently, and she responded to the pressure, taking two steps toward him. "It is a choice," he said again.

Understanding filled her.

Because he was giving her a moment now. To make the choice. Or to run.

It fully hit her now that it was a choice she had made. To stay here. To say yes to him.

She stood, and she didn't move.

She tilted her face upward, the motion her clear and obvious consent. He wrapped his hand more tightly around the chain, bringing her yet closer, and he claimed her mouth with his.

The gold was fine, delicate and such a soft metal. She could break free if she chose. But she didn't. Instead, she let him hold her as a captive, kissing her deep and hard. His one hand remained around the chain, and his other came up to cup her face, guiding her as he took the kiss deep, his tongue sliding against hers, slick and wonderful.

Hot.

Possessive.

He released his hold on her, taking a step back and beginning to unbutton his shirt, revealing hard-cut muscles that never failed to make her feel weak. To make her feel strong. Because wasn't the woman who enticed such a man to pleasure, to a betrayal of all that he was, even more powerful than he in many ways?

Maybe, maybe not. But she felt it.

This, this thing between them, was something that was hers and hers alone.

His.

Theirs.

Two people who belonged to a nation. But belonged to each other first.

She understood it.

He shrugged his shirt off his powerful shoulders and cast it onto the ground. Then, he wrapped his hand around the chain again and began to tug downward. "Kneel before royalty," he said, his voice rough.

And she did. Going down to her knees, the cuffs pressing against her ankles, the chain from her wrists pooling in her lap.

She looked up at him and watched, her mouth going dry as he undid his belt, slid it through the loops on his pants. She was captivated as the leather slid over his palm before he unclasped his pants, lowered the zipper.

And revealed himself, hot and hard and masculine. Hard for her.

A choice.

This was her choice. No matter the position of submission.

Just as when he had knelt before her, fastening the cuffs, it had appeared that he was the one submitting, but he had been in power. It was the same for her.

She reached up and circled her fingers around his length, stroked him up and down.

It was amazing to her that she had never been overcome by desire for a man in her life before, but everything about him filled her with need. He was beautiful. Every masculine inch of him. She stretched up, still on her knees, and took him into her mouth. He growled, the beast coming forward, and she reveled in that.

Because here was the power. Here was the mutual submission. That belonging that he had spoken of. She in chains, on her knees, but with the most vulnerable part of him to do with as she pleased. His pleasure at her command. His body at her mercy.

She was lost in this. In the magic created between the two of them. Even more powerful than it had been the first time.

Because she had all these physical markers of who she belonged to. And everything about his surrender proved that he belonged to her.

She kept on pleasuring him until he shook. Until his muscles, the very foundation of all that he was began to tremble. Until his hands went to her hair and tugged tightly, moving her away from his body.

"That is not how we will finish," he growled.

He lifted her up from the ground, setting her on the edge of the settee. Then he kissed her, claiming her mouth with ferocity. He moved his hand to her thigh and lifted it to his shoulders, looping the chain so that it was around the back of his neck. Then he did the same with the other, so that he was between her legs, secured there.

Holding her tightly, he lowered his head, placing his mouth between her legs and lapping at her with the flat of his tongue. Giving her everything she had given to him, and then some. He feasted on her until she was shivering. Until she was screaming with her desire for release. Begging.

Until she no longer felt strong, but she didn't need to. Because she felt safe. Because she felt like his, and that was every bit as good.

When she found her release, she was undone by it. The walls inside of her crumbling, every resistance destroyed. Defeated. And then, the blunt head of his arousal was pressing against the entrance to her body, and she received him willingly.

He thrust hard inside of her, her legs still draped over his shoulders, the angle making it impossibly deep. Taking her breath away.

Their coming together was a storm. And she didn't seek shelter from it. Instead, she flung her arms wide and let the rain pour down on her. Let it all overtake her. Consume her.

She held on to his shoulders, dug her fingernails into his skin as her pleasure built inside of her again. Impossibly so.

And when they broke, they broke together. But when they came back to earth, they were together as well.

And she realized that he was circled by the chains as well. As bound to her as she was to him.

And they lay there in the library, neither of them moving.

Neither of them seeking escape.

And whatever he had said about his brother mandating the marriage, whatever she had said about not being able to surrender to his country, she looked into his eyes then, and she saw it. Clearly for them both.

It was a choice.

She was choosing him. The same as he was choosing her.

And the only sharp part of the moment was wishing that he might have chosen her for the same reason that she was choosing him.

She had fallen in love.

As she looked into those fathomless black eyes, she knew that it was not the same for him.

CHAPTER ELEVEN

HE DIDN'T SHARE her bed that night.

It wounded her more than a little. She had hoped that… that she tested his control a little more than that. Especially considering he had reshaped her into a person she didn't recognize.

One who had agreed to stay here.

Who had agreed to marry a man she barely knew.

Except…

Didn't she know him? On a soul-deep level? It was terrifying how real it all felt. She loved him. He had taken such a large piece of who she was in such a small amount of time.

And with the same certainty that she loved him, she knew he didn't feel the same.

She wasn't even sure he could.

It didn't change her heart, though.

Maybe she could change his. She hoped.

First, though, she had to take care of her life.

She took a deep breath and fortified herself. Then looked down at her phone.

Violet knew that it was time to speak to her father. She had been avoiding it for weeks now.

And it wasn't that she hadn't received calls from her family in the time since her engagement to Javier had been announced. She had. The only calls she had been at home to were from her brother and from her sister.

Maximus had been stern, and she had waved off his concerns. Minerva had been... Well, Minerva. Thoughtful, practical and a bit overly romantic. But then, Violet herself was being a bit romantic.

And anyway, she had talked Minerva through her situation with Dante, when the two of them had been having issues, and so of course Minerva had been supportive of whatever Violet wanted.

But her parents... She had avoided them. Completely. Not today. Today she was ready to have the discussion.

Today she was ready to hear whatever the answers might be.

That was the real issue.

If she was going to ask her father for an explanation, she had to be prepared to hear the explanation.

But something had shifted in her last night. That decisiveness.

She was no longer hiding from the fact that she had chosen this. That Javier was her choice.

That being in Monte Blanco was her choice.

She took a fortifying breath, and she selected her father's number.

"Violet," he said, his tone rough.

"Hi," she said, not exactly sure what to feel. A sense of relief at hearing his voice, because she had missed him even while she had been angry at him.

At least, missed the way that she had felt about him before.

"Are you all right?"

"It's a little bit late for you to be concerned about that."

"Why? I didn't expect that you would be cut off from communication with me."

"I haven't been. I've been perfectly able to call and communicate with whoever I wished."

"You haven't come back to California. You haven't been at work. From what I've heard you've only given minimal instruction to your team. It's not like you."

"Well. You'll have to forgive me. I've never been kidnapped before. Neither have I been engaged to be married to two different men in the space of a few weeks. Strangers, at that."

"I meant to speak to you about this," he said.

"You meant to speak to me about it?"

"It was never intended to be a surprise. But I lost my nerve when it came to speaking to you after I struck the deal."

"I can't imagine why. Were you afraid that I would be angry that you sold me like I was a prized heifer?"

"I figured that if I could position it the right way, you would see why it was a good thing. Being a businesswoman is one thing, Violet, but a princess? A queen?"

"Well, I'm not going to be Queen now. I got knocked down to the spare, rather than the heir."

"What happened?"

Her father sounded genuinely distressed by that. "Do you really care?"

"It would've been better for you to marry Matteo. He is the King."

"No," she said, "it wouldn't be better for me to marry Matteo, because I don't have any feelings for him."

"Are you telling me you have feelings for… The other one?"

"Why do you care? You let him take me. You let me be kidnapped and held for reasons of marriage without explaining to me why. Without… Dad, I thought that I was worth more to you than just another card to be dealt from your businessman hand. You would never have done this to Maximus."

"Well, quite apart from the fact that neither of them would have wanted to marry Maximus…"

"Why not Minerva?"

"It was clear to me from the beginning that Minerva would not have made a good princess. But you…"

"I went on to build my own business. To build my own fortune. You didn't know that I would do that when you promised me to him at sixteen. And in the last decade you didn't have the courage to speak to me even one time about it."

"It won't impact your ability to run your business. I mean, certainly you'll have to farm out some of the day-to-day, but you're mostly a figurehead anyway."

"I'm not," she said. "I brainstorm most of the new products. I'm in charge of implementation. I'm not just a figurehead." Her stomach sank. "But that's what you think, isn't it? You think that I've only accomplished any of this because of my connection with you."

It hit her then that her father genuinely thought he had been giving her a gift on some level. That there was nothing of substance that she had accomplished on her own, and nothing that she could.

And he couldn't even see that. It didn't even feel like a lack of love to him. And maybe it wasn't.

It was a deeply rooted way that he seemed to see his girls versus the way he saw his son. Perhaps the way he saw women versus the way he saw men.

"It was a good thing that you did," she said, "when you took Dante in from the streets of Rome. You thought he was smart. You sent him to school. If he had been a woman, would you have just tried to make a marriage for him?"

"I know what you're thinking," her father said. "That I don't think you're smart. I do. I think you're brilliant, Violet. And I think you're wonderful with people. Women have a different sort of power in this world. I don't see the harm in acknowledging that. I don't see the harm in allowing you to use that in a way that is easier. You can try to compete with men in the business world, but you'll always be at a disadvantage."

"I want to be very clear," Violet said. "I am choosing this. Not for you. Your views are not only antiquated, they're morally wrong. That you see me as secondary to you, as incapable, is one of the most hurtful things I've ever had to face."

"I'm protecting you. No matter what happens with commerce, you'll always be a princess once you marry…"

"Javier. I want you to know that I'm choosing to marry him. Because I care about him. I'm not afraid of losing everything, Dad. Not the way that you are."

"That's because you don't know what it's like to have nothing," her father said. "I do. I didn't have anything when I started out. And I built my empire from nothing. You built yours off mine. Easy enough for you to say that you're not afraid to lose it."

"Maybe so," she said. "And I've always felt that, you know. That I built this off something that you started. And I suppose you could say that my marriage here is built off something that you started. But I'm the one that's choosing this. I'm the one that's choosing to make all that I can from it."

"Violet, I know that you're not happy with me about this, but clearly it worked out for the best."

She thought of last night. Of the passion that had erupted between her and Javier. Of the way that she felt for him.

It didn't feel like the best. It felt necessary. It felt real and raw and closer to who she was than anything else ever had. But it wasn't easy. And it wouldn't be. Ever. Because Javier wasn't easy. And she wouldn't want him to be, not really.

She wished that he might love her.

The strength of their connection was so powerful she had to believe... He was wounded. She knew that. He was scarred by his past.

He would fight against his feelings.

But he had accepted the marriage. He wanted them to choose each other, own each other.

She was certain of nothing, but she trusted that commitment.

She had to hope that someday it could become more.

"It didn't work out for the best because of you," Violet said. "You can't take credit for what I felt. And believe me, the relationship I have with Javier I built."

She hung up the phone then.

She didn't know what she was going to do about her relationship with her father going forward. Though living half a world away was certainly helpful.

The kind of distance required for her to get her head on straight. That was for sure.

And now she had to clear her mind. Because tonight there was going to be a dinner with foreign dignitaries. And Javier had told her that in light of the fact he had no people skills, she was going to have to do the heavy lifting for him.

Conviction burned in her chest.

He needed her to be his other half.

And so she would be.

She would choose to be.

Perhaps if she went first, if she forged that path with love, he would be able to find his way into loving her back.

* * *

An impromptu dinner with foreign dignitaries was not Javier's idea of fun. But then, few things were his idea of fun. And if he had his way, he would simply walk out of the dining room and take Violet straight back to bed. But tonight was not about having his way. Unfortunately.

She looked radiant. She had sent one of the members of the palace staff to town and instructed them to return with a golden gown from a local shop. And they had delivered. She was wearing something filmy and gauzy that clung to her curves while still looking sedate.

Her hair was slick, captured in a low bun, and her makeup was similar to how it had been the first day they'd met. More elaborate than anything she had done during their time together here at the palace.

He found he liked something about that as well.

That this was her public face. And that the soft, scrubbed-fresh woman with edible pink lips and wild dark hair was his and his alone.

She was standing there, talking to a woman from Nigeria, both of their hand gestures becoming animated, and he could only guess about what.

But Violet was passionate about her charities. About businesses that centered around women, and he imagined it had something to do with that.

"She is quite something," his brother said, moving to stand beside him.

"Yes," Javier agreed. "She is."

Not for the first time he thought that she would be better suited to the position of Queen than being married to him.

"Come," Matteo said. "Let us speak for a moment."

"Are you going to have me arrested and executed?" Javier asked as they walked out of the dining room and onto the balcony that overlooked the back garden.

"No," Matteo said. "Had I done that, I would have made a much larger spectacle."

"Good to know."

"I wanted to thank you for following through with the marriage."

"You don't have to thank me."

"I can tell that you have feelings for her."

Javier gritted his teeth. "She's beautiful."

"Yes," Matteo agreed. "She is. But many women are beautiful."

Not like Violet. "Certainly."

"Without you, I never could have done this," Matteo said. "All the years of it. Making sure that the damage that our father was intent on inflicting on the country was not as severe as it might have been. You have been loyal to me. Even in this."

Loyalty? Was that what he called this? He had been a fox curled around a hen. Waiting, just waiting for her to be left alone. Vulnerable and beautiful and his to devour.

It had taken nothing for him to abandon his promise. His honor.

To prove that he was morally corrupt in his soul. Incapable of doing right if he led with his heart.

"You consider it loyalty?" Javier chuckled. "I slept with your fiancée."

"It does not matter which of us marries her. Only that it's done. I told you that. And I meant it."

"I didn't know it at the time."

"I brought you out here to say that you must not think our bond is damaged by this. And it must not become damaged by this. I don't want your woman."

"I didn't think you did."

"I would ensure that you do not labor under the impression that I might. Which I feel could drive a wedge between us. As I can see that you are… Distracted by her."

"Now we come down to the real truth of it," Javier said. "Do you have concerns about what you consider to be my state of distraction?"

"Not too many. But you must remember that we have a mission here. A goal."

"I am very conscious of it. In service of that goal, she might have been a better queen than anyone else you could choose."

"She will do well in her position as your wife. As for me… I will keep looking."

"You will never be him," Javier said, looking at his brother's profile. "Don't ever doubt that."

"I doubt it often," Matteo said. "But isn't that what we must do? Question ourselves at every turn. I often wonder how I can ever be truly confident in anything I believe in. Because once I believed in him wholeheartedly. Once I thought that he had the nation's best interests at heart. Once I thought our father was the hero. And it turned out that he was only the villain."

Matteo gave voice to every demon that had ever lurked inside of Javier. When you had believed so wrongly, how could you ever trust that what you believed now was correct?

"We have to remember. An allegiance to honor before all else. Because if you can memorize a code, then you can know with your head what is right. Hearts lie."

Javier nodded slowly. "Yes. You know I believe that as well as you do."

"Good."

He turned around and looked through the window, saw Violet now standing in the center of a group talking and laughing.

"It's made easier by the fact that I have no feelings." He shot his brother a forced grin.

"Good."

Matteo turned and walked back into the party, leaving Javier standing there looking inside. Whether he had meant to or not, his brother had reminded him of what truly mattered. Not the heat that existed between himself and Violet. But progressing their country. Righting the wrongs of their father.

Javier had his own debt to pay his country. He had, under the orders of his father, used the military against its people. Had arrested innocent men who had spent time in prison, away from their families.

Who he knew his father had tortured.

He had been a weapon in the hands of the wrong man, with the wrong view on the world.

He was dangerous, and he couldn't afford to forget it.

Nor could he afford to do any more than atone for all that he'd been.

Nothing, nothing at all, must distract him from that mission.

Not even his fiancée.

"Someone else can go with me."

Violet was becoming irritated by the stormy countenance of her fiancé. He was driving the car carrying them down to town, wearing a white shirt and dark pants, the sleeves pushed up past his forearms. His black hair was disheveled. Possibly because earlier today they had begun kissing in his office, and she had ended up on his lap, riding the ridge of his arousal, gasping with pleasure until she realized that she was going to be late for her appointment at the bridal store in town.

"No," he said.

"You're not allowed to see the wedding dress that I choose anyway."

"It doesn't matter. I will wait outside."

"You're ridiculous," she said. "If you're going to go wedding dress shopping with me, you have to at least look a little bit like you don't want to die."

A mischievous thought entered her brain, and she set her fingers on his thigh, then let them drift over to an even harder part of him. "Are you frustrated because we didn't get to finish?"

"Obviously I would rather continue with that."

His tone was so exasperated and dry that she couldn't help but laugh.

"If it doesn't impact your driving…" She brushed her fingertips over him.

"It does," he said.

She felt even more gratified by the admission that she affected him than she could have anticipated. She let that carry her the rest of the way down the mountain and into town. It was important to her that she get a dress from a local designer. It was part of an initiative that she was working on with King Matteo's assistant.

Livia was a lovely young woman, with large, serious eyes and a surprisingly dry sense of humor. She was extremely organized and efficient, and Violet could see that Matteo took her for granted in the extreme.

But between the two of them they had begun to figure out ways to naturally raise the profile of the country, coinciding with her marriage to Javier.

Acquiring everything from Monte Blanco that they would need for the wedding was part of that.

When Violet and Javier pulled up to the shop, he parked and got out, leaning against the car.

She made her way toward the shop and looked back

at him. He was a dashing figure. And she wanted to take his picture.

"I'm putting you on the internet."

His expression went hard, but he didn't say anything. And she snapped the shot, him with his arms crossed over his broad chest, a sharp contrast against the sleek black car and the quaint cobbled streets and stone buildings behind him.

And he was beautiful.

"Thank you." She smiled and then went into the shop.

Immediately she was swept into a current of movement. She was given champagne and several beautiful dresses. It would be difficult to choose. But the dress that she decided on was simple, with floating sheer cape sleeves and a skirt that floated around her legs as she walked.

She took a photo of a detail of the dress on a hanger and took all the information for the bridal store.

Because when all this was over, anyone with a big wedding coming up this year would want a gown from this shop, from this designer.

When she reappeared, Javier was still standing where she had left him. Looking like a particularly sexy statue.

"All right. Now you have to come with me for the rest of this."

They went through the rest of the city finding items for the wedding. They created a crowd wherever they went. People were in awe to see Javier walking around with the citizens like a regular person. Not that anything about him could be called regular.

"They love you," she said as they walked into a flower shop.

He looked improbable standing next to displays of baby's breath, hyacinth and other similarly soft and pastel-colored things.

"They shouldn't," he said.

"Why not?"

"Nobody should love a person in a position of power. They should demand respect of him."

"You have some very hard opinions," she said, reaching out and brushing her fingertips over the baby's breath.

"I have to have hard opinions."

He touched the edge of one of the hyacinth blossoms and she snapped a quick picture. She enjoyed the sight of his masculine hand against that femininity. It made her think of a hot evening spent with him. It made her think of sex. Of the way he touched her between her legs.

As if he were thinking the exact same thing, he looked at her, their eyes clashing. And she felt the impact of it low in her stomach.

"I'm definitely feeling a bit of frustration over having not gotten to finish what we started earlier," he murmured.

"Me too," she whispered. "But we are out doing our duty. And isn't that the entire point of this marriage?"

The question felt like it was balanced on the edge of a knife. And her right along with it.

"It is," he said, taking his hand away from the flower.

"Right. Well. I think I found the flowers that I want."

She spoke to the shop owner, placing her order. And then the two of them carried on.

"I think we ought to have ice cream for the wedding," she said, standing outside the store. She was searching for something. For that connection with him that they'd had earlier. That they'd had back when it was forbidden.

"I don't want any," he said.

"I… Well. I mean, we can order some for the wedding."

"I think you can handle that on your own," he said.

Her heart faltered for a beat. It felt too close to a metaphor for all that they were right now. She could also love him alone. She was doing it. But it hurt, and she didn't know if she was ever going to be able to close this gap between them.

"Of course," she responded. "I… I'll go and order it."

She did. Then she ordered an ice-cream cone for herself and ignored the pain in her chest. She ignored it all the way through the rest of the shopping, and when they arrived back at the palace and he did not continue where they had left off in his office.

And she tried not to wonder if she had chosen wrong.

She had to cling to the story.

Because eventually the beast would be transformed by love.

The problem was that her beast seemed particularly resistant to it.

And she wasn't entirely sure she understood why.

CHAPTER TWELVE

THE DAY OF the wedding dawned bright and clear. Violet was determined to be optimistic.

It has been a difficult few days. Javier's moods had been unpredictable. Some days he had been attentive, and others, she hadn't seen him at all.

He hadn't made love to her since the day he had given her the jewels.

They hadn't even come close since the day in his office, where they had been thwarted by her schedule. Something she bitterly resented now.

This distance made her feel brittle. Made her feelings hard and spiky, cutting her like glass each time her heart beat.

What would it mean to be with him like this, if it were this way forever?

When she'd imagined marriage to him, she'd imagined more nights like the ones they'd shared in bed together. With passion ruling, not duty.

But if their marriage would be like this...

She didn't know if she'd survive it.

She had bought a beautiful dress, a beautiful dress to be the most suitable bride she could be. What else could she do?

She knew that she couldn't wear the cuffs the way that

she had done the day he had given them to her. But she did put two of them on one wrist and attached the gold chain, wrapping it artfully between the cuffs to make it look like an edgy piece of jewelry, rather than an intentional statement of bondage.

The day was made better and easier by the fact that her family was present. Minerva would be Violet's only bridesmaid.

Minerva looked radiant and beautiful in a green dress that skimmed over the baby bump she was currently sporting. She and Dante had taken to parenthood with zeal. They had been instant parents, given that it was a vulnerable baby that had brought the two of them together. They had adopted her shortly after they'd married, and then had their second child quickly after.

This third one had only waited a year.

"You look beautiful," Minerva said, smiling broadly.

"So do you," Violet said.

Falling in love with Dante looked good on her younger sister. Violet would have never matched her sister with her brother's brooding friend. She would have thought that somebody with such an intense personality would crush her sister's more sunny nature. But that wasn't true at all. If anything, Minerva was even sunnier, and Dante had lost some of the darkness that had always hung over him.

He had maintained his intensity; that was for sure.

Of course, when he held their children protectively, when he looked at Minerva like he would kill an entire army to protect her, Violet could certainly see the appeal.

Really, what could she say? She had fallen in love with a beast of a man who was as unknowable as he was feral. She could no longer say that the appeal of an intense partner was lost on her.

"You really are happy to marry him?" Minerva asked gently.

"Yes. It's complicated, but I think you understand how that can be."

Minerva laughed. "Definitely."

"How did you manage it? Loving him, knowing he might never love you back?"

The corners of Minerva's mouth tipped down. "Well. Mostly I managed it by asking myself if I would be any happier without him. The answer was no. I really wouldn't have been any happier without him. And the time I did spend without Dante was so... It was so difficult. I loved him so much, and I had to wait for him to realize that what he felt for me was love. He couldn't recognize it right away because... He didn't know what it felt like. More than that, he was terrified of it. And after everything he had been through, I could hardly blame him."

"Javier is like that," Violet said softly. "He's so fierce. A warrior at heart. And he believes that he isn't good. But that he has honor, and that's enough. He doesn't seem to realize that the reason honor matters to him is that he is good. And I think he's afraid to feel anything for me."

"Have you said that to him?"

Violet shook her head. "No. I don't want him to... I don't want him to reject me." It was one thing to be uncertain. In uncertainty, hope still blossomed inside her, fragile and small though it was.

But if she did say the words... If he rejected her definitively... Well, then she would not even have hope left.

"I understand that. But you know, it might be something he needs to hear. Because until he hears it, he's not going to know. Because he won't recognize it."

"I'm thankful for you," Violet said, wrapping her arm

around her sister's shoulder. "I don't know very many other people who would understand this."

"My love was definitely a hard one," she said. "But I don't think it was wrong to fight for it. I feel like sometimes people think… If it doesn't just come together it isn't worth it. But the kind of love I have with Dante… There's nothing else like it. There's no one else for me. He was wounded. He needed time to heal. And it was worth it."

Minerva put her hand on her rounded stomach and smiled. "It was so worth it."

Violet smiled, determination filling her. This would be worth it too.

The love that she felt for him was so intense, it had to be.

It had to be enough.

Javier waited at the head of the aisle. The church was filled with people. Some who were from Violet's world, and many from his. Though he realized he didn't actually know any of the people in attendance.

He was disconnected from this. From the social part of his job. A figurehead.

It had been interesting going out into town with her. She drew people to them like a bright, warm flame drawing in moths. He had never experienced such a thing, because he was the sort of man who typically kept people at a distance simply by standing there.

But not Violet.

Everyone seemed to want to be around her. To be near her. He could understand why she had managed to build an empire over the internet. With people who wanted to look like her, be like her. People who wanted to experience a slice of what she was.

She was compelling.

And after today she would be his.

He gritted his teeth, curling his hands into fists and waiting.

She would come.

And the momentary hitch of doubt that he had was assuaged by the appearance of her sister, who walked down the aisle with a small bouquet of flowers.

He had met her sister for the first time this morning. The other woman had seemed cautious around him, and a bit wary. Her husband had been more menacing. As had her brother.

Her father had seemed shamefaced, and Javier felt that was deserved. Her mother had simply seemed excited to be in a palace.

Javier had no concept of a family like this. Large and together, even though they disagreed on things, and it was clear that they did.

Though, he imagined that most families that appeared dysfunctional disagreed on small things, and not whether it was appropriate that one of them sold another into marriage. But at this point, what was done was done.

And she would be here.

She wanted him.

And she seemed committed to serving her role for the country.

That was her primary motivation. She had made that clear in the flower shop.

And it was a good thing. Because he could not afford distractions. He could not afford to start thinking in terms of emotion.

The music changed and he turned his focus again to the doorway. Watching with great attention.

And then, there she was.

The sight of her stole his breath.

She was…

She looked like she did for him. Only for him. Her dark hair was long and loose, the veil that she had soft and flowing down her back. She looked almost as if she didn't have makeup on at all. Rather, she glowed. Her lips looked shiny and soft, her cheeks catching the light. It was magic. And so was she.

He had held himself back these weeks, because it had felt like something he should do until it was done. But now, here she was. Now she was his.

There would be no turning back.

When she reached the head of the aisle, she took his hand. And he pulled her to him. It was all he could do not to claim her mouth then and there. Not to make a spectacle of them both in front of the congregation.

And that was when he noticed the bracelets.

She had them both on one wrist. But the chain was there as well.

And when she looked into his eyes, he felt the impact of it all the way down to his gut.

She nodded slowly.

An affirmation.

She was choosing to give herself to him. And she was saying that she understood. The bond, the loyalty that traditionally existed here in this country between a royal husband and wife.

But he did not know where ownership fit into that. He did not know where duty and responsibility fit in.

He had told her about it. Mostly because he had wanted to see her wear those for him. Those rubies and nothing more. But also he had… He hadn't understood. But suddenly, here, with those bracelets on her wrist, in a church, where they were about to make vows… Where she had brought the carnal into the sacred and blended them together, made them one, he could not understand how this bond could remain just another promise he decided to keep.

Because as she spoke her vows, low and grave in a voice that only he could hear, he felt them imprint beneath his skin. Down to his soul. And when he spoke his in return, they were like that gold chain on her wrist. But they wrapped around them both, binding them in a way that he had not anticipated.

He had thought he knew what this meant.

Because that day he had discovered the sorts of treachery his father protected. That day that he had realized that the orders he had taken for years had been in service of an insidious plan, and nothing that protected or bettered his people, he had sworn that he would uphold a set of principles. That he would not be led by his heart.

That he would not be led by anything other than a code of honor.

But now he had made vows to another person, and not an ideal.

When it came time to kiss her, it took all of his self-control not to claim her utterly and completely right there in front of the roomful of people. He touched her face, and he exercised restraint he did not feel, kissing her slowly but firmly, making sure that she knew it was a promise of more. A promise for later.

He had been restrained these past weeks.

But it was over now.

The vows were made. His course was set.

There was no turning back. Not now.

Whatever would become of this. Of them… It was too late.

You chose this.

He gritted his teeth against the truth of it.

It had been easy to say that he had done it for Matteo.

That he was doing it to atone for the sin of taking her in the first place. But the fact of the matter was he was far too selfish to turn away from her.

The idea of giving her to another man had been anathema to him. An impossibility. Had his brother insisted on marrying her, he would have...

He would have betrayed him. He would have stolen her. Secreted her out of the country. Abandoned his post. Abandoned all that they had built.

The truth of that roared in his blood.

Like the beast that he was.

But there was nothing to be done about that now. She was his, so it didn't matter. She was his, so it couldn't matter.

He pushed it all away as he continued to kiss her, and when he was through, the congregation was clapping, and they were introduced.

But he didn't hear any of it.

There was nothing.

Nothing but the pounding of his blood in his veins, the demand that burned through his body like molten lava.

He would endure the reception for as long as he had to. For as long as he had to pretend to care about flowers and ice cream and all manner of things that were only stand-ins for what he had truly wanted all along.

He didn't care to touch the petals of an alarmingly soft purple flower. He wanted Violet. Her skin beneath his hands. He didn't wish to lick an ice-cream cone. He wished to lick her.

And he would play the game if he had to, but that was all it was to him. A game. A game until he could get to her. Because that was all that mattered.

She talked to her family, and he knew that he could not rush her away from them. She was speaking, even to her father, and though there was cautiousness between them, he wondered if she might make amends with him. Javier didn't know how.

He asked her that very question once they got back to their room. In spite of the fact that his blood roared with desire, he had to know.

"I don't know if it will ever be the same as it was," she said. "But it was never easy. It was never perfect. I can always see those sorts of tendencies in him. Those beliefs."

"But you will forgive him."

"Yes. I think sometimes… If you value your relationship with another person enough, you have to be willing to accept that they are flawed. I don't know that I'll ever be able to make my father see the world, or me, the way that I want him to. I can keep showing him, though. And in the meantime I can live my life. But cutting him out of it completely wouldn't fix the wound. It wouldn't heal anything."

"It might teach him a lesson," Javier said.

"I think having to watch me join with you might have begun to teach him a lesson," she said.

"What does that mean?" he growled.

"Only that you are a bit more feral and frightening than I think he imagined my royal husband might be."

"The beast, remember?"

"Yes. I think… We are husband and wife now. And I would like to know… Why?"

"Why what?"

"Why did you become the beast? The sins of your father. We talked about that. But it's deeper than that. I know it is. Because you changed when you found that little girl…"

"What do you think I was doing all those years before? I was seeing to his orders. Arresting men when he demanded that I arrest them. And women. Separating families as he commanded. And he would tell me it was for a reason. Because they were traitors. Because it was upholding the health of the country. But I realize now they were freedom fighters. People who wanted to escape his oppressive regime, and it was oppressive. That innocent people were put behind bars, tried and... I helped. I upheld his rule of law, and I regret it."

"You didn't know."

"Maybe not. But when you have believed so wholeheartedly in a lie, you can never trust yourself again. You can never trust in the clarity of your own judgment because you have been so fooled. Because you were a villain and all the while imagined yourself a hero. And you will never, ever be able to walk through life without wondering which side you're on again. You will never be able to take it for granted."

"It takes such courage to admit that. You are brave. And I can see that you'll never take the easy way. You can trust yourself."

He shook his head. "No. I can't. I love my father and I allowed those feelings to blind myself to his faults."

"Well. So did I with mine."

"Your father is not a maniacal dictator. As challenging as he might be."

"No. I suppose not." She put her hand on his face, and he closed his eyes, relishing the feel of her delicate fingers against him. "You saved that girl, Javier."

"But so many more I did not save. So many I harmed myself. Arrested. Sent to a prison run by my father, where they were undoubtedly tortured. There is no salvation for such sins. My hands will not wash clean. But I can use them to serve."

"I'm sorry, but I know you, Javier. You're not a monster."

"I must assume that I am," he said, moving away. "The better to protect the world from any harm that I might do."

"I don't think you are," she said.

"This is not a fairy tale. The things that I have done cannot be undone. I can only move forward trying to do right now that I understand. Now that I have the power. It is not about being transformed by magic. Such a thing is not possible."

She moved to him and she bracketed his face with her hands.

He had no chance to respond to that, because she kissed his mouth, and he was dragged into the swirling undertow of desire by the softness of her lips, the slow, sweet sweep of her tongue against his. She was inexperienced, his beautiful goddess, but she had a sort of witchcraft about her that ensnared him and entranced him.

That made him fall utterly and completely under her spell.

How could the magic fail here? Because of him. That had to be it.

She was made entirely of magic. Glorious soft skin and otherworldly beauty wrapped around galaxies of light. She was something other than beauty. Something more.

Something that made his heart beat new and made him want to defy a lifetime of commitment to honor.

He had devoted himself to believing only in a code. A list of principles that helped him determine what was right and wrong because he knew full well that his own blood, his own heart could lead him in the direction of that which would destroy him and all those around him.

His belief in that had been unwavering.

When he looked at her, his Violet, his wife, he knew that he could believe entirely in her. In her magic. In the way her soft mouth rained kisses down over his skin, in the way her delicate fingertips brushed over his body. The way that she undid the buttons on his shirt and tackled the buckle on his belt. Yes. He could believe in that.

He could drop to his knees and pledge his loyalty to her and her alone, seal his utter and total devotion by losing himself in her womanly flavor. By drowning in the desire that rose up between them like a wave, threatening to decimate everything that he had built.

And he didn't care.

Just like he hadn't cared that first time they had kissed in the ballroom those weeks ago, when she had belonged to another man and his loyalty should have stood the test of time but crumbled beneath all that she was.

She was magic. And she was deadly.

And now, just now, he did not have the strength to deny her. To deny them.

And so, why not surrender? Why not drown in it? She was his, after all. He had gone down this path weeks ago, and it was too late to turn back. He had made her his.

His.

And tonight he would make that matter. He would revel in it.

He stole the power of the kiss from her, taking control, growling as he wrapped his arms around her and walked her back against the wall, pinning her there, devouring her, claiming her as his own.

He had spoken vows, but they were not enough; he needed to seal them with his body. He needed her to know.

He needed her to understand.

The way that she destroyed him. The way that he was broken inside. So that she would know. And he didn't know why he needed her to know, just like he didn't know why he had been in the library that night they had first made love. Why he had been looking through that same book that she was, trying to read the same story and find some meaning in it.

To try to see through her eyes the way that she might see him.

And it shouldn't matter. It never should have. Because she had been his brother's and he had been toying with betrayal even then.

But she's yours now.

Yes, she was his. For better or worse.

He feared very much it might be worse. Because he hurt people. It felt like a natural part of what he was. That monster.

But perhaps if it was only this, if it was only lust, he could control it.

He wrenched that beautiful dress off her body. She was an Angel in it, far too pure for him, and it nearly hurt to look at her. Burned his hands to pull the filmy fabric away from her. But it left her standing there in white, angelic underthings. Garments that spoke of purity, and he knew that he was unequal to the task of touching them. Just as he had been unworthy of touching her in the first place.

But he had.

And he would.

He tore them away from her body, leaving her naked before him. Except for those jewels. The necklace glittering at the base of her throat, the cuffs heavy on her wrist, the chain wound around them. And the ring, his ring, glittering on her finger, telling the world that she belonged to him.

He had never had her in a bed.

He hadn't realized that until this moment. And tonight he would have her in his bed. Their bed.

She would not have her own room, not after this.

It was often customary for royal couples to keep their own spaces, but they would not.

She would be here. Under the covers, in his bed with him. Her naked body wrapped around his. Yes. That was what he required. It was what he would demand.

He picked her up and carried her there, set her down at the center of the mattress and looked at her. He leaned over, spreading her hair out around her like a dark halo, and then he stood, looking at the beautiful picture that she made. Her soft, bare skin pale against the deep crimson red of the quilt. She took a sharp breath, her breasts rising with the motion, her nipples beading.

"Such a lovely picture you make, My Princess."

"I didn't think my official title was Princess."

"It doesn't matter. You are *my* princess. *Mine.*"

He bent down, cupping her breast with his hand, letting it fill his palm.

She was soft, so delicate and exquisite, and it amazed him that something half so fragile could put such a deep crack in the foundation of what he was. But she had.

He lowered his head and took one perfect, puckered nipple between his lips and sucked all her glory into his mouth. She arched beneath him, crying out in soft, sweet pleasure, and it spurred him on. He growled, lavishing her with attention, licking and sucking, stroking her between her thighs.

His wife. His beautiful, perfect wife, who threatened to destroy all that he was.

How had he ever thought that it was possible to maintain superior connections to this country. To duty and honor when the marriage bed presented shackles that could not be seen with the human eye. Perhaps that was why the cuffs existed. Not to create a sense that they were bound to each other, but to turn them physical. All the better to remove them when one chose to.

Because the ties that existed in his heart he could not see, he could not touch and he did not know how to unleash.

It was supernatural in a way that he would have said he did not believe in.

It was strong in a way he would have told anyone such a thing could not be.

And he was linked to her in a way he would have said he could not be to another human being.

Because he had given those things away so long ago. Because he had pledged loyalty to Matteo and not love. Because he had pledged his blood to Monte Blanco, but not love.

And what he wanted to give to Violet was deeper, and he was afraid that she was right. That magic had always only ever been love, and that it could turn and twist into something dark and evil, just like magic.

All that magic that she was.

All that... He did not wish to give the word a place, not even in his mind.

And so he covered his thoughts with a blanket of pleasure, wrapping them both in the dark velvet of his desire, lapping his way down her body, her stomach, down to that sweet place between her legs. He buried himself there. Lost himself in giving her pleasure.

Got drunk on it.

Because there was nothing to do now but revel in it. Afterward... Afterward there would be time for reckonings and for fixing all of this. But not now.

Now was the time to embrace it.

The only time.

Here in the bedroom.

And maybe that was what the cuffs were for.

To create a space where the world didn't matter. Where there could be an escape.

And maybe for other men that would have worked. But not for him.

Because he didn't know how to create space.

He only knew how to be all or nothing.

How to be an agent of his father, or a war machine acting against him.

How to be a man, vulnerable and useless. Or how to be a beast.

But he had the freedom to be that beast with her. And somehow, with that freedom he became both. Wholly a man and wholly an animal in her arms, and she seemed to accept him no matter what. She shouldn't.

She should push him away. She always should have pushed him away.

But she had gone with him, from the beginning.

She had chosen to be with him.

And when he rose up and positioned himself between her thighs, when he thrust into her body, and when her beautiful eyes opened, connected with his, he felt a shudder of something crack through his entire body like a bolt of lightning.

She lifted her head, pressed her soft mouth to his, and he felt words vibrating against his lips. He couldn't understand them. Couldn't do anything but feel them, as the sweet, tight heat of her body closed around his.

She clung to his shoulders as he drove them both to the pinnacle of pleasure. And when she released, he went with her. Pleasure pounding through him like a relentless rain.

And then, he heard her speaking again, her lips moving against the side of his neck, and this time, the words crystallized in his mind.

The words that he had been trying, trying and failing, not to hear. Not to understand.

"I love you," she whispered. Her lips moved against his

skin, tattooing the words there, making it impossible for him not to feel them. He was branded with them.

"I love you. I love you."

"No," he said, the denial bursting forth from him.

He moved away from her, pushing his hands through his hair. Panic clawed at him and he couldn't say why. He was not a man who panicked. Ever. He was not a man acquainted with fear. Because what did he care for his own life? The only thing he feared was the darkness in himself, and maybe that was the problem now. Maybe it called to the weakness that he had inside of his chest.

The desire to sink into her. To drop to his knees and pledge loyalty to her no matter what.

Even if she asked him to mobilize against his brother. Against his people.

And it didn't matter that she wouldn't.

What mattered was losing the anchor that kept him from harming those around him.

What mattered was losing the only moral compass he knew how to read.

What mattered was Monte Blanco and it was becoming impossible for him to hold on to that.

"I'm sorry," she said. "You don't get to tell me that I don't love you."

"I cannot," he said.

"Why not?"

"Haven't you been listening? Haven't you heard anything that I've told you? Love is the enemy. You're right. Magic. And magic can be dark as easily as it can work for good."

"So why can't you trust that between us it will be good?"

"Because I cannot trust myself," he said.

She put her hand on his chest and he wrapped his fingers around her wrist and ripped it away. She stared at him, the hurt in her eyes far too intense to bear.

Because he did not have the freedom to be himself with her. It was far too dangerous. And he had been lying. Evidence of his own weakness if it ever existed.

That he had wanted to pretend that what he knew to be true wasn't. That he wanted to give himself freedom when he knew that he could not afford it. This woman was a gift that some men could have. But not him.

Yet he had been weak, far too weak from the beginning to turn away from her. He'd been given every chance. Every roadblock in his personal arsenal had been set up. She had been intended for his brother, and if that could not keep him away from her, then nothing could.

She was dangerous. Deadly.

A threat to his own personal code in ways that he should have seen from the beginning.

Because she had been eroding the foundation that he had built from the beginning. Just a touch. A kiss. And then he had stormed into his brother's office to tell him that Matteo could not marry her. To tell him that he could not see through the plan that he had to make their country better, because Javier had wanted Violet for himself. He had never wanted to let her go. He would have gone after her. That much he knew.

But his brother had given him options that he had liked, and so he had taken them. Made it easy to keep on going down that slippery slope.

So he had done.

And now... Now he was sitting here in the consequences of it. She loved him. He could not give her that love in return.

He had broken not only his own sacred vows, but in the end he would break her too. And that was unacceptable.

But he had married her. And that was done. Consummated. Presented before the entire world.

But they did not have to live together as man and wife. He could give her the freedom that she had wanted. But he could not give her this.

"Love is not to be," he said. "Not for me."

"I know that you don't trust it," she said. "And I understand why. But you have to understand that what I feel for you has nothing to do with the way you were manipulated into caring for your father."

"Was I manipulated? Or did I simply want to accept the easiest thing. The easiest reality."

"Do you think that I'm going to trick you into doing something wrong? Do you think that I'm secretly here to destroy your country?"

"No," he growled. "No," he said again. "It's not that. It has nothing to do with that. But a man cannot serve two masters. And my master must be my people. It must be my country. It must be to duty, and to honor. That is where I must pledge my allegiance, and I cannot be split between a wife and a nation."

"Then make me part of your people. Make me one of those that you have a responsibility to. Surely that can't be so difficult."

Except that he knew it would destroy her. It was not what she wanted. It was not what she deserved. And without it she truly would be in captivity for all of his life. And he would be her jailer. And so he was trapped. Between violating all that he needed to be for his country and destroying the life of the woman who had married him.

He reached over to her and unclasped the first bracelet from her wrist. He unwound the chain that she had wrapped there, and then unclipped the second bracelet.

Her eyes filled with tears as she stared at him, but

he knew that it would be a kindness. It was a kindness whether she saw it that way or not.

"What are you doing?"

"You are not my prisoner," he said. "And I will not make you a prisoner."

"Now you say this? Now, after we've been married? After I told you that I love you? That's when you decide to give me freedom?"

"We must remain married," he said. "That much is obvious. My brother would take a dim view on there being a divorce so quickly. It would cause scandal. And... I do not wish to undo all that you have done for my country. But you may go back to California. To your life. There is no reason that you must stay here. You do not need to be under my thumb."

"What if I choose to stay?"

"What you choose is up to you. But that will not alter my behavior. That will not change the fact that this place is my priority. That it is where my duty lies."

"I love you," she said.

She got out of bed, standing there, naked and radiant in the center of the room. "I love you, and you can't make it so that I don't. I love you," she said, like a spell, like an incantation, like she was trying to cast it over him, like she was trying to change the very fabric of what he was. Destroy him, then remake him using those words to stitch him back together.

As if she might be able to use them to take the beast and turn him back into a man.

"And I cannot love," he said. "It is that simple."

"You can," she said. "You can. But you're not a beast to protect the world from you, you have to be a beast to protect yourself from the world. You're afraid, Javier. You're afraid of being hurt again, and I understand that."

Her words lashed against something inside of him that felt tender and bruised. And he hadn't thought that he had the capacity to feel such a thing.

"You don't know what you speak of," he said. "You are protected. Even the betrayal that your father meted out to you was not one that might put you in peril or threaten your comfort in any way. He sold you to a king. That you might be exalted. You have no idea what I am fighting against. You have no idea what real suffering is. I have seen it. I have caused it. And I have to guard against ever causing it again. Do not give me your quick and easy sound bites, Violet King. I am not one of your internet followers. I am not impressed by quick, condensed versions of truth that are easy to digest. I have seen human suffering on a level that you cannot possibly understand. And I am related to the cause of it. If my life must be devoted to the undoing of it so that those in the future can simply live, then it must be. But don't you ever accuse me of being afraid."

And for the first time he saw her crumple. For the first time, he saw her bravery falter, and he hated himself for being the cause of that. He had plucked the woman from her office some weeks ago and taken her off to a land that she had never even heard of, and she had remained strong. She had remained stoic. She had an answer back for everything he had said. But not now. He had finally taken that from her. He had finally destroyed some of what she was.

And there was no joy to be had in that.

It was confirmation. Of what he was.

That spark of light she had placed in him was now extinguished in her.

She had said he was not a monster, but he knew that he was.

That he would destroy her only more as the years wore on.

He hurt people.

He had caused pain under the rule of his father, and under the rule of his own heart, he would cause Violet pain as well.

"If you think that's what I meant, if you think that's who I am, then you haven't been paying attention at all. I thought that we knew each other. I thought that our souls recognized each other," she said, her voice breaking. "You saw me reading the book... And I knew that you would be reading it too. I knew it. You know the library was the first place that I looked for you that night we first made love. Because somehow I knew you would be looking at the same story I was, trying to see if you saw us in there."

"You misunderstand. I wasn't looking for answers because I already have them. I understand that this was significant to you. That this was a first for you. But I have lived life. I have already had all the revelations I will have. Perhaps you can think of me as a lesson learned."

"What an expensive lesson," she said, her tone full of venom. "Wedding vows seem a little bit extreme."

"As I told you, the wedding vows can remain."

"Why would I stay married to you? If you don't want to have a real marriage?"

He gritted his teeth, fought against the terror that clouded his chest at the idea of losing her. He liked much more the idea of being able to keep her while keeping her separate.

"Do what you must."

He gathered his clothes and began to dress.

"Where are you going?"

"Out."

"I would never have thought that you would transform

yourself into a basic sort of man. But that is very basic. Just out. No explanation."

"Because I don't owe you an explanation. Because you got the explanation that you were going to get already. That you thought there was more is your problem, not mine."

He gritted his teeth against the burning sensation in his chest and he walked out of the room, closing the door behind him.

Closing the door on them. On temptation.

Whatever she did now was her choice.

But he had done his duty, for honor.

Whatever she said, that was why.

He ignored the kick in his chest that told him otherwise.

He ignored everything.

Because that was the real gift of having transformed himself into a beast.

When he had done that, he had taken his feelings away as well.

So why did his chest hurt so much?

CHAPTER THIRTEEN

VIOLET WAS STUNNED. All she could do was sit there in the center of their marriage bed, alone. She had known that he would have an issue with her loving him. She had. But she hadn't known that he would do this.

Why now? Why had it come to this now?

All this time he could have set her free. He could have made this bargain with her.

And suddenly she felt very alone. Her whole family had been here for the wedding today, but she hadn't had enough time to speak to them. Would she have found strength from them?

She could call her sister. Her mother. Her father even.

She knew what Minerva would say, actually. Minerva would want her to do what made her happy. But Minerva would also say that sometimes difficult men needed you to believe in them until they could believe in themselves. Because that was what had happened with Dante.

But no one had helped Violet up until this point. This had been the most independent she had ever been. Yes, it was somewhat enforced by the entire situation, but it was still true. She had to stand on her own two feet since she had been brought here. It had been difficult.

Difficult to face the fact that her relationship with her family hadn't been what she thought. Difficult to be thrown in the deep end of independence, when she had been so surrounded by the people that she'd loved for so long. The people that she had depended on for her entire life.

But all of this had been about choice. A lesson in it.

Ironic that she'd had to be kidnapped and dragged across the world to really face the fact that she wasn't her own person. Not that what she had built wasn't hers to some extent.

But she had been propped up for so long by her father, and then was angry about the fact that he had been controlling things from behind the scenes when she had…

She had been fine with it as long as it had benefited her.

Allowing him to invest money when she had needed it.

Knowing that he was there as a safety net.

But nobody was a safety net for her in this. Because her heart was involved, her emotions. And there was no one who could fix it but her.

Her and Javier.

But he had broken it, because he was afraid. Whatever he said, he was afraid.

She understood what he thought. Understood why he felt the need to protect himself so fiercely.

There might not be real curses in this life, but there was pain that could feel like a curse. Betrayal that could make you feel changed.

And there might not be magic spells or incantations, but there was something even more powerful.

Love was the magic.

And she was going to have to figure out how to make it work.

She didn't have a spell. Didn't have anything to make the fairy tale literal.

But then, the beast wasn't on the outside. It was inside of him.

And it wasn't made of the sins of his father, wasn't made of tainted blood. It was made of fear.

And love couldn't exist alongside fear. Because they would always fight with one another. Love demanded bravery, and fear demanded that you hide.

He was hiding.

He was the strongest, bravest man she had ever known, but in the face of love, he was hiding.

If she could understand that.

Because he had just taken her heart and flayed it open. And she had already known that love could hurt, because the betrayal of her father had wounded her so badly, and she had to make the decision to forgive him in spite of that.

Was that what she had to do here? Forgive and love until he could do the same?

She didn't know.

She found herself wandering to the library, because it was where she had found him before. It was where she had found some of the answers she had been looking for. Maybe… Maybe she would find them again here.

Because she wanted to understand. Because she had so many questions.

Why had he done this now? Why had he turned away from her now? Told her she could live a wholly separate life from him, go back to California…

He didn't do it until he was sure that you loved him.

That truth sat there, like a rock in her chest. He hadn't done it until he was certain of her love.

He had not done it until part of him was certain that she would stay.

And so that meant she had to, she supposed. Even if it was the hardest thing she had ever faced in her entire life.

The idea of staying with a man who didn't love her.

She went straight to the back shelf, but she couldn't find it. The book with their story.

The book was gone.

And that, above all else, gave her hope.

"What are you doing down here?"

Javier looked up from the book and at his brother.

"Where else would I be?" He asked the question somewhat dryly, and yet to him, it made perfect sense that he was here. To him, it made all the sense in the world.

"Not Dad's favorite dungeon," Matteo said. "But still, definitely a logical choice for somebody who is punishing themselves."

"Is she still here?"

"Who?"

"My wife."

"As far as I know."

"Are you certain?"

"Honestly, I didn't consider the whereabouts of your woman to be my responsibility. I thought that was one of the perks of flopping her off on you. What has happened?"

"She's in love with me."

"Obviously," Matteo said.

"It's obvious to you?"

"Well. Not necessarily to me. But my mouse may have said something to the effect."

"Livia said something about it?"

"Only that she thought Violet seemed quite taken with you. And that it was probably a good thing she hadn't married me, all things considered."

"She's a fool."

"*Livia?* She's the least foolish woman I have ever known."

"No. Violet. She's a fool to love me. Anyone would be a fool to love either of us."

"It's true," Matteo said. "I don't disagree with you."

"So you understand that I told her I could not esteem her over the fate of the country."

"Is it a choice that must be made?"

"Yes. Because if the choice for Monte Blanco's well-being is not my ultimate motivation, then something else will replace it. And that makes me vulnerable."

"Vulnerable to what?"

He spread his arms wide. "To this," Javier said. "This. To being just like our father. A man with a favorite dungeon. A man who harms others."

"Is that what you think? That a mere distraction could turn you from the man that you are into the man that he was?"

"Haven't we always said that we must be careful to turn away from anything that might make us like him?"

"We must. I agree. But I suspect that you loving this woman will not bring it about. I think it is loving yourself above all else that opens you up to such concerns. Do you think that sounds right? Because our father never loved anybody. None of his corruption came from loving us so much. Or our mother, who we never even knew because she was dead before you ever took your first steps. No. Love did not cause what our father did."

"But I have to be vigilant…"

"Against what?"

"As we discussed, it would be far too easy to fall into another life. After all, wasn't it so easy to believe that our father was good because we thought we loved him?"

"What's the book?"

"Something that Violet was reading. A beauty and the beast story."

"What do you suppose you'll find in there?"

"An answer. Magic. I don't know. Some way to change myself, because I don't know how else I might. To be a man for her rather than a beast."

"Maybe you don't need to change it all. Doesn't the Princess in the story love him without changing?"

"But she deserves better. She deserves more."

"What did she ask for?"

"Nothing," he said, his voice rough.

"Then why not offer nothing but yourself?"

"Because that is something our father would do."

"No, our father would take the choice away from her. Which is what... Well, that's what I did, in the beginning, isn't it? Our father would do whatever he wanted regardless of what she asked for. So why don't you go back to her? And find out what it is she truly wants. Listen. Don't simply follow your own heart. That's what men like our father did. Consider another person. See where it gets you."

"Maybe to disaster. Maybe to hell."

"How does it feel where you are now?"

"Like *hell*," he responded. "Like I'm a foolish man staring at a fairy tale asking it for answers."

"Sounds to me like you don't have any further to fall. And I need you to be functional. So sort yourself out."

"Are you advocating for love and happy endings now?"

Matteo laughed, shaking his head. "Hell no. The opiate of the masses in my opinion. But if you wish to join the masses, Javier, then I won't stop you. And if it is what Violet wants, then all the better that she didn't marry me. Because I would never be able to give it to her."

"Are you such a hypocrite that you would advocate for me what you don't believe you can have for yourself?"

"Not a hypocrite. Just a king. A word of advice. Javier, you were not born to be the King so don't take on the re-

sponsibilities that I carry. Take on your own. You're a warrior. And you were born to be. That is your position in this
country. And the difference between you and our father
was always compassion. It was the sight of that little girl
being married off that changed you. That made you see.
It was always compassion that made you better. It was always caring. Because a man who is in and of himself a
weapon ought to have that sort of counterbalance, don't
you think? In my estimation, love will make you stronger
at what you do."

"And for kings?" Javier asked.

"A king should not be vulnerable." Matteo turned, then
paused for a moment. "But it might be the only thing that
keeps a beast from being dangerous. If you are so worried
about hurting others, perhaps you should think about that."

And with that, his brother left Javier there, sitting in
the bottom of the dungeon holding on to the book. And he
knew that he would find no answers there. None at all. No.
The only answers for who he was, who he might become,
who he needed to become, lay with Violet.

If only he could find the strength in himself.

But perhaps, until then, he could borrow strength from
Violet.

Suddenly the fairy tale made sense in a way that it had
not before. His fingertips burned, and he opened up to a
page with an illustration of the giant, hulking beast having his wounds tended by the delicate maiden.

Perhaps he was too focused on the transformation.

Perhaps he had not looked enough at what the story
was really about.

As she said, almost every culture had a version of this
tale. And in it, the beauty was seen by the reader to be the
weak one. Put up against a dangerous beast.

But he was the one who changed. He was the one who transformed, because of the power of her love.

In the end, it was the beauty who held all the power.

In the end, it was her love that made the difference.

And so, he would have to trust in her power. Trust that, like in the story, she was more than able to stand up to the challenge of loving him.

He was the one who had to find his strength.

She had already proven that she had more than enough for the two of them.

CHAPTER FOURTEEN

SHE HADN'T GONE back to California.

Her social media efforts had begun to create more tourism in Monte Blanco, and she was working with the tourism bureau and local business owners on strengthening the market. She was still involved in her own company, with her VP holding down the fort on the local level back in San Diego.

She had begun spending more time in the city. She had rented office space and had begun working in earnest on her project to bring work to Monte Blanco. Specifically for women. She was in talks to figure out manufacturing, something that she was arranging with Livia, and she had already hired a few women that she had met at a local shelter to work on data entry.

She was having to do some training, and she had hired people to do that as well.

And all of it was helping distract from the pain in her chest, though it didn't make it go away.

She was still living in the palace. It was just that it was so big it was easy to not see Javier at all. And he had allowed that to be the case. He hadn't come to her.

She wouldn't go to him. But she was there.

Because part of her was convinced, absolutely, that she needed to stay. That he needed to know she was choosing not to run. That he needed to know that she was choosing this life. That it was not a kidnapping, not anymore. It was just a marriage.

And she wasn't the one not participating in it. That was him. He was the one who was going to have to figure out exactly what he wanted and exactly how to proceed. She couldn't do it for him. And that, she supposed, was the most difficult lesson of all. That no matter how much she wanted to, she couldn't force a transformation if he didn't want it.

He had to accept her love.

And right now he didn't seem to be able to do that.

She looked around the small office space, up in the top of the small, cobbled building. Above the ice-cream shop. It was so very different from all that modern glass she had left behind in San Diego. But she wasn't sure she even remembered that woman. The one who wanted things sleek and bright. The one who had been so confident and set in her achievements.

She still felt accomplished. It wasn't that she didn't know that she had done impressive and difficult things. It was only that she had found something she cared about even more. She had been so focused for so long. And it hadn't allowed for her to want much else. That had been a protection. She could see now. Because caring this much about something else, about someone else, was extremely painful. But it had also pushed her to find a strength inside of herself that she hadn't known was there. And so for that she was somewhat grateful.

Grateful, if heartbroken.

Because no man would ever be Javier.

She knew that she would never find another man she wanted in the same way. That she would never feel this way for another man. Because she hadn't. Not for twenty-six years. She had had chance after chance to find another man, and she had never even been tempted. And she wouldn't be. Not like this. Not again. But that didn't mean she couldn't thrive. It was just that she would never fall in love again.

Tears pricked her eyes. She didn't want to fall in love again anyway. She just wanted to love him. And she wanted him to love her back. Even facing the fact that it was impossible now didn't make it seem real. Because she hoped... She just hoped.

She wanted to believe in the fairy tale. But she was afraid that the real world loomed far too large. That the damage inflicted on him by his father would be the ultimate winner.

And she didn't want to believe in a world like that. But she had to face the fact that it might be all she got.

She went downstairs, stopping in the ice-cream parlor and getting herself an ice-cream cone, trying not to cry when the flavor reminded her of Javier. The owners of the shop hadn't asked her any questions about why they hadn't seen Javier. Why it seemed that she was always alone, the Prince nowhere to be found after the two of them had been so inseparable at first.

Plus, she had a feeling she just looked heartbroken. She was trying her best to get on with things, but it was not easy at all. She was strong. But strength didn't mean not shedding tears. Strength didn't mean you didn't mourn lost love. Or in her case... Love that could have been if it weren't for a maniacal dictator who had taken the love of a young boy and used it so badly. Made him think that he was the monster, rather than his father.

When she went back out onto the street, she stopped. Because there, down one of the roads, she saw a silhouette that looked familiar. And she flashed back to that moment she had been standing in her office. But she had imagined then that he was dangerous. And now... Now the sight of him made her heart leap into her throat.

"Livia told me I might find you here," he said.

"Livia is a turncoat," Violet said.

"She works for my brother. Her loyalty is always going to lie there."

"Well. *Well*."

"I need to speak to you."

"Why?"

"I need to know... I looked for answers. I looked for answers that didn't have an enchantment or a spell. I don't know how to change."

"You don't know?"

"No," he said. His voice rough.

Her heart went tight, and she looked at his sculpted, haunted face. "Javier, it was never about the right spell. In all the stories, in all the lands, in all the world. It was never magic that changed the beast. It was love."

He shuddered beneath her touch. "I know. But I looked and looked at that book. At this story." He held the book up. "The beast isn't the strong one. It's the beauty. It's her love. And still I'm not... I'm not fixed."

"Yes," she said, moving toward him, her heart pounding hard. "But don't you know what changes him? It's not just her loving him. It's him loving her back. Love is the magic, Javier. We might not have sorceresses and spells, but we have love. And that's... That's what makes people change."

Hope washed through her as she saw a change come over his face, his body. As he moved into action, swept her into his arms and pulled her up against his body. "Is that all I have to do? Just love you? Because I do. Because I have."

"Yes," she whispered.

"What if I hurt you? I am afraid... I have caused so

much pain, Violet. All the years since don't make it go away."

"You have to forgive yourself. Because you're right, some things can't be undone. But people do change, Javier. You have. It doesn't wipe the past clean. But neither does a life of torturing yourself."

"If I hurt you… I am so afraid I will hurt you. More than I fear any other thing, more than I fear losing you, I fear hurting you. And that is what I could not accept."

"You won't," she said.

"You are so sure?"

"Yes," she said. "Because I saw the Prince beneath the beast the moment we first met. Even when I didn't know you, I trusted your word. You know the cost of selfishness, and you will never ask others to pay it. If you were your father, we would all know it by now. You simply have to believe it."

"What if I don't change?" he asked, the question sharp and rough. "What if love is not enough to change me?"

"I love you already. You're the only one who thinks you're a beast, Javier." She took a step back, putting her palm on his face. "*You* need to see the change. Not me."

"I love you," he said. "And I… You're right. I was afraid of what that might mean. Because I did love my father. Very much. But he was a monster. And I couldn't understand how I had been so blind to that. How I had seen only what I wanted to see. Because of how much I loved him. And I never wanted to be that way again. I never wanted to be vulnerable to making such mistakes. But I think… I think it is time for me to accept that I am a man, and no matter what, I will be vulnerable to mistakes. But with you by my side… You have a compassionate heart, Violet. And perhaps the secret is loving other people. Valuing their opinions. Not shutting yourself up in an echo chamber of your own desires so that nobody ever reaches you. So that no one can hold you accountable for what you do. Our love will make me better. Loving you… Matteo said something to me today. He reminded me that our father never loved anyone. That it wasn't love that made our father behave the way he did. It was the love of himself. The love of power above people. I trust that we will find right. Good. That you will help me."

The plea was so raw. So real. Straight from his heart.

"Of course," she said, resting her head on his chest. "Of course I will do whatever you want. I will be whatever you need."

"But what do you get from this? What do you get from me? I need you. I need you to be a moral compass. I need you to love me. I need you to change me. What I do, I do for you."

"You showed me my strength. You gave me the fairy tale I didn't even know I was looking for. And I became the heroine of my story in a way that I didn't know I could be. You are my prince. And you always were. Even when you were a beast."

A smile tugged at the corners of her mouth, and she kissed him. Deep and long. And when they parted she looked into his eyes. "And if am being honest. I quite like you as a beast. With cuffs and chains and the lack of civility. Because you've always held me afterward. Because you've always treated me with care. Because you know when to be both. A man and a beast. And I think that's better than just having one. It makes you perfect."

"I thought… I thought that my father had doomed me."

"No. The sins of our fathers might have brought us together. But they don't define us. It's about us. And it's about what we choose. It always has been.

"That's the real magic. That no matter where you end up in life… You can always choose love."

"I choose love," he said. "I choose you."

"So do I." She bracketed his face with her hands. "But I must warn you. I have a debt to collect, Prince Javier."

"A debt?"

"Yes. You owe me for the rest of my life."

"What is it that I owe you?"

"Only all of you. And I intend to collect some every day forever."

"Then you're in luck. Because I intend to give myself, all that I am, even the broken parts, forever."

"Excellent. I might still take you prisoner, though."

"I would happily be your prisoner."

"I shall have to figure out which of the dungeons is my favorite."

"Whichever one has a bed."

"Well. That I most definitely agree with. Did we break the curse?" she asked.

"I believe that we did."

"Magic," she whispered.

"Or just love."

EPILOGUE

"Princess Violet," came a rich, deep voice from behind her. "I believe I have a debt to collect."

A smile touched her lips, and she looked down into the crib at her sleeping baby, a girl they had named Jacinta, then back at her husband, who was prowling toward her, a wicked smile on his face. Man and beast become one.

That was how he loved her. And it was how she liked it. Fierce and tender. Dangerous but utterly trustworthy.

"Do you?" she asked. "Because last I checked I was still the richest woman in the world, and a princess on top of it. I doubt I owe anyone a debt." She had continued to run her company successfully from Monte Blanco, and with the country having become the most photographed tourist destination in the world, a phenomenon and a craze in the last five years, her brand—now primarily manufactured there—had only become more in demand.

"This is not a debt that can be paid with money. Only with your body." A shiver ran down her spine. "And with your heart."

Javier was the best husband. The best father. He loved her even more now that they'd been married half a decade than he had in the beginning, and she never doubted it.

"I wanted a kiss earlier," he said, gruffly, nuzzling her ear. "You were too busy with Jacinta and Carlos."

"Carlos was eating paper," she said, in a voice of mock despair over their three-year-old son's taste.

"And I find I am still in need of my kiss."

So she kissed him.

"I find that is not enough," he said, and from behind his back he produced the jeweled cuffs. Anticipation fired in her blood.

"This is one debt I'm eager to pay," she said.

When she had paid—enthusiastically, and repeatedly—she lay sated against his body.

"You are right," he said finally. "You are magic. You have transformed me multiple times, you know."

"Have I?"

"Yes. From beast to man. Heartless to a man with more love than he can contain. You made me a husband. You made me a father. You made me love. You made me whole."

"Oh, Javier," she breathed. "This is the very best magic."

"Yes, My Princess," he agreed. "It is."

* * * * *

KIDNAPPED FOR
HIS ROYAL DUTY

JANE PORTER

For Kelly Hunter, Carol Marinelli,
Abby Green & Heidi Rice.

Thanks for the inspiration and excellent
company last summer!

This one is for you!

PROLOGUE

THE BRIDE WAS GONE, hauled from the chapel the way a victorious warrior carried the spoils from war.

Poppy's wide, horrified gaze met Randall Grant's for a split second before swiftly averting, her stomach plummeting. She'd been trembling ever since the doors flew open and the Sicilian stood framed in the arched doorway like an avenging angel.

She gripped her bridesmaid bouquet tighter, even as relief whispered through her. She'd done it. She'd saved Sophie.

But it wasn't just Sophie she'd helped; she'd helped Randall, too. Not that Randall Grant, the Sixth Earl of Langston, would be grateful at the moment, because he was the groom after all, and no man wanted to be humiliated in front of two hundred of England and Europe's most distinguished, their guests having traveled far and wide to Winchester for what the tabloids had been calling the wedding of the year, and would have been the wedding of the year, had the bride not just been unceremoniously hauled away by a Sicilian race car driver. Correction, *former* race car driver.

Poppy doubted that the Earl of Langston would care about the distinction right now, either, not when he had a church full of guests to deal with. Thank goodness he wasn't a sensitive or emotional man. There would be no tears or signs of distress from him. No, his notorious stiff upper lip would serve him well as he dealt with the fallout.

But she also knew him better than most, and knew that he wasn't the Ice Man people thought. She shot Randall another swift glance, strikingly handsome and still in his morning suit, the collar fitted against his strong, tan throat, accenting the lean, elegant lines of his physique, and the chiseled features of his face. He looked like stone at the present.

Detached. Granite-hard. Immovable.

Poppy swallowed quickly once more, trying to smash the worry and guilt. One day Sophie would thank her. And Randall, too, not that she would ever tell him her part in the disaster. He wasn't just Sophie's groom—*jilted* groom—but her boss of four years, and her secret crush. Although he was a very good boss as employers went, and rather protective of her, if he thought she had something to do with this wedding debacle, he'd fire her. Without hesitation. And that would break *her* heart.

But how could she not write to Renzo?

How could she not send the newspaper clipping? Sophie didn't love Randall. She was marrying him because her family had thought it would be an excellent business deal back before she was even old enough to drive. It wasn't a marriage as much as a merger, and Sophie deserved better.

So while Poppy's conscience needled her, she also remembered how Renzo had shown marauder.

It had been thrilling and impressive—

Well, not for Randall. No, he had to be humiliated. But Sophie… Sophie had just been given a chance at love.

CHAPTER ONE

SHE KNEW SOMETHING.

Dal Grant could see it in Poppy's eyes, the set of her lips and the pinch between her brows.

She'd worked far too long for him not to know that guilty as hell expression, the one she only got when she did something massively wrong and then tried to cover it.

He should have fired her years ago.

She wasn't irreplaceable. She'd never been an outstanding secretary. She was simply good, and rather decent, and she had the tendency to keep him grounded when he wanted to annihilate someone, or something, as he did now.

Most important, he'd trusted her, which had apparently been the absolutely wrong thing to do.

But he couldn't press her for information, not with two hundred guests still filling the pews, whispering giddily while Sophie's father looked gobsmacked and Lady Carmichael-Jones had gone white.

Thank God he didn't have close family here today to witness this disaster, his mother having died when he was a boy, and then his father had passed away five years ago, just before his thirtieth birthday.

Dal drew a slow, deep breath as he turned toward the pews, knowing it was time to dismiss the guests, including Sophie's heartsick family. And then he'd deal with Poppy.

"What did you do?" Randall demanded, cornering Poppy in the tiny antechamber off the chapel altar.

Poppy laced her fingers together uneasily, Randall's words too loud in her head, even as she became aware of his choice of words.

He hadn't asked *what she knew*, but rather, *what did she do*? *Do*, as in an action. *Do*, as in having responsibility.

She glanced over her shoulder, looking for someone who could step in, intervene, but the chapel was empty now, the guests disappearing far more rapidly than one would have imagined; but maybe that was because after Randall announced in a cold, hard voice, "Apologies for wasting your time today, but it appears that the wedding is off," and then he'd smiled an equally cold, hard smile, the guests had practically raced out.

She'd wanted to race out, too, but Randall pointed at her, gesturing for her to stay, and so she had, while he waved off his aunts and uncles and cousins, and then exchanged brief, uncomfortable words with Sophie's parents before shaking each of his groomsmen's hands, sending every single person away. Sending everyone but her.

How she wanted to go, too, and she'd even tried to make a belated escape but he'd caught her as she was inching toward the vestibule exit, trapping her in this little antechamber typically reserved for the clergy.

"What did you do, Poppy?" he repeated more quietly, eyes narrowing, jaw hardening, expression glacial.

Her heart thumped hard. He was tall, much taller then she, and she took an unconscious step backward, her shoulders bumping against the rough bricks. "Nothing," she whispered, aware that she was a dreadful liar. It was one of the things Sophie said she'd always liked best about her, and the very thing that had made Randall Grant, the Earl of Langston, hire her in the first place four years ago when she needed a job. He said he needed someone he could trust. She assured him he could trust her.

"I don't believe you," he answered.

Her heart did another painful thump as her mouth dried.

"Let's try this again. Where is my bride? And what the hell just happened here, and why?"

Poppy's eyes widened. Randall Grant never, ever swore. Randall Grant was the model of discipline, self-control and civility.

At least he'd always been so until now.

"I don't know where she is, and that's the truth." Her voice wavered on the last words and she squirmed, hating that he was looking at her as if she'd turned into a three-headed monster. "I had no idea Renzo would storm the wedding like that."

His dark eyebrow lifted. "Renzo," he repeated quietly, thoughtfully.

She went hot, then cold, understanding her mistake immediately.

She shouldn't have said his name. She shouldn't have said anything.

"Poppy."

She stared at his square chin and bit her lower lip hard. It was that or risk blurting everything, and she couldn't do it; it wouldn't be fair to Sophie.

Instead, she tugged at her snug, low-cut bodice, trying not to panic, which in her case meant dissolving into mindless tears. She actually didn't feel like crying; she just felt trapped, but whenever trapped, Poppy's brain malfunctioned and she'd lose track of her thoughts and go silent, and then those traitorous tears would fill her eyes.

It had happened in school. It had happened during her awful summer camps before Sophie rescued her and invited her home with her for the summer holidays. Poppy had thought she'd outgrown the panic attacks, but all of a sudden her chest constricted and her throat closed and she fought for air. Her incredibly tight, overly fitted bridesmaid gown, the icy-pink shade perfect on women like Sophie with porcelain complexions and gleaming hair, but not on short, frumpy secretaries who needed a pop of color near the face to lift a sallow complexion, suffocated her.

"I think I might faint," she whispered, not quite ready to actually collapse, but close. She needed fresh air, and space…and immediate distance from her furious employer.

Randall's black brow just lifted. "You don't faint. You're just trying to evade giving an honest answer."

"I can't get enough air."

"Then stop babbling and breathe."

"I don't babble—"

"Breathe. Through your nose. Out through your mouth. Again. Inhale. Exhale."

He couldn't be that angry with her if he was trying to keep her calm. She didn't want him angry with her. She was just trying to help. She just wanted the people she loved to be happy. Good people deserved happiness, and both Sophie and Randall were good people, only apparently not that good together. And Poppy wouldn't have sent that note to Renzo about the wedding if Sophie had been happy…

Her eyes prickled and burned as Poppy's gaze dropped from Randall's gold eyes to his chin, which was far too close to his lovely, firm mouth, and then lower, to the sharp points of his crisp, white collar.

She struggled to keep her focus on the elegant knot of his tie as she inhaled and exhaled, trying to be mindful of her breathing, but impossible when Randall was standing so close. He was tall, with a fit, honed frame, and at the moment he was exuding so much heat and crackling energy that she couldn't think straight.

She needed to think of something else or she'd dissolve into another panic attack, and she closed her eyes, trying to pretend she was back in her small, snug flat, wearing something comfortable, her pajamas for example, and curled up in her favorite armchair with a proper cup of tea. The tea would be strong and hot with lots of milk and sugar and she'd dunk a biscuit—

"Better?" he asked after a minute.

She opened her eyes to look right into Randall's. His eyes were the lightest golden-brown, a tawny shade that Poppy had always thought made him look a little exotic, as well as unbearably regal. But standing this close, his golden eyes were rather too animalistic. Specifically a lion, and a lion wasn't good company, not when angry. She suppressed a panicked shiver. "Can we go outside, please?"

"I need a straight answer."

"I've told you—"

"You are on a first-name basis with Crisanti. How do you know him, Poppy?" Randall's voice dropped, hardening.

He hadn't moved, hadn't even lifted a finger, and yet he seemed to grow bigger, larger, more powerful. He was exuding so much heat and light that she felt as if she was standing in front of the sun itself. Poppy dragged in a desperate breath, inhaling his fragrance and the scent of his skin, a clean, masculine scent that always made her skin prickle and her insides do a funny little flip. Her skin prickled now, goose bumps covering her arms, her nape suddenly too sensitive. "*I* don't know him."

His eyes flashed at her. "Then how does Sophie know him?"

Poppy balled her hands, nails biting into her palms. She had to be careful. It wouldn't take much to say the wrong thing. It wasn't that Poppy had a history of being indiscreet, either, but she didn't want to be tricked into revealing details that weren't hers to share, and to be honest, she wasn't even clear about what had happened that night in Monte Carlo five weeks ago. Obviously, something had happened. Sophie didn't return home on the last night of the trip, and when they flew out of Monte Carlo, Sophie left Monaco a different woman.

Maybe most people wouldn't pick up on the change in Sophie, but Poppy wasn't most people. Sophie wasn't just her best friend, but the sister Poppy had never had, and the champion she'd needed as a charity girl at Haskell's School. Sophie had looked out for Poppy from virtually the beginning and finally, after all these years, Poppy had found an opportunity to return the favor, which is why her letter to Renzo Crisanti wasn't about sabotaging a wedding as much as giving Sophie a shot at true happiness.

Dal battled to keep his temper. Poppy was proving to be extremely recalcitrant, which was noteworthy in and of itself, as Poppy Marr could type ninety-five words a minute, find anything buried on his desk or lost in his office, but she didn't tell a lie, or keep a secret, well at all.

And the fact that Poppy was desperately trying to keep a secret told him everything he needed to know.

She was part of this fiasco today. Of course she hadn't orchestrated it—she wasn't that clever—but she knew the whys and hows and that was what he wanted and needed to understand.

"Go collect your things," he said shortly. "We're leaving immediately."

"Go where?" she asked unsteadily.

"Does it matter?"

"I've plans to go on holiday. You gave me the next week off."

"That was when I expected to be on holiday myself, but the honeymoon is off, which means your holiday is canceled, too."

She blinked up at him. She seemed to be struggling to find her voice. "That doesn't seem fair," she finally whispered.

"What doesn't seem fair is that you knew about Crisanti and Sophie and you never said a word to me." He stared down into her wide, anxious eyes, not caring that she looked as if she might truly faint any moment, because her thoughtlessness had jeopardized his future and security. "Collect your things and meet me in front of the house. We're leaving immediately."

Poppy was so grateful to be out of the antechamber and away from Randall that she practically ran through the Langston House entrance and up the huge, sweeping staircase to the suite on the second floor that the bride and attendants had used this morning to prepare for the ceremony.

The other bridesmaids had already collected their things and all that was left was Sophie's purse and set of luggage, the two smart suitcases packed for the honeymoon—and then off to one side, Poppy's small overnight bag.

Poppy eyed Sophie's handsome suitcases, remembering the treasure trove of gorgeous new clothes inside—bikinis and sarongs, skirts, tunics and kaftans by the top designers—for a ten-day honeymoon in the Caribbean. A honeymoon that wasn't going to happen now.

Suddenly, Poppy's legs gave out and she slid into the nearest chair, covering her face with her hands.

She really hoped one day Randall would thank her, but she sensed that wouldn't be for quite a while, but in the meantime, she needed to help Randall pick up the pieces.

She was good at that sort of thing, too.

Well, pretty good, if it had to do with business affairs and paperwork. Poppy excelled at paperwork, and filing things, and then retrieving those things, and making travel arrangements, and then canceling the arrangements.

She spent a huge chunk of every day booking and re-booking meetings, conferences, lunches, dinners, travel.

But Poppy never complained. Randall gave her a purpose. Yes, he'd been Sophie's fiancé all this time, but he was the reason she woke up every day with a smile, eager to get to work. She loved her job. She loved—no, too strong a word, particularly in light of today's fiasco, but she did rather adore—her boss. Randall was incredibly intelligent, and interesting and successful. He was also calm, to the point of being unflappable, and when there was a crisis at work, he was usually the one to calm her down.

She hated humiliating Randall today. It hurt her to have hurt him, but Sophie didn't love Randall. Sophie was only marrying Randall because her family had thought it would be an excellent business deal back before she was even old enough to drive. It wasn't a marriage as much as a merger and Sophie deserved better. And Randall definitely deserved better, too.

"I came to find out what was taking so long," Randall said from the doorway.

His voice was hard and icy-cold. Poppy stiffened and straightened, swiftly wiping away tears. "Sorry. I just need a moment."

"You've had a moment. You've had five minutes of moments."

"I don't think it was that long."

"And I don't think I even know who you are anymore."

She blanched, looking at him where he remained silhouetted in the doorway. "I'm not trying to be difficult."

"But at the same time you're not trying to help. I don't want to be here. I have my entire staff downstairs trying to figure out what to do with the hundreds of gifts and floral arrangements, never mind that monstrosity of a wedding cake in the reception tent."

"Of course. Right." She rose and headed toward Sophie's luggage. "Let me just take these downstairs."

"Those are Sophie's, not yours. She can make her own arrangements for her luggage."

"She's my best friend—"

"I don't care."

"I do, and as her maid of honor—"

"You work for me, not her, and if you wish to continue

in my employ, you will get your own bag and follow me. Otherwise—"

"There's no need to threaten me. I was just trying to help."

"Mrs. Holmes manages my house. You manage my business affairs," he answered, referring to his housekeeper.

"I just thought Mrs. Holmes has quite a lot to manage at the moment. She doesn't need another worry."

"Mrs. Holmes is the very model of efficiency. She'll be fine." He crossed the room and pointed to a small, worn overnight case. "Is this one yours?" When he saw her nod, he picked up her case. "Let's go, then. The car is waiting."

Poppy's brow furrowed as she glanced back at Sophie's set of suitcases but there was nothing she could do now, and so she followed Randall down the sweeping staircase and out the front door.

Mrs. Holmes was waiting outside the big brick house for them.

"Not to worry about a thing, sir," she said to Randall, before turning to Poppy and whispering in her ear, "Poor lamb. He must be devastated."

Poppy wouldn't have described Randall as a poor lamb, or all that devastated, but Mrs. Holmes had a very different relationship with Randall Grant than she did. "He'll recover," Poppy answered firmly. "He's been caught off guard, but he'll be fine. I promise."

Randall's black Austin Healey two-seater convertible was parked at the base of the stairs in the huge oval driveway.

He put Poppy's overnight bag in the boot, and then opened the passenger door for her. The car was low to the ground and even though Poppy was short, she felt as if she had to drop into the seat and then smash the pink gown's ballerina-style tulle in around her so that Randall could close the door.

"This is a ridiculous dress to travel in," she muttered.

She'd thought she'd been quiet enough that he wouldn't hear but he did. "You can change on the plane," he said.

"What plane?" she asked.

"My plane."

"But that was for your honeymoon."

"Yes, and it can fly other places than the Caribbean," he said drily, sliding behind the steering wheel and tugging on his tie to loosen it.

"Speaking of which, should I begin canceling your travel arrangements?"

"My travel arrangements?"

She flushed. "Your...honeymoon."

He gave her a look she couldn't decipher. "I may have lost my bride at the altar, but I'm not completely inept. Seeing as I made the reservations, I will cancel them."

Her hands twisted in her lap. "I'm just trying to help."

"I'm sure you are. You are a singularly devoted secretary, always looking out for my best interests."

She sucked in a breath at the biting sarcasm. "I've always done my best for you."

"Does that include today?"

"What does that mean?"

"What do you think it means, Poppy? Or have you suddenly become exceptionally good at playing dumb?"

Dal wanted to throttle Poppy; he really did. She knew far more than she was letting on but she was determined to play her role in whatever scheme she and Sophie had concocted.

He was disgusted, and not just with them, but with himself. He'd always believed himself to be an excellent judge of character, but obviously he was wrong. Sophie and Poppy had both betrayed his trust.

He hated himself for being oblivious and gullible.

He hated that he'd allowed himself to be played the fool.

His father had always warned him not to trust a woman, and he'd always privately rolled his eyes, aware that his father had issues, but perhaps in this instance his father had been right.

Dal's hand tightened on the steering wheel as he drove the short distance from Langston House to the private airport outside Winchester. There was very little traffic and the sky was blue, the weather warm without being hot. Perfect June day for a wedding. This morning everything had seemed perfect, too, until it became the stuff of nightmares.

He gripped the wheel harder, imagining the headlines in tomorrow's papers. How the media loved society and scandal. The headlines were bound to be salacious.

Unlike Sophie, he hated being in the public eye, detesting everything to do with society. In his mind there was nothing worse than English society with its endless fascination of classes and aristocrats, and new versus old money.

He'd spent the past ten years trying to avoid scandal, and it infuriated him to be thrust into the limelight. The attention would be significant, and just thinking about having cameras or microphones thrust in his face made him want to punch something, and he hadn't wanted to fight in years.

Dal had been a fighter growing up, so much so, that he'd nearly lost his place at Cambridge after a particularly nasty brawl. He hadn't started the fight, but he'd ended it, and it hadn't mattered to the deans or his father, that he'd fought to defend his mother's name. To the powers that be, fighting was ungentlemanly, and Dal Grant, the future Earl of Langston, was expected to uphold his legacy, not tarnish it.

The school administrators had accepted his apology and pledge, but his father hadn't been so easily appeased. His father had been upset for weeks after, and then as usual, his anger finally broke, and after the rage came the despair.

As a boy, Dal had dreaded the mood swings. As a young man, he'd found them intolerable. But he couldn't walk away from his father. There was no one else to manage the earl, never mind the earldom, the estates and the income. Dal had to step up; he had to become the dutiful son, and he had, sacrificing his wants for his father's mental stability, going so far to agree to marry the woman his father had picked out for him fifteen years ago.

Thank God his father wasn't alive today. His father wouldn't have handled today's humiliation well. God only knows what he would have done, never mind when. But his father wasn't present, which meant Dal could sort out this impossible situation without his father's ranting.

And he would sort it out.

He knew exactly how he'd sort it out. Dal shot a narrowed glance in Poppy's direction. She was convenient, tenderhearted and malleable, making her the easiest and fastest solution for his problem.

He knew she also had feelings for him, which should simplify the whole matter.

Dal tugged on his tie, loosening it, trying to imagine where they could go.

He needed to take her away, needed someplace private and remote, somewhere that no one would think to look. The Caribbean island he'd booked for the honeymoon was remote and private, but he'd never go there now. But remote was still desirable. Someplace that no one could get near them, or bother them...

Someplace where he could seduce Poppy. It shouldn't take long. Just a few days and she'd acquiesce. But it had to be private, and cut off from the outside world.

Suddenly, Dal saw pink. Not the icy-pink of Poppy's bridesmaid dress, but the warm, sun-kissed pink of the Mehkar summer palace tucked in the stark red Atlas Mountains... Kasbah Jolie.

He hadn't thought about his mother's desert palace in years and yet suddenly it was all he could see. It was private and remote, the sprawling, rose-tinted villa nestled on a huge, private estate, between sparkling blue-tiled pools and exquisite gardens fragrant with roses and lavender, mint and thyme.

The spectacular estate was a two-hour drive from the nearest airport, and four hours from the capital city of Gila. It took time to reach this hidden gem secreted in the rugged Atlas Mountains, the estate carved from a mountain peak with breathtaking views of mountains, and a dark blue river snaking through the fertile green valley far below.

He hadn't been back since he was an eleven-year-old boy, and he hadn't thought he'd ever want to return, certain it would be too painful, but suddenly he was tempted, seriously tempted, to head east. It was his land, his estate, after all. Where better to seduce his secretary, and make her his bride?

The jet sat fueled and waiting for him at this very moment at the private airfield, complete with a flight crew and approved flight plan. If he wanted to go to Mehkar, the staff would need to file a new flight plan, but that wasn't a huge ordeal.

Once upon a time, Mehkar had been as much his home as England. Once upon a time, he'd preferred Mehkar to anyplace else. The only negative he could think of would be creating false hope in his grandfather. His grandfather had waited patiently all these years for Dal to return, and Dal hated to disappoint his grandfather but Dal wasn't returning for good.

He'd have to send word to his grandfather so the king wouldn't be caught off guard, but this wasn't a homecoming for Dal. It was merely a chance to buy him time while he decided how he'd handle his search for a new bride.

CHAPTER TWO

POPPY CHEWED THE inside of her lip as the sports car approached the airstrip outside Winchester.

She could see the sleek, white jet with the navy and burgundy pinstripes on the tarmac. It was fueled and staffed, waiting for the bride and groom to go to their Caribbean island for an extended honeymoon.

She'd only learned that Randall owned his own plane a few weeks ago, and that he kept the jet in a private hangar at an executive terminal in London. Poppy had been shocked by the discovery, wondering why she hadn't known before. She'd handled a vast array of his business affairs for years. Shouldn't she have known that he owned a plane, as well as kept a dedicated flight crew on payroll?

"We're back to London, then?" she asked Randall as the electric gates opened, giving them admittance to the private airfield.

"Will there be press in London?" he retorted grimly.

"Yes," she answered faintly.

"Then we absolutely won't go there."

His icy disdain made her shiver inwardly. This was a side of him she didn't know. Randall had always been a paragon of control, rarely revealing emotion, and certainly never displaying temper. But he'd been through hell today, she reminded herself, ridiculously loyal, not because she had to be, but because she wanted to be. He was one of the finest men she knew, and it could be argued that she didn't know many men, but that didn't change the fact that he was brilliant and honorable, a man with tremendous integrity. And yes, she had placed him on a pedestal years ago, but that was because he deserved to be there, and just because he was short-tempered today didn't mean she was ready to let him topple off that pedestal. "But won't there be press everywhere?" she asked carefully.

"Not everywhere, no."

"You have a place in mind, then?"

He shot her a look then, rather long and speculative. It made her feel uncomfortably bare, as if he could see through her. "Yes."

Her skin prickled and she gave her arm a quick rub, smoothing away the sudden goose bumps. "Is it far?"

"It's not exactly close."

"You know I don't have my laptop," she added briskly, trying to cover her unease. "It's in London. Perhaps we could stop in London first—"

"No."

She winced.

She knew he saw her expression because his jaw hardened and his eyes blazed, making her feel as if he somehow knew her role in today's disaster, but he couldn't know. Sophie didn't even know, and Sophie was the one hauled away on Renzo's shoulder.

Randall braked next to the plane and turned the engine off. "You can cry if you want, but I don't feel sorry for you, not one little bit."

"I'm not crying," she flashed.

"But knowing you, you will be soon. You're the proverbial watering pot, Poppy."

She turned her head away, determined to ignore his insults. She'd take the higher ground today since he couldn't. It couldn't be easy being humiliated in front of hundreds of people—

"I trusted you," he gritted, his voice low and rough. "I trusted you and you've let me down."

Her head snapped around and she looked into his eyes. His fury was palpable, his golden gaze burning into her.

Her heart hammered. Her mouth went dry. "I'm sorry."

"Then tell me the truth so we can clear up the confusion of just what the hell happened earlier today."

"Renzo took Sophie."

"I got that part. Witnessed it firsthand. But what I want to know is *why*. Why did he come? Why did Sophie go? Why are they together now when she was supposed to be here with me? You know the story. I think it's only fair that I know it, too."

Poppy's lips parted but she couldn't make a sound.

His narrowed gaze traveled her face before he gave his head a shake. "I appreciate that you're loyal to Sophie. I admire friends that look out for each other. But in this instance, you took the wrong side, Poppy. Sophie was engaged to *me*. Sophie had promised to marry *me*. If you knew she was having a relationship with another man, you should have come to me. You should have warned me instead of leaving me out there, stupid and exposed." And then he swung open his door and stepped out, walking from her in long, fast strides as if he couldn't wait to get away from her.

Poppy exhaled in a slow, shuddering breath. He was beyond livid with her. He was also hurt. She'd never meant to wound him. She'd wanted the best for him, too. And beautiful Sophie would have been the best if she'd loved him, but Sophie didn't love him. There had been no love between them, just agreements and money and mergers.

Shaken, Poppy opened her door and stepped out. She needed to fix this, but how? What could she possibly do now to make it better?

She wouldn't argue with him, that was for sure. And she'd let him be angry, because he had a right to be angry, and she'd be even more agreeable and amenable than usual so that he'd know she was sorry, and determined to make amends.

Poppy went around to the back of the car to retrieve her bag, but a young uniformed man approached and said he would be taking care of the luggage and she was to go on board where a flight attendant would help her get settled.

Poppy wasn't surprised by the brisk efficiency. Randall's helicopter was always available and his staff was always the epitome of professional but it still boggled her mind that he had a helicopter *and* a private plane. It had to be a terrible expense maintaining both of these, as well as his fleet of cars. Randall loved cars. It was one of his passions, collecting vintage models as if they were refrigerator magnets.

"What about the car?" she asked him.

"I'm driving it back to Langston House," the young man answered with a quick smile. "Do you have everything?"

"Yes."

"Good. Enjoy your flight."

Poppy boarded the plane self-consciously, pushing back dark tendrils of hair that had come loose from the pins. She felt wildly overdressed and yet exposed at the same time. She wanted a shawl for her bare shoulders and comfy slippers for her feet. But at least she wasn't the only one in formal dress. Randall still wore his morning suit, although he'd loosened his tie and unbuttoned the top button on his crisp, white dress shirt.

A flight attendant emerged from the jet's compact kitchen galley and greeted Poppy with a smile. "Welcome on board," she said. "Any seat."

The flight attendant followed Poppy down the narrow aisle, past a small conference table to a group of four leather armchairs. The seats were wide and they appeared to be the reclining kind with solid armrests and luxuriously soft leather.

She gingerly sat down in the nearest chair and it was very comfortable indeed.

"Something to drink?" the pretty, blonde flight attendant asked. "A glass of champagne? We have a lovely bottle on ice."

"I'm not the bride," Poppy said quickly.

"I know. But the wedding is off so why not enjoy the bubbles?"

"I don't think that's a good idea. I don't want to upset Randall."

"He was the one who suggested it."

Poppy laughed, nervous. "In that case, yes, a small glass might be nice. I'm shaking like a leaf."

"From the sound of things, it's been quite a day. A little fizz should help you relax."

The flight attendant returned to the galley and moments later Randall and the pilots boarded the plane. The three men stood in front of the cockpit, still deep in discussion. The discussion looked serious, too. There wasn't much smiling on anyone's part, but then, Randall wasn't a man that smiled often. She wouldn't have described him as grim or stern, either, but rather quiet and self-contained. The upside was that when he spoke, people listened to him, but unfortunately, Randall didn't speak often enough, tending to sit back and listen and let others fill the silence with their voices. Sophie thought his silence and reserve made him rather dull, but there were plenty of women who found him mysterious, asking Poppy in whispers what was the Earl of Langston *really* like?

Poppy usually answered with a dramatic pause and then a hushed, *Fascinating*.

Because he was.

He had a brilliant mind and had taken his father's businesses and investments and parlayed them into even bigger businesses and more successful investments, and that alone would have been noteworthy, but Randall did more than just make money. He gave his time generously, providing leadership on a dozen different boards, as well as volunteered with a half dozen different charities, including several organizations in the Middle East. Randall was particularly valuable to those latter organizations since he could speak a staggering number of languages, including Egyptian, Arabic and Greek.

The Earl of Langston worked hard, very hard.

If one were to criticize him it would be that he worked too much. Sophie certainly thought so. Poppy had tried to educate Sophie on Randall's business, thinking that if Sophie was more interested in Randall's work and life, the couple would have more in common, and would therefore enjoy each other's company more, but Sophie wasn't interested in the boards Randall sat on, or his numerous investments. Her ears had pricked at the charity work, because Sophie had her own favorite charities, but the interest didn't last long, in part because Randall failed to reciprocate. He took Sophie for granted. He didn't try to woo her, or romance her. There were no little weekends away. No special dinners out. It was almost as if they were an old married couple even before they married.

Sophie deserved better. She deserved *more*.

Poppy hoped that Renzo marching down the aisle of Langston Chapel would ultimately be a good thing for Sophie.

But even if it was a good thing, it would be scandalous. It would always be scandalous.

Heartsick, Poppy closed her eyes and found herself wondering about Sophie. Was she okay? Where had Renzo taken her? And what was happening in her world now?

"Guilty conscience, Poppy?"

Randall's deep, husky voice seemed to vibrate all the way through her.

She opened her eyes and straightened quickly, shoulders squaring so that the boned bodice pressed her breasts up.

He was standing over her, which meant she had to tilt her head back to look up at him. He was tall and lean, and his elegant suit should have made him look elegant, too, but instead he struck her as hard and fierce, and more than a little bit savage, which was both strange and awful because until today she would have described Randall Grant as the most decent man she'd ever met. Until today she would have trusted him with her life. Now she wasn't so sure.

"No," she said breathlessly, worried about being alone with him. It wasn't that he'd hurt her, but he struck her as unpredictable, and this new unpredictability made her incredibly anxious.

The flight attendant appeared behind him with the flute of champagne. "For Miss Marr," she said.

Randall took it from her and handed it to Poppy. "We're celebrating, are we?" he said mockingly.

Her pulse jumped as their fingers brushed, the sharp staccato making her breathless and jittery. She glanced from his cool, gold eyes into the golden bubbles fizzing in her flute. "The flight attendant said you were the one that suggested the champagne."

"I was curious to see what you would do."

Her eyes stung. Her throat threatened to seal closed. "Take it back, then," she said, pushing the flute back toward him. "I didn't want it in the first place."

"I wish I could believe you."

The hardness in his voice made her ache. She'd thought she'd done the right thing by writing to Renzo, but now she wasn't sure. Had she been wrong about Randall and Sophie?

Did Randall actually love her? Had Poppy just inadvertently broken his heart?

It didn't help being this physically close to Randall when her emotions were so unsettled, either. Nor did she know how to read this new Randall Grant. He wasn't anything like the quiet, considerate man she'd worked for, a man who always seemed to know how to handle her.

"You like champagne," he said carelessly, dropping into the seat opposite hers. "Keep it. I have a drink coming, too."

"Yes, but I shouldn't drink, not when working. I don't know what I was thinking."

"You were thinking that you're a bundle of nerves, and a little bit of alcohol sounded like the perfect tonic."

"Maybe. But we don't drink together. I don't think you and I have ever had a drink, just the two of us. If there was wine, or champagne open, it's because Sophie was there and Sophie wanted a glass and we never let her drink alone."

"No, we never did. We both looked after her, didn't we?"

Poppy's throat thickened. "Please don't hate her."

"It's impossible to like her right now."

Poppy stared down into her glass. "Maybe it's better if we don't discuss her."

"Four hours ago she was to be my wife. Now I'm to simply forget her? Just like that?"

She looked up at him, struggling to think of something she could say, but nothing came to her and she just gave him a look that she hoped was properly sympathetic without being pitying.

"I'm shocked and angry, not broken. Save the sympathy for someone who needs it."

"Do you want her back?"

"No."

"I didn't think so."

"Why?"

"Because even if she did decide she'd made a mistake, I don't think you'd forgive and forget. At least not for a long time."

The corner of his mouth curled. "I don't like being

played for a fool, no," he said, giving her a long, penetrating look that made her squirm because it seemed to imply that he also thought *she* had played him for a fool. And if that was the case, then spending the next week working together was asking for trouble. He wouldn't be in a proper state of mind.

The flight attendant appeared with a crystal tumbler. "Your whiskey," she said, handing him the glass. "Captain Winter also wanted you to know that the new flight plan has been approved, and we'll be departing in just a few minutes."

"Thank you," Randall said, giving the attendant a warm smile, the kind of smile he used to give Poppy, the kind of smile that had made her put him on a pedestal in the beginning.

And just like that, tears filled her eyes and she had to duck her head so he wouldn't see. Because if she did look at him, he'd see more than she wanted him to see. Randall was startlingly perceptive. He paid attention to people and things, picking up on details others missed.

"I knew it wouldn't be long before you got weepy," he said, extending his long legs, invading her space. "Before this morning, I would have said you are nothing if not predictable, but you surprised me today. You're not at all who I thought you were."

She drew her legs back farther to keep her ankles from touching his, and told herself to bite her tongue, and then bite it again because arguing with him would only make the tension worse.

He gave his glass a shake, letting the amber liquid swirl. "Did you know about Crisanti?"

Poppy continued to bite her tongue, because how could she answer that without incriminating herself? Clearly in this case, the best answer was no answer.

"Poppy."

The flight attendant was closing the door and locking it securely, and the deliberate steps made Poppy want to jump out of her chair and race off the plane. She should go now, while she could do. She needed to escape. She needed to go. She couldn't stay here with Randall—

"My bride was carted off from the church today, and she didn't even make a peep of protest," he continued quietly, almost lazily, even as his intense gaze skewered her. She didn't even have to look at him to know he was staring her down because she could feel it all the way through her.

Poppy swallowed hard. "I think she peeped."

"No, she didn't. And neither did you." He growled the words, temper rising, and she jerked her head up to look at him, and the look he gave her was so savage and dark that Poppy's pulse jumped and her stomach lurched.

"You weren't surprised to see Crisanti marching down the aisle today," he added, lifting a finger to stop her protest. "Enough with the lying. It doesn't become you. You forget, I *know* you. I've worked with you, worked closely with you, and I saw it in your face, saw it in your eyes."

"Saw what?"

"Guilt. But I also saw something else. You were happy to see Crisanti arrive. You were *elated*."

"I wasn't elated."

"But you weren't devastated."

She placed the flute down on the narrow table next to her. "I'd like to take my vacation time, the time you promised me. I don't think it's a good idea to work together this next week. I think we both need some time, and time apart—"

"No."

"I can take the train back to London."

"No."

"I don't enjoy you like this—"

"Perhaps it's not about you anymore, Poppy. Perhaps it's now about me."

"I don't understand."

"I want to know what happened today. I want to know everything."

His voice was deep and rough and it scratched her senses. She dragged her attention up, her gaze soaking in his face. She knew that face so well, knew his brow and every faint crease at the corner of his eyes. She knew how he'd tighten his jaw when displeased, and how his lips firmed as he concentrated while reading. If he was very angry, his features would go blank and still. If he was relaxed, his lovely mouth would lift—

No. Not lovely.

She shouldn't ever think his mouth was lovely.

Even though she'd vanished, he still belonged to Sophie. He'd always belong to Sophie. They'd been engaged since Sophie was eighteen, with the understanding that they'd be married one day happening even earlier in their lives.

The fact was, Randall and Sophie had been practically matched since birth, an arrangement that suited both families, and the respective family fortunes, and Sophie insisted she was good with it. She'd told Poppy more than once that she hadn't ever expected to marry for love, and wasn't particularly troubled by the lack of romance since she liked Dal, and Dal liked her, and they complemented each other well.

A lump filled her throat because Poppy didn't just like Randall, she truly cared for him. Deeply cared. The kind of feelings that put butterflies in her stomach and made her chest tighten with tenderness. "It's not my place," she choked. "I wasn't your bride!"

"But you were part of today's circus. You took part in the charade."

"It wasn't a charade!"

"Then where is Sophie?"

His question hung there between them, heavy and suffocating, and Dal knew Poppy was miserable; her brown eyes were full of shadows and sorrow, and usually he hated seeing her unhappy. Usually he wanted to lift her when she struggled but not today. Today she deserved to suffer.

He'd trusted her. He'd trusted her even more than Sophie, and he'd planned on spending the rest of his life with Sophie.

Dal shook his head, still trying to grasp it all.

If Sophie had been so unhappy marrying him, why didn't she just break the engagement before it got to this point?

It was not as if he didn't have other options. Women threw themselves at him daily. Women were constantly letting him know that they found him desirable. Beautiful, educated, polished women who made it known that they'd do anything to become his countess, and if marriage was out, then perhaps his mistress?

But he'd been loyal to Sophie, despite their long engagement. Or at least he'd been faithful once the engagement had been made public, which was five and a half years ago. Before the public engagement was the private understanding, an understanding reached between the fathers, the Earl of Langston and Sir Carmichael-Jones. But for five and a half years, he'd held himself in check because Sophie, stunning Sophie Carmichael-Jones, was a virgin, and she'd made it clear that she intended to remain a virgin until her wedding night.

He now seriously doubted that when she'd walked down the aisle today she'd still been a virgin.

Dal swore beneath his breath, counting down the minutes until they reached their cruising altitude so he could escape to the small back cabin, which doubled as a private office and a bedroom.

Once they stopped climbing, he unfastened his seat belt and disappeared into the back cabin, which had a desk, a reclining leather chair and a wall bed. The wall bed could easily be converted when needed, but Dal had never used it as a bedroom. He preferred to work on his flights, not rest.

Closing the door, he removed his jacket, tugged off his tie and unbuttoned his dress shirt. Half-dressed, he opened the large black suitcase that had been stowed in the closet and found a pair of trousers and a light tan linen shirt that would be appropriate for the heat of the Atlas Mountains.

Hard to believe he was heading to Mehkar.

It'd been so long.

No one would think to look for him in his mother's country, either, much less his father's family. Dal's late father had orchestrated the schism, savagely cutting off his mother's family following the fatal car accident twenty-three years ago.

It was on his twenty-first birthday that his past resurrected itself. He'd been out celebrating his birthday with friends and returned worse for the wear to his Cambridge flat to discover a bearded man in kaffiyeh, the traditional long white robes Arab men wore, on his doorstep.

It had been over ten years since he'd last seen his mother's father, but instead of moving forward to greet his grandfather, he stood back, aware that he reeked of alcohol and cigarette smoke, aware, too, of the disapproval in his grandfather's dark eyes.

Randall managed a stiff, awkward bow. "Sheikh bin Mehkar."

"As-Salam-u-Alaikum," his grandfather had answered. *Peace be to you.* He extended his hand, then, to Randall. "No handshake? No hug?"

It was a rebuke. A quiet rebuke, but a reproof nonetheless. Randall stiffened, ashamed, annoyed, uncomfortable, and he put his hand in his grandfather's even as he glanced away, toward the small window at the end of the hall, angry that his mother's father was here now. Where had he been for the past ten years? Where had his grandmother gone and the aunts and uncles and cousins who had filled his childhood?

He'd needed them as a grieving boy. He'd needed them to remind him that his beautiful mother had existed, as by Christmas his father had stripped Langston House of all her photos and mementos, going so far as to even remove the huge oil family portrait only completed the year before, the portrait of a family in happier days—father, mother and sons—from above the sixteenth-century Dutch sideboard in the formal dining room.

Perhaps if Dal hadn't spent a night drinking, perhaps if Dal's phone call with his father the evening before hadn't been so tense and terse, full of duty and obligation, maybe Dal would have remembered the affection his mother had held for her parents, in particular, her father, who had allowed her to leave to marry her handsome, titled, cash-strapped Englishman.

And so instead of being glad to see this lost grandfather, Dal curtly invited his grandfather in. "Would you like tea? I could put the kettle on."

"Only if you shower first."

And Randall Grant, the second-born son who shouldn't have become the heir, the second son who had never flaunted his wealth or position, snapped, "I will have my tea first. Come in, Grandfather, if you wish. But I'm not going to be told what to do, not today, and certainly not by you."

Dark gaze hooded, Sheikh Mansur bin Mehkar looked his oldest living grandson, Randall Michael Talal, up and down, and then turned around and walked away.

Randall stood next to his door, his flat key clenched in

his hand, and watched his grandfather head for the steep staircase.

He should go after him.

He should apologize.

He should ask where his grandfather was staying.

He should suggest meeting for dinner.

He should.

He didn't.

It wasn't until the next morning that Randall discovered the envelope half-hidden by the thin doormat. Inside the envelope was a birthday greeting and a packet of papers. For his twenty-first birthday he'd been given Kasbah Jolie, his mother's favorite home, the home that had also been the Mehkar royal family's summer palace for the past three hundred and fifty years.

He wouldn't know for another ten years that along with the summer palace, he'd also been named as the successor to the Mehkar throne.

But both discoveries only hardened his resolve to keep his distance from his mother's family. He didn't want the throne. He didn't want to live in, or rule, Mehkar. He didn't want anything to do with the summer palace, either, a place he still associated far too closely with his beloved mother, a mother he'd lost far too early. It was bad enough that at eleven he'd become Viscount Langston following his older brother's death. Why would he want to be responsible for Mehkar, too?

Poppy glanced up and watched as Dal approached. He'd changed into dark trousers and a light tan linen shirt, the shirt an almost perfect match for his pale gold eyes. He looked handsome, impossibly handsome, but then, he always did. She just never let herself dwell on it, knowing that her attraction was unprofessional and would only lead to complications. Gorgeous, wealthy men like Randall Grant did not like women like her. Why should they when they could have the Sophie Carmichael-Joneses of the world?

"Your turn," Randall said shortly. "And once you change, please throw that damn dress away. I never want to see it again."

"Where is my bag?"

"In the closet in the back cabin."

Poppy located her worn overnight bag in the closet but when she opened it, she had only her nightgown, travel toiletries, a pair of tennis shoes and her favorite jeans. The jeans and tennis shoes were good, but she couldn't leave the cabin without a shirt.

Poppy sat back on her heels and tried to remember where she'd put the rest of her clothes. Had they gotten caught up in Sophie's things? Or had she left them at the hotel when they checked out this morning?

Suppressing a sigh, she returned to the chairs in the main cabin.

The flight attendant was in the middle of setting up a table for a late lunch, covering the folding table with a fine white cloth before laying out china plates with thick bands of gold, crystal stemware, and real sterling flatware.

"You didn't change," Randall said, spotting her.

"I don't have a blouse or top or...or bra...for that matter."

"You could borrow one of my shirts, and braless is fine. It's just me here. I won't stare."

There was nothing provocative in his words and yet her face and body flooded with heat. "Then yes, thank you. Because I'm ready to get out of this dress, too."

He rose from his seat, stepping around the table, and she followed him back to the cabin. The private cabin was small, and felt even tinier when Randall entered the room with her.

She stepped back so he'd have room to open his suitcase and find a suitable shirt for her.

"What are you wearing on the bottom?" he asked.

"Jeans."

He rifled through his clothes, selecting a white dress shirt with blue pinstripes for her. "This should cover you," he said.

"Thank you."

He nodded, and he turned to leave and she took a step to give him more room but somehow they'd both stepped in the same direction and now he was practically on top of her and he put out a hand to steady her, but his hand went to her waist, not her elbow, and his hand seemed to burn all the way through the thin silk fabric, and she gasped, lips parting, skin heating, her entire body blisteringly warm.

In the close confines of the cabin, she caught a lingering whiff of the cologne he'd put on this morning and it was rich and spicy and she wanted to step closer to him and bury her face in his chest, and breathe him in more deeply.

He smelled so good, and when he touched her, he felt so good, and it was frightening how fast she was losing those boundaries so essential to a proper working relationship.

"Looks like we're tripping each other up," he said, his deep voice pitched so low it made the hair on her nape rise and her breasts tighten inside her corset, skin far too sensitive.

"I'm sorry," she said breathlessly. "I didn't mean to get in your way," and yet she couldn't seem to step away, or give him space.

His hands wrapped around her upper arms and he gently but firmly lifted her, placing her back a foot, and then he exited the small cabin without a glance back.

Poppy exhaled in a rush, shuddering at the extreme awkwardness of what had just taken place. She'd walked into him, and then stayed there, planted, as if she'd become a tree and had grown miraculous roots.

Why?

Poppy carefully closed the door and then pressed her shoulder to the frame, wishing she could stay barricaded in the cabin forever. It was one thing to have an innocent crush on your boss, but it was another to want his touch, and Poppy wanted his touch. She wanted his hands on her in the worst sort of way. Which raised the question, what kind of person was she?

Poppy had always prided herself on her scruples. Well, where were they now?

CHAPTER THREE

POPPY STRUGGLED WITH the minute hooks on the pink dress, freeing herself little by little until she could wiggle out of the gown. The dress had been so tight that it had left livid pink marks all over her rib cage and breasts. It was bliss to finally be free and she slid the shirt on, buttoning the front. The fabric had been lightly starched and it rubbed against her nipples, making them tighten. She prayed Randall wouldn't notice. Things were already so awkward between them. She'd always thought they had the ideal relationship, professional but warm, cordial and considerate, but today had changed everything.

Today he overwhelmed her, and her brain told her to run but there was another part of her that desperately wanted to stay.

And be touched.

That was a very worrying part of her.

She'd have to work hard to keep that part in check, because elegant, refined Randall Grant was one thing, but dark, brooding Dal Grant was something else altogether.

Poppy finished changing, stepping into the soft, faded jeans that now hung on her hips thanks to four months of determined dieting, and after pulling the pins from her hair, she slipped her feet into her tennis shoes and headed back to her seat.

While she was gone, the flight attendant added a low arrangement of flowers to the center of the table, the lush red and pink roses reminiscent of the bouquet Sophie had carried this morning. The flowers made Poppy heartsick and guilty all over again.

"You look more comfortable," he said as she slid into her seat.

"I am."

"Tell me your sizes and I'll have some basics waiting for us when we land."

"I can shop for myself, thank you."

"There won't be shops where we're going."

"Where are we going?"

"Jolie."

The flight attendant appeared with the salad course, and Poppy waited for Randall to reach for his fork before she did the same. "Is it a country house?" she asked.

He didn't pick up his fork, or answer right away, instead he glanced away, his long black lashes lowering, accenting the high, hard lines of his cheekbones.

She'd always thought he had the most impressive bone structure, with his lovely high cheekbones, strong jaw and chin coupled with that long nose. Sophie had always disdained of his nose—not refined enough—but Poppy had disagreed, thinking he had the nose of a Roman or Greek.

"Something like that," he finally answered, his dark head turning, his light gold gaze returning to her, studying her for a long moment, making her feel strangely lightheaded. And breathless. Far too breathless.

Poppy inhaled slowly, trying to settle her nerves. She'd had a crush on him for four years and she'd managed to keep her feelings in check. There was no reason to let herself get carried away just because he was suddenly single.

And free.

Her heart did a funny little beat, the kind of beat that made her feel anxious and excited, but neither emotion was useful. She needed to settle down and be calm and steady and strong.

"You're not doing much to clarify things." She tried to smile, a steady, professional smile. "Where is it exactly?"

"Out of the country."

Did he just say out *in* the country, or out *of* the country? It was a tiny preposition, but a significant difference. "Where is the nearest airport?"

"Gila."

She touched the tip of her tongue to her upper lip as her mouth had gone dry and her stomach was doing a wild free fall. "I'm not familiar with Gila."

"The capital of Mehkar?"

For a moment she still didn't understand, unable to process what he was saying, and then everything inside her did a horrifying free fall. "We're going to *Mehkar*?"

"Have you been before?"

"No."

"It neighbors Morocco—"

"I know where it is, but we can't go to Mehkar!"

"Of course we can. We're en route now."

"But how? Why? It's hours away and I have no passport, just an overnight bag with virtually nothing in it at all."

He shrugged carelessly. "Sophie had nothing when she left the church, did she?"

Poppy's throat sealed closed and she stared at Randall, heartsick. He stared right back, his light gold gaze hard, so hard that it made him look like a stranger.

"You're not worried about her, are you?" he added, his voice dropping, deepening, an edge of menace in his tone.

A shiver raced through her. In the past hour Randall Grant had gone from chivalrous to dangerous.

"Answer me," Randall demanded, leaning forward, his anger altogether new. The Randall Grant she knew was impossibly calm, impossibly controlled.

"I didn't agree to leave the country," she said, voice rising, tightening. "I didn't agree to go to Mehkar. I'd like to return to London immediately. I have work to do—"

"You work for me."

"But the work I need to do for you is all there," she said, making a jabbing motion behind them. "So, please ask your captain to turn around and take me back to Winchester, or to London, so I can take care of the one hundred and one things that need to be done by Monday."

"You can do them in Mehkar."

"But I can't."

"You can, and you will, because it's your job to handle this crushing mountain of work I've tasked you with."

"I never said it was crushing."

"You make it sound crushing."

"I do have a lot of responsibility, and I take my work seriously. Nor do I want to let you down."

His firm lips quirked, but it wasn't a friendly smile. "I don't think that's true at all." His gaze slowly traveled across her face, as if examining every inch. "In fact, I know it's not true."

Heat rushed through her and she felt every place his gaze touched grow uncomfortably warm. "No?"

"No." He was about to add something else, but the flight attendant appeared to remove their salad plates even though neither of them had barely touched the greens.

Randall remained silent the entire time she was gone, and stayed silent while their next course was placed before them. Poppy stared down at her seafood risotto, feeling increasingly queasy. Seafood risotto was Sophie's favorite, not hers. Poppy didn't like seafood, or risotto.

She looked up at Randall to discover that he was watching her intently, his dark head tipped back against the pale leather seat, lids lowering, lashes dropping, concealing part of the golden glimmer. "If you valued your position with me, Poppy, you would be loyal to me. Yet, you're not."

For a second it seemed as if all the oxygen in the plane disappeared and she stared at him, lips parting, but no air moving in or out of her lungs. No air, and no words, either, because what could she say? How could she defend herself?

"Have you found a new position, Poppy?"

She shook her head, eyes stinging.

"Are you interviewing?"

She shook her head again.

"Résumés out...inquiries...networking?"

Poppy's stomach twisted. "No. I am not job-hunting. I like my job."

"Is that so?"

"Yes."

"Then maybe it's time you showed me some loyalty, Poppy Marr, and tell me what you know about Sophie and this Crisanti fellow."

She deserved that. Because she had taken sides, hadn't she? She'd taken Sophie's. Sophie was her best friend. Her only friend. If Sophie was queen, Poppy would be her lady in waiting. "I would like to help you," she said, stomach still churning, nerves and nausea. It didn't help that the smell of the risotto was making her want to gag. She carefully pushed her bowl away. "But I don't really know much of anything."

His set expression indicated he didn't believe her. "But you know something," he said. "So let's start with that. How long has Sophie known Crisanti? Where did she meet him?"

"I don't want to do this, and it's not fair of you to ask me when you know Sophie is the only one who has ever looked out for me—"

"Are you saying I haven't?"

He'd spoken lowly and yet his words vibrated all the way through her. She clutched the edge of the table, panicked and overwhelmed, not simply by what he was asking, but by the unreality of their situation.

She'd harbored the crush for years, falling for him almost from the very start as he was handsome and intelligent and wildly successful and best of all, he was kind to her, and always so very thoughtful, mindful of her feelings even when things were stressful at work.

It was on one of those terribly stressful days that Poppy had overshared with him, blurting out her fears and insecurities that she'd always be single, because men wanted women like Sophie, women who were strong and confident, women that made men feel like men.

Randall had sputtered on muffled laughter and then he shook his head, eyes smiling. "You can't compare yourself to Sophie. That's not fair of you. Sophie is Sophie Carmichael-Jones for a reason. There's only one of her, but also, there is only one of you. The key, Poppy Marr, is to be you."

"I don't think that's enough," she answered tearfully.

"Trust me, it's more than enough."

And as he'd looked at her, his gold eyes still smiling, she'd melted into a puddle of aching gratitude, want and wishful dreams. *Imagine* having Randall Grant as your champion. Imagine him in your corner, as your partner. Poppy had never been more envious of Sophie in all her life.

Poppy swallowed hard now, a lump in her throat. "You've always been very, very kind to me. Probably better than I deserve."

"So why only protect Sophie? Why not try to protect me?"

"But I did!" she choked. "I wasn't just trying to help Sophie. I was trying to help you, too!"

"So how did you help us?" he asked softly, silkily. "What did you do?"

He'd done it. He'd trapped her, cornered her, and she'd all but confessed.

Horrified, Poppy tried to run, but Randall caught her by the wrist as she attempted to leave the table. His fingers tightened around her slender bones, and he pulled her toward his side.

"Tell me," he said quietly, tugging her closer to his chair. "Let's have the truth."

She tried to pull free, but he was so much stronger than she was, and then he began to stroke the inside of her wrist with his thumb, lightly running the pad of his thumb over her wildly beating pulse. It was the most electric sensation, her nerves jumping, dancing, sending little rivulets of feeling everywhere.

"Sit," he said, drawing her toward him, and then pulling her down so that she perched on the arm of his chair. "Talk. The truth now."

But how could she think, much less say anything coherent, when his thumb was caressing her wrist, making her tingle all over?

She looked up into his eyes and her breath caught as she saw something in his eyes she'd never seen before.

Heat. A fierce, raw, masculine heat that was completely at odds with the man she knew.

But then his thumb caressing her pulse was equally at odds with Randall Grant, the Earl of Langston. The Earl of Langston was elegant, disciplined, restrained. The Earl of Langston did not want *her*.

"I can't think when you're doing that," she said under her breath.

"And I can't have you running off every time the questions get uncomfortable." He moved his hand, sliding it from her wrist up over the flat of her hand so that they were palm to palm, his long fingers pressing against hers, parting them.

She shivered at the press of his hand to hers. It felt wildly indecent.

"I would say this is far more uncomfortable than any of your questions," she whispered, trying to slip her hand out, but only succeeding in dragging her palm down his, sending sparks of sensation up her arm, through her breasts and into her belly below.

His fingers laced through hers, holding her still.

She looked down at their joined hands because there was no way she could look into his face right now. "I don't think this is proper."

"It's a little late to worry about propriety, Poppy. So tell me what you did. You don't need to tell me why. I think we both know the why."

She closed her eyes, mortified, not sure if he was suggesting what she thought he was suggesting.

She prayed he wasn't suggesting...

She prayed...

Just then the plane lurched and dropped, caught in a violent stream of turbulence, and Randall clamped his arm over her thighs, his hand locking around her knee, holding her steady. "I have you," he said.

And he did, she thought wildly, eyes opening as heat and desire rushed through her.

He'd touched her before—a hand to her elbow as he assisted her across a gravel car park, or a touch to her shoulder when entering a crowded lift to nudge her forward—but never like this. Never anything like this, and she was suddenly riveted by the sight of his hand on her knee, his fingers as lean and strong and elegant as the rest of him.

She'd imagined this, though, hadn't she?

Poppy smashed the little voice but it was too late, the little voice wouldn't be silenced. It was beyond inappropriate to have feelings for him in the first place. Randall Grant was Sophie's fiancé and her employer, and Poppy would rather cut off her right arm than embarrass Sophie, or Randall. But that didn't mean the feelings weren't there, suppressed. Buried.

She worked hard to keep them mashed down, too. And

one of the ways she contained her feelings was by keeping a proper distance from him.

She didn't let herself stand too close, or bend too low.

She didn't look him in the eye more than was necessary.

She dressed conservatively, even frumpishly, so no one could accuse her of trying to play up her assets—not that there were too many of those.

And she called him Randall, not Dal like his other friends, because she wasn't his friend. She was his secretary and on his payroll, and those were key distinctions.

She couldn't ever risk forgetting herself.

She couldn't risk dropping her guard, letting him see that beneath her professional demeanor was a real woman...a woman who wanted nothing more than to see him happy. Because Randall Grant was many things—brilliant, wealthy, strategic, successful—but he wasn't happy. In fact, he didn't seem to allow himself to feel emotions at all.

Perhaps that was what troubled her most. He would give the shirt off his back to someone in need, but he never asked for anything in return.

He never took anything from anyone, or wanted anything for himself.

He just existed in his space and sphere, brilliant and handsome and impossibly solitary.

Sophie had never seemed to notice. In her mind, Dal was just one of those introverts...a loner...and content to be alone, but Poppy didn't agree. Of course she kept her opinion to herself. But instinct told her that Randall Grant hadn't always been so alone, and that his isolation was perhaps the result of his being raised by a difficult father.

"I think you should let me go, Randall." Her voice was soft, almost broken.

"Maybe, but I don't think I shall. I quite like having you close. You have no defenses right now, making it impossible for you to lie."

"You're more of a gentleman than that."

"Oh, Poppy, you don't know me at all."

"That's not so. I know you quite well—"

"You've made me into someone I never was. Your impression of me is sweet, and flattering, but absurdly false. I am no gentleman, and am anything but chivalrous."

"I'd like to return to my chair now."

"Why? Isn't this what you always wanted? Haven't you wondered what it would be like to be Sophie, engaged to me?"

Poppy stiffened. She couldn't move, or blink, or speak. She couldn't do anything but sit frozen while shame suffused her heart. *He knew?* Dear God, did he really know? All these years she'd thought she'd been so good at hiding her feelings, hiding her attraction, and yet apparently she hadn't hidden anything well at all.

But then she forced the thought back, not willing to go there, not willing to be stripped emotionally bare before him. "How much whiskey did you drink?" she flashed, praying he hadn't heard the wobble in her voice.

"The one glass. I'm not drunk." He leaned back against his leather seat, infuriatingly relaxed. "And you can play it cool, and pretend you don't know what I'm talking about, but we both know the truth. I'm not trying to shame you—"

"It certainly feels like it, and I don't appreciate it. I was supposed to be going on holiday in the morning. I haven't had a proper vacation in years and this should have been the start to a vacation and instead you have me trapped on your plane, listening to your insults."

"It's not an insult."

"For you to imply that I've been dying for you to kiss me, yes, that's an insult because until five hours ago you were marrying my best friend."

"I never said Sophie knew. You were remarkably good at concealing your feelings when she was around."

"I don't have feelings for you!"

His expression of amused disbelief made her want to throw up.

"Can we agree on soft spot?" he suggested with the same insufferable smile.

Poppy shuddered. She averted her face, trying to hide behind her shoulder. "I miss the old you, the nice you. Can you please bring Randall Grant back?"

"Randall Grant is dead."

Her head jerked up and her gaze met his.

He nodded, expression almost sympathetic. "Yes, dead, because he never existed. I am Dal Grant, and have always been Dal. You made me into this Randall who was good and kind and considerate, but that's not me. It never has been."

"Fine. You're Dal Grant. Congratulations." She yanked on her hand, struggling to free herself, struggling with a new, feverish desperation. "Now, let me go."

"Not yet."

"Why not?"

"Because we need to finish establishing a few things—"

"I think we've established quite a lot already. You're Dal, not Randall. You're not a nice man and you never have been. You think I betrayed you—"

"I *know* you betrayed me."

"And you want me to betray Sophie."

"But you don't want to do that."

"Of course I don't. And I won't."

"Because she was your champion. She protected you from the time you were just a charity case at Haskell's—"

"Stop, just stop."

"I understand more than you think I do. I know more than you think I do, too. I know you grew up poor and insecure, and how you believed that you had to be perfect, or close to perfect, because one misstep and you could lose it all. Your scholarship at Haskell's. Your friendship with Sophie. And then later, your job with me. Sophie once said that the reason you were so dependable was because you knew life was precarious and fraught with uncertainties. You'd told her that the best way to survive, and maybe the only way to survive, was by being necessary to those around you. So you became Sophie's rock. And then my rock."

"You were Sophie's rock, too," he continued, "but she's gone now, and that leaves just you and me."

She flushed deeply, even as her body throbbed with awareness. Randall's arm still lay across her thighs, and his hand continued to cup her knee, and her pulse was beating so hard that her head felt woozy. "I don't like the way you make that sound."

"How am I making it sound?"

"As if there is something…illicit…between us. But there is nothing illicit. There is just a work relationship, and this—" she broke off, gesturing to the chair and the place she sat "—is not proper or professional and I'm asking you to let me go so that I can return to my chair."

"Did you not invite Renzo to my wedding today?"

Her stomach rose and fell and she stared into Randall's golden eyes, stricken. Had Renzo contacted Randall? Had there been communication of some sort between the two men?

But no, that couldn't be. There was no way.

He was making wild guesses, trying to unsettle her, and it was unsettling, but he didn't know anything and she could not, absolutely could not, give him details. Let him speculate all he wanted, but it would be disastrous if she confirmed her part in today's debacle.

Stay calm, she told herself. *Don't panic.*

And don't feel, and don't think about how warm Randall's hand is, or how heat seemed to radiate from him to her, seeping into her skin, making her aware of how large his hands were, and how the pressure of his forearm across her thighs made her feel tingly, and tingly wasn't good. Tingly was dangerous.

"It's not disloyal to care for us both," he added after a moment.

"I won't say more. I'm done talking."

"I could get you to say more. I could get you right now to tell me everything." He must have seen her expression because his mouth eased and his eyes warmed. "One kiss—"

"For God's sake, stop!" Tears filled her eyes and reached up to wipe them away before they could fall. "I know you've had a bad day. I know this has to be one of the worst days of your life, but why must you torture me? I love Sophie, and I love you—"

She broke off, horrified to have said so much, to have admitted the depth of her feelings. She closed her eyes, teeth biting into her lower lip to keep it from trembling, and yet she couldn't stop the tears from falling, one after the other, but she gave up trying to catch them, or stop them.

It didn't matter.

Nothing mattered anymore.

"I quit," she whispered. "I'm done. Consider this my formal resignation. As of now, I no longer work for you and the moment we land, I'm gone."

CHAPTER FOUR

DAL RELEASED HER, and Poppy returned to her chair, but Dal was fully aware that she didn't eat anything, choosing to simply stare out the window, the very picture of martyred innocence.

But she wasn't innocent. She was responsible today for his being on this plane, now, a single man, and he wasn't just holding her accountable. He fully expected her to solve his problem, saving him from failing his father.

Dal had never been close to his father but he'd made a vow to his father when he was dying, and he fully intended to keep the promise.

Which meant, he needed a wife. Quickly.

Thank goodness Poppy was available. She wasn't the wife his father had wanted for him, but she'd definitely do in a pinch.

Sadie, the flight attendant, appeared to check on them and when she saw that neither of them had eaten the risotto she asked if there was something else she could bring.

"The cheese plates," Dal answered. "And whatever chocolates you might have. It's an emergency."

Poppy muttered something unflattering beneath her breath and Dal looked at her, eyebrow rising. "You once said chocolate helps everything."

"Well, not *this*."

"I think you're wrong. I think once you eat some proper food and then have some excellent chocolate you'll calm down and realize you don't want to walk away from me in Mehkar, at the Gila airport—"

"Why not? It's supposed to be a gorgeous country."

"Without a passport, or money, or bra. Mehkar is not as

conservative as some of our neighbors but it's still an Arab country with a traditional culture."

"I can't believe you felt the need to mention the bra."

"Men are men."

"Well then, once we land, and you get out, send me back to England in your plane. That way I won't be stranded and my lack of undergarments won't create alarm."

"And what will you do once you're back in London?"

"Go on the holiday. Sleep in. Enjoy the freedom of being unemployed."

"And then when you're properly rested you'll begin looking for a new job."

"Yes."

He studied her thoughtfully. "But won't it be hard to get a decent position without references? I'd think you'd need me to put in a good word for you. You did work for me for four years after all."

"That's not fair."

"What happened today in the chapel wasn't fair, either."

"Sophie always did say she knew you better than I thought. Clearly, she was right."

His secretary was so disillusioned that he almost felt sorry for her. "It will be better tomorrow."

"What will be?"

"The disappointment. You'll realize it's just a temporary setback, and life goes on."

Poppy glared at him, her brown eyes flashing. "Thank you for that extremely deep and insightful philosophy lecture."

Sadie returned with two cheese plates, each plate filled with cheeses, crackers and fruit, along with a bowl of chocolates. She set the plates down, centered the bowl of chocolate and disappeared.

Dal watched Poppy try to ignore the chocolates and cheese plate. It was almost comical because he knew how much she loved both things. "You really will feel better if you eat something."

She refused to look at him, her smooth jaw set, lips pursed, expression mutinous. He'd never seen this side of her. She had a temper. He was pleased to see it, too. He'd worried that she had no backbone. He'd worried that Sophie had taken advantage of her generous nature.

"There is no reason to continue the starvation diet," he said. "The wedding is over. No one is going to compare you to Sophie's stick friends."

Poppy gave him an indignant look. "They're not sticks. They're models."

"They're annoying."

"You really think so?"

"You've never noticed that they live on their phones? For them, social media is more important than real human interaction."

"It's because they get paid for their Instagram posts. The more likes they get, the bigger the bonuses."

He rolled his eyes. "I find that very hard to believe."

"It's true. I didn't know it until one of them explained that modeling has changed. Lots of their jobs are pictures for their Instagram accounts."

"I'm still not impressed."

"Are you being serious? You really didn't like them?"

"Did you?" he retorted.

He seemed to have caught Poppy off guard and she paused to think about her answer. After a moment her shoulders shrugged. "They were nice enough to me."

"But?"

"I wasn't one of them."

"Of course not. You weren't an actress or a model—"

"Some of them are just horsey girls. They live for polo."

"You mean, rich men who play polo."

"You don't sound very complimentary."

"I knew I was marrying Sophie, not her social scene."

Poppy regarded him for another long moment, her wide brown eyes solemn, her full mouth compressed, and he was glad she was nothing like Sophie's other friends. He was glad she was short and curvy and fresh-faced and real. She was Poppy. And she was maybe the only person in his life who could make him smile.

"But maybe that was part of the problem," she said now, picking her words with care. "Maybe you needed to like her world better. Sophie is quite social. She likes going out and doing things. She was never going to be happy sitting around Langston House with you every weekend."

"It's a wonderful house."

"For you. It's your house. But what was she supposed to do there all day?" When he didn't answer she pressed on. "Have you ever looked at her? Really looked at her? Sophie is one of the most beautiful, stylish women in all of England. *Tatler* adores her—"

He made a dismissive noise.

Poppy ignored him. "Everyone in the fashion world adores her. Sophie is smart and glamorous and she is very much admired, but you…you only saw her as the woman who would beget your heirs."

When Dal's mocking smile disappeared Poppy felt a stab of pleasure, delighted that she knocked his smug, arrogant smile off his smug, arrogant, albeit handsome, face, but then when he rose and walked away, the pleasure abruptly faded.

Chewing the inside of her lip, she watched him walk to the back, heading for his private cabin in the rear of the jet. After he disappeared into the cabin, the door closing soundlessly behind him, she sank back into her seat, deflated, as if all the energy had been sucked from the cabin.

So much had just happened that she couldn't process it all.

Poppy didn't even know where to begin taking apart the conversations and the revelations, never mind examining the intense emotions buffeting her.

Randall—Dal—knew about her infatuation, and had implied that Sophie probably knew, too. And then Poppy, in a burst of uncharacteristic temper, had quit.

Poppy sighed and rubbed her brow, gently kneading the ache. Was she really going to leave him, after four years of working for him? After four years of trying to deny her feelings?

And did it matter that he knew her secret?

On one hand it was incredibly uncomfortable that Randall—Dal—knew, but on the other, so what?

She had feelings for him. Why should that make her feel ashamed? Why were feelings even considered shameful? She'd been emotional in her entire life. From the time she was a little girl, she'd felt things intensely. Her sensitive nature had made her a target for the girls at Haskell's. They'd enjoyed teasing her about being a charity case. They'd enjoyed mocking her lack of coordination and athletic ability. They'd enjoyed her discomfort at being forced to remain at school for holidays because her parents couldn't afford to bring her home.

And then wonderful, lovely, courageous Sophie stepped in and made the teasing and bullying stop. But she didn't just make the teasing stop; Sophie changed Poppy's life when she confessed that she respected Poppy's kindness and good heart. Suddenly, Poppy wasn't embarrassing but someone that Sophie Carmichael-Jones admired.

So of course Poppy had never acted on her feelings for Randall. She would never, ever be disloyal to Sophie. At the same time, what harm had there been secretly caring for Randall? Her devotion made her a better assistant. Her dedication making her more sensitive and attuned to his needs.

But now her secret was in the open. Did it have to change everything? Did she *want* it to change anything?

Did she want to say goodbye to Randall?

Poppy didn't know the answer to the first two questions but she knew the answer to the third. She didn't want to leave Randall. And the way she felt about him, she'd never want to leave him, but how could she continue working for him like this?

It wouldn't be the same. She'd feel self-conscious and he'd be awkward. Better to end things while she still cared about him. Better to say goodbye while she wanted the best for him.

But just admitting that she had to go broke her heart.

Dal closed his computer, rose from his desk and put away the computer in his briefcase. The jet had just begun the final descent for Gila and he'd not only canceled the essential pieces of the honeymoon but had also created a short list of possible countess candidates to share with Poppy when he returned to the main cabin.

The list was for show. There was only one woman he was considering to be his wife, and that was his secretary, but if he told Poppy she was the one and only name, she'd be terrified. Far better to ease her into her new reality, and it would be her reality because Dal had to be married by the time he turned thirty-five, and his birthday was just sixteen days away.

Which meant he had sixteen days to find a new bride and marry her as he wasn't going to lose Langston House, or the earldom, or any of the other Grant estates, because he'd failed his father.

He'd grown up with enough abuse. He wasn't going to let his father win, even if he was in the grave.

So he'd marry Poppy and prove his father wrong and then Dal would finally be free of this burden he'd carried that he wasn't his brother Andrew, and that he wasn't fit to be the Earl of Langston, and he didn't deserve the Langston House and estates.

Now he just needed to convince her that she was the perfect future countess.

Dal left the back office and returned to his seat in the main cabin. As he took his seat, Poppy stirred sleepily in her chair. Her lashes fluttered open for a moment before closing again. "You," she murmured crossly.

"Yes, me," he answered, his gaze sweeping her, studying her for the first time in an entirely different light.

She wasn't his secretary anymore, but his future wife, which meant not just overseeing Langston House and the thousand different domestic tasks that encompassed, but also bearing him the necessary Grant heirs.

It wouldn't be difficult taking her to his bed. She was pretty and tidy and wholesome, although at the moment she looked flushed and rumpled from sleep, her brown hair down tumbling to her shoulders while a rebellious tendril clung to her pink cheek.

His dress shirt overwhelmed her small frame, but it was refreshing seeing her in something other than her conservative navy and brown skirts, which she paired with equally conservative cardigans. In warm weather she swapped the jumpers for trim white blouses with oval collars and half sleeves. Her work wardrobe was neither well cut nor flattering, and while the pinstripe shirt wasn't flattering, it revealed her curves. Poppy Marr was voluptuous with hourglass curves. Full breasts, tiny waist, rounded hips. He suddenly wished she wasn't wearing jeans so he could see her legs. He'd very much like to see her in nothing but his shirt, and then without the shirt altogether.

"What do you want now?" she demanded, stretching and covering a yawn.

"We should be landing soon."

"Good."

He'd never noticed how firm her chin was until now. It matched her new backbone. He liked the spirit. Spirit was sexy and strong and his future countess would need to be strong.

"I'm not sending you back to England," he said casually. "You owe me two weeks after giving notice. It's in your employment agreement. You can't just quit and walk away."

Her dark lashes slowly lifted and she stared at him, clearly unhappy. "You're going on holiday. You don't need me."

"I'm not on holiday, and I do need you."

"For what?"

"To help find your replacement. I can't possibly interview for a new secretary and a new wife at the same time."

She stared at him blankly. "You're already trying to replace Sophie?"

"She's gone, isn't she?"

"Isn't that rather…callous?"

"Did you expect me to mourn her?"

"She was loyal to you for five and a half years!"

"But she decamped at the last possible second, and the fact is, I need a wife, quickly."

"You've never needed anyone, and yet now you must have a wife, immediately."

"It does sound ridiculous put like that, but that pretty much sums it up."

"I don't understand."

"It's a very convoluted story so I'll give you the short version. I must be married by my thirty-fifth birthday or I lose the earldom, the house and everything attached."

She was still for a moment before she sat upright in her chair. "Your birthday is July sixteenth."

"Correct."

"That's just…a few weeks away."

"Correct again."

She impatiently shoved hair behind an ear, away from her flushed cheek. "This sounds like something from a novel."

"I'm fully aware of the ridiculousness of my situation, but my father set up the trust that way. When he died just after my thirtieth birthday, I inherited the title, but there were provisions."

Silence followed his words. Poppy looked absolutely appalled.

Dal shrugged, adding. "My father thought he was being clever. Exerting control from beyond the grave, and so forth."

"When did you find out? At the reading of the will?"

"No, although wouldn't that have been a shock? Surprised my father didn't think of that. But no, I've known since my early twenties, and did my best not to think about it until I was nearly thirty."

"Did Sophie know this?"

"Sophie was part of my father's plan. He hand-selected her for me."

"This just keeps getting worse."

"She didn't ever tell you?"

"Heavens, no. But probably because she knew I'd disapprove. No wonder she ran at the last second. I would run, too. Poor Sophie."

"Sophie benefitted from the arrangement...until she didn't." He shrugged carelessly. "But now there is a serious time crunch. I have to be married in sixteen days. It's hard enough closing a big deal in two weeks, but to find a wife in the same amount of time? It's not going to be easy."

"And there is no way out of this?"

"No. But trust me, I tried. I've spent a fortune in legal fees and finally accepted that marriage really is the only solution."

She bit her lip and looked away, a sheen of tears in her eyes. "I am so upset."

In his shirt, with her thick hair loose and her slim legs curled up in the seat of her chair, she exuded youth and a sweet, innocent sensuality that teased his senses.

"Don't be," he answered her, forcing his attention from her lips to the sweep of her cheekbone and the strands of dark hair framing her pale oval face. "There is no point in both of us being upset."

"I know I shouldn't say it, but the more I learn about your father, the more I dislike him."

"He was a very tortured man."

"It sounds as if he did his best to torture you."

This was not a comfortable conversation. Dal couldn't even remember the last time he'd discussed his father with anyone. "I'd like to believe it wasn't intentional. I'd like to think he just…couldn't help himself."

She rubbed her eyes and drew a deep breath and turned to look at him, focused now on the goal. "So you need a wife."

"Yes."

"Have you given thought to possible women you could see…proposing to?"

"Yes. I've thought about it carefully and made a short list." He reached into his pocket and pulled out the sheet of paper where he'd scrawled the names, handing it to her.

He sat back, studying her face as she skimmed the list. For a moment her expression was blank and then her head shot up, her rounded eyes matching her dropped jaw.

"I don't appreciate the joke," she said shortly, folding the sheet of paper in half and thrusting it back at him. "Take it."

"I couldn't be more serious."

"Obviously you don't really mean to marry in the next two weeks."

"Why not? You don't think any of the three could be suitable?"

"Perhaps the first two," she said bitingly, "but not the third. She's not rich or a Sloane Ranger."

He unfolded the sheet of paper and glanced down at the three names.

Seraphina Woolton
Florrie Goodwin
Poppy Marr

"But number three is smart and generous and easy to like," he answered, rereading the names.

"That would be very nice if you were a vicar, or a primary school teacher, but you're not. You're from one of the oldest, most prominent families in England and you need an appropriate wife, someone sophisticated, respected and connected."

"I do?"

"Obviously. It's what your father dictated, and it explains why you and Sophie had all those contracts and agreements."

"Yes, but that was with Sophie, and exclusive to my engagement to her. There is nothing that stipulates who my replacement bride should be."

"You started with a very small list, and it's just grown shorter as we're crossing number three off."

"Are we?"

"Yes. Poppy Marr is not an option, which means we'll need to focus on Seraphina and Florrie."

"But Poppy Marr *is* an option. All three names on that list are options. I thought quite seriously about each possible candidate—"

"Please don't use the word *candidate*. It's dreadful. It's as if you're trying to hire a woman to fill a position."

"Being the Countess of Langston is a job."

"Then definitely take Poppy Marr off your list. She's not interested in that position."

"Why not? We work well together."

"Because this new *job* requires skills that are outside my area of expertise." Her cheeks flamed and her eyes glowed bright. "Nor have I any interest in acquiring the skills necessary to be the Countess of Langston."

Heat surged through him, and he hardened as he pictured her fulfilling her marital duties. His trousers grew uncomfortably tight as he imagined introducing her to those duties. "I would teach you."

"No."

"I'd be patient."

"We're ending this discussion now. It's not going to happen. It's not even a remote possibility. I'm not interested in jumping from your office to your bedroom. I like the you in your office."

"Randall," he said dismissively.

"Yes, Randall. Polite, controlled, chivalrous. I don't trust Dal at all."

"That's probably wise."

"Excuse me. Who are you? I don't even know you anymore!"

"I suspect it's because you never did."

"If that's the case, does anyone know you?"

His wry smile faded. That was an excellent question, and he had to think about it for a minute before answering. "Probably not."

More silence followed, and then Poppy broke it with a heavy sigh. "You have no idea how sad that makes me."

"And you, my dear Poppy Marr, have just moved into melodrama."

"Just because I feel things doesn't mean I'm being melodramatic."

"I have found that emotions unnecessarily complicate things."

"Probably because you were taught that emotions were bad things."

"No one has ever told me anything about emotions. My views are based on firsthand experience. Excessive emotion is toxic and damaging."

"What about good emotions? What about love and joy and—"

"That's Gila in the distance," he said mildly, cutting off her impassioned stream of words. "You can see the skyline on the horizon."

She shot him an indignant look, letting him know that she didn't appreciate him interrupting her, before craning her head to see out the window.

He watched as the city loomed nearer, surprisingly eager to see how much he recognized of the Mehkar capital. He'd heard that elegant, historic Gila had become a new, modern, urban city, but the change hadn't registered until now when he saw the dozens of new skyscrapers dotting the skyline.

As they approached the airport, they flew over lakes and glittering pools, and oases of green amidst the marble and glass. The captain turned just before they neared the historic neighborhoods, the ones Dal knew best as it was home to the royal palace, the place where his mother had grown up.

His mother loved to show off her hometown when they used to visit every year. They never went to Kasbah Jolie without first visiting their grandfather and family in Gila. One of their grandfather's drivers would take them out in one of the classic cars he loved, and they'd travel the wide, pristine boulevards lined with stately palm trees, boulevards that led to museums and palaces as well as her favorite shopping district.

To a boy, Gila represented family and history and culture. It never crossed his mind that it was a playground to others—sensual, sexy, hedonistic. It wasn't until he was at Cambridge that his friends talked about going to Mehkar on holiday, that Gila with its white marble and endless man-made lakes, was nonstop entertainment. His friends never understood why Dal wouldn't want to go on holiday to an exotic desert country famous for its hotels, restaurants, shopping and nightlife.

"I had no idea Gila was so big," Poppy said after a moment.

"There has been a lot of new development in the past twenty years. The people of Mehkar love their sports, and their toys."

"Sophie's friends used to come here for the polo tournaments."

"But not Sophie?"

"No. She always said she wanted to visit. Mehkar was on her bucket list." Poppy gave him one of her reproving looks. "But you should have known that, though. You were her fiancé, and engaged forever."

"Not forever, just five and a half years."

"Which is pretty much forever to a twenty-six-year-old." She continued to frown at him. "If you didn't discuss travel, and bucket lists, what *did* you discuss?"

He didn't immediately reply. The jet was dropping lower, and faster, a rapid descent, which meant they'd be on the ground soon before making the quick transfer to his helicopter, and Poppy would be making the transfer with him, too.

"Sophie and I didn't talk a lot. But I think you know that," he said as the wheels touched down in an impossibly smooth landing. They were still streaking down the runway, but soon they'd begin to slow.

"You can't blame her," Poppy answered. "Sophie wanted to be closer to you. You just wouldn't let her in."

And that was also probably true, he thought, but he didn't want to continue discussing Sophie. Sophie was part of the past. She'd chosen a different path, a different future, and it was time for him to focus on his future.

The jet turned at the end of the runway and began the slow taxi toward the small, sleek, glass and steel terminal.

"Women feel close through word and language. We bond through talking—"

"I'm not ready for another lecture on emotions," he interrupted firmly in the authoritative voice he used when he needed to redirect Poppy, and he needed to redirect her now.

"I'm trying to help you."

"That may be the case, but I'm not in the right frame of mind to be presented with my overwhelming failures as a man."

"You're not a failure. But you could work on your emotional intelligence—"

"Poppy!"

She pressed her lips together, her expression defiant, and he drew a deep breath, trying to hang on to his patience.

"I thought you said you had only sixteen days to find a wife," she said in a small but still defiant voice.

Where had this new Poppy come from? She was beyond stubborn, and while he appreciated persistence, now was not the time. She had no idea how unsettled he felt. It was difficult returning to Mehkar. He was already dreading getting off the plane and transferring to the helicopter. Mehkar represented his mother and his carefree summer holidays with his brother at Jolie. He'd never truly dealt with their deaths. He'd just stopped thinking about them and now he was thinking about them and it wasn't a good day to be feeling overwhelmed.

Dammit.

Why had he thought that going to Kasbah Jolie was a good idea?

How had he thought this could be positive?

He shouldn't have come. He should have stayed put at Langston House and weathered the media storm and focused on wooing Poppy there. Instead, he was here, jumping from the proverbial fire into the frying pan.

Dal could see the helicopter ahead. He also saw the cars and the crowd and the royal security details. The black helicopter wasn't just any helicopter but the royal Mehkar helicopter, the elegant gold crest as familiar to him as his mother's face and name. His heart thudded, his chest tight and hard as he battled memories and a past that gave him nothing but pain.

Maybe one day he'd be able to remember his mother without feeling the grief. Maybe after he'd spent a week at Jolie he'd be more peaceful when he thought of Mehkar. In his teens he used to dream of the summer palace and gardens, and when he woke up, his lashes would be damp and his stomach cramping as though he'd swallowed glass.

All through his twenties he'd continued to miss his mother profoundly. He'd missed his brother, too, but it was his mother that he had been closest to. His mother had been the anchor when his father struggled. Andrew had somehow been able to block out their father's volatility, but Dal, the sensitive second son, hadn't been able to unplug from the drama and chaos.

Dal wasn't proud of the boy he'd been. Sensitive boys were no good to anyone and it took his father ten years to stomp the sensitivity out of him, but Dal survived, and became a man, and a relatively successful, stable man.

The jet came to a stop. His flight attendant, Sadie, rose from her seat to open the door. But Dal didn't move, not yet ready.

He turned to Poppy, who was reaching for her seat belt. "So we're in agreement, then? You give me the full two weeks I'm due, and then if you still want to leave, I'll personally put you on a plane home. But I need the two weeks, and I need you available, round the clock if need be."

Poppy's gaze met his. She held his gaze, too, not afraid to let him see the full measure of her disapproval. "Round the clock sounds excessive. I'm not your nursemaid, I'm your secretary. And at the end of the two weeks, I will most definitely still go, so don't just focus on finding your wife. Work on the replacement for me, too."

"I trust you to find me a suitable secretary."

"You're leaving the entire task to me?"

"You know what I like, and what I need."

Her brows arched over her clear brown eyes. "You might regret this."

"Possibly. But I'm in a bind, Poppy, and you're the only one that can save me."

"Now you're laying it on a tad thick."

The corner of his mouth lifted. "You like to be needed."

Two spots of color burned in her cheeks. "But I draw the line at becoming a business transaction."

He said nothing and silence stretched and yet she never once looked away.

"I don't think I've ever refused you anything," she said after a moment, "but I am now. I won't be manipulated. You have two weeks and then I'm gone."

It had taken every bit of Poppy's courage and strength to stand up to Randall—Dal—and define her terms, because if she didn't make it absolutely clear, then she'd find it very hard to resist him.

It had nearly melted her when he'd said he needed her. She liked being needed, and once upon a time, she would have given everything to hear him say that he needed *her*.

But things had changed, circumstances had changed, and she couldn't continue in his employment, not when he knew she had feelings for him. He'd use the knowledge to his advantage. He'd be able to manipulate her far too easily.

As it was, he was intimidating. Not frightening intimidating, but thrilling. He was so very handsome, and so very polished and so very accomplished.

Every time he entered a room, he seemed to light it up. She loved the way he moved, and the way he frowned and the way he'd focus on whatever he was reading.

She loved the way he held his teacup—

Oh, heavens, she loved him. She did. And it had been excruciating trying to manage her feelings and her attraction when he'd been engaged to Sophie. How could she possibly manage her envy and jealousy as he began to court someone new? She'd hate the new woman. She'd resent her far too much. It wouldn't be comfortable for any of them.

Poppy rose from her seat and smoothed her men's shirt, and then her hair, tucking it behind her ears to control the thick wave.

Dal was leaving the jet, descending the stairs, and she kept her eyes on his broad shoulders as she followed him down the five steps and onto the wide red carpet banded by gold. The brilliant crimson carpet was something of a shock, but even more surprising was the sheer number of people gathered on the tarmac.

There were rows of robed men, and then rows of armed men, and even a couple of men with what looked like musical instruments.

Dal, for his part, did not look pleased by the welcome. From the set of his shoulders and the rigid line of his back, she knew he was tense and angry. She fully expected him to step onto the carpet and proceed toward the helicopter. Instead, he turned to her and offered his hand, to aid her down the last few steps.

She felt a little silly accepting his help when she was

wearing jeans and tennis shoes, not the staggeringly high heels Sophie preferred. But his fingers closed around hers, and he gave her hand a quick, reassuring squeeze as she stepped from the stairs onto the carpet.

And then he let her hand go and he started walking down the carpet, which stretched from the plane to the side of a huge black helicopter with a gold emblem on the helicopter's door. The same gold emblem filled the middle of the crimson carpet, and two rows of men in long white robes and headwear stood on either side of the carpet.

It was intimidating as hell, she thought, swallowing nervously, picking up her pace to catch up to him. "Dal," she whispered, taking in the men farther back, the armed ones, with their big guns and vests and helmets. "Who are all these people?"

"The welcoming committee," he answered.

Well, the welcoming committee was bowing now to Dal, every head nodding as he passed. A shiver coursed through her as she trailed after him. It was the strangest greeting she'd ever seen, and beyond formal, reminding her of the ceremony reserved for England's royal family.

Poppy didn't know what Randall had done to earn such a welcoming, or what the emblem of sword, lamb and crown represented, but clearly the government of Mehkar was aware of his arrival today, and clearly the government of Mehkar wanted Dal to know they respected him.

At the helicopter Randall stopped and clasped hands with a robed man that looked close to Randall's age. The man said something to Randall in a foreign language, and Randall answered in the same language, and then they shook hands, and the handshake became a swift hug, and then the hug became a longer, warmer embrace.

When Randall stepped back, there was a sheen in his golden eyes, and a flicker of emotion that Poppy had never seen before. But then the emotion was gone and Randall's features were hard, and his expression remote. He assisted Poppy into the helicopter and she glanced back at the men Randall had called a welcoming committee, and it was only then that she noticed the rows of cars farther back, black limousines with tinted windows.

"That was quite impressive," she said, sliding into the seat by the far window and reaching for the harness.

"It was," he agreed as the pilot shut the helicopter door.

She felt dazed by the pomp and ceremony. "Who do you have to know to get a welcoming like that?"

"The king."

Her eyes widened. "He's one of the men you work with?"

"In my international work? No. My relationship with King Hamid is personal. I've known him my whole life." Randall hesitated. "King Hamid is my mother's father."

It took her a second to put the pieces together. "He's your *grandfather.*"

Randall nodded once. "My mother's father."

"That's why you received such a royal welcome."

"Here in Mehkar I am not Randall Grant, the Sixth Earl of Langston, but rather Sheikh Talal bin Mehkar."

It had been a day of shocks and surprises and this one was just as stunning. Poppy stared at him, bewildered. "You're a...*sheikh?*"

CHAPTER FIVE

POPPY'S HEAD THROBBED, the thumping at the base of her skull making her feel as if her head would soon explode. He was a sheikh *and* an earl? How was it possible?

Furthermore, how could she not know? Did *anyone* know?

It was one thing not to know that he had a private jet stashed in London, but another not to know his mother was a princess from Mehkar!

But thinking about it, Poppy realized she'd never read anything in the papers about his mother's family. There was very little in the society magazines about who she was, or where she came from, and Poppy knew because she used to read everything she could on Dal, and there were stories about his father, and his father's family, and lots of stories about Langston House itself, but very little about his mother. Some articles did briefly mention the tragic car accident that took the life of his mother and brother, but that was all that was ever said.

Now Poppy wondered if it was the Fifth Earl of Langston who'd kept his wife's name from the papers, or if it had been the royal family of Mehkar?

Poppy glanced at Dal. He was giving that impression of stone again, the same look he'd had this morning in the chapel. Detached. Immovable. It wasn't really a good look. It made her worry even more. "Dal?"

"Mmm?"

"Are you okay?"

"Never better," he answered mockingly.

She sighed and looked out the window, her stomach doing a little free fall when she did.

She'd been in helicopters before. She'd traveled with Randall in his helicopter dozens of times over the years, accompanying him to meetings, taking notes, pulling together his travel details, but the London-based helicopter was small compared to this one, and that one never flew over jagged mountains marked by narrow, deep ravines.

She tried not to look down. She didn't want to see just how close they were to the mountains, or how far from civilization, either.

There was nothing here.

Just scrub brush. The occasional flock of sheep. What seemed to be a sheepherder's hut made of mud and stacked stone.

Poppy exhaled softly, fingers curling into her palms, telling herself to relax. Not worry. But how could she not be concerned? The Randall Grant she thought she knew was gone, and this new man was even more complex and mysterious. "I know you said you didn't want to discuss Sophie anymore," she said carefully.

"Right."

"But I've been thinking about what you said, and how you feel betrayed by both Sophie and me, and I want to explain—"

"I wanted to hear earlier. But that was earlier. I've realized it doesn't matter. It won't change anything."

"But won't you always wonder?" When he didn't answer she drew a shaky breath. "Sophie met him in Monaco, during her hen party. It was on the last night. I don't know all that happened, only that he was there, and then he wasn't."

"She went with him?"

She couldn't meet his eyes. "I didn't know then that she had. I thought she'd maybe gone to get air, or maybe popped up to the room to freshen her makeup. We waited for her in the casino. We were drinking bubbly and playing roulette and I kept looking for her as I'd saved her seat as it was next to mine."

"She didn't return."

"She was back in her bed when I woke up the next morning."

"But she wasn't there when you went to bed."

Poppy drew a deep breath. "No."

"What time was that?"

She hesitated, debating telling him the details, wondering whether or not the details mattered now, after everything else that had happened.

"Late."

"Midnight? One? Two?"

Later than that, she silently answered, seeing herself in the opulent hotel room, sitting in the upholstered chair closest to the door, holding her phone, keeping vigil.

The other girls had all gone to bed.

Poppy couldn't, imagining the worst. Poppy was just about to dress and go down to the hotel reception and ask if she should contact the police when the text arrived.

Am fine. With Renzo. Go to sleep.

After getting Sophie's text, Poppy pressed the phone to her brow and squeezed her eyes shut, heartsick instead of relieved.

The fact that Sophie knew she'd be worried was small comfort.

Everything had changed.

Poppy continued her vigil until four-thirty when she finally fell asleep in that overstuffed chair. She was still curled in the chair when she woke an hour later and discovered the room dark, and Sophie tucked into her bed, pretending to sleep.

"We never discussed it," Poppy said carefully, and that

much was true. As they packed for their return to London, Sophie acted as if nothing had happened. And maybe nothing did happen. Maybe nothing would have happened. Maybe Sophie would have married Randall Grant this morning if Poppy hadn't sent the newspaper clippings to retired racecar driver, Renzo Crisanti, letting him know just who he'd taken to his bed five weeks before her wedding to the Earl of Langston.

On one hand, it was a terrible thing for Poppy to do.

On the other, it wouldn't have signified if Renzo hadn't stormed into the church and carried Sophie away with him.

Clearly, Sophie meant something to Renzo, and clearly Sophie had some interest in Renzo, too, because she hadn't kicked and screamed on the way out of the church.

It had been quite a scene, and profoundly uncomfortable, but the morning's events reassured Poppy that she'd done the right thing. She'd given Sophie not just a chance at love, but passion, too—

"Convenient," Dal said drily, sardonically. "Whatever you do, don't discuss the one thing that needs to be discussed."

The helicopter dipped and she grabbed at the harness straps connected to her lap belt and gave it a desperate tug. Thankfully, she was still secure, even though she felt as though her entire world had turned upside down.

Dal's gaze met hers, but he said nothing. He didn't need to, though. She could feel his fury.

Poppy looked away, out the window, fighting the emotion that threatened to overwhelm her as it crossed her mind that her note to Renzo hadn't just wrecked Sophie and Dal's wedding, but it'd wrecked her life, too.

Dal clenched his hand. He was so angry. So incredibly angry. He longed to smash his fist into Renzo Crisanti's face. He'd like to follow that blow with a series of hard jabs. Crisanti had no right. But then, Sophie had no right, either.

Jaw gritted, Dal glanced from the jagged red mountain range beneath them to Poppy's pale, stricken face and then he couldn't even look at her because she would marry him.

She didn't know it yet, but she didn't have a choice.

They traveled the rest of the way in tense silence, and then they were landing, heading for a sprawling pink villa. Tall, rose-pink walls surrounded the estate, while inside the walls it looked like a miniature kingdom complete with stables and barn, orchards and garden, and three different pools. They swooped lower, still, and her stomach dropped, too.

While the Gila airport transfer had been formal and choreographed, the arrival at the Kasbah was loud and joyous and chaotic. People were everywhere, and there was so much noise. Shouts and cheers and laughter and song.

Dal hadn't expected such a welcome, and from the look on Poppy's face, neither had she.

Poppy kept her smile fixed as she was greeted by one bowing, smiling woman after another, the women in long robes in bright jeweled colors. She was aware that the women greeted her only after first bowing to Randall. He, of course, received the biggest welcome, and it was a genuine welcoming, every staff member clearly delighted to see him. Several of the older men and women had tears in their eyes as they clasped his hand. One small, stooped woman kissed his hand repeatedly, tears falling.

Randall, so stoic in England, seemed to be fighting emotion as he leaned over to kiss the elderly woman's wrinkled cheek and murmur something in her ear.

Poppy got a lump in her throat as she looked at Randall with the tiny older woman. He wasn't affectionate with any of the staff in England, which made her even more curious about the elderly woman, but before she could ask, he brusquely explained the history as they walked toward the villa, shepherded by the jubilant staff.

"Izba was my mother's nanny," he said. "She used to look after me when we would visit Jolie. I hadn't expected her to still be alive."

"She was so emotional."

"She raised my mother from birth, and was closer to my mother than her own mother. Izba would have followed my mother to England, too, if my father had permitted it."

"Why wouldn't your father allow it?"

Randall shot her a mocking look. "He wanted my mother's wealth, not my mother's culture or family."

"It's not right to speak ill of the dead, but your father was—" She broke off, holding back the rest of the words.

"He was hard to love," Dal agreed. "And while he and I didn't have a good relationship, he was loving toward my brother. Andrew was his pride, his joy. My father was never the same after he died."

Poppy knew there had been a brother, but she'd never heard Randall speak of him, not in the four years she'd worked for Randall.

She shot him a troubled glance now, but before she could ask another question, they were climbing broad stairs and then passing beneath a graceful pink arch to enter a walled courtyard dominated by a huge blue fountain. White and purple bougainvillea covered the walls with pots of blooming lemon and orange trees in the corners of the courtyard. Two dark wooden doors were set in one of the long walls, and Randall opened one of those doors now.

"This is your suite," he said, leading her into a living room with a high ceiling covered in a dark carved wood. Windows lined one wall with the rest painted a warm golden khaki that made the floor-to-ceiling green-gold silk drapes shimmer in relief. The couch was covered in a vivid turquoise velvet; the two armchairs facing the sofa were covered in a luxurious silver silk. The lamps were silver, too, as was the giant sliding screen door that Randall pushed open to reveal the bedroom.

Again, one wall was nearly all floor-to-ceiling windows with views of the mountains and valley below. The bed dominated the large room, the bed itself enormous and low, covered in pristine white with two rows of plump white pillows. A long leather ottoman was placed at the foot of the bed while two silver nightstands were at the head of the bed. The ceiling had the same dark carved detail as in the living room, while a huge antique silver chandelier hung from the center of the ceiling, making the room glitter with soft iridescent light.

The space was expansive, furnishings were simple and yet the overall effect was sophisticated and glamorous. Poppy had slept in some beautiful rooms, but nothing came close to this understated luxury. Silks, satins and velvet. Furniture and wood covered in silver and gold.

"You're sure you want me in here? This looks like a room reserved for family."

"All rooms at the Kasbah are for family, and our special guests."

Something in his tone made her pulse jump. "When did I become a special guest?"

"When your job shifted from performing routine, mundane tasks to aiding me in a critical mission."

"Finding you a new secretary is a critical mission?"

"Absolutely. I'm a very busy, very important man. Surely you know that by now?" And then he smiled, his mocking, self-deprecating smile, and she felt a funny flutter in her chest. He was making fun of himself, teasing her in his self-deprecating manner, and she'd never been able to resist him when he made her smile.

"Can we please start with the search tomorrow? I'm beyond exhausted."

"Is this your way of saying you're not up for a big banquet tonight with live entertainment and a stream of visiting dignitaries?"

Poppy grimaced, unable to imagine a worse ending to what had been an absolutely horrendous day. "We're not really doing that, are we?"

"I am Prince Talal."

She saw the gleam in his golden eyes and the ache was back in her chest.

But then, she'd never been able to resist much about him. Even on the first day of work, she'd felt giddy in his presence. She'd thought that eventually she'd outgrow the juvenile reaction. Instead, she just developed deeper feelings, and a stronger attachment. "If you are indeed the prince, then you can excuse me from the lovely, but possibly lengthy, festivities."

"What if the festivities were short?"

"I've rather had it. I just want to go to bed and stay there forever."

"In that case, go to bed after dinner. Tomorrow is going to be a busy day. We have work to do, and since you're only here for fourteen days, we can't afford to waste any time."

"I'll be up early," she promised, unable to imagine life without him. It would be hard not seeing him almost every day. After she was gone, there would be no bounding out of bed, eager to get her day started.

"I'll have a tray sent to you," he said. "In the meantime, you'll find all the basics you'll need for the Kasbah in here." He opened one of the doors of the huge wardrobe. "I'm sure one of the dresses should fit, and then tomorrow one of the ladies' maids can adjust the others, and if need be, I can bring in a seamstress to make up anything else you might need."

"I don't need a lady's maid. I'm quite used to fending for myself."

"It would offend them if you refused assistance."

"Can you not explain that I'm English and eccentric?"

"Oh, I'm sure they'll realize just how eccentric you are, but please don't reject them. They've been trained by Izba, and Izba will want you happy."

Poppy sighed and rubbed at her forehead. "Fine. But there is no need to bring a seamstress in. I'm only here a short time and tunics are sort of a one-size-fits-all kind of dress. I should be fine without alterations."

"Sounds good. Sleep well, and I'll see you in the morning." Then he was gone, leaving her alone in the spacious suite.

Poppy had just opened the wardrobe to look for a nightgown when a light knock sounded on the door and then her door opened.

"Good evening," a young woman greeted Poppy in careful, stilted English. "May I please help you?"

"Thank you, but—" Poppy broke off, remembering Dal's warning and not wanting to offend anyone, much less within twenty minutes of arriving. "Yes, thank you. I was going to take a bath and then go to bed."

"I shall make your bath."

"Oh, no, I can start it myself. But I would like something for dinner. Perhaps salad or a sandwich?"

The young woman stared at Poppy clearly not understanding. "No bath?"

"Yes, I'll have a bath, but I can start it myself. I'd prefer if you could check on dinner."

"Please, more slowly." The girl's face crumpled. "My English is not so good."

So that was it. The poor girl didn't understand her. Poppy managed a tired smile. "Okay. Yes, I'll have a bath. Thank you."

* * *

Dal slept deeply, sleeping through the night and then until late in the morning, the blackout curtains in his room keeping the light out, allowing him to sleep far later than usual.

When he woke he was disoriented for a moment—the blackness of the room didn't help—and then it all came back to him.

The wedding.

The flight to Mehkar.

The helicopter ride to the Kasbah.

Dal left the bed and drew the heavy blackout curtains open, revealing brilliant sunshine. He could feel the heat trying to penetrate the thick glass windows. Thank goodness for thick stucco walls and triple glazed glass. The Kasbah remained cool even when temperatures soared outside.

He walked around his room, looking at it properly. This wasn't his room, at least, not the room he'd had as a boy. This room had been his grandfather's. It was the room reserved for the head of the family.

Apparently, here at Jolie he was the head of the family.

He felt like a disgrace.

He should have called his grandfather personally to let him know he was returning. He should have gone to the palace in Gila and met his grandfather for coffee or tea. He should have invited his grandfather here…

Dal opened the door to one of his terraces and stepped outside. Despite the heat, the air smelled fragrant, sweet.

He'd wondered if Jolie would still smell the same. It actually smelled better than he remembered—lavender and thyme, jasmine and orange blossoms.

He glanced down at the patio far below, and then at the tower off to his right. Past the tower he could see one of the tall external walls.

The Kasbah had been in the family hundreds of years, originally built as a fortress with thick external walls and tall towers offering vast, panoramic views ensuring that no one approached the Kasbah unseen.

The external walls were over fifteen feet tall and the same soft rose-peach hue as the palace itself, but once inside the huge gates, the hard surface of the walls disappeared, becoming a living garden, the plaster covered with flowering vines and lush scarlet, pink and white bougainvillea.

The Kasbah had been designed to protect the royal family in the event of a siege, with everything necessary for survival, but for a young boy that hadn't been its charm. Dal loved the towers and the secret rooms, the cool cellars and sunlit terraces with low couches piled high with silk pillows. He loved the clay pots used to cook his favorite dishes, chicken and lamb fragrant with saffron, fruit and spices.

The staff at Jolie was friendly, too, and in his mind, the staff had felt like family, always nodding and smiling and greeting him with warmth and pleasure.

Langston House was different. Even as a young boy he was aware of the difference and how no one smiled at Langston House. At Langston House the staff did not feel like family. They were servants. Menial. It was how his father liked things, the separation between classes, the distance between upstairs and downstairs. His father was the Fifth Earl of Langston, after all, raised with a clear sense of distinction and entitlement.

Dal's chest tightened up again, and he shifted in his seat, wishing he could just walk away from his past, and his father, but that would be the ultimate failure. His father had never expected Dal to succeed at anything, which is why Dal intended to keep his promise to his father—that he'd marry by thirty-five.

It was the only promise he'd ever made to his father and he'd honor the vow because then he'd be free.

And Dal longed to be free, not just of his father but the past.

With no time to waste, he rang for coffee and Poppy.

Poppy had thought her suite of rooms was lovely, but they were nothing compared to Dal's magnificent suite, which literally took up the entire second floor of the villa, bordered on all sides by sundrenched terraces and patios and fragrant, private gardens.

Like her, he had a living room and bedroom suite, but he also had a dining room, and office, all four rooms with the same floor-to-ceiling windows and doors that filled her suite with light.

He had papers, a notebook, pen and computer on a table outside, the area shaded by an elegant pergola covered with blooming jasmine.

"Is it too warm for you out here?" he asked, gesturing for her to sit in the chair by the laptop.

"It's comfortable now," she said, "but it'll definitely be quite hot later."

"I promise we'll move inside to an air-conditioned room before you melt."

She sat down in the low wooden chair with the teal pillows. "What am I to call you here? Dal? Prince Talal? Izba referred to you as Sheikh Talal, as well as His Highness. You have so many names."

"Not that many. My staff at the Kasbah will either call me Prince Talal, or Sheikh Talal. My family in Mehkar calls me Tal, although when we were in Gila, at the airport, my cousin addressed me as His Highness due to protocol."

"Your cousin? Which one was he?"

"The last man on the carpet."

"The one you hugged."

"Yes." Randall's mouth curved but his eyes were shuttered. "The last time I saw him he was just six years old. Now he's a man."

"How old were you the last time you were here?"

"Ten."

"You've both grown up."

"We have," he said, but there was no joy in his voice, just loss, and regret. And then his broad shoulders squared and his voice firmed. "Now to your question, you may call me anything you want, provided it's not Randall."

"You dislike your proper name that much?"

"My father is the only other person who has ever called me Randall."

She felt a shiver of distaste. No wonder he didn't like it. "I wish you'd told me that earlier."

"I tried. But you insisted Dal was too personal."

"I'm sorry."

"It's fine. Clearly, I survived the horror."

She shot him a swift look and was relieved to see that faint ironic smile of his. A smile she was learning that he used to hide hurts and needs, and all those emotions he viewed as weak. "But this is exactly what I mean. You have to talk. Tell people things. If I knew that the only other person who called you Randall was your father, and your father and you were not close, and it wasn't a positive or comfortable association—"

"You're getting a little carried away. You haven't inflicted any damage. I'm no more scarred than when you first met me."

She must have looked sufficiently startled because he grimaced. "That was supposed to make you smile."

Her brows pulled. "Do you think you're very scarred?"

"I was being amusing. Don't read too much into it."

But she couldn't help reading into it. She'd heard some horror stories about Randall's father, the Fifth Earl of Langston, and she'd long suspected that Dal's isolated nature was due to his father's volatility. Poppy carefully chose her next words. "Were you close to your mother?"

"Yes."

"What did she call you?"

"Tal."

All these years she'd thought she'd known him. She'd prided herself on knowing him better than anyone, but as it turned out, she didn't know the real Dal Grant at all. "Who are you?" she asked, smiling unsteadily.

His smile faded and he glanced away for a moment and when he looked back at her, his expression struck her as rather bleak. "Interesting question, Miss Marr. I'll have to get back to you on that one."

And then just as quickly, the darkness was gone and he was back to business. "Let's get started, shall we? I know you follow all of Sophie's friends, so how about we start by pulling up Seraphina's Instagram page—"

"No."

"No?"

"I'm not going to pore over Seraphina's social media. Or Florrie's. I promised I'd help find a new secretary, not a replacement for Sophie."

"I'd like your input on both."

"This makes me uncomfortable."

"It should. If you hadn't interfered yesterday, I'd be a married man today."

"You just think I did something, but you have no proof."

"And when I have proof? What then? How will you make it up to me?"

She shook her head, lips compressed.

"Poppy, I made my father a promise, and I'm not going to break that promise."

"Then perhaps you need a better list," she said, picturing Seraphina and Florrie. Both had been at Langston House yesterday for the wedding. Florrie was single at the moment—in between polo player lovers—and Seraphina was dating someone. It was in the early stages of the relationship but she apparently liked him and had told everyone he could be the one. Although that wasn't the first, or second, or even third time she'd said such a thing. "Only Florrie is currently single. Seraphina is seeing someone. She brought him to the wedding yesterday."

"I didn't notice."

"I'm not surprised. It was a tad hectic." She studied Dal, who looked handsome and rested this morning, his crisp white linen shirt the perfect foil for his black hair and golden eyes. "So tell me, how do you intend to proceed with your wooing?"

"I'll make a phone call, explain that I'm in need of a countess, and ask if she's interested."

"That's it?"

"Should I ask her to fill out an application and give five references?"

"Dal, this isn't the way to a satisfying relationship."

"You're a relationship expert now?"

She ignored the jab. "I'm not the one rushing into marriage, and I know it's been difficult these past few days, but you can't truly want a shallow, materialistic woman who is only marrying you for the title and money?"

"But that's exactly what I'm offering, and all I'm really offering—"

"That is not so. She gets you. *You.* And yes, you're a horrible, ridiculous, stubborn, awful man, but you're still you. Why give yourself to someone who doesn't care about you?"

"Because she'll be happier with the title and houses and bank account than she will with me."

"I don't know why you're saying these things."

"Why not let her enjoy herself? As long as she gives me heirs, she can do what she wants."

"I don't want to hear any more."

"It shouldn't upset you. You crossed yourself off the list of candidates. Who I marry, or how I choose my wife, shouldn't trouble you in the least."

"But of course it does! I care about you. I care about your happiness, or lack of happiness. I care that you lock yourself away from the world and just work, work, work. I care that you lost Sophie, and now you're in this position, but at the same time, I'm glad you didn't trap Sophie in a cold marriage. That wouldn't have been fair to her. She deserves so much more. And you deserve more, too, but you won't demand more and that absolutely baffles me."

She lifted the computer, rose and walked away.

Dal didn't stop her, letting her march away with the laptop as if she was the injured party.

She wasn't injured. She was lucky. She would soon have everything she wanted, and more.

A husband, a family, financial security, as well as respect. Once she was his wife, she'd have power and prestige. People would fall all over themselves wanting her approval, trying to ingratiate themselves.

She would be fine. He, on the other hand, was not. Normally, he was quite good at compartmentalizing emotions and suppressing anger, but he felt barely in control at the moment. He was being tested as his past, present and future collided together in a sickening crash of memories and emotions.

When he'd pictured Kasbah Jolie yesterday, he'd pictured a remote estate, someplace peaceful, and he'd imagined he'd arrive with very little fanfare, but the transfer in Gila had been anything but understated. The royal carpet, the line of dignitaries, the military guard behind, the royal helicopter itself. He hadn't wanted any of it. His flight crew had contacted the executive terminal at Gila and arranged for a helicopter for the Earl of Langston, but at no time had they dropped his Mehkar title. They couldn't have, as they didn't know it.

Which meant someone at the Gila airport had contacted the palace, and the king had ordered the welcome.

Dal frowned, his chest as heavy as his gut.

His grandfather knew he was here, aware that Dal had not just come home, but had once again shut him out, choosing to retreat to the mountain palace rather than attempt any form of reconciliation.

Dal didn't know why he was treating his grandfather the same way his father had—with callous contempt and utter disregard. What was wrong with him? Why couldn't he be kind to the one man who'd always been kind to him?

Dal planned on accomplishing two things before he left Mehkar: he'd be married, and he'd finally make peace with his grandfather.

CHAPTER SIX

Poppy settled down to work at the desk in the library on the main floor. The room had a soaring, dark-beamed ceiling, arched windows and walls the color of deep red rubies. The beamed ceiling had been stenciled in gold, and the big light fixtures were gold, and then there were the floor-to-ceiling shelves filled with leather-bound books that looked to be hundreds of years old.

Poppy had discovered the room earlier this morning and couldn't wait to return. She opened her laptop, checked the internet and was pleased to see that it worked just as well here as it did at home. It wasn't long before she had accessed all her files through the cloud storage system on the laptop. All of Dal's companies used the same cloud storage, making it easy to use any computer, anywhere.

She checked her email, and then scanned BBC's news and then reached out by email to several prominent employment agencies, sharing the details about the secretarial position to be filled, and how they were hoping to fill the job as soon as possible.

She received a reply from each almost immediately. One wanted her to fill out a more complete questionnaire, while the other promised to begin forwarding résumés later that afternoon.

With no résumés to review yet, Poppy wasn't quite sure what to do with her time next.

And then she thought of Sophie. Where was she? And how was she?

Poppy opened her email and sent Sophie a quick message.

I'm with Dal in Mehkar. Where are you? How are you? Fill me in, please!

And then, because her curiosity was getting the best of her, she went back online and studied Florrie and Seraphina's social media accounts.

Florrie had shared a photograph taken outside Langston House before the wedding had begun. She was with Seraphina and several other beautiful girls and they were all smiling for the camera.

Seraphina was a dark brunette and Florrie was a golden blonde. They were both gorgeous and glamorous, and they knew how to wear clothes well.

But that didn't make them good matches for Dal.

Poppy was staring at the photo hard, so hard, she didn't hear Dal enter the library.

"Are you trying to decide which one is better for me?" he asked, leaning over her desk chair to get a better look at the photo of four smiling women.

She closed the computer quickly. "What are you doing here?"

"Checking on your progress. Any good résumés yet?"

"One agency asked me to fill out a questionnaire, while the other has promised to begin forwarding résumés straightaway."

"Was the questionnaire complicated?"

"No." She wiggled in her chair, not willing to admit that she'd somehow managed to forget all about completing the form. She didn't know how she could forget.

"So you are all done with everything right now?"

"I'm caught up for the moment, if that's what you're asking."

"Yes. Great. I'd like your help in my search." He lifted a hand to stop her when she started to protest. "And I know you don't want to. Sophie was your friend and you're very loyal to her, but Sophie is no longer in the picture and I need a wife."

"But how can I help you when you won't even help yourself?"

"What does that mean?"

"You can't treat your next fiancé the way you treated Sophie. It was criminal. You were the King of Cold, the Master of Remote." She shrugged at his frown. "It's true, Dal. I'm telling you the truth. Please don't propose to another woman without being willing to give her more."

Dal couldn't believe they were back to discussing this intangible "more" again. It was beyond infuriating.

It was also beyond infuriating to have to play this game with her. He wasn't even considering Florrie or Seraphina as a future wife. There was only one woman on his list and that was Poppy. But if he told Poppy that, she'd have a nervous breakdown, and they didn't need that. He had to get married, but he preferred marrying someone stable. And most days Poppy was stable. She was also dependable, and someone he trusted. Perhaps Sophie had done him a huge favor.

"I'm not sure I know how to go about demanding more," he said flatly, battling to hide his irritation. "I am not sure I even know what this 'more' would look like."

"More is just more, Dal. More companionship. More conversation. More laughter. Possibly more tears—"

"Not that, please."

She sighed, but continued on. "More would also be more friendship, and more support, more encouragement, more happiness."

"That's a great deal of more."

"Yes, it requires some thought and effort, but that's how you develop a relationship. It's how people get to know you, and you would get to know them. It takes time, too." Her wide brown eyes met his. "And it's not something money can buy. So you can't throw money at it. If anything, money makes it worse."

"How so?"

Her brows pulled, her expression troubled. "Money is power, and power thrives on inequality. True friendship, just like true love, doesn't care about position, or prestige. It wants what is best for the other person."

Her words grated on his nerves, putting an uncomfortable knot in his chest. He didn't know why her thoughts bothered him so much, but it took every bit of his control not to retort sharply, mockingly. He didn't like the world of feelings and emotions. He didn't enjoy the company of emotional people. Poppy was the sole exception, and maybe that was because at work he could normally steer her in a different direction, and she'd oblige him. But here, here was proving to be a different matter.

"Please don't make me lose all respect for you," he said with a hard, sardonic smile. "Feelings are massively over-rated."

"But I didn't specifically say *feelings*," she answered quietly. "I was very careful not to use the word *feelings*. Apparently, that's all you heard, though."

"I think I stopped listening when you said I couldn't solve the problem by throwing money at it."

"You can make all the jokes you want, but you can't change the truth, and the truth is, you have to open up more, and give more and be present in the lives of those who love you."

He shot her a wry glance. "You make me sound like an ass."

"Well, you can be intolerable at times."

"And yet you're still fighting to save me."

"Just for another two weeks."

"So altruistic, then, trying to whip me into shape for the next secretary."

"I'm more concerned about the next fiancée. She's the one that would get the short end of the stick because she will expect a relationship. The secretary won't."

"Have you always been so pragmatic?"

"Charity girls can't afford to wear rose-colored glasses."

And yet Poppy did. Poppy was the least practical, most idealistic woman he'd ever met. He functioned best when his world was cool, precise and analytical...the complete opposite of the world Poppy inhabited.

"Perhaps you didn't get the memo," he answered, aware that she'd had a difficult past. Poppy had lost her mother to cancer and then her father died ten years later, leaving Poppy all alone. Or, she would have been alone if it wasn't for Sophie. "You love your fairy tales and rainbows."

"You forgot lemon drops and fireworks. I love those, too." Then she shrugged. "I know it's hard for you to stomach, but my parents met in school, fell in love and never dated anyone else. They were totally devoted to each other, as well as really happy together...despite Mum's cancer, and the creditors constantly calling."

Her shoulders shifted. "And then when they were both gone, Sophie gave me a second home. She looked after me and showed me what real friendship is. I learned that love isn't just a romantic thing. Love is kindness and commitment and doing what's best for the other person. And that's what I want for you. I want you to have a kind wife. A woman who will commit to you and do what's best for you, and in return, you would be kind to her, and loyal to her and put her needs first, too."

"If you care so much about my happiness, why not just marry me? Wouldn't that be the simplest thing to do?"

For a long moment she said nothing, and then her throat worked and her voice sounded low and rough. "I've never had much in life in terms of material things, but I was loved, dearly, by my parents, and if I ever marry, it will be for love. A marriage without love is doomed from the start."

By the time Poppy made it back to her room, she was absolutely worn out.

These intense conversations with Dal drained her, and part of her wanted to just give up on him and stop trying to help, but the only way she could handle the idea of leaving him was by thinking she was leaving him better off than he was now.

The man didn't need more money. The man didn't need more people to bow and scrape. What Dal needed was honesty. He needed someone to care enough about him to tell him the truth. He needed to be pushed to try harder and give more and be more…and she knew he could, because during the past four years she'd seen a softer side of him. She'd experienced his kindness and patience firsthand. He knew how to talk and be good company, too. But she also knew that it had to be his choice, on his terms, or he'd just shut you out and become that remote, unfeeling ice man that Sophie dreaded.

Poppy showered and then wrapped a cotton robe around her and headed to the wardrobe to see what she'd wear for dinner.

Poppy knew from this morning that the wardrobe was full of long tunics in every color of the rainbow. She'd stroked the vivid fabrics, pausing at a brilliant green gown with gold embellishments from the plunging neckline all the way down the gauzy fabric, and then an ivory one, and another ivory one this time with hot pink fringe all around the sleeves and edges of the long, narrow skirt. The dresses were like art, each unique but stylish and impossibly pretty. Poppy didn't know how she was supposed to choose just one to wear when they were all so beautiful.

She now flipped through all the dresses again, this time stopping at a rich gold dress with full three-quarter sleeves. The sleeves were dotted with a graphic black-and-white sunburst pattern, with black-and-white trim down the front, and along the hem of the straight gold skirt.

But Poppy's favorite part of the dress were the two playful black-and-white fringe pom-poms that hung from the V-neckline.

"Would be beautiful on you, my lady," a soft voice said from behind her in slow, broken English.

Poppy turned around and smiled as she spotted Izba in the doorway.

"These gowns are exquisite," Poppy said.

Izba stepped into the room and closed the door behind her. "His Highness Talal's mother designed them," she said, crossing to the wardrobe and reaching into the closet to draw out a white lace kaftan with coral-red embroidery on the shoulders and vibrant coral-red fringe at the sleeves and hem. "She thought clothes should make a woman happy."

Izba spoke with a quiet sincerity that put a lump in Poppy's throat. "Talal's mother was very talented," Poppy answered huskily.

The elderly woman's dark brown eyes shone and she carefully hung the white lace gown up. "She was most beautiful woman in Mehkar, but with the most beautiful heart in the world." She turned around to look at Poppy. "Which dress you wish to wear for tonight?"

"I don't know which one to pick. What do you think I should wear?"

Izba's lips pursed and her dark gaze swept Poppy before she faced the closet again. She studied the rack for a long moment, cheeks puffing, until she reached in and lifted out a dark cherry gown with big cheerful silver flowers embroidered across the bodice before becoming delicate trailing flowers down the skirt. The sleeves were plain except for a thick silver bank of embroidery at the cuff.

"These are poppies," Izba said in her careful, stilted English. "Just like your name, yes?"

Poppy didn't know why she wanted to cry. Instead, she nodded and smiled. "That's perfect."

"Perfect," Izba echoed carefully, smiling affectionately. "Once you are dressed, I will fix your hair."

"Oh, I don't need help with my hair."

"His Highness expects us to help you."

"Yes, but his—" Poppy broke off, unable to call Randall anything remotely like His Highness, and she searched for the right words. "His…your Prince Talal…knows I am accustomed to taking care of myself. I prefer taking care of myself."

Izba's already wrinkled brow creased further. "But as his wife—"

"Oh! No. *No.* I think there's been a mistake, and I understand the confusion, but I'm not his wife. I work for Talal. I'm his secretary."

Izba stared at her, dark eyes assessing. "You are not just friend. You are to marry the prince."

"No! Oh, Izba, no." Poppy swallowed hard, thinking this was incredibly uncomfortable but she had to make the older woman understand. "Believe me, I am not marrying Prince Talal. I serve as his secretary, nothing more." She drew a quick breath. "I've agreed to help him find a wife, but Izba, it's not me."

Before they came to Jolie, Dal would have described Poppy as pretty, in a fresh, wholesome, no-nonsense sort of way with her thick, shoulder-length brown hair and large, brown eyes and a serious little chin.

But as Poppy entered the dining room with its glossy white ceiling and dark purple walls, she looked anything but wholesome and no-nonsense.

She was wearing a silk gown the color of cherries, delicately embroidered with silver threads, and instead of her usual ponytail or chignon, her dark hair was down, and long, elegant chandelier earrings dangled from her ears. As she walked, the semi-sheer kaftan molded to her curves, highlighting her full, firm breasts and swell of hips.

"It seems I've been keeping you waiting," she said, her voice pitched lower than usual and slightly breathless. "Izba insisted on all this," she added, gesturing up toward her face.

At first Dal thought she was referring to the ornate silver earrings that were catching and reflecting the light, but once she was seated across from him he realized her eyes had been rimmed with kohl and her lips had been outlined and filled in with a soft plum-pink gloss. "You're wearing makeup."

"Quite a lot of it, too." She grimaced. "I tried to explain to Izba that this wasn't me, but she's very determined once she makes her mind up about something and apparently, dinner with you requires me to look like a tart."

Dal checked his smile. "You don't look like a tart. Unless it's the kind of tart one wants to eat."

Color flooded Poppy's cheeks and she glanced away, suddenly shy, and he didn't know if it was her shyness or the shimmering dress that clung to her curves, outlining her high, full breasts, but he didn't think any woman could be more beautiful, or desirable than Poppy right now. "You look lovely," he said quietly. "But I don't want you uncomfortable all through dinner. If you'd rather go remove the makeup I'm happy to wait."

She looked at him closely as if doubting his sincerity. "It's fun to dress up, but I'm worried Izba has the wrong idea about me."

"And what is that?"

"She seems to think you're going to…marry…me."

When he said nothing, she added, "I know I'm not on your 'list' anymore, and so I'm not suggesting you're encouraging her, but it's awkward trying to convince her that I'm not going to be your new wife."

"I'll have a word with her," he said, and he would have a word with Izba, but not about this. The fact was, Poppy would be his wife. She was going to marry him. He knew exactly how to get her acquiescence. Women thought they needed words. But even more than language, they needed touch.

He was trying to hold off on seduction, though. He didn't want to trick her into being his wife, nor did he want to use her body against her. But she would capitulate, if he seduced her. She was already his even without a single touch.

His goal was to get her to think marriage was her idea. It was far better to let her believe the idea was hers. She'd be a far happier, and more malleable bride that way.

"Thank you." She glanced down, fingertips grazing the silver beadwork near her shoulder. "Did you know this is your mother's design?"

"What do you mean?"

"Every dress in the wardrobe in my room was designed by your mother. Izba said she was an aspiring fashion designer when she married your father."

"I didn't know," he said after a long moment. "I had no idea." He frowned at the candle on the table, surprised that such a little detail should knock him off guard, but it did. It might be a small thing, but it said so much about who she was, and the dreams she'd had.

"She had tremendous style," he said gruffly. "I always knew she was different from other mums, but I don't think I appreciated the differences until it was too late."

"I wish I'd had the chance to meet her. She sounds so lovely."

"She was." And then because he found the memories unbearable, he smashed the past, making the memories vanish. As the memories faded, so did the ache. The ache didn't completely disappear, but at least it was manageable.

He signaled to one of the stewards standing in the corner. "Let's eat."

Dinner was a feast, with salad after salad, followed by warm, fragrant pilaf and delicious pan-seared salmon, and of course there was dessert, the waiter tempting Poppy with the description of the honey and mint syrup cake served with a small scoop of spiced vanilla ice cream on the side.

Poppy was full from dinner and was going to reluctantly pass on the cake, until Dal suggested she skip the ice cream and try a slice. He said the cake had just been baked; he'd smelled it earlier in the oven and it was his favorite cake because it was topped with a thick, crunchy layer of slivered honey-glazed almonds.

Poppy couldn't resist the description and the cake was even better than Dal described. She ate her slice, and had just popped a stray slivered almond into her mouth when Dal leaned back in his chair and told her he'd spoken with Seraphina earlier.

Poppy almost choked on the almond. She coughed to clear her throat. "You called her?"

"I did," he said casually as if this was no big deal.

"When?"

"This afternoon." His broad shoulders shifted carelessly. "She was surprised to hear from me, but she quickly warmed up. It seems she and her new boyfriend had a fight on the drive home from the wedding." He looked at her, lashes lowering, concealing the gold of his eyes. "She's not sure if it's going to work out between them."

Poppy's heart fell. She didn't know why she felt such a rush of disappointment. She should want this for him. He needed a wife. Quickly. If tall, slim, Sloane Ranger Seraphina could fit the bill, why shouldn't he marry her?

"That's good," she said faintly, struggling to smile. Many would consider Seraphina an excellent substitution for Sophie. Seraphina's family was far wealthier than the Carmichael-Joneses, and Seraphina was wildly popular, always in the press, photographed at all the right events, and big parties and fashion shows.

The fact that she was as shallow as a plate was only problematic if one wanted a wife with emotions…

"You don't sound very convincing," he said, reaching for his wineglass. "I thought you'd be pleased. I'd much rather narrow down my list to just one and focus on courting her, rather than jumping back and forth between two women."

"You don't want to even give Florrie a chance?"

"I was under the impression that you didn't think Florrie would be a suitable match."

"I never said anything against her."

"But you implied she's one of those horsey girls, always at a polo match."

"Did I? I don't remember."

"I ride, but I'm not by any means an equestrian. If polo is her passion, she wouldn't be happy with me."

"And Seraphina is a clothes horse, always seen in the front row of some fashion show or other."

"Yes, but I wouldn't be expected to attend the fashion shows with her. That's something she could do on her own, and no one would think twice about her being in Paris or Milan or New York without me."

"Don't you want to be with your wife?"

"No."

"Dal!"

"Don't you want your wife to want to be with you?"

"Not really. I enjoy my own company. Besides, if Seraphina is currently disgruntled with the new boyfriend, she'll welcome my attention and it shouldn't take much effort to close the deal with her."

"I've never heard a worse proposal."

"I'm not a romantic man."

"That might be why you lost Sophie."

He gave her a look that wasn't pleasant. Clearly, he didn't appreciate her honesty, but honesty is what he needed. "Women aren't things to park on shelves or in closets. They want and need time and attention."

"The *more* you're constantly harping on."

"Or in your case, some. *Some* time. *Some* attention." She was angry now, and she didn't even try to hide her irritation. "Never mind a token of affection, because I know you gave Sophie almost none."

"Sophie didn't like being touched."

"Sophie *craved* affection. You're the one that rejected her."

"She recoiled every time I reached for her."

"But did you talk to her before you reached for her? Did you take her to dinner? Did you send her flowers? Did you plan anything fun? No. It was strictly business, and cold as hell."

"And you've thought this all these years?"

"Yes."

"Why didn't you say something?"

"Because it wasn't my place, and she didn't complain, not until this last year, and then she wasn't complaining as much as…panicking. I thought maybe the sheer size of the wedding was overwhelming her, but clearly it wasn't the wedding. It was you."

"Of course you'll be Team Sophie until the bitter end."

"I'm on your team, too. That's why I'm spoiling my delicious dessert, trying to make you understand that it takes two to make a marriage. You can't just put a ring on someone's finger and be done with it."

"I did care about Sophie. I cared a great deal. But the fact is, I couldn't seem to make her happy. It was as if she didn't want to be happy with me—"

"You're just saying that now."

"You wanted honesty. I'm being honest. She didn't want to marry me. But she couldn't stand up to her parents."

"And when did you realize this? Five and a half years ago?"

"No. This past year. I tried to plan several special occasions for us—theater, shopping, dinner. She agreed to each and looked beautiful every time we stepped out, but there was no...conversation. There was no...warmth. Even her smiles looked forced as if she was suffering and barely tolerating my company."

"Martyred for the cause," Poppy muttered.

Dal glanced at her, eyes narrowed. "What did you say?"

She was so annoyed with him, and all of them. Money and power changed people, inflating their sense of worth, and bringing out the worst in them. "Your fathers shouldn't have arranged the marriage, not against your wishes."

"I didn't protest very much. It was easier just to make him happy. Less conflict, and honestly, I didn't care who I married."

"Why not?"

"I don't feel emotions like you. I don't feel love, and I wouldn't have ever married for love."

"Well, Sophie did, and she tried to fight it." Poppy saw Dal's startled expression. "I overheard them once, Sophie and her parents. It was a terrible row. They said terrible things to her, squashing her completely." She swallowed hard. "I think that's why she stuck up for me, from early on. Because she never had anyone who stuck up for her."

And this was why Poppy did what she did, sending newspaper clippings to Renzo Crisanti.

She wanted Sophie to have a chance at happiness. She wanted Sophie to have more.

Just as she still wanted Dal to have more.

"You're making me feel like the devil," Dal said roughly.

"That's not my intention."

He shifted at the table, features tight, jaw jutting. "I had no idea she'd been pressured to marry me. It disgusts me to think that she was being forced into a marriage with me."

"You both deserved better."

He rose from the table and crossed the room, hands in his trouser pockets. "No wonder you looked elated when Crisanti showed up. You were thrilled she'd escaped the marriage. You were thrilled she was escaping marrying me."

"Yes," she answered. "I was. No woman should be forced into marriage with a man. Not even if it's in marriage to you."

"Thanks…?"

"You know I mean it in the nicest, sincerest way, because you're aware of how I feel about you. I have that… soft spot. I see all the good things in you that Sophie couldn't see."

"Really? What did you fall in love with, since it clearly wasn't my title and wealth?"

"You give to others, constantly, generously. You provide leadership to developing countries. You donate money to developing businesses, particularly businesses headed by women. But you don't just give money, you give time, and wisdom, and you listen to these people. You truly care."

"So why did you take yourself off my list?"

"Because you care about everyone but yourself. You don't love yourself. You barely like yourself, and it would be difficult, if not impossible, being your wife when I know you'd never love me—"

"But I'd want you."

"Not the same thing."

"Physical pleasure can be incredibly satisfying."

"But it's not love, and I want true love, and I'm holding out for a man who will move the moon and stars for me."

He made a rough, mocking sound. "I understand that I expect too little from marriage, but you, my darling Poppy, expect too much."

"Maybe. But I'd rather believe in happy-ever-after then be bitter, cold and cynical."

"Like me?"

"I think you're cynical because it's easier than trying to muddle through with emotions. Far better to be coldly intellectual than a flesh and blood human being—"

"Just because I don't believe in romantic love doesn't mean I don't bleed when cut."

"I've never seen you bleed, or grieve. You lost your fiancée yesterday and yet you never shed a tear."

"Maybe because she wasn't the right one for me. Maybe because I'm relieved that I have an unexpected opportunity to find the right woman and make this work."

"You're not acquiring a company, Dal. You're talking about marrying a woman!"

"And I think you're angry because you'd like to be that woman, only you're too afraid to allow your dreams to become reality—"

"A life with you isn't my dream. You would never, ever be able to give me what I need!"

He crossed the room, walking toward her with such deliberate intention that it made her heart race. "That's just another excuse. You are full of them today. Why don't you stop acting like a little girl and fight for what you want?"

She backed up a panicked step. "You're not what I want!"

"Bullshit." And then he trapped her against the wall, wrapped an arm low around her waist and pulled her close.

Poppy knew a split second before his head dropped that he was going to kiss her, and she stiffened, shocked, surprised, but also curious.

And then his mouth covered hers and she felt an electric jolt shoot through her. He was right about her fantasies. She'd imagined this for years. She'd had a few dates here and there but she was essentially an inexperienced, twenty-six-year-old virgin. It had been easy remaining a virgin, too, because Dal was the only man she wanted, and how could any other man measure up to him? No one was as handsome. No one as intelligent. No one as powerful.

And now he was holding her, kissing her and tremor after tremor coursed through her. The kiss felt like a claiming. There was nothing tentative in the way his mouth slanted over hers, his mouth warm, his breath cool. Her senses felt flooded and her brain struggled to take it all in…his smell, his warmth and then there was that delicious pressure of his body so hard and lean against her, his chest a wall of muscles.

His head finally lifted and he stared deep into her eyes. "Tell me you didn't want that to happen."

"Do you enjoy humiliating women?"

"I wanted it to happen." His narrowed gaze examined every inch of her face. "Because I've spent years trying not to imagine that kiss."

It was true, too. Dal would have never kissed her while engaged, or married. He would have never acted on any kind of impulse—there would be no impulse—if he wasn't single, but he was single now and she was single, and she was more than available. When she looked at him, she practically offered herself up to him. The sacrificial maiden, the innocent virgin—

He stopped himself, brow furrowing as he glanced at her. "Are you a virgin?"

Her cheeks burned with color. Her eyes flashed dangerously. "That is none of your business."

"So it's a yes," he answered, fascinated by the bloom in her cheeks and the bruised pink of her lips. Emotion darkened her eyes now, making her wonder what she'd look like after she'd shattered with pleasure.

"There is no need for you to be horrible," she protested breathlessly.

She was aroused but fighting it.

He respected her more for fighting it. "Not trying to be horrible," he said, thinking she needed another kiss, as did he. "Just trying to figure out why you still want to fight the attraction. There's no reason. Sophie is gone. I'm single. You're single."

"You are so incredibly unromantic."

"Lust isn't always romantic, but it's real."

"Well, I don't lust for you. I have feelings for you. A huge difference."

"But that's where you're wrong. You might have feelings for me, but you also desire me. I can prove it."

Her eyes had clung to his as he spoke, her wide, dark eyes showing every single thing she was feeling. She was aroused and curious but also remarkably shy and innocent. Holding her against him, he could feel how her slim body hummed with tension, as well as the wild beating of her heart. She was as soft as he was hard, as warm as he was cold, and as he gazed down into her lovely expressive eyes, he thought Sophie had indeed done him a favor.

Dal could imagine Poppy as his wife. A sweet, kind, warm wife. The kind of woman who'd be a sweet, kind, warm mother, too.

"Let's revisit the subject of lust," he said, just before his head dipped and his mouth covered hers to part her full, soft lips and plunder the inside of her hot, sweet mouth. His tongue teased hers, stirring her senses, making her clutch at his arms and whimper against his mouth.

He pressed her closer, shaping her to him, his hand settling on her pert, round derriere. He cupped her bottom, caressing the generous curve, and she shuddered and arched against him, her entire body trembling as if he'd set her on fire.

He shifted around so that he could lean back against the wall while he positioned her between his thighs. He felt hard and savage as he drew her hips against his hips, letting her feel the heavy length of his erection.

She sighed against his mouth, and her breasts peaked against his chest. He relished the feel of her tight nipples and he stroked up, from her hips over the small of her waist to caress the side of her full breast.

She shivered again and made soft, incoherent sounds that heated his blood and made him want to rip her dress off and devour her here.

It had been so long since he'd been with anyone, and forever since he'd felt this way. He'd forgotten what desire felt like. He'd forgotten the insistent throb of need, and the need to claim. And he didn't want just anyone, he wanted her, all of her, and the more she gave, the more he wanted to take. His thumb found her breast, her nipple pebbled tight, pressing through the thin silk of her kaftan. He rubbed the tip, pinching it, just to hear her gasp and feel her hips twist against his.

He ached, and his erection throbbed and he felt more alive than he had in years. Not just years. But decades.

He stroked Poppy's full, round breast again, and beneath her breast, before palming the fullness, savoring the shape and weight. He loved her curves, and her sensual nature, amazed that she'd hidden both all these years with her ugly practical wardrobe and shy, retiring smile.

Poppy was not shy or retiring at all.

Poppy was a goddess and he could not wait to take her to bed.

She was exactly what he needed. And he would have her. It wasn't a matter of if, but when.

Reluctantly, he lifted his head. Her dark eyes were cloudy and her gaze unfocused. She swayed in his arms, off balance.

"We'll marry end of this week," he said tightly, reining in his hunger so that he could attempt to be logical and rational. "I don't know if you want to stay here for a honeymoon, or if you'd want to travel somewhere else."

She blinked up at him, still dazed. *"What?"*

"It will just be a very simple ceremony. A civil ceremony. And then with formalities done, we can do what we want. Honeymoon here, or travel to someplace you've never been."

She gave him a shove, freeing herself. "I'm not marrying you!"

"You are, and you want to. Stop fighting the inevitable."

Her face flushed pink. "Excuse me, but what planet are you living on? I never agreed to marry you, and just because I kissed you doesn't mean we're suddenly a couple."

"We should be."

"Because I kissed you back? Ha!" She took another quick step back, arms folding over her chest. "I have kissed dozens of men and I've never married any of them!"

"I don't care if you kissed three hundred. You're a virgin. You want me. You belong to me."

"Ahem. I don't belong to you, or with you. In fact, I gave notice that I'm leaving you. So, maybe you need to go out there and find someone you can actually date, and court and hopefully marry before you lose your precious earldom and your historic Langston House!"

Poppy practically fled back to her room, nearly bumping into Imma as she threw open her door.

Poppy wished Imma a good night and then once alone, began to pace her floor before flinging herself on her bed, replaying the entire scene with Dal in her head. What a scene it was! The words he'd said, those obnoxious, arrogant words, and then the kiss…

Oh, the kiss…

But no, she wouldn't think about the kiss. That was the most impossible thing of all, too much like the fairy tales she'd loved as a girl because those stories about good and evil, lightness and darkness, helped explain the world and the things that had happened in her world—the financial struggles, her mother's prolonged battle with cancer, a battle they'd thought she'd won, *twice*, only to relapse and die just after Poppy's thirteenth birthday. It had just gotten worse after that. Her father couldn't juggle his job and fatherhood and on the advice of friends, had found a boarding school that offered scholarships to promising young women in need.

She was in need, but poverty was the least of her woes.

She missed her mother and her father and what she'd thought of as family.

But just when she didn't think she could take any more, there was Sophie, lovely, strong Sophie, who took Poppy under her wing, becoming her champion when Poppy was at her lowest.

Sophie had given Poppy her hope back, and hope was everything. Hope made one look forward. Hope helped one to focus on what lay ahead rather than what was behind. Hope made all things possible, and had more than once lifted her from despair.

Hope also meant that she could dream of happy endings, if not for her, then for Sophie, which is why Poppy had written to Renzo in the first place. Poppy had wanted to save Sophie from a loveless marriage. She wanted Sophie to have the life she deserved, which meant true love. Passionate love. Forever love.

The kind of love Poppy's parents had. Poppy's father had dearly loved her mother, taking her to every chemo and radiation treatment and staying with her after.

His love had been fierce and unwavering even to the bitter end.

The love and tenderness he'd shown her mother allowed her mother to say, even after she'd been taken to hospice, that she'd met her prince and had lived happily-ever-after. Their relationship hadn't been one of lust but trust and respect, and that was the marriage Poppy wanted. That was truly the ultimate fairy tale. Dal's idea of marriage made her ill, which is why she would never, ever agree to marry him, or to even be a candidate on his "list." She didn't even believe in lists. Or candidates. She believed in love, real love, true love.

And yet his kiss, that kiss, pure magic…

So unbelievably—

No.

No. She wouldn't think about it, not anymore.

Poppy jumped off her bed, unable to remain inside her bedroom a moment longer but not sure where to go, and then glancing out one of her windows, she spotted the enormous lap pool, gleaming with all the pool lights on.

She rifled through her wardrobe until she found the drawer with the swimsuits and grabbed the black bikini with the gold beads on the straps and hips. She topped the suit with a feather-light green gauze tunic and headed downstairs to the long lap pool illuminated for the evening.

Thankfully, there was no one outside, and she could commandeer any one of the dozen lounge chairs.

She picked a chair in the corner and kicked off her leather sandals and peeled off her tunic, dropping them onto the chair before diving into the pool.

She swam under water as far as she could before she had to surface to get air. Turning onto her back she floated for a moment, feeling some of the tension melt away.

And then from beneath her lashes, she spotted a shadowy figure on one of the terraces above, and she knew from the width of the shoulders who it was.

Poppy turned over onto her stomach and dove back down, swimming below the surface as if she could hide from him.

Maybe he didn't see her.

Maybe he'd ignore her.

Somehow she doubted it. There was too much unsettled between them. And that kiss had been so explosive. She'd always wanted to kiss him but that kiss…that hadn't been what she'd ever imagined.

That kiss had been pure sex, pure sin, and if she hadn't fled when she did, she would have given herself up to him.

Dal watched Poppy swim in the glowing pool below.

She looked beautiful and sensual floating in the water, her dark hair glistening in the light of the pool. He very much wanted to go down and dive in and draw her toward him, continuing what they started.

She'd feel warm and soft, and slick in the water. He could imagine cupping her full breasts and then her rounded derriere.

She was almost naked. He wanted her naked. He wanted her stripped and exposed so that he could drink her in.

She was lush and ripe and unbearably sweet. Her kisses earlier had driven him half-mad. They were ardent and innocent at the same time, and her passionate response had woken a hunger and even now, a half hour later, he still burned.

Everything in him wanted to go down to the pool and take her, and claim her. But he wasn't going to just seduce her. That would be too easy. He wanted her to want him, and want to be with him, but not just for one night. For all nights. Forever.

She needed to marry him. She needed to agree to be his wife.

As his wife, he would spoil her and shower her with gifts and things, endless beautiful things. He'd also give her security and stability. As well as pleasure.

Always pleasure.

But first, the wedding ceremony.

There would be no sex, not until he had his ring on her finger.

CHAPTER SEVEN

POPPY SPENT THE next morning going through the various résumés and applications that had been forwarded, rejecting the ones that would not be a good fit, and then setting aside the possibilities. She even followed up on the references of two different women who'd stood out.

After finishing with the applications, she answered new emails that had come in during the night. There were a few from concerned associates, as well as three very bold inquiries from one member of the press. The reporter was with an American tabloid and asked if Poppy could jump on the phone with her for a quick call, and if that wasn't possible, perhaps Poppy would send a few words…maybe a quote? The online magazine was also quite happy to cite her as an anonymous source, and they did pay, too…all very hush-hush to ensure that the earl would feel no embarrassment.

Poppy deleted the emails from the reporter immediately, determined not to say a word about them to Dal and was just about to close her laptop when an email popped into her inbox from Florrie.

Had such a lovely message from Dal this morning, but having difficulty reaching him on his phone. He said he has tickets for Royal Box for the Gila Open in Mehkar. Beyond excited. Send me deets, please! And the poor darling! How is our gorgeous earl holding up?

Poppy read the email twice, unable to believe her eyes.

Dal had been in contact with Florrie now, too. And he hadn't just checked in with her, he'd dangled VIP polo tickets to a woman who was completely mad about ponies.

It was a brilliant move—Dal was nothing if not shrewd—but also utterly infuriating because just last night Dal had been seducing her!

Livid, Poppy marched up the flights of stairs, rapped on his door before entering his room, laptop tucked beneath her arm. "I hope you're dressed," she said curtly, "because we have work to do."

Dal was lying stretched out on the couch in the living room, reading, one arm propped behind his head. He looked up from the book, a black eyebrow lifting. "What work would that be?"

"Your work. I get emails about your business affairs all the time. People still think I'm your secretary."

"That's because you are." He sat up, stretching, which just made the soft knit fabric of his shirt pull tighter across the hard planes of his chest. "So what is so urgent?"

She stared at him baffled by his nonchalance. "I have never seen you lie down in the middle of the day and read."

"I was focused all morning. Why not take a break before lunch and get caught up on this book I've been wanting to read?"

"Indeed?"

"You seem quite tense. Is everything all right?"

"I've just been working for you. That's all."

"Good. Since you're still on the payroll."

She bit her tongue to say something she might regret. And then she had to wait another ten seconds to get her racing pulse to slow. Finally, when she trusted herself to speak and not shout, she said, "I've made good progress on finding my replacement. How is it going finding the replacement for Sophie?"

"Better than I hoped."

"Really?" She decided she'd play dumb. Let him be the one to tell her about his clever invitation to Florrie. "Any exciting developments?"

"Well, I kissed you last night—"

"That's not an exciting development."

The corner of his mouth curled. "It was for me."

"How is it going with the other two on your list?"

"I haven't kissed them, but that's probably due to the lack of proximity and other logistics."

"Would you kiss all three of us if you could?"

"Absolutely."

She hated hearing him say that, she did. Poppy clenched her hands into fists. "Why?"

"Because as you so kindly pointed out, physical attraction is part of marriage—"

"I did not point that out. I said nothing about attraction or sex."

"You did infer that compatibility is important, and part of the 'more' relationships needed."

"Successful relationships."

"Right, and that's what I'm to want for myself because I deserve it. I deserve that elusive 'more.'"

She hated that he kept quoting her, and doing it literally word for word. "'More' is not elusive."

"Isn't it? It's an intangible, something one cannot easily quantify when making an offer, or proposing marriage."

"You should stop talking. You're making me hate you."

"And yet you were the one that told me to communicate. I'm trying to communicate."

"I think you're trying to annoy me."

"Why would I do that?"

"I'm not sure. I haven't figured that part out yet."

"Well, when you do figure it out, let me know. I hate having you upset with me when we only have thirteen days left together."

And just like that she felt her heart mash and fall. She ground her teeth together to keep from making a sound.

"You will be missed," he added kindly. "More than you know."

Poppy smiled to hide how much his reminder hurt. He made her feel crazy, but at least she was able to be crazy and near him. "So you don't need me today? There's nothing you want me to do?"

"Why don't you take the afternoon off? Have some time for yourself. Read or swim or feel free to explore the estate." He was smiling up at her, the smile of a man who acted as if he genuinely cared about her best interests.

He didn't, though. Because if he did, he wouldn't have kissed her like that last night. He wouldn't have held her so firmly, his hands low on her hips, making the inside of her melt and ache, while making the rest of her shiver and tingle. She'd felt his desire, but most of all, she'd become painfully aware of her own. She wanted him…almost desperately. She'd always wanted him, but it had been a cerebral thing, not a body thing, but last night had woken her up and set her body on fire.

Poppy headed for the door, her sandals making a light tapping sound against the marble floor, the tapping echoing the hard, uncomfortable thudding of her heart.

All these years she'd wondered what it would be like to kiss him, and now she knew.

And now she'd never forget.

She paused in the doorway to look back at him. "Oh! Before I forget, Florrie emailed me. She'd love those tickets to the polo match in Gila and is eager for all the *deets*."

And then, flashing him a great, wide, *furious* smile, she walked out.

Dal listened to Poppy's footsteps retreat.

Gone was his tidy, buttoned-up secretary with the tight chignons and conservative skirts and blouses. In her place was this passionate, fierce, fresh-faced beauty who didn't

hesitate to give him her opinion. He'd always enjoyed working with Poppy, even when she had her mini meltdowns
and crises of confidence, because she was fundamentally
one of the best people he'd ever known, but now he enjoyed
looking at her. And teasing her. And making her blush.

And shiver and arch in his arms.

She'd been impossibly appealing last night; so appealing that he'd barely been able to sleep, his body heavy and
aroused for far too much of the night. Which is why he'd
deliberately kept her at arm's length this morning. It had
been an endless night and he wasn't ready to be tempted.

But clearly, she didn't like that he'd kept his distance,
and she definitely didn't like the email from Florrie.

His lips twisted. Poor Poppy. He'd told Florrie that Poppy
would be the one to help her get the tickets because he knew
Poppy wouldn't like it.

His smile deepened, remembering her extreme vexation.
He wasn't a nice man, but he was good at getting what he
wanted, and he wanted Poppy, fierce, passionate, beautiful
Poppy, who wasn't afraid to stand up to him, and talk to
him and make him feel like a man, not a machine.

Poppy took a bath before dinner feeling incredibly con-
flicted about the night ahead. At any other time in her life
she would have been thrilled at the idea of having a lovely,
long evening with him, where it would be just the two of
them, but her fantasy Randall was nothing like Sheikh
Talal, who did what he wanted and kissed her when he felt
like and generally ignored all the rules for polite behavior.

Poppy towel-dried and stepped into the bedroom where
Imma had placed a variety of kaftans on the bed for her
to choose from.

She wasn't in the mood for the navy or green one, even
though both were lovely, and the black looked far too de-
pressing even with all the silver and blue beadwork. She

reached for the plum gown with the gold and cream and quickly dressed. She tried drawing her hair into a pony-tail but it didn't look right with the formality of the gown. Sighing, Poppy released her hair, combed it hard, hating the thick waves, but left it down.

Imma told her dinner would be on the rooftop and di-rected her up the three flights of stairs in the central tower. Poppy stepped out of the dim, cool tower into the golden light of dusk, thinking she had never seen a more magi-cal setting for a meal. It was a rooftop dining room, open to the sky. It was heading toward twilight now, but it'd be dark within the hour. The walled patio already gleamed with candlelight, pillars of candles along the waist-high walls, while glittering silver lanterns dotted the side tables.

Stewards stood at attention, one with a tray of cocktails, another with appetizers. A third gentleman held a folded silk pashmina should she become cold later.

It wasn't just luxurious, but wildly romantic, although she'd never tell that to Dal. He was already powerful and overbearing. She didn't need to feed his ego, or his ridicu-lous marriage plans.

She was not going to marry him. Nor was she on his list. She'd never be on a *list*.

Dal emerged from the opposite tower just a minute after she did. He was wearing elegant black trousers and a fitted black dress shirt open at the collar. He wore no tie and his black hair was combed but he hadn't shaved before din-ner, giving him a hint of a shadow on his strong jaw and a wicked glint in his golden eyes.

She hated the shiver that raced down her back, as well as the bubbly, giddy sensation she got when he lifted two glasses from the silver tray, carrying one of the pretty icy-pink cocktails to her. "The Kasbah Jolie signature drink."

"What is it?" she asked warily, taking the frosty glass rimmed in sugar.

"I have no idea. There is a new chef and he seems to be having a great deal of fun naming everything Kasbah this, and Kasbah that."

It seemed that tonight Dal was determined to be charming and she couldn't help smiling. "Cheers to the innovative chefs." And then she clinked her glass to his and sipped the drink, and the icy-cold pink martini-style cocktail was absolutely delicious. She could taste pomegranate juice, grapefruit juice plus vodka and something else. "Compliments to the chef."

"Come this way," he said, taking her elbow and steering her across the enormous roof to a private alcove facing the mountains.

Screened by a hedge of jasmine, he set down his drink and reached into his pocket and drew out a small black velvet box.

Poppy's breath caught in her throat as she spotted what looked like a jeweler's box. This wasn't…it couldn't be…

"I haven't showered you with gifts. I thought it was time," he said. "I hope you like them, and I think you should put them on now."

Like them. Put them on now.

Obviously, it wasn't a ring, then, and she didn't know why she felt a stab of disappointment. She didn't want to marry him. She didn't want to be wooed by him. So why did she care that he was giving her some pretty trinket instead of a diamond ring?

She hated herself for feeling like crying as she cracked open the lid, and catching a sparkle of white fire, she popped the lid open all the way. More glints of light and fire. "Oh, Dal." Nestled in black velvet was a pair of large gold and diamond chandelier earrings, dazzling earrings, the kind that only movie stars and princesses wore. Without even meaning to count, she added up all the diamonds sparkling up at her, with eight large oval diamonds in each earring, with dozens of smaller diamonds covering the gold setting. "I am praying these are not real diamonds," she said.

He looked scandalized. "I have never bought anyone fake stones."

"But these must be a fortune."

"I can afford a fortune." He took one out of the box and loosened the back. "And you deserve a fortune."

"I don't."

"Let's see what they look like on you," he said as though she hadn't spoken. "You're not wearing anything tonight."

"The silver earrings Izba had for me last night wouldn't have looked right with this gown."

"I know. I told her to make sure you couldn't wear the silver earrings tonight."

"You're awfully bossy."

"That shouldn't be news to you," he said, stepping closer so that he put the diamond chandelier on her. His fingertips felt deliciously warm and her ear felt deliciously sensitive. She suppressed a shudder of pleasure as he twisted the back to keep the heavy earring from falling out.

"Now the other ear," he said.

More tingling sensations as he attached the second earring and then gave her head a little shake, hearing the stones click, and feeling the earrings move. "How do they look?"

"You look beautiful."

"I'm afraid this is far too extravagant. I'll wear them tonight, but I can't keep them."

"Don't say things like that. It's not polite."

"You can't give me gifts that cost hundreds of thousands of pounds."

"You're supposed to love them, not argue with me."

"Maybe Florrie and Seraphina like presents like this—"

"Oh, they most definitely do. They wouldn't dream of refusing a token of my affection."

"I'd rather have your real affection."

"You do. You had proof of that last night."

"You're making me very angry," she said.

"Don't be angry. It's a lovely night. Just look at the sunset."

She turned to look out over the valley. The setting sun had painted the red mountains rose, lavender and gold. "It is beyond breathtaking," she said after a moment.

"It is quite spectacular," he agreed. "I wish I hadn't waited so long to return. It's good to be back."

She glanced up at him. "Did you think it wouldn't?"

In the elegant black evening shirt, his skin looked more olive and his eyes appeared an even lighter gold. It was funny how she'd always thought of him as so very English, and yet here in Mehkar, he exuded heat and mystery, as well as an overwhelming sensuality.

"I was worried," he admitted after a moment. "I was worried about what it'd be like here without Andrew and my mother. I'd never been here without them, but you've made it easy for me."

"Are you going to see your grandfather while we're here?"

"I should, but haven't made any plans to do so yet."

"Tell me about your relationship with him."

"There's not much to understand. I live in England. He lives in Mehkar."

"And yet you're here in Mehkar, and we were in Gila, albeit briefly."

"It's complicated," he said brusquely.

"That's your code for you don't want to discuss it."

"It really is complicated. I don't even know how to talk about it. One day this place was my home. It was my favorite place in the world. And then suddenly it wasn't part of my life anymore, and the people here were cut off, too. It was bad enough losing my mum and brother, but to lose your grandparents and cousins and aunts and uncles? It hurt more than I can say. It's still not easy to talk about."

"Who cut them off? Your father or your grandfather?"

He shoved a hand through his black hair, rifling it. "Does it matter?"

She looked down into the shimmering pink of her cocktail, the color so very similar to the walls of the Kasbah. "I guess I have this crazy idea that if I understand your past, then maybe I'll understand you."

He gave her a look she couldn't decipher. "I've spent all these years burying the memories. I don't know that it's wise to dig them all up."

"Buried memories mean buried emotions—"

"My favorite kind," he said darkly.

"Don't you want to feel anything?"

"No. But apparently, you do." He finished his drink and set the glass down on the wall next to his hip. "It was June eleventh. We'd just finished the school term and were out on holiday. Mum came to pick us up, as she always did. We were on our way to the airport to come here when the accident happened." He paused before saying slowly, clearly. "The accident that killed my mother and Andrew."

It took her a moment to piece it together. "You were on your way here? To Jolie?"

"We always flew here straightaway on our last day of school. It was our tradition. We couldn't wait to come. At least I couldn't wait. Andrew had wanted to stay home that summer with Father but Mother insisted. Grandfather wanted to see Andrew." He frowned, brows flattening. "Andrew was the oldest of my grandfather's grandchildren, important to both sides of the family."

He looked up right into her eyes, expression still intense. "Until that day, I'd had a very different childhood from Andrew. He was the heir. I was just a boy…a free-spirited, rather sensitive, second son."

She didn't know what to say, so she didn't try to speak.

Dal added after a moment, "It wasn't ever the same after that. Not in Winchester. Not here."

"It wouldn't be, would it?" she said sympathetically before adding, "So you chose not to come back?"

"It was my father's decision to cut contact with my mother's family. After the funerals, I didn't see or hear from anyone from Mehkar for ten years."

"Why?"

"My father blamed my mother for the accident, and so by extension, he blamed her family."

"Was she at fault?"

"No. The other driver was distracted. They said he was on the phone, ran a red light and smashed into our car head-on."

"Mother died immediately. Andrew died at the hospital. And I survived with just cuts and bruises."

"Your poor grandfather," she sighed. "It must have been devastating to lose his daughter and his eldest grandson on the very day they were to return home."

"I'm sure it wasn't easy for him. My grandmother, his wife, had died just months before in an accident. He'd been eager to have my mother return for the summer."

"So your grandfather has never reached out to you since your mother's funeral. If you were eleven that has been nearly twenty-four years!"

"No. He reached out. I was rude. I rebuffed him, and even though I was at fault, I have chosen not to apologize or make amends."

"Why?"

"I don't know."

"I don't believe that. I think you do know. And I'd like to know."

"So you can have additional proof of what a cool, unfeeling ass I am?"

She gave him a reproving look. "I already know who you are, and what you are, which is why I want to know why you—someone I know does have feelings, only you keep them very deeply buried—would rebuff someone you apparently once loved very much?"

His shoulders shifted impatiently. "Because I did love him. And I didn't understand why he left me there, in England. I hated England. I hated my father—" He broke off, jaw grinding, shadows darkening his eyes. "It doesn't matter, and I shouldn't admit that I hated my father. My father had problems. He couldn't help himself."

"But you can help yourself. Reach out to your grandfather. See him. Apologize. Make amends."

"I can't."

"You *can*. Don't be stupid and proud. Tell him you're sorry, because one day he won't be here and then it'll be too late."

Dal didn't say anything for the longest time. He finished his drink and she finished hers and they watched the shadows swaddle the mountains, the rose and gold light fading to lavender and gray.

After a long silence Dal glanced at her, lips curving. "You're the only person that ever tries to tell me what to do."

"You could be a really, truly lovely man if you tried."

"That sounds terribly dull."

"I like dull men. I'm looking for a dull man, someone who will cuddle with me on the sofa while we watch our favorite program on the telly."

"You would hate that after a while."

"Not if it was a good program."

"You almost make watching television sound fun."

Fun. In all her years of working for him, she'd never once heard him the use the word *fun*. Discipline, duty, responsibility, yes. But fun? Never. "You have changed," she said. "You're already very different from just a few days ago."

"It seems I had to. Randall Grant was an arse."

"Is Dal better?"

"He's trying."

She glanced at him from beneath her lashes and felt a little shiver as he looked right back at her, his golden gaze locking with hers and holding. He didn't look away, not even when one of the stewards invited them to the dinner table.

"Why didn't you try before?" she asked softly. "Why didn't you try for Sophie?"

"I don't know. Maybe because she didn't bring out the best in me. Not like you."

"I bring out the best in you?"

His dense black lashes dropped, his lovely mouth curving. "Perhaps I should say you bring out the *better*."

Her chest squeezed, her insides wobbly. He made her feel so much and it wasn't fair. When he dropped his guard and had a real conversation she felt close to him. Connected. *Too connected.* How was she to leave him when he felt like hers?

One of the stewards approached them and spoke quietly in Arabic to Dal. Dal answered and then turned to Poppy. "I have a phone call I must take. It won't take long, just a couple minutes. Please have another drink and I'll meet you at the table."

True to his word, he was gone less than ten minutes, and when he returned she was waiting at the beautiful table with the rose-pink tablecloth and the gleaming white candles.

"I tried to make it quick," he said, sitting down at the table with her.

"Is everything okay?"

"It was Florrie."

Poppy's chest squeezed tight. "Oh?"

"She's heading to Gila for the polo tournament and she had some questions about the tournament and packing and appropriate dress for the royal box."

"I didn't realize you were a fashion consultant."

He leaned back in his chair, his lips quirking. "You're jealous."

"I'm not."

"No, you shouldn't be. I've asked you to marry me—"

"You've never asked. You told me we were to marry. That's not a proper proposal."

"So is that all that's keeping you from saying yes? Are you wanting romance? Flowers? Candlelight?"

She became very aware of the romantic dinner under the stars, and the fragrant roses on the table, along with the candles glimmering everywhere.

"You threw your list together," she said. "There was very little thought put into it, and I wish you would have considered more possibilities. Women who are not Sophie's friends. Women who might actually want to stay at home with you and have dinner with you, or maybe grab a book and read in the evening near you—"

"I don't need a nanny, Poppy."

"No, you just need a woman with hips and a womb."

When he didn't contradict her, she felt her temper spike. "You are so infuriating! You know you haven't tried hard to find a great wife. You're simply settling—"

"Not settling at all. You're on the list."

"At the number three position, which makes me think that the names on your list are there by default. I'd hazard to guess that all three names made it because that's all you could remember in a pinch."

He grinned at her, a sexy, powerful, masculine smile. "Your name was not added because I was in a pinch. *You* were added because we suit each other—"

"So annoying," she muttered under her breath.

"Why can't you accept a compliment?"

"Because I know you. You don't compliment people, and you most certainly don't compliment *me*."

"Let me put it another way. I can barely tolerate most people but I haven't just tolerated your company for the past four years. I've enjoyed it."

"And you wonder why I have absolutely no desire to marry you!"

"It wouldn't hurt for you to be a little more logical and a lot less fanciful."

"How about we focus on the two women still on your list? You can't court both Florrie and Seraphina at the same time. It's not practical when you're down to fourteen days, and so I recommend at this point in time you focus on one. With Florrie en route to Gila, just settle on her and be done with it. I am sure once she learns that you're not just the Earl of Langston but Prince Talal she'll jump through the hoops and marry you right away."

"I had no idea Florrie was your clear favorite."

"She's not my favorite. In fact, of the two, she's my least favorite."

"Is she? Why?"

"She's—" *The least monogamous woman I know.* But Poppy bit back the words, uncomfortable with the truth. "She just doesn't seem quite ready to settle down."

"I don't know. Maybe she hasn't yet met the right person."

"Maybe," Poppy answered sourly.

"What else do you know about them? Who would I enjoy more? No. Scratch that. Which one would be a more natural mother?"

Poppy shuddered. "Neither. They are both too self-absorbed."

"You're sounding very catty right now, Poppy. It's not attractive. I thought these were your friends."

"Sophie's friends."

"Is there nothing positive you can say about either?"

Poppy ground her teeth together and lifted her chin. "Seraphina loves fashion and clothes. She spends twenty thousand or more each season on new clothes."

"You're supposed to be giving me positives."

"That is a positive. She's always beautifully dressed. Oh. And she keeps herself very slender. Very, very slender."

"Is that your way of saying she has an eating disorder?"

"No. It's my way of saying she just doesn't eat. She has a liquid diet. Mostly green drinks and cleansers. Things like that."

"I'm sure she'd indulge in cheese plates and chocolate now and then."

Poppy frowned, trying to remember when she'd ever seen Seraphina actually eat anything. She nearly always had a bottle in her hand, or purse, filled with one of those drinks that smelled of lemon and parsley, cucumber and ginger. "I've never actually seen her eat anything sweet. Or anything with carbs. Or any kind of meat."

"So she won't share a steak and kidney pie with me?"

"Oh, no. Never. The crust alone would make her faint."

"What about Florrie? Would she eat a steak and kidney pie?"

"Probably."

"That's good news."

"Yes." But Poppy couldn't feign enthusiasm. Florrie would not be a good wife for Dal. She wasn't even a good girlfriend. She didn't understand the meaning of faithful, juggling her polo player lovers with disconcerting ease.

"Now, come on, Poppy. What's wrong with Florrie? If I didn't know you better, I'd think you were jealous and wanted to be my countess."

He was right, of course. She was jealous, but she'd never

let him know that. "Fortunately, you do know me better and know I've absolutely zero desire to be your countess."

"Why?"

"I hate that you dangle money and possessions and make it sound as if those material things are the basis for a good marriage, when we both know that nothing is more important than affection, kindness and respect."

"If I wasn't the Earl of Langston, but a vicar in a Cotswold parish, would you consider my proposal?"

Her cheeks burned with embarrassment but she held his gaze. "If you were a vicar in the Cotswold, would you love me?"

"I don't know how to answer because I don't believe in love. It's a fantasy concocted in the twentieth century by advertising giants to sell more things to more people."

"That is such rubbish."

"But I do believe passion and desire are real."

"And I believe that passion without love is just sex. And I wouldn't ever marry a man just to have sex. I could have sex *now* if that's what I wanted."

"Sex with whom?"

She lifted her chin, absolutely brazen. "You."

Her words stole his breath. And all rational thought. Her eyes shone with light while her cheeks glowed with color and her expression was nothing short of defiant.

Who was this woman? When had she become so confident and provocative?

It didn't help that the lush outline of Poppy's breast was playing havoc with his control.

He'd managed his physical side for five and a half years, clamping down tightly on all needs or wants, shutting himself down so that he could be the elegant, chivalrous man Sophie desired.

But with Sophie gone, and Poppy here, he felt anything but elegant and chivalrous.

What he felt was ravenous, his carnal side awake and hungry. After years of not feeling or wanting or needing, he needed now. He needed her. And his body ached morning, noon and night with desire.

Just watching her bite her full lower lip now made him want to kiss that tender lip, and then lick the seam of her lips so that she'd open for him and let him have his way with her.

His tongue in her mouth.

His tongue on her breasts.

His tongue between her legs, lathing her clit.

Dal hardened all over again, his skin so tight he felt like he'd explode.

"You have no idea what I want to do to you," he said huskily, picturing stripping her naked so that her full breasts were bared, her nipples peaked. He'd work her nipples, pinching, teasing, sucking, until she was wet for him and arching, hips lifting, begging.

He wanted to be between her thighs.

He wanted to clasp her hips and hold her still while he devoured her.

He wanted to feel her shattering and hear her cry and know that she was his, and only his.

"Not interested," she said. "I don't want to sleep with you, or marry you. You're not my type—"

"You don't have a type, Poppy. You haven't dated once in all the years you've worked for me."

"Not true. I had a boyfriend three years ago—"

"A boyfriend?"

"Yes. A boyfriend. He was lovely, too, until well, he wasn't so lovely anymore."

"And just how long was he your boyfriend?"

"I don't remember."

"That means he wasn't around long enough to truly signify."

"That's not what it means. It just means I decided to move forward and put the past behind me."

"I have a feeling he was your boyfriend for all of three weeks."

"It's not really any of your business whether he was my boyfriend for three minutes or three years. What matters is that I don't want to be your girlfriend, or your wife, or anything at all because your values are not my values. You don't want what I want in life. We'd be a disaster together."

"Even though you like how I can make you feel?"

Color stormed her cheeks and her eyes snapped fire. "You must be confusing me with someone else on your list because I care about you, and yes, I enjoyed kissing you last night, but I'm not going to give up my freedom and future just because I felt a twinge of lust!"

CHAPTER EIGHT

BACK IN HER ROOM, Poppy allowed Imma to help her ease the stunning plum kaftan off her head. While Imma hung the gorgeous gown back up, Poppy removed her dangling gold and diamond earrings, tucking them into a drawer next to her bed before taking off her makeup.

But even a half hour after changing into her pajamas, she felt hot and riled up. Dal was beyond annoying. He was the worst. The absolute worst.

Poppy stripped off her nightgown and put on her swimsuit and cover-up, and headed for the pool.

She swam a lap under water, and then another lap under water before surfacing to float on her back.

The warm water soothed her, relaxing her tense muscles, while the gentle lap of water against her skin made her feel buoyant and free.

She heard a scraping sound and opened her eyes to discover Dal sitting down on the foot of her lounge chair.

He was still dressed for dinner, which reassured her somewhat because that meant he wasn't planning on swimming. Maybe if she closed her eyes and ignored him, he'd leave soon.

She flipped over onto her stomach and did a slow, easy breaststroke toward the opposite end of the pool. She pretended she was alone, without a care in the world, even though she could feel his eyes, his gaze, following her every kick and stroke.

At the far end she reached for the wall and turned around, facing him.

He looked at her, his handsome face expressionless.

She almost wished for one of his small, mocking smiles.

The smiles and ironic laughter were easier than this tension between them now.

"What do you want?" she called, even as she stretched her arms out along the tiled pool edge, and leaned back so her legs could float up.

"You."

"But I don't want you."

"Liar."

The low, husky pitch of his voice sent shivers racing through her, making her tummy clench and her knees press tight.

She couldn't engage, couldn't encourage him; it would be disastrous to provoke him at this late hour.

Poppy forced herself to relax. She closed her eyes, let herself float where she was, and as she breathed in and out, she pictured him getting up and walking away. In fact, she willed him to leave, pouring all her concentration into making him disappear, but when she opened her eyes, he was still there.

"I can prove it to you," he said.

"We're not children. There's no need to prove anything to anyone."

"You can't hide forever from the truth."

"But I can get some laps in, can't I?"

"I'll wait."

"I have a lot of laps."

"I'll count them for you."

She shot him a frosty look, not comfortable with this game.

She dove under water and swam half the length of the pool before needing to surface for a breath. When she glanced over her shoulder toward the lounge chair where she'd left her things, she realized he was gone. For a split second she felt relief, and then she noticed the pile of clothes set next to her tunic on the lounge chair.

He'd undressed.

Poppy spun in the pool, discovering him behind her. "What are you doing?" she demanded breathlessly.

"Joining you for a swim."

"Are you...naked?" she asked, afraid to look down.

"Have you never gone skinny-dipping?"

"No." Her voice came out strangled. "So you are naked."

"Would you feel better if I told you I was wearing briefs?"

"Yes."

"Then I'm wearing briefs," he answered, reaching for her and drawing her toward him with the assurance of a man who knew exactly what he was doing. He drew her through the water until her breasts brushed his chest.

His body was so large and warm, and it felt unbelievably good to be pressed to him, skin to skin. Her breath caught when his large hands circled her waist, drawing her hips even closer to his.

He wasn't naked. But he was hard...very thick and very erect. Her eyes widened as he rubbed her across him, the tip of his shaft finding the apex of her thighs and all the sensitive nerves there.

Her lips parted. She made a soft hiss of sound.

He lifted an eyebrow. "Did you say something?"

"This isn't a good idea," she choked, even as he did it again, and the thick blunt tip against her core made her want to swoon.

Maybe he wasn't wearing briefs after all...

"I don't think this is a good idea," she said hoarsely, even as her pulse raced and her skin felt exquisitely sensitive.

"We're just playing," he said.

She stared at him, mesmerized, at the gleam of water on his shadowed jaw, and the way the pool light reflected onto the hard features of his face. "But this kind of play is dangerous."

"You're safe with me."

"I don't think that's true at all." In fact, she knew it wasn't true, and yet it was hard to move away from him when everything in her wanted this with every fiber of her being.

But that didn't make it right, a tiny part of her brain shrieked. Sugar is delicious, but too much will make you sick.

And he most definitely wasn't sugar.

He was spice, wicked, sexy spice and beyond addictive.

"You want danger," he murmured, his lips brushing her ear, and then finding the hollow below.

Pleasure shrieked through her and she gasped, lips pressing to the warm wall of his chest.

"But you want danger that won't destroy you," he added, his teeth catching at her earlobe and giving it a tug. "And you know I would never destroy you. I'd just teach you all the things you've always wanted to know."

"Like what?"

"This," he answered, his head dropping so that his mouth covered hers in a light, teasing kiss. Last night's kiss had been fierce and hot, but this kiss was tender and light and unbearably erotic.

His lips brushed hers, and then again, sending ripples of pleasure from her lips into her breasts and belly and beyond.

The fleeting caress seemed to wake nerve endings she didn't even know she had and she lifted her mouth to his, wanting more.

She felt his smile as he kissed her, his lips just barely parting hers, and the tip of his tongue lightly touching the inside of her lower lip.

Oh, that felt so good. Goose bumps covered her arm and made the fine damp hair at her nape rise. Her breasts swelled, aching, too.

"One more of those," she pleaded.

The soft, warm kiss flooded her with heat, and then as his tongue did a slow, lazy exploration of her mouth she pressed herself closer, thinking it was just a kiss and yet so much more.

She wanted so much more.

And when his hand moved to her breast, playing with the taut nipple through her wet suit, she nearly groaned at the pleasure. His hand felt so good on her, and the way he touched her sensitive nipple made her tummy tighten and her lower back prickle as she felt close to popping out of her skin.

"And you say desire isn't important," Dal said, lifting his head to look into her eyes.

She blushed and tried not to squirm as he tugged and kneaded her nipple, each small pull creating more tension inside her and adding to the heat between her thighs. "Desire is important," she whispered breathlessly as he pinched and played with her, the sensation so new and erotic that she couldn't focus properly.

"So you agree."

"I agree it's part of love."

"You can desire someone you do not love."

"Well, I couldn't," she answered, gasping as he pushed the scrap of fabric covering her breast away, exposing her nipple.

She saw his eyes darken in appreciation, his hard jaw jutting just before he bent his head and took the tender pebbled peak in his mouth.

His mouth felt surprisingly cool against her warm skin, and then as he suckled her she grew hot and wet in a way that had nothing to do with the pool or the warm, cloudless night. She clung more tightly to him, her fingers biting into his shoulders as her body came to life, shivering and shuddering from the intense sensation streaking through her.

She strained to be closer, seeking more contact and more

friction. As he drew on her nipple, she pressed her hips to him, wanting the rough rasp of his chest hair and the thick press of his erection.

He wrapped her legs around his waist, securing her ankles behind his back. "Don't move," he commanded.

"You're not in charge—" she began to protest but then broke off as his fingers slipped inside her bikini bottoms, finding the cleft where she was so wet and hot.

She shuddered as he stroked her there, finding her tender nub and then down and circling back again. He then drew his fingers away, and he looked down at her, a black brow lifting.

Her hips rocked helplessly. She felt beyond bereft, her core clenching, her body straining for touch, for relief.

"Are you in charge, then?" he asked quietly, silkily, combing her dark, wet hair back from her face.

Her cheeks burned. She burned. She felt as if he'd set her on fire and was now watching her incinerate.

"Maybe I spoke too soon," she said faintly.

"Louder?"

"You are in charge. There. Happy?"

"Not yet. But I will be, soon."

And then he slipped his hand back beneath the elastic of her bikini panty, stroking between her thighs, learning the shape of her. It was all very nice but she wanted him to do what he'd done before. Touch her there, at that place where all the nerve endings seemed to be.

She opened her thighs wider, pressing her hips at him, unable to ask for what she wanted, but he didn't seem in a hurry to caress the nub. Instead, he traced the outer lips and then inner lips before slipping the tip of his finger inside her. She hissed a breath, lips parting as he withdrew and then did it again, just touching her with the tip, making her shudder, making her want to press his finger deeper.

"It will sting when I possess you on our wedding night,"

he said, kissing the side of her neck, finding more sensitive spots she didn't know existed. "But it will only hurt that first night."

"We're not marrying," she breathed, twitching as he found her nub and gave it a caress.

"You should give up now," he said, stroking the nub again, making her tighten and dance against him. "You won't win."

"You can't buy me, and you can't seduce me," she choked.

"Maybe I can't buy you, but I can seduce you. I am seducing you." And then as he caressed her clit, he slipped the fingertip back inside her, making her whimper.

He deftly stroked both, and she didn't know which pleasure to focus on. Both sensations felt so good, the bright, sharp pleasure at the top of her thighs, or the sensitive shivers from teasing her below.

She felt her body try to tighten around his finger, the sensations so new and exciting but also overwhelming.

He kissed her then, and she wrapped her arms more tightly around his neck, kissing him back. He sucked her tongue into his mouth, drawing on her tongue in a tight, hot, erotic rhythm that had her hips rotating. She felt like she was on fire, sensation flooding her. It was hard to focus on any one pleasure when it all felt so good together—her tongue in his mouth, his hand between her thighs, stroking her. She felt the pressure build and tighten, everything in her tensing, and then he slipped a finger inside her even as his thumb played across her nub and suddenly she couldn't control the pleasure, couldn't keep it together, and she cried out against his mouth, shattering in her first climax ever.

For long moments after, she was breathless and dazed. She felt boneless and weak and she rested her head against his chest as he rearranged her in his arms, letting her legs settle and her body relax. Another few moments later, she felt sufficiently recovered to push away, needing distance now, uncomfortable with what had just happened.

"Do you have a preference for the kind of ring you'd like?" he asked.

Poppy blinked, her brain still fuzzy and disconnected from the pleasure. "Ring?"

"I'll give you the ring tomorrow, and we'll marry a week from today. That gives us a full week before my birthday. I don't want to leave it to the last minute this time."

"That is surely the least romantic proposal I have ever heard of in my life."

"I gave you romance at dinner. I just proved we have chemistry. And there is a great deal of it between us. Now we just need to finalize the details so we can move forward with our lives—"

"You're mad," she interrupted, floating farther away.

"Possibly. It runs in the family."

"Don't say that. It's not funny." Poppy had first learned of Randall's father's illness from the housekeeper at Langston House years ago. The housekeeper had wanted Poppy to understand why control was so important to the Sixth Earl of Langston. It seemed that the Fifth Earl had none.

"I'm entirely serious. My father was quite ill."

"I know."

"Sophie told you?"

"I don't think Sophie knows."

"But you do?"

"Mrs. Holmes told me."

"Why would she do that?"

"It was the day after your father's funeral. You'd told me to return to London and she asked me not to go."

"Why? Was she afraid I'd hurt myself?"

Poppy flinched. "No. She just didn't want you alone. She thought you needed a friend with you."

"And you were my friend?"

She lifted her chin, unwilling to let him see he'd hurt her. "I was the only one there. You'd managed to scare everyone else off."

"You make me sound like a monster."

She heard the bruised note in his voice. She glanced away, over the sparkling surface of the water, trying to think of something to say.

"Sophie used to call me the Ice Monster." His voice had grown even deeper. "You used to laugh."

"It was that or cry," she flashed, glancing down at her hands skimming back and forth just below the surface of the water. "But I'm no Belle, and you're no Beast and I can't save you—"

"Not asking you to save me. I'm asking you to marry me."

"In your case, it's one and the same, isn't it? You don't want me. You don't even want to marry. You're just trying to protect your title and lands."

When he didn't answer, she persisted. "Is it really so terrible to lose the earldom and estates?"

"Yes."

"Why? You don't need the money. And you don't seem to care at all for the title. If you have all this here in Mehkar, why do you need Langston House and the rest? Most of your investments aren't tied to the property, and the title is just a title."

Good for Poppy for asking the question. But then, he would have been surprised if she'd hadn't eventually asked it.

He certainly would have asked it if he were her, because she was right. The income wasn't significant, and Dal wasn't attached to the title, but the house was his home and then there was the real issue, the issue of duty. The issue of commitment and honor. Responsibility.

Duty and responsibility had been drummed into him every single day following his mother and brother's funeral.

His brother Andrew had understood duty. His brother, Viscount Andrew Ulrich Mansur Grant, was to have been the Sixth Earl of Langston, and Andrew loved everything about being the firstborn. He understood the responsibility but he didn't find it crushing. He knew he'd one day marry someone who benefited the estate, rather than someone he fancied. He would have been an excellent earl, too.

Dal had not been a good replacement for his brother. He was hapless—the Fifth Earl's description—and overly intellectual, so his father had been forced to shape Dal into a proper heir, even if it broke both of them.

And it had nearly broken both of them.

"From the time I was eleven, I understood my sole life mission was to marry and have children. Not just an heir and a spare, but numerous spares in the event something awful happened." He lifted his head, his gaze finding Poppy's. "Because awful things did happen. Cars crashed and mothers died and older brothers die in hospitals during surgery."

"Heirs and spares," he added mockingly, bitingly, "were not children to be loved, but insurance policies. Annoying but essential."

Wives were not to be cherished, either. They were brood mares, and income. The Grants of Langston had filled their coffers for the past hundred and fifty years by marrying foreign heiresses: Greek, American, German and in the case of Randall's mother, Arab. The wife didn't have to be beautiful, or even accomplished. According to the Fifth Earl of Langston, Randall's wife needed to be healthy—to bear those heirs—and wealthy. Her dowry was the most important thing she brought to the marriage.

Randall had been shocked and disgusted as a boy, but the years of lectures and discipline had numbed him to all but duty. Duty was the only thing that mattered, because once he fulfilled his duty, he would be free, no longer haunted by the fact that it was Andrew who should have been the Sixth Earl, not he.

"Who I am in Mehkar has no bearing on who I am in England, nor does it change my duty. My duty is to marry and continue the Grant family. It's my sole responsibility. I've known since my mother and brother's funeral that I have no other reason for being alive."

"That is probably the vilest thing I have ever heard you say."

He shrugged. "I will fulfill the promise made to my father, not to save the land or pocket the income, but because I am determined to get this monkey off my back."

"It's not a monkey, it's a curse!"

"I won't let it be a curse in the future. I'm a different man than my father and I'll make different choices." He hesitated. "You have no idea how different I want the future to be, and with you, it will be a new future. With you, I can move on."

"I hear about what you need, but what about what I need? Or do women not matter in your world? Are we just things…property and possessions?"

"You want security in life, and I'm offering it to you."

"You're not offering security. You're taking my freedom and the opportunities before me."

"I can take you places, show you the world."

"I don't want the world. I want a comfortable little house and a garden where I can plant my flowers."

"And in that house there will be a couch, and a telly and a husband that will kiss and cuddle you."

"Yes."

"You have not spent the past four years working for me to sit with some fat, balding bloke who only wants to watch football—"

"He's not going to be fat, or balding, and he's most definitely not going to be obsessed with football." Her chin jerked up. "He will be obsessed with me."

"Right."

"I'm serious."

"It will never happen."

"Why not?"

"Because you're going to marry me, and be my wife, and we're going to have the life you wanted…the life we wanted…the life where you insisted we have more!"

"Marrying you would not be more. Marrying you would be less."

"Coward!"

"Your idea of marriage makes my skin crawl."

"Liar."

"Listen to me. Listen, Randall Michael Talal Grant, Earl of Langston, Sheikh of Mehkar, I have no desire to be your countess, or your princess. I fancied you, yes. I had a crush on you, yes. But I never once wanted to trade places with Sophie because I knew then what I still know now. You will never love anyone but yourself. You can't. You don't know how."

CHAPTER NINE

SHE HEARD THE helicopter early, just after dawn. Poppy left her bed to stumble to the window arriving just in time to see the black helicopter with the gold emblem rise from the gardens, lifting straight up.

She saw the pilot, and then she spotted Dal in the back-seat.

She felt a shaft of pain. Where was he going? And why was he leaving her here?

She struggled to breathe as the helicopter flew away, her chest unnaturally tight.

It had been an awful night. She hadn't been able to sleep, not after the terrible fight with Dal in the pool.

She'd said hurtful things to him, and she'd regretted them immediately. She'd spent much of the night lying awake, wanting to go to him and apologize, but pride and self-preservation kept her in her bed.

If she went to him, she'd apologize and then possibly kiss him, and if she kissed him, then she'd want him to touch her, and hold her and then it would be all over.

He'd win. And she couldn't let him win. This wasn't a business deal. This wasn't a financial transaction. This was about her life and her future. It was about all the values she held dear: love, and hope and faith.

Love, hope, faith and family.

He'd give her the children but he couldn't give her the other things she craved.

And so she'd forced herself to stay in her bed, aware that Dal was upset, but it wasn't her problem. She cared about him—oh, so very much—but she couldn't allow him to just ride roughshod all over her.

But oh, last night…

She tipped her head to the glass and closed her eyes. His proposal had been so incredibly uncomfortable. And her furious refusal, that was even more uncomfortable.

So where had he gone today? What was he thinking? What was he doing?

Poppy dressed and went to her living room and rang for coffee. It was Izba who came to the door, not Imma or Hayek.

"Where did Talal go?" Poppy asked her.

"Gila."

"Gila," Poppy repeated numbly. "Did he say how long he'd be gone?"

The old woman's face creased. "Three days. Maybe four. He said there is a big tournament in the city. Polo, I think he said." She tipped her head, expression curious. "You don't like polo, Miss Poppy?"

Poppy felt a lump fill her throat. "No," she answered huskily. "Not as much as some women I know."

So he'd gone to Gila. Gone to Gila to see Florrie.

Poppy felt ill, so ill that she stripped off her clothes and climbed back into bed.

She heard the helicopter late on the third night after he'd gone. Poppy glanced at the small clock next to her bed. Nearly midnight.

Relief filled her. Relief followed by pain.

He'd left her three days ago and he hadn't said goodbye. He hadn't emailed her, either, even though she'd checked her inbox obsessively.

But now he was back home.

And then she realized what she'd thought. Home.

She turned on her side, pulling the cover up over her shoulder as if she could tuck herself in. But even beneath the covers she was cold. And scared. Had he proposed to

Florrie? Or God help her, had he married Florrie while he was there?

She tried to make herself fall back asleep but she couldn't. She lay in bed, heart pounding, stomach knotting, so anxious. So heartsick.

A half hour passed, and then another. It was close to one in the morning now but she was wide awake and close to tears.

Unable to endure another moment of misery, she left her bed and pulled on a pale green cotton robe and headed for Dal's suite one floor above hers.

She knocked on the door. There was no answer. She gently turned the handle and it opened. She entered the living room, crossing soundlessly the long narrow living room to his bedroom. The door there was open and she stepped inside his bedroom, her gaze going to his bed. It was empty, the bed made. A lamp was burning on a corner table and the sliding glass door was open.

"Dal?" she whispered.

She saw a shadow move on the balcony and then he appeared in the doorway.

"What's wrong?" he asked.

"I couldn't sleep. I was worried about you."

"As you can see I'm fine."

She reached for the sash on her robe, giving it an anxious tug. "How was Gila?"

"Good."

"What did you do there?"

"I saw a lot of family. I think I forgot just how big the family is."

"Were you able to spend time with your grandfather?"

"Yes."

"Did you attend the polo match?"

"I went for a little while."

He just went for part of the match? What else did he

do, then? And did he see Florrie? Did he take her out on a date? Did he kiss—?

Poppy stopped herself there, not wanting to imagine all the possibilities. Not even wanting to know if there had been a date. Too much could happen, and the details would just make her feel half-mad.

"You were gone for three days," she said, hearing the hurt and accusation in her voice but it was too late to take the words back.

He shrugged. "I had things to take care of. Arrangements to make."

For his wedding.

He hadn't said the words, but she was sure of it. Pain exploded inside her chest, and she balled her hands, her nails digging into her fists. "Is there anything I can help with?"

"No, you're doing what I needed you to do. You've given me five strong résumés. Someone from HR in the London office will call the five, interview and then rank them for me, and then hire the one they think is the strongest."

As her eyes adjusted to the night, she could see he was leaning on the frame of the glass door, his shoulder at an angle, muscular arms crossed over his bare chest. He was wearing dark, loose pajama bottoms. He had such a big, hard, gorgeous body and his mind was brilliant—sharp, swift, incisive. She'd loved working with him, and learning from him and hearing his ideas. He was bold and brave, conscientious and fair. His new secretary was going to be very lucky to have him as a boss. "Sounds as if my job is nearly done."

"Indeed. We will probably have someone hired by the end of this week."

She swallowed around the lump in her throat. "It's all coming to an end so fast now."

"It seems everything is working out."

"Does that include your search for a new bride?"

"Yes."

"You must be relieved."

"I'll be relieved when the wedding is over."

"Do you have a date set?"

"I don't want to leave it to the last moment."

"You have nine days until your birthday."

"Yes, so probably three or four days from now." His big shoulders shifted. "Something like that."

So soon.

"That's wonderful," she said even as she found herself wishing she hadn't come here, to his room. She should have waited until morning to ask about his trip. She could have waited to hear this news.

She hated his news. It broke her heart. "Was it good to speak to your grandfather?"

"Yes. Just seeing him again has made the trip here worthwhile."

"I'm glad." She swallowed again, fighting the prickle and sting of tears in the backs of her eyes. "Did you tell your grandfather about your plans to marry?"

"Yes."

"What did he say?"

"He said that he respected me for fulfilling the promise I made my father, and hoped that my future wife will bring honor to the family and the people of Mehkar."

"Have you introduced her to him yet?"

"No, and I won't. Not before the ceremony. This is my choice, not his, and I'm not looking for his approval."

She was silent a moment, trying to imagine Dal with his grandfather, the king. "What is he like? Your grandfather?"

"Perceptive. Powerful. Quiet. Dignified."

"Easy to talk to?"

He laughed softly. "He wasn't at first, but by the time I left, it was better. He has aged. He has worries." He straightened and entered the room. "I suppose we all do."

She watched him cross the floor and take a seat on the side of his bed. "What are you worrying about?"

"My worries are mostly behind me. I've done what I needed to do. Now I can breathe easier." He looked at her. "I'm just sorry you lost sleep over me. That must have been truly aggravating."

"Don't be angry with me."

"I'm not. I'm not angry with you, or anyone. I think for the first time in years, I'm finally at peace."

She wanted to ask him why. She wanted to know if Florrie was wearing his engagement ring. She wanted to know so many things but knew she didn't have the right to ask anymore. She'd essentially found her replacement. She wouldn't be working for him soon. He'd be married to Florrie—

"I hated you leaving the way you did," she whispered. "And then you didn't even email me once."

"I was busy."

"You were punishing me."

"If there is to be no future together, we need to create distance. I left to give us distance, and allow us both to take a step back."

"Is that why you're at peace?"

"I'm at peace because I know, no matter what happens in the next week, I have the answers I need." He reached up to drag a hand through his thick hair, ruffling it. "In Gila, my grandfather and I talked quite a lot about my father. My grandfather had offered to bring my mother home from England more than once, wanting to rescue her from her difficult marriage. She refused. She believed my father needed her, and that it wouldn't be fair to take the children away from him, and so she stayed."

"Your poor mother."

"That is what I always thought, but my grandfather said my mother loved him. Apparently, she was the only one who could manage him." He smiled grimly. "Rather like you with me."

"You're not a monster."

"He didn't want to be, either."

"Don't compare yourself to him! You're not your father. He had struggles you don't have. His mood swings, and mania, that was his illness. It's not yours."

"Emotions make me uncomfortable."

"Because of him."

"His emotions were out of control, so I trained myself never to lose control."

All of a sudden she understood. "You're not him, Dal. You're not ever going to be him. And you didn't inherit the illness, either."

"But my children could."

She felt another sharp stab of pain. My God. She'd never thought of that, or imagined that he'd harbor secret fears that his children could. "Or not," she said quietly, evenly, finally seeing what she'd never seen before.

"I spent my twenties waiting for the disease to strike. I kept waiting for signs or symptoms…highs, lows, anger, despair. But I felt nothing. All those years, and I felt absolutely nothing. I was numb. Even at my father's funeral. And I thought that was good."

"Being numb can't feel that good."

"But at least I had dignity."

"Is that what you call shutting everyone out?"

"It's how I survived. I can't apologize for being me. It's the only way I knew how to get through the grief, and the pressure and the unbearable responsibility."

"You have had tremendous pressure," she said. "But you're not alone. You have people who care for you. Deeply."

For a long, agonizing moment there was only silence.

Poppy's heart pounded. She felt as if she'd been running a very long, hard race.

His lashes slowly lifted and his light gaze skewered her. "No games," he said quietly.

"No games," she agreed breathlessly.

"Tell me why you came to me tonight. I want the truth."

She couldn't look away from his burning gaze, couldn't think of anything but him, and wanting him, and needing him and needing to be there for him.

"Don't marry Florrie," she whispered.

And still he said nothing, just looked at her with his intense, penetrating gaze, the one that had always made her feel as if he could see straight through her.

"I don't know if it's too late," she added, breathing in short, shallow, painful gulps of air. "But I want you to have options, and I should be an option. I shouldn't have taken myself off your list. If anyone believes in you, it's me."

"You weren't going to marry without love."

Her eyes burned and the almost overwhelming emotion in her chest put a lump in her throat. "But I'm not marrying without love. We both know I have always loved you."

CHAPTER TEN

POPPY HAD FINISHED dressing an hour ago and was now waiting for Dal to appear. Her gown was quite simply the most beautiful thing she'd ever seen, high necked with a thick gold collar and then gold starburst embellishments and embroidery down the bodice. The long, wide sleeves reminded her of a royal cape, and the soft silk and chiffon dress was fitted through the hips, the skirt straight and sleek, making her feel like a queen. There was more of the exquisite gold starbursts down the front of each sleeve.

Her hair had been pinned up with gold strands twisted in the loose curls. Her hair glittered, and heavy gold diamond earrings swung from her ears.

Looking in the mirror, she didn't even know who she was anymore.

Poppy turned away from her reflection, uneasy with her image. She didn't feel beautiful or regal, and yet the woman in white and gold looked every inch a princess.

How had this happened? How had any of this happened?

If she didn't love Dal so much, she'd pack her bags and run. She didn't know where she'd go, only that she was terrified of losing herself.

Poppy tried not to pace her private courtyard, but it was hard to just sit still when she felt wound so tight.

It had been three days since she'd agreed to marry him, and since then she'd been filled with anxiety and excitement, hope and dread.

She loved him, yes, but at the same time she feared a future where she'd give, give, give and he'd…what?

Would he ever love her? Would attraction and physical desire be enough?

Hopefully, making love would give her the closeness she craved, but not knowing made everything harder.

She couldn't help thinking that it would have been better if they'd made love before today. It would have been better to know more before the ceremony, just so she'd know how to manage her heart.

The wedding was a very simple service. There was no music or fanfare. There was little but the ring ceremony and exchanging of vows.

The paperwork that followed took far more time than the ceremony.

Poppy felt painfully overdressed for such a business-like ceremony. She told herself that she wouldn't cry, and so she didn't cry. It was her own fault for having any sort of expectations in the first place.

Dal had never said he cared for her. Today's ceremony was about convenience, and the brevity of the ceremony reflected the business nature of their union.

This was strictly business.

He'd married her because he'd run out of time. He'd married her to keep his title and lands.

And she? She'd agreed because she hadn't wanted to lose him. And yet, she'd never had him; at least, she didn't have what she wanted from him. His heart. His love.

His gaze narrowed on her face. "From your expression you'd think we had just attended a funeral instead of a wedding."

"I'm sorry. I'll try to look more celebratory. And maybe I will feel more celebratory once all the paperwork is finished."

"There is always paperwork after a wedding."

"But my impression is that there is considerable more after ours."

"You agreed to this, Poppy. You understood what we were doing today."

"Yes, I did agree. But I could have done this in T-shirt and jeans. I would have probably been happier in a T-shirt and jeans. I know Izba wanted me to look attractive for you, but the dress, shoes and jewelry was overkill."

"She dressed you as if we were marrying at the palace in Gila."

"I wish you had spoken to her."

"I did. I asked her to help you get ready. If you don't like the dress, blame me. I suggested it. It was my mother's wedding dress. The earrings were my mother's, too."

Poppy felt awful. Her eyes suddenly stung and she pressed her nails to her palms. "I didn't know."

"We could have married in Gila. The palace is impressive. There would have been a great deal of pomp and fuss. My family would have preferred we hold the ceremony there, but I didn't want to make this about the family. I wanted this to be about us. I wanted to spend the day with you. After the circus of Langston House, I thought you'd agree. I realize now I was wrong."

"You married me because you had no other choice."

"I married you because you were my first choice."

She bit into her lower lip to keep it from trembling. "You don't have to try to make me feel better—"

"Open and honest communication, remember? I'm telling you the truth. Whether or not you want to believe me is up to you."

It seemed impossible that he would actually want her. She had worked closely with him all these years and he had never been anything but professional and polite. She'd been the one to have feelings for him, not the other way around. But in the end, it didn't really matter about first choice or third choice; hierarchies and rankings were insignificant now that they exchanged their vows and signed the paperwork. They were married. He was her husband and she his wife and he'd fulfilled the terms of the trust with a week to spare.

"Now what?" she asked him. "A game of pool or ping-pong? Or are you going to get back to work?"

He regarded her steadily for a moment before smiling. "You are really upset."

"Yes, I am, and you can turn it into a joke but—"

He silenced her by taking her in his arms, his mouth covering hers. Heat surged through her, heat and longing, the longing so intense that it made her heart ache.

She'd wanted him forever and she'd married him to protect him, but in marrying him, she'd left herself so vulnerable.

He would have access to all of her now—not just her mind and emotions, but her body. And while she craved his touch, she feared it, too. She feared that once he took her to his bed, he'd see the side of her that she worked so hard to hide.

That she was afraid she wasn't enough.

That she was afraid she'd disappoint him.

That she was afraid he'd regret marrying her when he could have married almost any other woman in the world.

"Stop thinking," he murmured against his mouth, pulling her even closer to him, his hand sliding down her back, a caress to soothe, but the caress inflamed as his palm slid over her rump.

The heat in her veins made her sensitive everywhere, and as he stroked her hip, his tongue parted her lips, claiming her mouth with an urgency that she felt all the way through. Her belly clenched and her thighs trembled and she leaned into him, aroused, so aroused, and yet also so worried that she wouldn't keep his interest.

Little kept the Earl of Langston's interest.

Tears filled her eyes, slipping beneath her closed lashes.

Dal lifted his head, brow furrowing as he stroked her damp cheek. "Why the tears, my watering pot?"

She sniffed and tried to smile, but failed. "I have so many emotions and they're not listening to me today."

He gently wiped away the second tear. A glint of humor warmed his golden eyes. "I don't think your emotions ever listen to you. They're not very obedient, I'm afraid."

He elicited a smile, and her lips wobbled but it was a real smile. "You're making me laugh."

"As if laughter is tragic."

She felt another bubble of reluctant laughter. "Why aren't you falling apart?"

"Because it'd be unmanly to cry on my wedding day."

Poppy snorted.

He smiled down at her. "That's better. No more tears. Izba won't forgive me if we ruin your makeup before the *zaffa*."

"*Zaffa?* What is that?"

"It's the wedding ma—" He broke off at the distant sound of drums.

Poppy stilled, listening to the drums. They were loud and growing louder, and then it wasn't just drums but bagpipes and horns.

She looked up at Dal, confused. "Wedding what?"

"Wedding march." He smiled into her eyes. "I hope you weren't expecting an exciting game of ping-pong, because the festivities are just beginning. After the *zaffa* there will be a party and dinner. It could be a late night."

Somehow Dal had managed to get fifty of his closest Mehkar family members to the Kasbah without her knowing.

She found out later that he'd had them flown to a nearby town and then they had bused in. He had also bused in the musicians and belly dancers and the fierce-looking men carrying flaming swords.

While she'd been dressing and having her hair and makeup done, dozens of Dal's staff had transformed the huge lawn into the site for the Arabic wedding and party. The *zaffa* swept them from the house, down the external stairs, to the grounds below. There was another ceremony after the noisy, colorful, chaotic march. Dal and Poppy had been led up an elevated platform, or *kosha*, to two plush, decorated chairs. Once seated, glasses were passed to all the guests and everyone toasted them, drinking to their health.

After the toast, the royal family's Iman spoke to them about the importance of honoring and respecting each other, and then she and Dal switched rings from their right hand to the left index finger before they were pulled to their feet to dance their first dance ever When the band struck up the second song, the dance floor filled with Dal's family.

Poppy was introduced to so many people, and pulled into so many hugs and kisses, she couldn't keep the guests straight, although Poppy remembered two—the cousin who'd greeted Dal at the Gila airport, and then the tall, somber patriarch of the family, Dal's grandfather, the King of Mehkar.

She'd dropped to a deep curtsy before the king, unfamiliar with proper protocol but also profoundly honored that the king would choose to join them today. It couldn't have been an easy trip for a man in his mid-to late-eighties.

The king drew her to her feet, and then lifted her face to his to scrutinize her thoroughly. She blushed beneath his careful inspection, even as it crossed her mind that the king had the same beautiful golden eyes that Dal did.

Dal, she thought, would look like this when he was older, and suddenly she couldn't help but smile at the king.

Dal's grandfather's stern expression eased, and while he didn't quite smile at her, there was warmth and kindness in his eyes as he murmured words in Arabic before kissing each of her cheeks.

"My grandfather welcomes you to the family. He said you will bring us many blessings and much joy."

And then the king moved away and the dancing continued, only interrupted for the cutting of the cake and then again when Dal invited his family and guests to the supper.

It was later in the evening when Dal took her hand and lifted it to his mouth, kissing her fingers. "In our culture the bride and groom always leave before the guests. It is their job to continue the party for us."

And then just like that, they were walking away, hand in hand, as the assembled guests cheered and the drummers drummed and the horns sounded.

A lump filled Poppy's throat at the joyous noise. She glanced back over her shoulder and blinked, not wanting Dal to see that she was crying again on their wedding day. "That was amazing," she whispered. "Beyond anything I could have imagined." She looked up at him and then away, eyes still stinging with tears. "Thank you."

His fingers tightened around hers. "You didn't think I would let our day go without a celebration?"

"I don't know. Maybe I did."

He stopped her then, on the stairs in the shadows, and drew her into his arms for a slow, bone-melting kiss. A shiver of pleasure coursed through her as heat and desire filled her, the warmth sapping her strength so that when his tongue stroked the seam of her lips, she felt weak and breathless. Senses flooded, she opened her mouth to him, giving herself to him, wanting to feel everything she could possibly feel on such a beautiful night.

Below them, laughter and music rose up from the garden where the band continued to play and Dal's family talked and danced inside the colorful tents. And then far above their heads came a crackle and pop, and then another loud pop and fizz.

Poppy opened her eyes to see fireworks fill the dark

sky with brilliant crimson and gold, green and silver light. The inky sky came alive with the shooting, exploding sparkling light.

Poppy's breath caught at the unexpected beauty. But then everything about today was unexpected. The simple, practical civil ceremony this afternoon, followed by the exotic, thrilling Arab ceremony and party and now this: gorgeous, spectacular fireworks. She absolutely adored fireworks, too.

"Is this another tradition in your culture?" she asked, gaze riveted to the brilliant display above them.

"No. It's something I did for you. You once told me fireworks made you happy. I wanted you to feel happy."

Her eyes burned and her throat ached, a lump making it impossible to speak. All she could do was nod and blink and try to keep from falling apart.

He'd thought of her. He'd wanted her happy. Even though he didn't say the words she wanted to hear, he'd tried to make today special for her.

"Thank you," she whispered, standing on tiptoe to kiss him before turning in his arms to watch the fireworks shoot into the sky and explode.

When it was all over, the guests gathered on the lawn cheered and Poppy applauded and Dal grinned, looking handsome and boyish and impossibly pleased with himself.

He should be, she thought, running up the stairs with him, heading now for his room, which he'd told her would be their room. He stopped her on the terrace before they reached the tall glass doors, and picked her up, swinging her into his arms, carrying her over the threshold into his darkened bedroom, which had been filled with dozens of flickering candles.

Dal could feel Poppy stiffen as he carried her into the bedroom, her heart racing so hard he could feel it pounding in her rib cage.

"Don't be scared," he said, placing her on her feet. "Nothing terrible is going to happen."

He saw her nervous glance at the bed and he reached out to stroke her warm, flushed cheek. "That won't be terrible, either, but we're not going to bed yet. I thought we should change and have some champagne and dessert. We left the party before the dessert was served."

She gave a half nod, her expression still wary. He didn't blame her. It had been an overwhelming day and he'd known what would happen today.

He'd kept the *zaffa* and party secret from her, wanting to surprise her, but maybe it would have been better to let her in on the plans so that she wouldn't have been so sad earlier after the civil ceremony. He'd hated the shadows that had darkened her eyes when she'd thought the civil ceremony was all that had been planned. It had made him realize how sensitive she really was, and how much she'd need emotionally. But that would be the problem.

He could give her things, and place credit cards without limits in her hands, but he'd never give her the intimacy and emotional closeness she craved, but God help him, he would try.

"I'll open the champagne while you change," he said. "I believe Izba is waiting in the bedroom to help you out of your bridal gown and into a more comfortable dressing gown."

Dressing gown was overstating things, Poppy thought, inspecting herself in the mirror. Dressing gown implied weight and coverage, but this sheer ivory kaftan with the scattered circles of diamonds and gold beads hid nothing. Oh, there was fabric all right; the gown was wildly romantic with shirred shoulders and a plunging neckline that went nearly down to her waist, but if it wasn't for the strategic draping Dal would be able to see absolutely everything.

As it was she had a hard time keeping her nipples from popping through the fabric, never mind the dark curls at the apex of her thighs.

"Izba, I can't go to him like this," Poppy muttered, blushing. "I'm practically naked."

"It's your wedding night," Izba answered soothingly. "And you look so beautiful."

"Beautifully naked." She frowned as she walked, aware that any light shining behind her would give away everything. "Was this another of his mother's gowns?"

"No. His Highness brought this one back from Gila for you. It was custom made." She gave Poppy a pat on the back. "Go to him. Don't be shy. He loves you very much—"

"He doesn't love me, Izba."

"Nonsense."

"He doesn't. He told me so." Poppy's voice suddenly broke. "But I knew it. I've known it. And I'm not going to cry about it. I'm not crying today."

"He wouldn't marry you if he didn't love you."

"He married me because he *had* to be married. He needed a wife by his thirty-fifth birthday."

"His Highness can have any woman. Many women would marry him. But you are the one he wanted."

Poppy wanted to explain that he hadn't had real choices, nor the time to explore all his options. Sophie disappearing from Langston Chapel had put him in a bind, and so Dal had settled…he'd settled for her. "It's more complicated than that," she said faintly. "His Highness had tremendous pressure on him—"

"Stop making excuses for him. He's a man. And he wouldn't have married you if this isn't what he wanted, not just for him, but also, to be the mother of his children."

The ever-important heirs and spares, Poppy thought with a panicked gulp.

She shot Izba a quick, nervous smile and then exited the bedroom before she lost her courage altogether.

Dal had dimmed the lights while she was gone, and he was waiting for her on his grand terrace. He gestured for her to come to him and she hesitated, suddenly shy, aware that she was next to naked.

His gaze met hers and held.

He gestured again, a masculine gesture of power and ownership.

She didn't want to go to him, but at the same time, she couldn't resist. She walked slowly, self-consciously, aware of the way he watched her, a hot, possessive light heating the gold of his eyes.

The soft chiffon and silk gown floated around her ankles as she crossed the floor. Izba had unpinned her hair, taking out the gold beads, and she could feel her hair brushing her shoulders.

"Why are you looking at me like that?" she breathed.

"Because you're gorgeous and you're mine."

Her tummy did a flip. "I think I need that champagne."

He carried their glasses to the low couch and sat down. He placed one glass on the table and then patted the cushion next to him with his free hand. "I have your glass here. You just have to come to me to get it."

"You like being in control, don't you?"

The corner of his mouth lifted. "No. I love being in control."

"So what are your plans for me?"

"Come here, and I'll tell you."

It seemed like it took her forever to reach his side, but at last she was there, heart racing, her mouth so dry. As she carefully sat down next to him she held out her hand for the champagne. He handed her the flute and she took a hasty sip, the cold, tart bubbles warming and fizzing all the way down. She took another sip for courage and then another to help her relax.

Dal reached out and removed the glass from her trembling fingers. "Easy," he cautioned. "You don't want to get sick."

"It's just champagne."

"Exactly."

She drew a quick breath, wondering how this would go, and what it'd be like to consummate the marriage. "You said it will sting."

"It's what I've been told."

"Will it be bad?"

He reached out and pushed her heavy hair back from her face. "I am not an expert in virgins. The whole idea of deflowering a woman has never appealed to me."

"I thought men loved the idea of being the first."

"I think those must be very insecure men."

"You wouldn't care if I'd been with other men?"

"Do you care that I've been with other women?"

"Yes."

His eyes flashed fire, and his head dropped, his mouth covering hers. The kiss was hot and slow, and so incredibly sensual it made her head spin.

She reached for him, holding on to his shoulders, pulling herself closer, needing more of his warmth, and strength and skin. She remembered the night in the pool and how he'd felt against her, and she wanted that pressure and pleasure now.

"Please take your shirt off," she murmured. "Let me feel you."

"If you want it off, you take it off," he answered, his deep voice pitched low.

She felt a frisson of nervous excitement at the hungry, predatory gleam in his eyes as she rose up on her knees to better reach the middle button on his shirt since the top ones were already undone.

When she struggled to get the button unfastened he lifted her off her knees and placed her on his lap, so that she was straddling him, her sheer gown floating out on either side as if they were wings of a jeweled butterfly. Poppy could feel the hard press of his arousal through his trousers. She was wearing nothing beneath her delicate gown and his thick, blunt head pressed against her core.

He was hard, and hot and she shuddered as he shifted his hips, his length rubbing against her where she was open and sensitive.

"My shirt?" he drawled, leaning back to watch her at her task.

Her hands shook as she struggled to unfasten one button and then another. Again, he shifted his hips, the rocking motion deliberate, and this time she pressed down on him, welcoming the feel of his thick tip pressing between her folds, nudging her bud, flooding her with pleasure.

Poppy glanced up into his face. His black lashes had dropped over his eyes, concealing his expression, and yet the sensual set of his full, firm mouth sent twin shots of lust and adrenaline through her.

He was so beautiful. So incredibly handsome and physical.

She'd never met any man half so appealing. Had never met any man she'd wanted the way she wanted him. She'd fought her attraction for years, but there was no more fighting her desire, or him. She just wanted to be his. She wanted to belong to him.

"Are we going to just leave the shirt on?" he asked, arching a brow. He didn't sound annoyed, or impatient. If anything, he sounded very pleased with himself, and her and all of this.

"Focusing now," she answered, forcing herself to finish

with the unbuttoning of the shirt, even though she could barely focus thanks to the heat of his thighs and the way the hard length of him seemed to be making her melt.

And then at last his shirt was open and she leaned forward, her breasts brushing his chest, to push the smooth fabric off his shoulders and then down each arm until his arms were free and his muscular torso was beautifully bare. Her breasts brushed against him again as she reached for the shirt and tossed it away.

"You are a tease," he growled.

"Me? You're the one making me do all the work," she answered, even as she flashed him a shy, breathless smile.

The air practically crackled and hummed with desire. Dal had to fight to keep his hands at his sides and not touch Poppy as she finished stripping the shirt off his arms.

Her full breasts had swayed and bounced beneath the sheer ivory chiffon fabric, her dark pink nipples teasing the hell out of him, the tips pebbled tight. It didn't help that she was impossibly hot and wet. He wanted to bury himself inside her, thrusting hard and deep, but she was inexperienced and even though it had been years since he'd made love, he wasn't going to rush their first night. He wanted her to see herself as he saw her—seductive, stunning, powerful, feminine. Perfect.

He reached up to touch her, finding her breast through her sheer beaded gown. Her nipple puckered tighter at the touch and she gasped a little as he pinched the tender peak. He watched her face as he stroked her and then took her breast into his mouth.

She groaned as he sucked and kneaded the warm, sensitive peak with his tongue and lips. He reached up to cup her other breast while he continued sucking. She rocked against him, hot and damp and aching for relief, and it crossed his mind that he'd never seen anything half as erotic as Poppy rocking on his lap.

He wanted so badly to be inside her. He wanted to feel her tight heat wrap his length, and when his control threatened to snap, he swung her into his arms and carried her into the bedroom, placing her in the middle of the bed.

She fell backward with a soft sigh onto the sheets. She was still breathing hard, her beautiful, dark eyes wide and luminous, her cheeks flushed, her luscious lips parted and pink. He leaned over her, drinking her in, thinking she was the most beautiful woman he'd ever known.

Poppy.

His wife.

His pleasure.

Poppy reached for him, bringing his head down to hers so he'd kiss her again. She loved the way he kissed. She loved the way he touched her. He was touching her now, caressing her breast through the filmy gown and then lower, stroking her flat stomach, across her hip and down the outside of her thigh.

Her legs trembled as he slid his hand between her thighs, parting them.

"Don't be nervous," he said.

"I'm not," she lied.

He dipped his head to hers, his mouth covering hers in a slow, hot, dizzying kiss. She relaxed as he caressed the inside of her thigh, stroking down to the back of her knee, and then up again.

She could feel his fingers trailing over the inside of her thigh again, so very close that his knuckles brushed her dark curls. Her breath caught as his knuckles lightly trailed across her mound, the light, teasing caress sliding the delicate gown across her, as well.

She was ready to have his hands on her, skin against

skin, ready to feel him touch her as he had in the pool, with his clever expert fingers against her where she was aching and wet.

"You're torturing me," she complained when his knuckles brushed over her again, the sensation too light to bring relief and yet too firm to be ignored.

"I don't want to rush you."

"I've been aroused for hours."

"Not hours," he answered, his fingertips trailing over her, pressing the now beaded chiffon over her tender folds and then holding it against her core. "Maybe a half hour."

She felt herself throbbing as he cupped her, his palm capturing her heat and dampness. She could feel her moisture on his hand.

Dal reached for the filmy hem of her gown and lifted it up, drawing it up over her knees, and then her thighs and then over her head, leaving her naked.

She felt his gaze as it took her in. He was studying her so intently she felt as if he was memorizing her. And then his hand returned to her knee, skimming down her shin to her ankle, and then back over her calf.

He caressed her leg until she relaxed and he opened her legs wider, and leaning over her hips, he placed at kiss just above her pelvic bone, and then another one lower, in the middle of her curls.

She shivered at the warmth of his breath and then shivered again when he parted her curls, exposing her tender skin and slick inner folds before placing a kiss right to the heart of her.

His mouth felt cool where she burned, his tongue flicking her and curling around her, toying with the delicate skin, stirring every nerve, making her feel wanton and desperate and yet also empty.

She reached for his belt, tugging it free. He lifted his head, and she nodded. "Please lose the trousers."

He did, very quickly, and with the trousers removed his heavy shaft sprang free.

"I don't think that will fit," she said hoarsely.

"It will. You'll see," he answered, lowering himself over her, kissing her, his tongue stroking the seam of her lips and then the inside of her mouth before catching the tip of her tongue, making her squirm.

With his knee he pressed her legs apart, making room to settle his hips between her thighs. She felt his shaft rub against her as he positioned himself near her core, the tip gliding across her wet entrance, making her feel delicious things.

He didn't try to enter her, instead focusing on kissing and touching her neck, her earlobe, the sensitive skin beneath her breast. She liked the feel of his strong thighs between hers, his legs hard with muscle and slightly rough with hair. Little by little his powerful thighs opened her wider, and the smooth, thick head of his shaft settled at her core, pressing in.

Dal lifted his head. "Look at me," he said quietly. "It's just me and you, and it will only sting this once."

And then he was pressing into her, a slow, steady thrust that made her eyes water and her breath catch, from the fullness and pressure of him filling her. It was a lot of sensation. It felt like too much sensation. The stretching was no longer remotely comfortable.

"Breathe," he murmured, kissing her lips. "That's it, breathe."

As she breathed in, he thrust deeper, breaking through the resistance. It hurt. It did. She blinked rapidly at the burn, and then the strange fullness of him lodged so deep inside her.

It wasn't what she'd imagined.

It was more than she'd imagined.

More pressure, more warmth, more fullness, more pain.

"Breathe," he said again.

She struggled to smile. "Don't worry, I'm not going to faint."

"It will feel better when I move. Let me move. It'll help ease the tightness."

"If I didn't like you so much I'd hate you."

He kissed the corner of her lips, and then her full lower lip, and then pressing up so that his weight was on his arms, he pulled out of her and then gently thrust back in. He did it again, and then again, and he was right; she wasn't as uncomfortable anymore. In fact, as he moved she began to feel something that rather resembled pleasure.

She closed her eyes to concentrate on the sensation and yes, it was a nice sensation, better then nice, as with each of Dal's deep, slow thrusts she felt heat grow and sensation coil, and she reached for him, hands sliding up his lean chiseled torso, fingers spreading wide across his warm satin skin. She could feel the hard, taut muscles beneath his skin and the way they tightened with every thrust of his hips.

Every time he buried himself in her, he stroked a sensitive spot inside, and it made her breath catch and want to press up against him to hold him there. "Yes," he said hoarsely, "just like that," as she rocked her hips again.

The next time he stroked down into her she rocked up and the pleasure was even more intense. She clenched him with her inner muscles, trying to hold him. He growled with pleasure. Poppy felt a thrill like nothing she'd ever felt better.

It was, she thought, rather amazing how their bodies came together, his hardness buried deep in her wet, slick heat, and this simple joining could make her never want to let him go. She wrapped her arms around him, holding tighter, his tempo quickening, stroking her faster and harder. The feel of him in her was maddening and delicious. Her body burned and glowed and she arched up as he pressed deep, her heels digging into the bed to give herself traction.

"Can you come?" he asked.

"I don't know," she said, because there was so much pressure and tension and desire but she couldn't focus on anything but the hard, silky feel of him filling her.

Suddenly, his hand was there between their bodies, and his fingers found her nub and he stroked the sensitive spot as he thrust deeply. The sensation felt so perfect; everything about this was perfect, and as he filled her and touched her, she felt overwhelming love.

He was everything to her. He was the very center of her world.

His deep thrusts were sending her over the edge. She couldn't fight the building sensation anymore. With a cry, she shattered, the climax stunning and intense. He thrust into her one more time, burying himself so deeply that she felt his muscles tighten and contract as his orgasm followed hers.

For several moments after, Poppy didn't know where she was, or who she was. She'd felt thrown to the stars and she'd somehow floated back.

Slowly, reality returned and she turned her head to look at Dal, who was lying on his back next to her.

He was the most beautiful person in the world. There was no one more dear or special to her.

Her eyes filled with tears. She blinked hard, trying to keep them from falling. "I love you," she whispered. "I love you so much it hurts my heart."

He gazed back at her, his golden gaze shuttered.

She held her breath, waiting to hear what he would say. But he just looked at her for a long moment, then leaned over, kissed her. "I hope today was special."

"It was," she answered, trying not to feel empty after feeling so incredibly much. He wasn't being cold, she told herself. This was just him. Dal wasn't good at expressing emotion. He'd never say the words she wanted to hear. "It was magical."

He kissed her again and pulled her close to his side and he was soon asleep. Exhausted, Poppy lay next to him, emotions unhinged, thoughts racing, still too wound up to sleep.

Everything had changed in one day.

She'd done what she'd intended to do. She'd protected Dal, but she'd left herself completely open and vulnerable.

This life with Dal would not be easy on her heart.

Sunlight pierced the gap between the heavy drapes that had been drawn across the windows. Poppy rolled onto her back, stretching and yawning.

She winced a little as she rolled onto her back, feeling a new soreness between her thighs. She flashed back to the intense lovemaking and blushed, remembering his mouth and lips on her, exploring her, and then the way he'd filled her, burying himself in her, making her feel more connected to him than she'd ever been with anyone.

Poppy reached out to see if Dal was still with her, but he was gone.

She turned to look at the place he should have been, and could still see an indentation from his big frame.

She stroked the sheet in his spot. It was cool. He'd been gone a long time.

Poppy slowly sat up, drawing the covers with her. Last night had been a revelation. She hadn't expected the closeness, nor had she realized that a man's body could feel like that…the sinewy pressure of Dal's thighs, and the warm, hard planes of his chest. She could still remember how she'd clung to him, arms wrapped tightly, feeling as if she'd never get close enough. Poppy didn't know if this was how everyone felt when they made love, but the intensity of it had been shattering. She'd anticipated pleasure, and she'd expected new sensations, but she hadn't expected that the desire would become pure emotion.

When he'd filled her, and held her and thrust so deeply into her, she'd wanted to burst out of her skin and crawl into his.

She wanted him, all of him, his mind, body and soul.

It was why she'd told him she loved him. She wanted to be part of his heart, and safe in his heart and feel secure forever.

But she didn't feel secure.

If anything, making love had made her feel more alone and isolated than before.

It was late afternoon before Poppy saw Dal. He found her down by the pool, reading beneath an umbrella. He leaned over her, kissed her and then sat down on the chair, apologizing for being gone all day, explaining that he'd spent much of the day making sure his family returned safely to Gila, and then a problem had come up in the London office and he'd been on conference calls ever since.

It wasn't until he sat down next to her that she realized he was wearing the traditional white robe of his people.

"Where has Randall Grant gone?" she asked, and she wasn't just referring to the clean, elegant lines of the robe, but the gradual transformation that had taken place since they flew out of Winchester. In England he'd been so private and contained. He wasn't just more open here; his personality was warmer, too. He smiled here, and made jokes and teased her. And made love to her. Her cheeks heated remembering last night.

"Do you want him back?"

"Not necessarily. Although he is the you I know best."

"There is just one of me. But the me here is more relaxed. Happier, too," he added, leaning forward to kiss her, a hot, erotic kiss that made her tummy tighten and her breasts peak. She was breathless when he pulled away.

"Are you happy here?" he added.

"It's beautiful but very remote."

He studied her face for a moment. "Was it not a good day?"

"It was a rather long day. I got lonely."

"I'm sorry. I expected to be free sooner." He pressed another lingering kiss to her lips before rising. "I'm going to go shower and change. Join me soon. I've asked for some drinks and a light meal to be sent to our room since I haven't eaten anything today."

She reached for his hand, catching his fingers, preventing him from leaving. "What's happening at the office?"

"A problem, not an emergency. Nothing you need to worry about."

"Is there anything I can do?"

He squeezed her hand and then let it go. "I have one of the administrative assistants in the office taking care of some things for me and soon we'll have your replacement. It's just a temporary stress, nothing to trouble you."

And then he was gone, striding toward the Kasbah, his long white robe swirling, reminding her of a powerful desert warlord just returning home while she very much felt like a concubine with no purpose other than being available to please her master.

She grimaced, frustrated, not wanting to be shut out from his life, or his business. She'd worked with him for years and had enjoyed the partnership. What were her responsibilities in this new role of hers?

Poppy pushed off the chair and went to her room to shower and change before going on upstairs.

"Where did you change?" Dal asked her when she entered his suite of rooms.

"My room."

"This is your room now," he said. "I expected you would have the staff move your things today."

"You never said anything."

"You are my wife. This is the master bedroom suite. This is where you belong."

"How do I know if you don't tell me?"

"I'm telling you now."

Poppy compressed her lips, not liking his autocratic tone. "This is all new to me, Dal. You're going to have to communicate a little bit."

"You're upset with me?"

She fought to keep her voice steady, not wanting to sound hysterical on their second day of married life. "You were gone when I woke up. You didn't leave a note, or tell me when you'd return."

"I didn't know myself."

"In England you communicated far better."

"In England you were my secretary."

"Maybe I liked being your secretary better than your wife!"

He gave her an intense, brooding look. "Really?"

Her pulse quickened, her chest tightening. "I don't want to be shut out of your life."

"You're not. You are the very center of my world now." And then as if to prove his point, he swept her into his arms, carrying her to the bed where he tossed her, pinned her down and kissed her fiercely, deeply, the scorching kiss torching her senses.

As he kissed her, he slid a hand between her legs, caressing her thighs until she opened them for him. He leaned over and kissed the top of her thigh, and then the inside of her thigh and she trembled.

"I'm not sure I can handle *this*," she murmured unsteadily as she felt his fingers slide over her, lightly tracing her folds and then lightly, lightly parting her before placing a kiss on her, and then another kiss, followed by a flick of his tongue across her clit.

She gasped as sharp, delicious sensation shot through her and when he covered her there with his mouth and sucked, her hips jerked up of their own accord. Dal shifted his weight, clamped an arm across her pelvis, holding her open and still while he kissed, sucked and licked her to an orgasm so powerful she dug her nails into his shoulders and screamed his name.

The orgasm was so intense she felt almost broken. The intensity of the sensation made her feel emotional and un-done. Flushed, spent, she felt him stretch out next to her and pull her to his side. He left his arm around her, his palm covering her breast.

"I want to be in you," he said, "but I don't want to hurt you. Maybe tomorrow."

She nodded, glad he couldn't see the tears filling her eyes.

She hadn't thought sex would feel like this…physical and carnal but then afterward, painfully empty.

It was hard to love someone who didn't love you back.

"Poppy?" he asked, shifting her so that she lay on her back. He pushed her thick hair from her face and then un-tangled a strand still clinging to her damp cheek. "What's wrong?"

"Nothing."

"Something is. You're far too quiet."

She looked up at him, seeing his strong brow and the high, hard lines of his cheekbones. She loved his face. It was so very beautiful and familiar. But the rest of this…it was new and overwhelming. In bed, he was overwhelming. The sex was overwhelming. His body was so big, and powerful and sexual. He was so very sexual. But then after all the physical intimacy there was no emotional intimacy. If any-thing, after sex, she felt even further from him than before.

"Is this what you thought marriage would be like?" she asked carefully.

"No. It's better." He smiled crookedly. "You're not just my friend, but now you're my lover."

"So you're satisfied? Happy you married me?"

"No regrets." He rolled onto his back and pulled her toward him so that she was lying against his side, her cheek on his chest. "And you? Regrets, my sweet Poppy?"

It took her a moment to answer. "No regrets," she said unsteadily. "But I think I may be a little homesick. We've been gone a long time."

His hand stroked her hair and then trailed down her spine. "What do you miss most? Winchester? London?"

"My flat."

His hand stilled in the small of her back. "Why your flat?"

"It was cozy and familiar. I felt...safe...there."

"But Poppy, your home is with me now. I have promised to take care of you, and I will. You must know you are safe with me."

She nodded, eyes closing, holding back the hot emotion, because despite his words, she didn't feel safe. She didn't feel secure. She didn't have what she needed—love.

Sex was good and fine, and pleasure was definitely nice, but what she needed most in the world was to be truly needed, to be truly special, to be truly loved.

CHAPTER ELEVEN

THEY FELL INTO a pattern over the next week, a pattern Poppy did not enjoy. Dal would be sequestered in his office working while she drifted around the Kasbah trying to find ways to occupy herself. She'd asked if she could work with him, or assist him like she used to, but he curtly reminded her she was his wife now, not an employee.

After that he seemed to withdraw even more, at least during the day when he was distant and unavailable. But then in the evening he emerged from his office and was warm and charming and always he'd make love to her. The sex was incredibly hot, and he never failed to make sure she climaxed, but the long days of being alone followed by the carnal lovemaking was breaking her heart.

He'd take her body, and pleasure her body, but that was all he wanted from her.

And that was also all he'd give her.

"We will leave here soon for Gila," he said on the ninth night of their honeymoon, in that quiet aftermath that followed their lovemaking. "I thought perhaps we could look for our home in Gila together. Would you enjoy that?"

Her brow creased. "Are we going to live in Gila?"

"I'd like to have a home in the capital. Maybe something modern, or if you prefer classical architecture—"

"What about England? What about our home there?"

"My intention is to divide our time between the two. I want my children to know Mehkar and be comfortable in both places."

"They would be my children, too," she said in a small voice.

"Of course. I meant our children."

She wasn't so sure he did.

Poppy couldn't sleep that night, but she didn't lie awake tossing and turning. No, she spent the long, quiet hours of the night making a brutal but necessary decision.

She'd given Dal what he'd needed. She'd protected his lands and title. But now it was time she protected herself.

In the morning she would leave, and she wouldn't go in tears. She was going to leave strong and proud and focused on her future for a change, not his.

He was at his desk when she entered his office. He didn't even look up for a minute, so engrossed in the document he was reading.

She watched him read, feeling a pang of love and regret, recognizing the Randall Grant focus.

No one could compartmentalize like Dal.

She shifted the hands holding her purse and worn travel bag but made no other sound. Finally, he glanced up at her, his strong black brows flattening over his light eyes.

"What's happening?" he said brusquely.

She didn't take offense. She knew it was his tone when concentrating. His sharpness wasn't aimed at her but rather the annoyance of breaking his focus. He wouldn't like what she had to say, but it was time, and she'd made her mind up. "I'd like to leave now."

For a moment there was just silence and then he slowly rose. "What did you say?"

"You told me when you found a new secretary, you'd put me on a plane. You have a new secretary. I know she's working in the London office right now, but she replaced me a week ago."

"You're my wife, Poppy, not an employee."

"Please have your helicopter come and take me to Gila. I intend to sleep tonight in my own bed, at home."

"I don't understand."

"I know you don't, and I don't expect you will, but this marriage helped you, but it's not good for me. Please do the right thing for me, and let me go. If you care for me at all, you'll send me home now."

He moved away from the desk, walking slowly toward her. "I won't send you back to England like this—"

"So you don't care for me."

"I won't send you because I do."

"Then you're not listening. I'm not happy here. I'm not happy living like this. I don't regret marrying you, and I won't call it a mistake, because I gave you what you needed...the title, the house, the estates...so please give me now what I need. My freedom."

Dal was grateful for twenty years of lessons in control and discipline because it allowed him to keep his expression mercifully blank. He was stunned, though. Inwardly reeling.

"I am listening," he said casually, calmly, as he approached her. "I always listen to you, even when you think I'm sleeping. I am there in bed with you, hearing you breathe, hearing you weep—"

"If you've heard me cry at night, why didn't you say something, or do something? Why just let me cry myself to sleep?"

"Marriage is new, and an adjustment. I thought you needed time."

"No, I didn't need time. I needed *you*." She nearly backed up a step as he closed the distance, stopping just a foot in front of her. Her chin lifted, her dark eyes bright with anger and pain. "*You*, Dal," she repeated fiercely, "not time. All I've had here is time."

"But you have me. I sleep with you every night. I hold

you through the night. I am not far during the day, and when you need me, you can find me. Just as you found me today."

Silence greeted his words. Her eyes narrowed a fraction and then her lips curved but there was no warmth in her eyes. "This you," she said at last, nodding at him, "the one you're offering, the one you're giving, it's not enough. I'm sorry if it hurts, but it's the truth."

He'd never seen this side of her. He didn't know what to make of her anger. "People are not perfect. They will inevitably let you down. I'm sorry if I've disappointed you—"

"There are small disappointments, life's little irritations and then there are tragedies. I can handle the irritations. I expect the irritations and annoyances. But me marrying a man who doesn't love me…that borders on tragedy."

She'd stunned him again. He couldn't think of a single appropriate thing to say. Poppy, for her part, was so still and pale she reminded him of a wax figure.

"Please put me on the plane—"

"No. Absolutely not."

"So you don't care for me. I am just another of your toys and possessions."

"I don't know where this is coming from, and I don't know what has made you feel so insecure—"

"You have, Dal! You with your lack of words and lack of emotion. You only make room for me in bed. But out of bed, there is no place for me in your life!"

"You are bordering on hysteria."

"Of course you'll mock me and shame my emotions, but at least I have emotions! At least I feel, and at least I'm able to be honest about what I need. I need a man who will love me. I need a man who will share with me and sacrifice for me." Her voice cracked, broke. "But from the beginning it's been about you, and as long as I stay here, it will only be about you, and I was wrong to think I could do this…live like this. So let me go now while we both have some dignity."

"I'd rather lose my dignity than you."

"You've already lost me."

"No, I haven't. You're hurt and angry, but we can fix this."

"It's impossible to fix us. We can't be fixed. You can't be fixed—"

"I am not a machine! I have feelings—" he broke off, grinding his teeth together, trying to hold the blistering pain. "And maybe it shocks you, but your words hurt. Your words wound. But I'll take the words and the wounds if it will allow us to grow stronger together."

She averted her head, lips quivering. "I don't want us to be together. Not anymore."

"I don't believe you. I can't believe you. After four years—"

"I didn't know the real you! I didn't know us."

He felt like he was in quicksand and sinking fast. Emotions were not his strength. Tears and sadness and grief and need…they baffled him. He'd never been allowed to feel or grieve, and he'd learned to survive by being numb. But he wasn't numb right now. His chest burned. His body hurt. She might as well have poured petrol on him and then struck a match. "Perhaps what you should be saying," he said tightly, "is that you didn't know you."

She looked at him then, tears in her eyes. "But I did know me. I knew what I needed. And every time I refused your proposal it was because I knew what I needed…and that was love."

"Poppy, I am trying, with everything I am——"

"It's not enough." Her chin lifted, eyes glittering with tears. "Call for the helicopter. I'll be downstairs in the garden, waiting."

* * *

Poppy walked away then, quickly, her heels clicking on the marble, her eyes scalding.

That was beyond brutal. That was awful, so very awful. She'd said hard, harsh things, not to hurt him, but to make him understand that this wasn't a game. She was done. She felt broken. He had to let her go.

She sat in the garden on a bench waiting for the helicopter, her bags at her feet. She would stay in the garden until the helicopter arrived, too. It might take days, but eventually he'd know she was serious.

Thirty minutes later Dal emerged from the Kasbah with his large black suitcase. She watched him cross the lawn and then he squeezed onto the bench next to her. She refused to make eye contact. This wasn't an act. It wasn't a game. She was leaving him today.

"The helicopter should be here in the next five to ten minutes," he said, breaking the silence.

"Good."

"The jet has been fueled and is ready in Gila."

"Thank you."

"I needed to file a flight plan and I told them London."

"That's correct."

"Good. Glad to know I've done something right."

She shot him a furious glance. "I don't feel sorry for you. You're a grown man, a very successful man. You have extensive experience in mergers and acquisitions. You're accustomed to the bumps and disappointments. You'll bounce back in no time."

He met her gaze and held it. "You're not a merger, or an acquisition. You are my wife, and you're hurt, and I'm sorry. Your happiness means everything to me."

"Those are just words."

"But isn't that what you wanted? Words? Tender words? Affectionate words?"

"You can't even say them!"

"Love, you mean?" His black eyebrow arched. "I do love you, Poppy, and yet I find the word hard to say, but that doesn't mean I don't feel it."

"Huh!"

He caught her jaw, turned her face to him. "I'm not a machine. I feel emotions. In fact, I feel them so intensely they scare me. I have spent my entire life trying to contain my emotions, determined that they wouldn't dictate my future. And every time I said I wanted you, I meant it. I wanted you then, and I want you now."

"Sexually," she said, bitterly.

"Sexually, emotionally, spiritually. I want you as my partner, my best friend—"

"Your *only* friend."

"The mother of my children," he continued calmly.

She gave her head a toss. "For the all-important heirs."

"Not heirs," he corrected, "but us, our family. You'll be an incredible mother. And I'd like to be a father, although I'm not sure I'll be good at it in the beginning. I'll have to learn, but I can."

"You never talked about family before. You and Sophie—"

"Because I couldn't imagine raising a family with Sophie. I couldn't imagine a life with her. But I can with you. I can imagine everything, and I want everything, and I do mean everything. You, Poppy, have made me want more."

She bit her lip and looked away, tears in her eyes. "It's too little, too late, Dal. You've hurt me—"

"I did. I know I did, and I'm sorry. Poppy, I am an arse. I'm ruthless and relentless but none of this should surprise you. You know me. And you married me, knowing me."

"True, and I've realized you haven't changed. You'll never change. I'm not going to change, either. I will always want more and you will want less."

"If I wanted less, why did I marry you? If I wanted less, why didn't I pick one of those silly party girls who would have been grateful for my wealth and position, instead of throwing it in my face? If I wanted less, why did I choose the woman who wanted *more*? Who demands more? Who insists I demand more, too? If less was my future, then why have I struggled to grow and change for you?"

She said nothing.

Frustration filled him. "Poppy, who would I be without you?" And then he fell silent, his question hanging there between them for what felt like forever.

Finally unable to bear the silence a moment longer, she said, "You are the Earl of Langston and the Prince of Mehkar."

"Actually, I'm not the Earl of Langston anymore."

She looked at him, aghast.

He shrugged. "You're not the only one who can make grand gestures. I can, too, and I've chosen to walk away from the title and the house and everything it entails. It was a bit more complicated than I imagined, but it's done now. It's what I've been working on since our wedding."

"The problem in London?"

He nodded.

"But you married me to secure—"

"You. I married you because I couldn't imagine going through life without you. Poppy, I don't care about titles and houses. I don't need anything but you."

"Then why the rush? Why the pressure?"

"I wanted to keep the promise I made to my father. And I did. And now I'm free."

She looked away, blinking back tears.

"I am not good with words, my sweet Poppy, but you

are my other half. You are my heart and my soul. You are
my family and my future. Please don't leave, and if you're
determined to go, then plan on taking me."

She brushed away her tears. "You won't like my crowded,
untidy little flat."

"I will if that's where you want to be. If that's what feels
like home."

"The flat's so small there's barely room for me, never
mind you."

"We'll downsize."

She spluttered on laughter. "You have no idea what
you're saying. You're accustomed to huge houses and servants and people bowing and scraping."

"Not anymore. I've given it up."

"What about here in Mehkar? Are you still Prince Talal,
or have you dispensed with that, too?"

"No, I'm still Prince Talal." He grimaced. "And I should
probably tell you something that I ought to have told you
long ago."

"Oh, no." She looked at him, immediately wary. "I don't
know if I want to hear this." She looked into his eyes, worried. "What is it? What else have you done?"

"I haven't done anything yet. You see, I am my grandfather's heir. When he dies, I will be king."

"Oh, Dal."

"I know it's a lot to process—"

"He's healthy, though, isn't he? At least he seemed relatively fit and strong when he was here for the wedding."

"He's as healthy as an eighty-four-year-old man can be."

"That's good."

He regarded her a moment, the corners of his mouth
curving. "You took that better than I expected."

"You must know I don't really wish to be a queen. I just
want a cozy little house in the Cotswolds—"

"With a couch and a telly." He smiled and kissed her.

"I promise you'll have the house you've always dreamed about. And the television set, too."

"Are you making fun of me?"

"Absolutely not. I'm just trying to reassure you that I'm listening and attentive to your needs."

She groaned and rolled her eyes. "You are impossible."

"Yes, I know. But isn't that what you always liked about me?"

EPILOGUE

TALAL'S CORONATION WAS nearly ten years to the day of their wedding at Kasbah Jolie.

It was early July and impossibly hot. The Gila palace was air-conditioned but with so many guests crowded into the reception room, the air conditioner couldn't quite do its job.

Poppy was miserable in her gold gown and heels. Not because the kaftan was tight; if anything it was made of the lightest, softest silk imaginable, but she was very pregnant, nine months pregnant, and her ankles were swelling and she was desperate to be off her feet.

Thank goodness she knew what to expect. This was her fourth pregnancy and she always felt irritable at this stage, ready for the bump to be gone and the baby to be in her arms. She was always anxious as the due date grew closer, worried about any number of things that could go wrong. Fortunately, the first three deliveries went without a hitch and all three were really good children, and very excited about the new one, because finally the three boys would have a baby sister.

Poppy struggled to not fidget as Dal accepted his new crown, and the duties it entailed.

But it was hard to stand perfectly still with the odd contractions. They were false contractions, she was sure. She'd had them with the last two pregnancies and she knew now not to be alarmed.

She pressed her elbow to her side, pressing against the tension that wrapped her abdomen.

She must be overly hot and overly tired because that one felt like the real thing.

And then her water broke and Poppy's head jerked up.

Dal was suddenly looking at her and she didn't remember speaking, or making a sound, but suddenly he was there, at her side, his arm around her.

"What's happening?"

"My water just broke," she whispered, aware that all two hundred plus people in the reception room were watching. "But it's too early. She's not due for another couple of weeks."

"Apparently, no one told her that," he said, smiling warmly into her eyes.

Poppy's heart turned over. Ten years of marriage and he still made her melt. "I'm sorry we're disrupting the ceremony."

"I'm not. I can't wait to meet her. You know how much I've wanted a daughter."

Another contraction hit and Poppy gasped and squeezed his arm. "It seems she's in a rush to meet you, too!"

"I'm not surprised. If she's anything like her mother, she's going to be fierce and loyal and impossibly loving." He wrapped his arm around her waist, supporting her. "I love you, Queen Poppy, completely and madly, you know."

"What has happened to my safe, predictable Englishman?"

"Gone, I'm afraid."

She gripped his arm as another contraction hit.

"And so are we," he added, swinging her into his arms. "Because I don't trust our little princess not to make an appearance here and now."

* * * * *

MILLS & BOON

THE HEART OF ROMANCE

A ROMANCE FOR EVERY READER

MODERN

Prepare to be swept off your feet by sophisticated, sexy and seductive heroes, in some of the world's most glamourous and romantic locations, where power and passion collide.

HISTORICAL

Escape with historical heroes from time gone by. Whether your passion is for wicked Regency Rakes, muscled Vikings or rugged Highlanders, awaken the romance of the past.

MEDICAL

Set your pulse racing with dedicated, delectable doctors in the high-pressure world of medicine, where emotions run high and passion, comfort and love are the best medicine.

True Love

Celebrate true love with tender stories of heartfelt romance, from the rush of falling in love to the joy a new baby can bring, and a focus on the emotional heart of a relationship.

Desire

Indulge in secrets and scandal, intense drama and sizzling hot action with heroes who have it all: wealth, status, good looks…everything but the right woman.

HEROES

The excitement of a gripping thriller, with intense romance at its heart. Resourceful, true-to-life women and strong, fearless men face danger and desire - a killer combination!

To see which titles are coming soon, please visit

millsandboon.co.uk/nextmonth

JOIN US ON SOCIAL MEDIA!

Stay up to date with our latest releases, author news and gossip, special offers and discounts, and all the behind-the-scenes action from Mills & Boon...

 @millsandboon

 @millsandboonuk

 facebook.com/millsandboon

 @millsandboonuk

It might just be true love...

GET YOUR ROMANCE FIX!

Get the latest romance news,
exclusive author interviews, story
extracts and much more!

blog.millsandboon.co.uk

MILLS & BOON

MODERN

Power and Passion

Prepare to be swept off your feet by sophisticated, sexy and seductive heroes, in some of the world's most glamourous and romantic locations, where power and passion collide.